THE LAST OF THE SAVAGES

THE
LAST OF THE
SAVAGES

a novel by

Jay McInerney

ALFRED A. KNOPF   NEW YORK
1996

THIS IS A BORZOI BOOK
PUBLISHED BY ALFRED A. KNOPF, INC.

Portions of this work were originally published in *Esquire.*

Library of Congress Cataloging-in-Publication Data

McInerney, Jay.
    The last of the savages : a novel / by Jay McInerney.
        p.   cm.
        ISBN 0-679-42845-3 (alk. paper)
        I.   Title.
PS3563.C3694L37   1996
813′ .54—dc20   96-2112
                                                        CIP

Manufactured in the United States of America
First Edition

... one is a rebel or one conforms, one is a frontiers-
man in the Wild West of American night life, or else
a Square cell, trapped in the totalitarian tissues of
American society, doomed willy-nilly to conform if
one is to succeed.

—Norman Mailer

The author wishes to thank Lucius Birch, Mildred and Robert Bell, William Eggleston, Sam Henderson, Matthew Johnson, Warner F. Moore II, Charlie Newman, Pallas Pidgeon, Julia Reed, Dorothy Stevenson (aka Bug), Maxine Smith and Donna Tartt. Special thanks to Morgan for office space. And of course— Fritz.

THE LAST OF THE SAVAGES

I

The capacity for friendship is God's way of apologizing for our families. At least that's one way of explaining my unlikely fellowship with Will Savage.

Though we hadn't spoken in weeks, maybe months, I thought of him the moment two New York City police detectives showed up at my office. I was taken aback, naturally, when my secretary announced them. The kind of law we practice here doesn't bring us in contact with the police. But their visit had nothing to do with Will Savage—they wanted to ask me about Felson. Ah, yes, officers. Please, sit down.

Saul Felson was in the tax department at my firm. Family man, active member of his temple, a doggedly brilliant lawyer who, even by the conservative standards of our white-shoe firm, was so colorless as to seem virtually transparent. Kind of a geek. We occasionally worked together, but I didn't know him well—I don't think anyone did—and nothing I could tell the detectives might explain how he'd ended up dead of multiple stab wounds in a seedy motel in the Bronx. Everyone's quite shaken, of course, and the partners will all be attending the funeral. I have to admit the whole affair has given me an acute intimation of mortality. At forty-seven, he was just a year older than me.

Lately I've been wondering if Felson had a best friend. The visit from the detectives reminded me of the day the FBI came to interview me about mine.

By now, I'm used to answering questions about Will; it seems to be part of my life's work. The first person ever to formally interrogate me was the rock critic for the Boston *Phoenix*, looking for colorful anecdotes with which to embroider the nascent Savage legend.

Camouflaged by a heavy beard and outfitted in the olive army jacket which was then the uniform of strident antimilitarists, anticonformists and all the other bushy antinomians, he sampled many of the world's beers that afternoon at the Wursthaus in Harvard Square. I think I was wearing a Levi's jacket and fashionably flared and faded jeans, but as far as he was concerned I might as well have been in chinos and a blazer. In any case he was disappointed to discover that Will Savage had such a straight, musically obtuse friend.

For all the time I spent with Will and all his efforts to educate me, I'm still apt to confuse Johnny Jenkins with Pinetop Perkins. So shoot me. I appreciate a good hook and a big backbeat, I can hum along with half the songs in the Stax and Chess catalogs, but I can't necessarily deliver a lecture on the difference between R and B and soul—a fact that irritates and amazes those who worship Will, who think he is a great man because of the careers he helped to create, the empire he constructed, the millions he accumulated and, in true rock-and-roll fashion, the millions he pissed away. I can only say that I believe in the achievement because I believed first in Will, and because I think I understand what it meant to him. The music was not an end in itself but the expression of a deeper program. Will was always trying to free the slaves.

Halfway through his pilsner, the rock critic asked if it was true that Will had picked up the scar on his cheek in a knife fight with Bukka White, the great Delta bluesman. It was the first time I'd heard this story, which became one of the cornerstones of the Will Savage myth—along with the one about his contest with Jimi Hendrix to see who could swallow more reds without passing out, in which Will was said to prevail.

"No," I said. "He got it in a car accident." Then, realizing how bland that sounded, I added, "He crashed into a cement mixer one night when he was drunk."

This fact didn't make it into the article; certainly the rumor must have seemed more interesting than the truth. I actually met Bukka once, with Will, in Memphis. Big, powerful-looking man, even at seventy, hands like sledgehammers. He wouldn't have needed a knife.

Just to fuck with the guy—and with Will, who had sicced him on me—I claimed that Will was known to his closest friends and associates as Memphis Slim, until that moment a private moniker which I had bestowed on him at school. This faux fact was duly reported in the article, without attribution, and subsequently attached itself to Will.

"I guess," opined the rock critic, closing his notebook, his dark mustache frosted with the foam of his Czech pilsner, "you didn't pick up much from your time with Will." This was after I blanked on something he asked me about Lee Dorsey—or was it Tommy Dorsey?

Choosing to ignore the implication that Will now belonged to the true believers, I said: "Will taught me about history."

Looking stunned, he ordered up a Belgian beer to assuage his incredulity. "*History?*"

At the time—this was the early seventies—history was a discredited subject. Not that it has ever quite recovered from that devaluation—but at that precise *historical* moment it was deemed irrelevant to the accelerating millennial blitz, or, at best, just kind of a drag. And Will, of all people, seemed like an avatar of the orgy of the eternal present.

"He's a southerner," I explained.

I wasn't just being perverse. Almost from the moment he could speak, Will knew the names of the battles his ancestors had engaged in—Vicksburg, Gettysburg, Chicamauga—and where their lead-pocked bones were interred. Not that he was a history buff particularly; Will had just about no use for orthodox scholarship. But he came from a haunted family, a vanquished land, and even as he stormed the crenellated walls of convention, he inadvertently taught me about the past's implacable claims on the present—that it is if anything more tangible than the vibrant, breathing moment. I tried to explain some of this to the rock critic, but either I wasn't clear or he was fuddled from his malty geography lesson.

In spite of his atrocious hygiene, craven hagiolatry, caustic French cigarettes and High Germanic critical vocabulary, I preferred the rock critic to the FBI agents who showed up at my door a few weeks later. I was in my first year of law school; they were waiting outside my door when I returned to my room from Torts one afternoon.

"Patrick Keane?"

They introduced themselves. Ominously, one of them was named Lynch. Fellow Hibernians both, they seemed to count on this for some sort of rapport. The old sod and all. But this was the era of civil war both in Vietnam and at home. As conventional and politically bland as I might have seemed to my peers, I recognized the enemy by their gray suits and ties, black brogues and crewcuts. Back when hair length was such a foolproof signifier it was easy to tell who was who. Though my own hair was only moderately moppy—halfway down the ears, volume and wave just barely suggestive of an Afro—friends of mine had been clubbed and teargassed in the streets, and a college classmate was in prison in Texas because state troopers had found a joint in his car. When I extended my hand it was shaking. A real child of the times, of course, wouldn't have offered his hand at all, but in politics I'm a follower of Henry Clay.

"How 'bout we take a walk," suggested Special Agent Lynch. Not seeing any choice, I nodded pragmatically. I imagined myself whisked into a car, slowly roasted under fluorescent light in a smoky, windowless room. I felt his paternal arm on my shoulder, urging me forward. The other agent walked behind us, the better to club or chloroform me. I forget what the most popular song was that year, but *paranoia* was definitely the number-one hit word, the dark mantra of the drug culture. Under the circumstances I seemed to have difficulty remembering how to walk—I couldn't quite get the traditional rhythm down—and breathing seemed likewise a new and intricate activity. Could this be about the peace rally I had attended the previous fall?

"So, how you like it here at Ha'vad?"

"The law school's excellent," I said, trying to muster some hauteur.

"Not bad for an Irish kid from Taunton."

I was silent, disliking his implication that I had more in common with him and his sidekick than with the scruffy princelings around us.

"Tell me about Will Savage."

All in a moment I felt relieved, and in the next instant disloyal for *feeling* relieved, and worried that Will was *really* in trouble this time. "Did something happen to him?"

"Not yet, so far as we know. But maybe you can help us help him out of some serious trouble."

I had a hard time looking at the special agent because my gaze was alternately drawn to a purple, pea-sized growth on his cheek and to the perfect mesa on the top of his head—a flattop haircut being nearly as rare by then as a powdered periwig. Even as I equivocated, trying to divulge as little information about Will as possible, I was plagued with the notion of picking that rotten pea from his face, and strafed with images of tiny airplanes taking off and landing on the special agent's head.

"How would you describe Mr. Savage's politics?"

"I think they're, uh, pretty . . . standard," I equivocated, "for someone of his age and . . . educational background." A year of law school had not been wasted on me.

"Would you say that advocating the violent overthrow of the American government is pretty standard, Mr. Keane? Is that what they teach you here at *Ha'vad?*"

I am pleased to recall that I dropped my mask and looked at him with open disdain, citizen to citizen. Maybe I had been dodgy about Will's politics, but I thought this was laying it on a bit thick. "Will doesn't believe in violence," I insisted. Of course, he'd been known to carry a gun when traveling the chitlin circuit with his soul and blues acts; but it was strictly a capitalist tool, reserved for those occasions when the local promoters were reluctant to share the take.

"We have proof," said Flattop, "that he's affiliated with groups that do."

"Will doesn't affiliate with groups," I said, even more confident in this than in my previous assertion.

"Have you ever heard of the Black Power Solidarity Committee?"

At first this sounded merely ludicrous, something the director of the

FBI dreamed up in an apocalyptic fever. On reflection, however, I realized I'd met the entire politburo of the committee in question, in a hotel suite in Miami a few years before. It *was* ludicrous, but that didn't prevent it from being frightening—like many things that happened then.

I had just finished my freshman year at Yale and was enjoying a brief vacation courtesy of Will, who was attending a convention of radio announcers. He'd taken over a vast suite in a hotel in Miami Beach, at the edge of the then-crumbling deco district. I spent my days on the beach with the codgers and the Cuban muscle boys while Will confined himself to his rooms, receiving visitors, conferring with his entourage, smoking dope and stroking the phones. Returning to the hotel from a day on the sand, grilled to an unflattering shade of pink, I emerged from the elevator to discover three black men in leather jackets loitering in the turquoise hall.

"We s'posed to meet Will Savage."

I pointed to the door. Trying to be helpful, trying to show that I *knew* there was nothing out of the ordinary about three black men—even three black men who, under slightly different circumstances, might look menacing—visiting Will, I went over and knocked on the door myself. *Hey, man, we're all cool round here.*

"Who is it?"

"It's Patrick," I said. As the door yielded, I felt myself pushed from behind, across the threshold into the sentinel bulk of Jack Stubblefield, former football player and Will's devoted vassal. There was a brief scuffle as I tried to regain my balance and the men behind me surged forward, and finally we were all standing uncomfortably close inside the door, me and Stubblefield facing the intruders—only one of us ready and willing to fight them off.

"Who the fuck do you think you are?" he said.

A tall, thin man in a red beret glared at him. "We want to talk to Savage."

"Who's asking?" None of us had noticed Jessie Petit, a wiry, white-haired black man in his fifties, who was standing in front of the bedroom door. A revolver dangled from his right hand as casually as a cigarette. I wanted to be excused from this class immediately.

When the guy in the beret cut his eyes away from us, I looked over my shoulder and saw Will emerging from the bedroom. Although he was still thin at the time, Will always walked with the stately deliberation of the much bulkier man he would become. He was wearing a black silk robe with Chinese ideograms crawling up the facing like white spiders. Within the nest of dark hair and beard, his face seemed sleepy and slack, but the eyes were a brilliant, supernatural blue, as startling as the sudden flash of the light on top of a police car.

"What is it?" he demanded.

"It's about your contribution, man," the spokesman finally said. "We're here in the name of the Black Power Solidarity Committee."

"Let them in, Jack," Will ordered.

Stubblefield backed up a few steps, creating a narrow right-of-way.

"Come in," Will said, "have a seat." The invitation seemed more an act of noblesse than a capitulation, and perhaps for this reason the three were reluctant to acknowledge it.

"We don't need your fucking hospitality, man. What we want right now is your contribution to the committee, on behalf of all the black artists and—"

His speech was interrupted by Taleesha Savage, who slammed the bedroom door and stood beside Jessie. Glancing at the tableau, she hastened to her husband's side, her manner wary and protective as she put her arm around his waist. She was a striking creature, tall and lithe and feline in her grace—though at this moment her expression conveyed a hint of razory, sheathed claws, which she wouldn't hesitate to deploy in protecting her mate.

"Gentlemen, my wife."

The two junior committee members registered their surprise; only the man in the beret seemed stoic about the fact that Will Savage's wife was as black as himself.

Stubblefield, meanwhile, was moving slowly along the wall into the living room. My heart nearly stopped when I saw the shotgun leaning against the couch.

"On behalf of—"

"I'm afraid I don't have much cash," Will said, interrupting the speech again. He'd probably heard it already; everyone at the convention was talking about the mysterious group of shakedown artists claiming to represent exploited black musicians. The rumor was they'd tried to kidnap Jerry Wexler.

As Will reached into his pocket, the man on the beret's right thrust his right hand under his jacket.

"There's no need for that," Will said.

He pulled a roll of bills from his pocket and counted them out. "About a thousand, eleven hundred."

"You gotta do better than that."

"Don't you tell him what he's gotta be doing," Taleesha snapped.

"I'll write you a check," Will said cheerfully. "Five thousand?"

"Yeah, and then you call your bank to cancel the motherfucker soon's we out the door."

"If I write you a check," Will said quietly, "you can be goddamn sure that it's good and it will stay good." Will's voice, formerly that of the relaxed and gracious host, was now icy with disdain. He sounded exactly like his father—perhaps his great-great-great-grandfather, the slave owner, who'd killed a man in a duel over an obscure point of honor. He was a hippie one moment and a Savage the next, though of course he was both all along. The hippie had been happy to make a contribution of his own volition; the Savage was outraged that his sincerity would be called into question.

This was a strange compound, and one that Stubblefield still didn't understand. After the committee had sullenly accepted the check and backed out of the room, he expressed his outrage that Will had given them anything. "I could have got to the twelve gauge," he whined. "And Jessie had the thirty-eight."

"They have a legitimate grievance," Will said, his former serenity restored. "Black artists have been getting ripped off in this business since it started."

"Not by you," said Taleesha.

"Maybe not." He shrugged. "By people like me."

"They're running a fucking protection racket," Jack said.

Will lit one of his corona-sized joints and inhaled. "We can all use a little extra protection." It sounded like a line from a song.

The G-men didn't believe for a minute that anyone would casually give six thousand dollars to an unknown bunch of black radicals.

"You're saying they held him up at gunpoint?"

"No, not exactly. He felt like giving it to them."

The special agent whose head looked like an aircraft carrier shook his head in disgust. "What the hell's a clean-cut kid like you doing with a dangerous radical like Will Savage?"

This would not be the first or the last time I heard some version of that question.

II

Will Savage and I were thrown together as juniors at prep school, late arrivals to the class of '67, strangers to a cold New England campus which glows warmly in the memories of a half-dozen generations of American plutocrats. Although our new school was only forty miles from my home and a thousand miles from his, I'd traveled much farther than Will. He was the fifth Savage to matriculate, and the observatory bore the name of his maternal grandfather; I was a scholarship student from a New England mill town down the road, a dying redbrick museum of the Industrial Revolution ringed by fast food and auto dealerships. Will was from Memphis, Tennessee, the first real southerner I'd ever known.

His luggage preceded him. When the housemaster showed me and my parents to the cell that would be my home for the next academic year, two large trunks layered with faded steamer stickers were stacked in the middle of the room, taking up most of the space between the two beds. I unpacked my plaid suitcase while my father made nervous conversation and my mother tried not to cry.

"Your room at home is much nicer," she said, as if trying to assure herself that this snotty school wasn't too good for her son even as she was mourning the perceived necessity of my leaving the nest.

"It's not exactly the Ritz-Carlton," my father agreed. Scared as I was, I wanted to be here, and I wanted to be alone in my new room. I resented this mild criticism. Already, I realize now, I was disowning them in my heart.

My mother is, shall we say, a noticeable woman: nearly six feet tall, she has a bust like the prow of a ship. The fact that she had always been a doting and devoted mother did not prevent me from feeling, somewhere around the dawn of puberty, acutely embarrassed by her sheer physical volume, bright clothing and clarion voice, its broad adenoidal vowels redolent of the tenements of South Boston. She compounded the crime of being the parent of an adolescent by being so damnably conspicuous. My father, as if to compensate, tended to recede; he is, in fact, two inches shorter than my mother, and this, too, was a source of chagrin. Fathers were supposed to be taller and, when visiting their sons' prep schools, were not supposed to wear checked sports jackets worn shiny at the elbows, nor polyester ties. This much, even *I* knew. I was, in short, an ungrateful little shit.

As we'd walked across the lawn to the house, I felt the casual reconnaissance of three young men with lacrosse sticks languidly flicking a ball back and forth, and felt myself wanting. My clothes, my hair, my very walk, did not pass muster. For this I blamed my parents. Now, on the verge of leaving home for the first time in my life, and actually forever, I was most worried that my new roommate would arrive before they left. And a taxi did pull up just as my parents were climbing into our Impala, my mother weeping, supported by my father, who was holding the passenger door open for her. A tall boy hopped out of the cab whistling, wearing aviator sunglasses, a transistor radio pressed to his ear. My father, who despite my partial scholarship was straining his resources to send me here, honked the horn as he slowly pulled away. Brimming with impatience and shame, I raised my hand in farewell but didn't look back. If this show of indifference was performed for the sake of the new arrival, I don't think he noticed, bopping up the flagstone walk ahead of me.

A head taller than me, with shaggy dark hair, he wore ripped khakis and a much worn button-down shirt, the tail of which flapped behind him; he suffered his clothing the way you might inhabit an old summer cottage, cheerfully indifferent to the sagging porch and peeling paint. This was in fact the last gasp of his sartorial conformity; within the year my new roommate would shed the inherited uniform of the preppie and start dressing in rainbow hues and, later, after that psychedelic decade of our youth, in black.

I dawdled up the stairs in his wake. When I reached our room, he was deeply occupied in the task of setting up a stereo. After I introduced myself, he stood up and held out his hand. When he focused on me the effect was quite startling; beneath his dark eyebrows his eyes were bright blue verging to violet, like an acetylene flame.

"Will Savage," he drawled, shaking my hand firmly, almost violently, before turning back to electronics. "Gonna wire us up for some sound here," he said. "You like the blues?"

"Sure," I said, not entirely certain who or what the blues might be. I was relieved to find my new roommate friendly, if somewhat distracted. Within minutes we were listening to an eerie, piercing lament. He sat on the bed cross-legged, nodding behind his sunglasses, explaining with evangelical zeal that the singer—the greatest ever American musical genius—had died at the age of twenty, poisoned by a jealous woman.

"This is the purest art this damn country has produced, man. Listen up. It's like the distilled essence of suffering and the yearning to be free. That's why it could only have been produced by the descendants of slaves."

Will's enthusiasm was initially more convincing to me than the music itself. He listened with rapturous concentration, closing his eyes and tilting his head back, his face contorting in a kind of map of the song's emotional arc. "We're all slaves," he announced suddenly, "but we don't know it." He pointed to the record player. "Him, *he* knows it."

When, after the song ended, I ventured that I liked the Beatles, he sneered. "This is the real thing," he said. "At least the Stones acknowledge their sources."

The music unsettled me, as did the fierce, restless blue beam of his attention when he asked me about myself and absorbed my answers. He seemed intensely interested in my story in spite of my own vague sense of shame at its cheap, Sheetrock and Formica stage sets and lack of high dramatic interest. I simultaneously inflated and disparaged the details of my background. I told him my father worked for General Electric— marginally true: he sold their washers and dryers. I said grandiloquently that my life had been largely lived through books to date, that I liked the novels of Ayn Rand, Salinger and Sir Walter Scott—though I had read only *Waverly*—and the poetry of e. e. cummings and Dylan Thomas.

"He's cool," said Will of the latter. "Old Bobby Dylan copped his name."

I nodded sagely, having absolutely no idea what he was talking about. But I could tell he was impressed with the breadth of my reading, and for the first time it occurred to me that all those lunch hours spent in the library in order to avoid getting beaten up on the playground might yield social as well as academic dividends.

Will's chosen field of erudition was harder to define and—for me— to understand: it revolved around the music scene in his hometown of Memphis, although the music, in his analysis, was part of a larger movement of personal and social liberation. I knew about Elvis, of course— the whole planet knew about Elvis.

"Even before civil rights," he told me, "the musicians were breaking down the barriers, secretly integrating the city. I'd hide under the covers in my parents' house in East Memphis and listen to Rufus Thomas on WDIA in Memphis and WLAC out of Nashville and when I was older I'd sneak down to Beale Street with Jessie Petit—our yardman till my old man fired him—we'd split a pint and listen to the rhythm and blues and I'd say to myself, Shit, the segregationists are right—if white folks find out what they're missing they ain't never going to work for the man anymore. That's why the old man sent me here, they wanted to get me away from that Memphis scene. But the shit's out of the box now and it's spread way beyond Memphis." As if throwing me a sop, he added, "The Beatles are part of it, they're messengers."

He stood up to change the record. "My parents gave me this fucking stationery, has our family *crest* on it. Like I'm going to be writing lots of letters home about the glories of the old school." He paused and looked off. "Tell you what—I'm gonna design me my own crest with the motto, Free the Slaves. And let me tell you, Pat—the slaves are you and me."

I began to worry at this point that my new roommate was crazy.

"You Catholic," Will asked suddenly.

The question threw me. "Is the pope?" I finally responded. This was one of the characteristics of my upbringing I was sort of planning on leaving behind. Growing up Irish Catholic in the fifties and sixties, it was impossible not to feel slightly déclassé among the Protestants, who seemed to be the real natives of the Republic, and who were still being regaled in their own churches with stories of papist idol worship and voodoo.

"Wish I was," said Will. "Next best thing to being Jewish, which is the next best thing to being a Negro. At least you've got a real identity."

I had never considered this aspect of the matter. Will wanted to know all about confession, and in the light of his intense curiosity—caught in the disconcerting focus of those raptorish blue eyes—I suddenly saw one of the more tedious rituals of my life as faintly exotic and interesting. This was one of Will's gifts, within the limits of his choppy attention span: to make you seem interesting to yourself by virtue of his inquisitiveness. Within minutes he'd forced me to reassess two of my manifest handicaps—my bookishness and my Catholicism.

"Do you confess *everything*? Like even your *thoughts*?"

"You're supposed to." Flexing my new independence, I added, "I don't." This was true; ever since the virus of sex had invaded my body I had been unable to make a really honest confession.

As if reading my mind he said, "So if you think about laying a chick, that's a sin?"

"Can you believe it?"

Men of the world, we both stretched out on our beds and contemplated this absurdity. All the tormented hours I'd spent trying to reconcile my unbidden sexual fevers with the supposed dictates of my faith suddenly seemed like so much moral persnicketiness.

Will said, "No wonder Catholic girls are so screwed up about sex."

Were they? I wondered. And how did he know?

"What are you," I asked.

"Episcopalian, Methodist, what's the diff?" He gave the impression that he considered himself cursed at birth. "I come from one crazy-assed family. From the Mississippi Delta by way of Charleston. You know about the Delta?"

"More or less," I muttered. I knew only that it was a geological feature associated with the river. And at that time the delta you heard most about was the Mekong.

"Some say it's the flatness of the land and the isolation and the heat. I say it's karma." He paused and looked out through the wall; this, I would soon discover, was a habit of his—to fall into a reverie in mid-speech. He seemed to count on the fact that you would wait for him to continue, or rather, he didn't really care. "I fully expect to be dead before I'm thirty," he said suddenly. "Drinking and firearm violence run in the family."

He frowned, pushed the hair out of his eyes. Then he announced: "My little brother's dead." Clearly it was something he'd been saving, a fact he considered vital to his own story.

Not knowing what to make of any of this, I said I was sorry. Then, amazing myself, I said that I had a sister who died.

"How did it happen," Will asked.

"We were playing kick-the-can and she ran across the street and got hit by a car." I couldn't quite believe I was lying so fluently. I'd never had a sister—my mother had been unable to conceive after my birth—and I was borrowing her from my friend Jeff Toomey. "She was seven," I added.

"A.J. was fourteen," Will said after a respectful pause. "I was supposed to come east last year but he got killed in a hunting accident and I had to stay home with my mother. It was my fault," he added, tantalizingly, and then we were called down for our first house meeting.

That night we were walking to the dining hall together when Will stopped to stare at a cement mixer on the site of the future science building. There was nothing to see but a hole in the ground and a big yellow cement mixer. "What is it," I asked.

He didn't answer right away. "I don't know, I've always had a thing about them."

"Cement mixers?"

He nodded.

I looked around, worried that somebody might see us here staring at a big yellow truck. "Well, so did I when I was a *kid*." This was the first chance I'd had to act superior to Will, but he didn't seem to notice.

"I dream about them sometimes."

Again I worried that there was something wrong with my roommate. He certainly *seemed* a little crazy. It would be a terrible curse, starting out my new life with a cracked roommate. Finally we resumed walking.

"Someday I'm going to buy one and make a little room in the back cylinder," he said, "and cut a window to look out while somebody drives me around."

My faith in Will's social value was restored when an older boy with a southern accent greeted him warmly in the food line, inquiring about mutual acquaintances.

Everything was so new to me that I no longer clearly remember the sequence of events, but a day or two after we arrived we passed a group of five or six boys lounging in the shade of the big chestnut tree observing us with intense indifference. A small, acne-speckled kid I would later know as Henson said, "Johnny Reb and the Townie," and the others laughed. At that moment I longed to be transported back to my second-rate hometown high school, where at least I could look down on the boys who tormented me. It had been crazy, hubristic, to think I could fit in here.

Will walked up to the group and stood looking down at Henson, who cocked and bobbed his head nervously. Then he turned to the largest boy, whom I already recognized as Jack Stubblefield, a linebacker on the football team, and punched him in the face. Stubblefield fell like a tree, wobbling and bowing slowly to the ground, and Will started calmly back to the house.

"Are you crazy," I asked, exhilarated, after I caught up. "Why'd you hit the big guy? He didn't say anything."

"Ever heard of Lester Holmes," Will asked. "Guitar player, played with

Elmore James and Muddy Waters, I met him a couple of years ago on Beale Street. He told me he'd been thrown in the pen, he was in a cell with about ten other mean, hungry-looking specimens. Right away he could see he was in for some shit. So he said to me, 'You know what I did?'"

By now we had reached the room. Will sat down on the bed, swiping the hair away from his face. A sixteen-year-old suburban kid, I didn't have any idea of the things that might happen to a caged man.

"He said, 'I go up to the biggest, baddest nigger in that cell, boy about ten foot tall, face like King Kong. And I punch him hard as I can right square in the face and knocks him cold. And none of them boys in that cell bothered me the rest of the night including old King Kong.'"

"But, Jack Stubblefield . . ."

"Biggest gorilla in the cage."

"What if he reports you?"

"That's not how it works, Patrick."

In fact the incident seemed to have precisely the effect that Will anticipated. He was treated with cautious respect and, as his friend, I was spared some of the ritual indignities of the new boy. Stubblefield glowered and sulked for a few days, as the bruise on his dumb handsome face ripened purple, and finally he and his gang confronted us one night when we were returning from the dining hall. Striding up to Will, he demanded an apology. Will said he was perfectly willing, if Henson first apologized to us. Henson, the spotty, jumpy little court jester who'd precipitated hostilities, whined in protest, but finally bowed to his leader's command, staring at the ground and gouging the turf with the toe of his Weejuns as he did so. Then Will said, "Sorry I hit you, Stubblefield," and honor was satisfied.

That autumn I took on new colors, seeking to transform myself and to erase the green trail of my blood and upbringing. I talked my mother into sending me part of the housekeeping money for clothes, which I slowly acquired from the prep shop in town. Playing soccer, I earned a certain minor jock status. In these attempts to pander to the elitist tone of the campus I was out of step with the approaching egalitarian drumbeat of the times, despite the fact that I heard the beat every day from the little shelf speakers of Will's stereo.

Will, who already was almost everything I wanted to be, was also transforming himself, sloughing off the dry shell of familial expectation. His disrespect for authority seemed almost pathological, and he seized on small points of discipline against which to rebel—as when he wore a jacket and tie but no shirt to chapel one day, observing the letter if not the spirit of the dress code, for which act of sedition he received a week's detention. If he had been thrown out for drinking or fighting or bad grades—this would have been understood at home. His grandfather had been tossed out of four schools, including this one. But Will was reading *Siddhartha* and D. T. Suzuki and Kerouac, listening to James Brown as well as his beloved Delta blues, imagining a world which the Savages did not own—although he also had the *Wall Street Journal* delivered to our dorm, presumably to check on the progress of stocks in his trust fund.

Will's hair grew longer and shaggier; the administration threatened to expel him unless it was cut. One Saturday afternoon he arranged for a barber to come out to the campus and had Stubblefield and Henson escort him, in handcuffs—for I refused to participate—to a chair in the middle of the quad, where he had an inch cut off his locks in front of the hundred or so students who had heard about the event. It was the first act of political theater I ever witnessed. That Will was able to enlist Stubblefield and Henson was no more amazing than the fact that he managed to escape punishment for this antic.

These changes in each of us were probably more gradual and subtle than they seem now, for we became even closer friends over the course of that academic year and the next. I helped him with the subjects he was too bored to follow in class. And there was one major subject which we never tired of discussing. After lights-out we whispered into the night about whom we would and wouldn't screw, and what we would give to do so. I was deeply, achingly in love with Elizabeth Montgomery, the good suburban witch of *Bewitched,* while Will had a special boner for the duskier Natalie Wood. Besides these public stars, the wives of teachers and housemasters came under intense scrutiny, since there were no other live victims for our fantasies. One night he whispered across the chilly room, "Would you take an F in history to pork Carsdale's wife?"

"God, are you kidding? Absolutely." But in this case I was lying. As much as I might have liked to pork almost anybody, I knew I needed to succeed in school in order to realize my ultimate desires. I would've traded away any number of girls to get into Princeton or Yale.

One evening Will said that the thing that he liked about soul music and the blues, as opposed to, say, "fucking *folk* music," was that it was all basically about sex, not just the words but the actual music itself, and from that moment I started to listen to his records with keener interest. So it wasn't only about freedom, but about sex, this music he was so passionate about. He also told me about his older brother's dirty books—*The Story of O* and *My Secret Life,* part of the same private library where Will had also discovered *On the Road* and *Black Like Me.*

Another night we argued about whether black or white lingerie was sexier. I said black, since I was pretty sure no one I knew wore a black bra or panties; the secret garb of hookers and starlets, they seemed, like sex itself, incredibly strange and kinky. Will argued for white, though I think he took the position just for the sake of debate. It must have been one of the only times in his life he picked white. As I recall he extolled the virginal properties and the thrill of metaphoric soiling and defloration. It certainly didn't occur to me at the time to ask what color of hypothetical female flesh we were trading in. Neither one of us, as it turned out, had conventional tastes, although we weren't about to fess up to it back then.

As in most worldly matters, our relationship was lopsided, since Will's experience far surpassed my own, and even far surpassed the experience I claimed. He'd gone to third base twice and gotten two hand jobs by the time I met him. Or so he said. One of the triples was with a Negro girl who lived on their place in Mississippi. Perhaps most incredible of all—he had also been the fleeting recipient of an actual blow job until his partner, whom he'd gotten drunk specifically for the occasion, threw up in his lap. Brimming with wild surmise, I stayed awake long after he told me this story; I could hardly imagine ever asking anyone to put her mouth on my thing, any more than I could imagine a girl who would do so without being asked. It seemed extraordinary—indicative of a hidden, waiting world that was far more mysterious and splendid than I had ever thought possible. I listened to the rhythm of Will's raspy breathing as I masturbated beneath the starched tattletale sheets, as earnestly and devoutly as I had once upon a time said my prayers.

III

Memphis possesses a jagged vitality that seems more western than southern, as if its inhabitants have never been told that the frontier has moved on and, finally, disappeared. Although physically situated in Tennessee it is the spiritual capital of Mississippi, the metropolis to which planters sent their wives for finery and their sons for dissipation; and to which the sons and daughters of their slaves migrated to escape the brutal drudgery of the cotton fields. The city was once abandoned to fever, and a riverine funk still hangs over the housing projects of the South Side as well as the mansions to the east. At least that's one theory, that it is the big river that makes people there a little crazy—the car-crashing debutantes, the love-triangle murderers, the dipsomaniacal aunts, the suicide uncles, Elvis.

"Why don't you come home with me for Thanksgiving," Will asked one day. We were dawdling on the squash court; Will had an excellent forehand but evidently felt that running for the ball was beneath his dignity.

I didn't particularly want to admit that my parents probably wouldn't stand for it or that in any case we couldn't afford the plane ticket. As if anticipating the latter obstacle Will blithely offered to pay the fare.

Stunned, the best I could manage was "Have you asked your parents?"

"I don't have to ask them. It's my money." When he saw that I didn't recognize this distinction, he said, "I made it."

Walking back to our room, Will stopped in front of the construction site, apparently mesmerized by the sight of the cement mixer churning away. When Will became fascinated by something he was beyond embarrassment. No matter how bizarre his enthusiasms, he believed in them utterly.

Worried that Will might forget or withdraw his offer, I finally succeeded in prying him away. And as soon as we got back to the room, he immediately dug around in the back of his closet and retrieved a crumpled shopping bag. When he dumped its contents onto his bed, I was astonished to see hundreds of bills of various denominations. From this gray-green pyramid Will picked out a handful of tens and twenties and held them out to me.

"I can't," I said.

"Why not?"

"Put it back in the bag, for God's sake. What if Matson or somebody walks in and sees this."

"It's my money."

"Where'd you get it?"

"Just take it. You want to come, right?"

In the end I constructed a flimsy rationale: I would accept the money if Will would clear it off the bed and promise to hide it somewhere else in the future. We'd both be in deep shit, I knew, if anybody found that kind of cash in the room.

"How much is there," I asked, leaning against the door, holding it shut, as he casually stuffed the bills back into the bag.

"I don't know." He shrugged. "A few grand?"

On at least two occasions that semester I'd overheard Will discussing what sounded like large sums of money on the hall telephone; he had transparently changed the subject as soon as he saw me. Now, I didn't inquire further into the source of Will's shopping-bag funds, because I didn't want to know and because I really did want to go to Memphis.

A kid whose name I have forgotten snapped our picture outside the dorm just before we set off for Logan Airport. It's framed alongside the family portraits on my library table, and I've often thought the caption should read, *My real life begins.*

A thin black man waiting beyond the gate called out, "Hey, Mr. Will."

"Hey, Joseph." Will was clearly delighted to see him; just as clearly, Joseph was embarrassed by Will's hearty clap on the back. "If you want to know anything about us," he said, "just ask Joseph."

Will glared at me when I surrendered my suitcase to Joseph, refusing to relinquish his own battered canvas-and-leather duffel. "We can carry our own bags," he said, then made a point, after we reached the car, of sitting up in the front seat, beside Joseph. They talked about their respective families while I sat in the back watching the unfamiliar landscape unscroll. When we passed through a neighborhood of sprawling ranch houses set on expensive-looking lots with incongruous architectural flourishes—cupolas and columned porticoes—Will turned and said, "Down here, anything without wheels, they put columns on it."

Attached to the street by a long lasso of a driveway, Will's house was in an older neighborhood: a brick mansion of Georgian heritage surrounded by four or five acres of mature trees and gardens. A satellite dwelling was set behind the main house. "That's the old man's quarters," Will said, pointing as we drove slowly up the long drive. "After my little brother got killed he moved out there. He comes down to the main house mostly to eat supper and harass the rest of us."

We were greeted with great enthusiasm by Beauregard, a black Labrador retriever, who thrust his head into our crotches and thrashed the air wildly with his clublike tail. Two English setters barked from their kennel stalls behind the garage. The humans were more elusive.

Our first stop was the kitchen, where Will embraced Eula, about whom he'd told me more than he had about his parents. Now the cook, she was once Will's nanny. "Eula here raised me up," he said.

"Don't be telling folks that." She laughed, freeing herself from Will's arm. "They be thinking it's my fault how you turned out. Now go see your mama."

Will's mother was a brittle and elegant ash blonde who received us in the sitting room attached to her bedroom, a pastel chamber lined with floral chintz. She wore a brilliant dressing gown and seemed vaguely convalescent, but I was to discover over the succeeding days that her delicate femininity was annealed to a core of steel. She accepted and returned Will's kiss on the cheek without exactly hugging him, then turned to me. "And you must be Patrick. I've heard *so* much about you, you'd *practically* think Will hadn't met another living soul out east."

"We're *room*mates, Mama," Will said, in answer to this . . . was it a complaint?

"Well, of course you are, dear. And I *couldn't* be more delighted." She patted the settee beside her. "You must be absolutely *exhausted* after your trip. Now Patrick, set down and do tell me every little thing about yourself."

Will motioned me toward the door. "We're going to get something to eat, Mama."

"Your hair is dreadful," said his mother. "You look like that awful singer who lives in that awful house out on Fifty-one Highway."

No mention was made of Will's father, and it was only at supper that he made his appearance.

Will's description had led me to expect a monster, whereas Cordell Savage was a smaller man than I'd anticipated, shorter than Will—a recent development, I gathered; shaking Will's hand in the dining room he said, "Just because you're taller doesn't mean you won't get your damn hair cut first thing tomorrow, you hear?" Like his son, he was dark and handsome in a slightly menacing way—with heavy brows and the same blue, metal-cutting eyes. My own reception was far more generous, and once he heard it was my first visit to the South he greeted me like an official ambassador. " . . . And welcome to my home—I'm still titular head of the household though I've been exiled out back to the summer palace."

"You moved out there your own self."

"Boys who backtalk their fathers sleep under the stars."

"Fine by me," Will muttered faintly; I could see that for all his rebellion he was still afraid of his old man.

Cordell gave me the grand tour and pointed out a few of the highlights of his castle—portraits of noteworthy ancestors, including a Confederate general, whose full-dress uniform with saber hung from a mannequin in the library, and an alcove devoted to athletic trophies, medals and photos of Will's older brother holding various sticks and balls. "Elbridge is a hell of an athlete," he remarked, as Will slouched lower, appearing almost invertebrate; if there were a competition in sullen adolescent posture my friend could have won the gold medal at that moment.

Alongside Elbridge's trophies were artifacts from the ancient Egyptian city of Memphis, with which Cordell seemed to feel an almost mystical connection. The shelves and vitrines in the paneled library displayed ceramic and granite vases, limestone panels incised with hieroglyphics, wooden and cast-bronze figures with human and animal heads, dusty clay lamps and hundreds of amulets: mystical eyes called *uzats,* which protected the wearer against ghosts, snake bites and envious words; a red carnelian girdle tie of Isis, which washed away the sins of its possessor; and dozens of *scarabaei*—dung beetles with the heads of men and rams and bulls in jade, amethyst, crystal and obsidian, which were prophylactic against annihilation.

He handed me a beautiful object which he informed me was an alabaster kohl jar, carved approximately in the shape of a woman. "Feel that," he said. "Feel the coolness, the smooth curve of the stone. Imagine: four thousand years ago someone held that object just as you're holding it now."

"My father believes he's a reincarnated pharaoh," Will noted.

"All of civilization," Cordell said, "descends from the great alluvial delta of the Nile."

"Which Dad confuses with our own Mississippi Yazoo Delta."

"There are intriguing parallels," his father said. "The founders of our city had a great many reasons to name it after the ancient capital of Egypt."

"The institution of slavery," Will said, "for instance."

"The concept of hierarchy," Cordell countered, "is how I prefer to think of it."

"Easy to do when you're high up in the archy."

"I've had about enough of your talk for now, young man."

I felt acutely uncomfortable witnessing this. I couldn't believe how far Will was pushing it, and I faulted him for the bickering. I found Mr. Savage a terribly intriguing and presentable father.

Supper was served by Joseph, who now wore a white uniform and an impassive expression. Cordell told a great many stories about the family, several concerning a heavy-drinking uncle who had formal engraved cards printed that read: *Meredith Tolliver Savage apologizes for his behavior of _____ night and regrets any damage or inconvenience he may have caused.* He described the cyclical nature of the Savage family fortunes: his great-great-grandfather, a planter, who'd invested heavily in Confederate war bonds; a grandfather who recouped in real estate and poker; his hard-drinking father, who "lost his shirt in '29 and then lost his britches in '31, when cotton fell to five cents"; and more elliptically, his own restoration of the Savage wealth and former properties through a series of entrepreneurial adventures.

"Marrying Mama didn't hurt," Will remarked.

"You should pray to be so fortunate," Cordell said ambiguously, "in your own choice of helpmeet."

"I don't expect to ever get married," Will said.

"Don't be ridiculous," said Mrs. Savage. "Of *course* you'll get married."

"You'd recommend it, would you, Mother?"

"Everyone gets married," she replied stoically.

After dinner Will and I played pool in a paneled room consecrated solely to that pastime, and I remarked that his father wasn't so bad.

"Hey, if the devil wasn't charming," Will said, flipping his hair away from his eyes, as he lined up a shot, "we'd all be living in the Garden of goddamned Eden."

The next day was Thanksgiving. Cordell's parents, I gathered, were both dead, and Will's mother was estranged from hers. Thanksgiving dinner was postponed until the arrival of Will's older brother, Elbridge, who drove in from Sewanee. A handsome sophomore at the University of the South, L.B., as he was diminutized, was clearly the golden boy of the family, adored by parents and younger brother alike.

Cordell seemed indulgent and easy with his firstborn, in contrast to his prickly, almost hostile attitude toward Will; Elbridge was allowed to drink beer at the table and use the milder profanities, a fact I couldn't help noticing when Will's father rebuked him for saying "goddamn" just moments after Elbridge had. Not the least impressive of Elbridge's attributes, along with his racing-green Austin-Healy 3000, was the girl he'd brought home in it. Her name was Cheryl Dobbs, and she was the most beautiful human I'd ever seen. Although it was hard to imagine what might constitute a normal night around the Savage dinner table, Cheryl Dobbs was blatantly a social disruption; Mrs. Savage was overly solicitous in a manner which I would later understand to indicate disapproval, while I went out of my way not to look at her, and thereby was constantly aware of her presence. I could see that Will was stricken, too. Mr. Savage was gallantly flirtatious. "Where exactly do they grow girls as pretty as you," he asked. I blushed at this direct reference to her appearance, which was affecting us so powerfully. It seemed a violation of taboo.

Cheryl told us she'd grown up in a small town in Kentucky. A senior in high school, she'd met Elbridge at a Sewanee football game.

"Cheryl's a champion majorette," Elbridge informed us.

The putative champion blushed. "Go on, L.B., you're just embarrassing me now."

"How about a demonstration?" Cordell suggested.

"Now?" she asked, in a voice which suggested she was not entirely averse, looking around the table for guidance.

"Let the poor girl eat her supper," said Mrs. Savage.

Cheryl looked to Elbridge, who seemed amused at the notion. "Go right ahead, honey." Then I saw him wink at Will.

"My baton's just upstairs in my valise," she said, jumping up from the table, her eyes shining. "Won't be but just a minute." She disappeared, leaving an awful void behind her.

"The halftime show is a great American tradition," said Cordell Savage. "A great southern tradition."

"She's a very traditional girl," Elbridge said, smiling cryptically. I wondered if he was being condescending.

Within minutes Cheryl had returned with her baton, ripely overflowing a spangled cheerleader's outfit. She stood next to Elbridge, all shy and eager. "Usually I have my music," she apologized.

"We'll just sing along in our own heads," Mr. Savage proposed.

I turned around in my chair as she took up a position between the table and the sideboard. The performance was excruciating. That she was skillful did nothing to lessen the embarrassment I felt for her. On the other hand, it was a relief to have license to stare at her; seeing her engaged in this lumpish dance humanized her in my eyes.

Thoroughly unaware of my tortured attitude, she marched in place, twirled and threw her baton, cartwheeled across the carpet, tossed her hair like a brilliant yellow banner and finally landed in a split, the long scissors of her bare legs glinting on the faded Tabriz. We all clapped, even Mrs. Savage; her husband whistled through his teeth. Cheryl bowed and resumed her seat, glistening beneath a fine sheen of perspiration like some freshly rinsed fruit.

Two hours later we were skirting the southern edge of Memphis in the Cadillac, Will driving like a crazy man, running stop signs, a beer clenched between his thighs. A terrifying driver, he seemed to feel obliged to tempt fate every time he got behind the wheel. Later in life he would have a driver, which is the only reason he's alive today.

After dinner he had changed into black jeans, a black turtleneck and pointed black boots. He then opened a locked drawer in his desk, from which he extracted another paper bag filled with wadded-up currency—singles, fives, tens and twenties. "I've got more, about ten thousand buried out back," he said, stuffing bills into his pockets, "and way more than that down in Mississippi."

"From what?"

"You'll see."

In the car, Will talked of Cheryl and her virtues while I clutched the dashboard in preparation for disaster. "Man, can you believe Elbridge," Will asked in a tone of stunned admiration. "Lucky bastard."

We finally came to rest in front of a squat cinder-block bunker on a block of derelict frame houses. A brilliant mural in pink and black depicted flamingos—as stylized as the totem animals of a cave painting—high stepping to the notes of a stick-figure band. The sign over the door identified the place as THE HOT SPOTTE. A huge black man in an electric-blue sharkskin suit guarded the door. After a moment he recognized Will, who shook his hand and shouted a greeting above the din.

Inside, the establishment seemed to be on fire. From what I could see through the thick smoke, the bar was lined with black men in hats who looked us over skeptically. Two couples danced to the music from the jukebox; after three months as Will's roommate, I recognized the voice of Jackie Wilson.

I'd never seen the inside of a bar before; if I'd been suddenly, inexplicably transported to the Elks Lodge in Des Moines, Iowa, I would have felt a frisson of exotic danger. But this was like standing on the thundering lip of Victoria Falls, teetering above the steamy abyss. The walls were covered in red shag carpet, and the patrons were dressed with a meticulous flamboyance that made me feel distinctly underdressed. Will had disappeared. I tried to find a posture that would seem natural and fixed my attention on a tiny stage where three musicians were setting up their equipment. Painted on the bass drum was the legend LESTER HOLMES & THE SOULFULS. When Will finally returned, he was holding two beers and a ratty cigarette. He handed me one of the beers and lit the cigarette as a fourth man with tight glistening curls and a sequined jacket hopped up on the stage to scattered applause.

Will handed me the cigarette. When I reminded him I didn't smoke he shouted, "It's grass." Had I been anywhere else I would have declined, or argued, but instead I inhaled the weedy smoke, perhaps sensing that it might make me feel less out of place, eager for any ritual that would ease my profound discomfort.

"Lester's going to be as big as James Brown if I have anything to say about it," Will shouted. I nodded vigorously as if this were my firm conviction, too, and took another drag; minutes passed, it seemed, before I suddenly examined the statement and found it improbable. Then in another moment it seemed the most reasonable assertion in the world, and when Lester began to play I decided he was indeed the greatest singer and guitar player I'd ever heard. The music entered my body and took over my heartbeat and respiration. I felt as if I were somehow participating in its creation, sensed that every brain stem in the room was synchronized to this powerful rhythm, all of us part of a single nervous system. Lester and the band were the nucleus, and we were all orbiting electrons.

"Lester's drawing blood from that *gui*tar," Will said, accenting the first syllable in the Deep South manner. The audience talked back, exhorting him to *Say it* and *Sing it.* I found it hard to take my eyes off him, his sinuous moves inducing a kind of hypnotic rapture. A woman bobbing in front of the stage kept calling out, "Ride my alley, Lester."

Between songs, another fan called out, "You fast, Lester."

"Lightning would be faster," he growled into the mike, " 'cept it zags."

I've always been a highly self-conscious person, but that night was one of the few times in my life I experienced a warm dissolution into a pool of collective consciousness; it provided me with a sympathetic point of reference for the strange fervor that's driven Will for thirty years, and has enabled me to see the continuity in his quest from juke joints to private-jet debauches, from shooting galleries to Zen monasteries. Briefly, I think, I got it. Somehow connected to everything, I felt liberated from the narrow box of my own small existence. And if the exhilaration of that moment faded with the night, I can recall the force of it still. It was like the rocket transport of sex, like emerging from Plato's cave into the brilliant sunlight of life itself.

Suddenly we were helping the band load equipment into an ancient pickup truck. Then quite naturally we found ourselves in the front room of a small frame house. Just like that. I thought this a wonderful way to move around the planet, eliding and deleting the boring intervals of transport, zapping from one high point to the next. When I later tried to explain this feeling to Will he nodded approvingly, holding his hair back from his face as he did so: "You segue from one hit to the next, without commercial interruption."

I was straining to hear Lester's bass player above the din: "I use to play spiritual," he shouted, "but I had to quit. You can't play the blues on Saturday night and go to church Sunday and sing God's music. You gots to be pure. Your heart gots to be pure. The preacher he say to me—'I know what you was doing last night and it ain' right. You got to do one or t'other.' So now I jes' play these nasty old blues."

The new venue was not nearly large enough to contain all of us, though it did, as if its plywood and tar-paper skin were infinitely elastic. Everyone danced to the music from the record player, including several small children and a white-haired relic with gold teeth. The floor throbbed beneath our feet, rough planks showing between odd sheets of brown speckled linoleum. If anyone thought I looked ridiculous they were polite enough to keep it to themselves.

The women made a show of fighting one another to dance with us. Will graciously declined these invitations. He did not dance, he just swayed. For all his apparent ease, and his intoxication, he maintained a habitual remoteness. Spending much of his life among black people, he preserved his dignity and possibly his life by never pretending to be anything but a white man. He seemed to belong, but not by virtue of aping the behavior of the local populace, nor of a moist heartiness. I was just the opposite, slapping backs and attempting to reproduce the moves of those around me. A few hours before I'd been sucking up to the plantation owner and studying his manners; now I wanted to have soul. Set me down on the street with a one-legged man, Will once said of me, and I'll be limping inside of a block.

Under the benign influence of cannabis, I felt I could do no wrong, and the funky, foreign smell of all those bodies packed together seemed a powerful intoxicant in itself. I'd been dancing with a girl named Belinda, who kept ignoring the tall interloper with a keloid scar across his chin who tried to claim her after the first dance. Refusing to look at me, he tugged on her shoulder and hissed until she finally slapped his hand away and told him to leave her alone. When the tempo dropped with the opening notes of "I've Been Loving You Too Long" I reached out to embrace my partner for a slow dance. She grabbed me and pressed me into the soft wilderness of her breasts while thrusting the hard ridge of her pelvis into mine.

When I was suddenly, violently dislodged from this refuge, I could not understand by what agency, until I saw the skinny, shiny-faced man with one hand wrapped around Belinda's neck and the other pointing a knife at me. He said, "How you like to get stuck, white boy?"

Even before I had time to be afraid Lester Holmes had grabbed him from behind and shaken the knife from his hand. "This boy's a guest in my house," he said, cuffing the attacker with an open hand. "He don't know nothing. Just a dumb little shit. If you can't hold on to your woman, that ain't no doing of his."

"I ain't his woman," shouted Belinda, who had retreated out of reach. Returning to the fray, she reached over and punched the captive in the face.

Lester escorted the man out and the music resumed, but without me. If I'd felt like a dreamily detached spectator at my own near evisceration a moment before, I was now scared straight. I saw Will standing in the corner, conferring languidly with Ronald, Lester's bass player. As I approached, Will tipped his beer bottle illustratively at me. "These Yankees come down here, Ronald, don't know how to behave themselves, messing around with some other cat's woman, getting in knife fights and all."

The bass player smiled broadly, nodding his head up and down. And I was stung, because it occurred to me that Will possibly had more in common with this Negro musician twice his age than he did with me. Though I'd just been forced to acknowledge that I was a white boy in a room full of coloreds, I'd thought I had at least one natural ally in the room. Now I was not so sure. Maybe I was all alone. Maybe Will didn't even like me. Maybe no one could ever understand anyone else, all of us trapped forever alone in our own hard skulls. . . .

I was stoned, my addled and unfamiliar mind making sharp turns, unnatural leaps. Seeing my distress, Will punched my shoulder. "We just might make a hipster out of you yet."

"So why aren't you dancing?" I said, wanting to question his own credentials.

"I don't dance," he said emphatically, the way a Baptist might declare that he didn't drink.

"That's true," Ronald agreed. "He don't." His tone seemed to indicate that he regarded this as an impressive if bizarre achievement.

"I *might* dance," Will said. He stroked his hair away from his forehead thoughtfully. "If that little girl over there in the door would dance with me, I just might."

Ronald laughed mirthlessly through his nose. "Shit, boy. You ought'er just said Ann-Margret. Fact, you got a way better shot at her. That's Lester's niece Taleesha. Lester don't let nobody near her. A little princess, that girl. Her daddy's a big nigger in town, own a couple funeral parlors. And her mama was Lula James, the blues singer."

"No shit?" Will's interest was if anything redoubled. "Whatever happened to her?"

"Tha's a good question. She done married this funeral parlor gentleman, and he made her give up the music, get respectable you might say. Well, she had a baby, that you're looking at right now, and a couple more, but I guess she couldn't stay respectable and finally she just up and left and ain't nobody seen her from that day to this."

I'd noticed the girl in question, slouched against the wall, looking on but not partaking of the festivities, perhaps the only person in the place besides Will who hadn't danced. I couldn't judge her age. Though she was at least my height she had the awkward posture and the uncertain gestures of a brand-new adolescent, of someone unused to new limbs. Her elongated and delicate features seemed suggestive of ancient Egypt. Motionless, she was a serene statue presiding over the Dionysian frenzy. Then, thrusting a sharp elbow into the air, she stuck a finger in her nose and probed, finally removing it to inspect her findings. Observing this secret bit of grooming from across the room, Will and Ronald hooted with laughter.

Looking back, I think it was this memory that in later years gave me the confidence to live up to Taleesha's assumption that I was an elder statesman, immune from the violent tides of blood and passion, though she was only a few months younger, and somehow always made me feel a little like a foolish boy.

"How old is she," Will asked.

"Old enough to nasty," I said with the false bravado of a virgin.

"I done told you, man, Lester don't let nobody mess with his niece, man."

"We'll just see about that," said Will, staring intently. And I realized then that he was extremely stoned. With Will, it was hard to tell; for all the massive quantities of stimulants and depressants he ingested, you had to know the signs: long pauses and ellipses, and, in this case, a certain glazed concentration. Suddenly the girl looked our way. She rose out of her slouch, stiffening as if for battle, and sneered at us before turning away.

A body detached itself from the rhythmic mass and crashed into me. The man apologized profusely, exhibiting the thorough and decorous contrition of the happy drunk. I was exhausted and eager to leave. "If you're gonna ask then ask her already."

Ronald smiled, showing an irregular row of brown teeth. "I got a dollar says no way."

"I'll take it," said Will. He finished his beer, stroked his hair back with both hands and started over with a determined stride that carried just the hint of a waddle. Years later, when he became very large, I realized he had finally grown into that walk—the confident fleshy march of a man on whom cars and planes and bankers wait—as if his body had known all along its eventual shape.

The girl stiffened and seemed to grow taller and sterner and older as he said whatever he was saying. At one point she spoke. I was just about to turn my attention elsewhere when she slapped him. It was so quick and unexpected I wondered if I'd imagined it. Will stood there, nodding his head. Then he bowed slightly from the waist and retreated.

Ronald was slapping his thigh. He pocketed his dollar and told Will he'd better leave before Lester returned from out back.

"I'm not worried about Lester," Will said, and he probably wasn't. "But my friend here's tired."

We breaststroked our way through the humid murk. Belinda caught up to me on the porch and tried to convince me to stay, or to take her wherever we were going. She kissed me wetly and ran her hand between my legs, but Will was revving the car and in the end I was a little afraid—of her, of sex, of the mysterious chasm of race. I told her, improbably, that I'd come back for her tomorrow and jumped in the car.

We peeled out, spitting gravel back across the lot, and raced away with the windows wide open.

"That was wild," I howled over the rush of the cool air.

Will nodded. He was silent, withdrawn.

Finally I shouted, "What the hell did you say to that girl, anyway?"

He kept driving as if he hadn't heard me, and it would be years before I heard the punch line.

IV

ate at night, there are two kinds of errant sons—those, like me, who try to sneak in quietly, and those who defiantly jam the brakes and slam the doors as if to insist they'll never stoop to stealth. Will was the latter. He slammed the car door twice for good measure, possibly in the hope that the sound would carry up the hill to the little house where the lights were glowing ominously.

It seemed as if I'd just finished undressing and fallen backward onto the bed when I was startled bolt upright by a pounding on the door of my room and a series of shrill squawks. Finally I recognized Mr. Savage's voice between the duck calls. "Rise and shine. Coffee's on the stove and the ducks are on the water."

It was still pitch dark when we piled into the station wagon. Elbridge rode shotgun, while Will and I collapsed groggily in the backseat with Beauregard the lab, who was as excited as Will was sullen.

The external world seemed incredibly strange: the cold morning air freighted with smells of leaf decay and wet dog fur, the cinematic flashes of landscape scooped up fleetingly in the cone of the headlights. Drunk and stoned, within minutes I fell asleep.

Later, I was prodded awake by Will and presently found myself on the edge of a dock, looking out into the blackness. At Mr. Savage's instigation, I stepped uncertainly down into the varnished ribs of a boat that resembled a large canoe with a flat stern. Our guide—a silent, camouflaged figure—huddled over what looked like a lawn-mower engine.

Will's father sat beside me as we spluttered across the water, Will and Elbridge following in a second boat. Now and again, like a wading giant, a dark cypress would loom up out of the oblivion. "This was all dry land here," Cordell announced over the gurgle of the engine, "and then round about 1811 there was an earthquake, maybe the most violent earthquake on this continent ever. Felt the tremors all the way to Boston and New Orleans. At the time this was the hunting grounds of the Chickasaws. A clubfooted chief named Reelfoot was their top dog, and according to legend he stole a Choctaw princess for his wife, whereupon the Great Spirit stamped his giant hoof, crushing the old clubfoot and creating this lake." He laughed. "Or so they say. There was a white settlement across the river called New Madrid, and when that earthquake hit they figured it was Judgment Day for sure. The earth rolled like a storm sea and belched out sulfur and smoke. Darkness fell for a week. Right out of the Book of Revelation—all fire and brimstone and sulfurous stink."

He was interrupted by a thump on the bottom of the boat as the stern rose and fell over an obstruction in the water.

"Cypress knee," he said. "And there's still stumps from the forest that was here before the quake. The land downstream rose up and the land here dropped fifty feet. They say the Mississippi ran backwards for three days, which is how the lake was formed. God knows how many Indians drowned right underneath us."

All at once I could see the dead warriors, fish nibbled and bloated in their buckskins, rising from the muddy bottom. I almost leaped out of the boat when we hit another cypress knee.

When we passed close to a rectangular blind rising on stilts out of the black water, he observed, "Plenty of white men have died since, disputing the fishing and hunting rights." Something in the way he said it suggested that this was a different order of mortality.

Twenty minutes later I was shivering in a duck blind situated at the edge of a spongy island which was an ancient Chickasaw burial mound, clutching a 12-gauge Winchester pump. Will's father had explained its operation, but I had no idea if, when the moment came, I would remember what to do, or if I could stand up to the kick. Cordell was still in the boat with the guide, laying out decoys. Gradually their silhouettes grew more distinct beneath a pewter sky turning pink to the east. And suddenly Will, who I thought was dozing in the corner of the blind, raised his gun to his shoulder and aimed it directly at his father's head.

Shocked by this tableau—son posed for patricide—I couldn't quite believe what I was seeing. In a moment the gun again was resting over his shoulder, and I wondered if my senses, still scrambled from the night, had conjured a hallucination out of the morning haze. Until I looked at Will's face.

"If we'd only stayed out another hour," he snarled, "we could have missed this fucking adventure."

Coming ashore, Mr. Savage said he'd keep an eye on me and sent his sons into the adjacent blind with the guide. Both nervous and eager, I was determined not to disgrace myself. And finding it impossible to reconcile last night's world with this morning's, I opted out of choosing and gave myself over to the tutelage of Cordell Savage.

The chatter of invisible ducks drew closer. "On a passing shot," he whispered, "pick your bird, start from behind, swing your barrel through him and fire. On an incoming bird, just try to put the bead below its beak."

Beauregard's cheerful panting increased in tempo. "Stay down until I give the signal." Ducks called all around us, squawking in casual, interrogative tones. A loud, brassy invitation issued from the blind beside us—the guide with his call, trying to lure them in. Sky and water were now clearly distinct. Cordell peered intently through the slit of the blind and finally said, "Now!"

Rising, I looked into a sky full of violent wings—shots booming all around me—and fired into the maelstrom. The impact knocked me backward. By the time I'd recovered my balance, Mr. Savage had lowered his gun, and Beauregard was paddling in the water, where four ducks were floating.

"Got a double," Elbridge called from the other blind. I was fairly certain that none of the birds was mine. My mentor saved me the trouble of pretending. "Don't worry," he said. "You'll get the hang of it."

For the first time I could take in my surroundings: I found myself in a Pleistocene swamp, a miscegenation of land and water for which "lake" seemed a dubious label.

Half an hour went by without any further activity. By now the sky was bright, the sun invisible behind low clouds. Mr. Savage pointed out a bald eagle wheeling overhead. "Benjamin Franklin opposed adopting the bald eagle as our national symbol," he whispered, "he wanted the damn wild turkey—can you imagine?—because he said the eagle lived in part by killing other birds." He snuffled in amusement, wiped his nose ostentatiously on his sleeve. "Seems highly appropriate to me."

He sucked thoughtfully on his cigarette. "I know Will didn't want to come out here today," he whispered, glancing over at me. "Two years ago he was supposed to hunt quail down the Delta with me and some old boys. He was out late with this caretaker we had. I inherited Jessie with my marriage and I finally had to fire his ass on account of his trying to turn my boy into a goddamn juvenile delinquent. I swear to God it's a wonder Will's skin isn't black as coal the amount of time he spent in the damn servants' quarters and sneaking around Beale Street instead of asleep in his room."

He raised his head above the edge of the blind in reconnaissance before resuming his story.

"Anyway, Will stayed in bed and I brought his younger brother along. We were hunting horseback. Charlie Ledbetter had taken his gun out of the scabbard for some damn reason when his horse stepped in a hole and went down. Gun went off. Hit young A.J. square in the chest. Lifted him right out of his saddle." He fell silent at the sound of an approaching flight, which eventually faded to the east. "I think Will blames himself," he said. "Which isn't to say he doesn't blame me."

We were silent for some time again before he spoke. "He ever tell you that story?"

"No sir," I said. "Not exactly."

"Not a day goes by I don't wish it was me on that buckskin mare." He turned and looked at me seriously for the first time. It was a long searching look, a blatant appraisal, and I can't imagine what he might have seen to please him, for I was nervous and hung over and tired all the way to the ends of my hair and to this day I can't comfortably meet the sustained gaze of a man like Cordell Savage. But it was at that moment, I believe, he decided to deputize me as his representative to Will. He offered me a cigarette, a Lucky Strike, and for the second time in less than twenty-four hours I accepted a ritual smoke, though the two implied promises seemed incompatible and even contradictory.

My pact with Will's father was sealed with my first kill. When a string of high fliers approached our blind from the south, he let me take the shot. I stood and tracked the lead mallard, swinging from behind and pulling the trigger as the bead cleared the outstretched green head. To my astonishment the duck folded neatly and tumbled out of the sky at a forty-five-degree angle, seeming to fall for many miles before crashing into the cattails on the island behind us. Beauregard was already thrashing through the rushes; I was right behind him, oblivious to the harsh abrasion of the saw grass.

Holding the limp, broken body of the mallard in my hand I was briefly touched with remorse. I stroked back the feathers of the bird and saw, amidst the forest of quills, three shiny lice writhing on the translucent pink skin. Sinking to my knees, I threw up, retching stealthily under cover of the cattails as Beauregard barked and licked my neck. When I was finally purged I heard them calling my name. Wiping my mouth, I stood up holding my trophy overhead, and slogged back to the blind, affecting a triumphant mien that became real once Mr. Savage clapped me on the back and said, "That was a fine shot, boy."

"Come on, I wanna show you something." Will was shaking me. I woke with a start in the shotgun seat of the Cadillac, apparently in the same neighborhood where we had dissipated ourselves the night before. In the fading light of the afternoon, three sullen Negroes in fedoras slouched in front of a dilapidated storefront, smoking and surveying us with suspicious insouciance.

I followed Will, who nodded and walked past them into the store. A pool table took up half of the room within; a couple of pinball machines and a card table with folding chairs completed the furnishings. The two men playing pool looked up. "If it ain't my man Will," said the small, white-haired man who'd been shooting. He walked over and exchanged a complicated, slapping handshake with Will, who in turn introduced him to me, sans hand jive. "Patrick, Jessie Petit. Jessie's my chief operating officer."

"That's what he says." His broad smile revealed a gold front tooth. "It's the same old shit, the black man works his ass off, the white man sits on his and collects the take."

"You could always," Will suggested, "go back to work for my old man."

"Well, there's white men and then there's white men."

"Now I suppose you're going to tell me what a bad week we've had."

Jessie laughed an exaggerated, mock-servile laugh. "Well, now you mention it, Knife White hit the box this week and that set us back some."

"Seems like somebody's always hitting big," Will said jovially.

They continued in this obscure vein until two young women entered and, upon seeing us, started to back out; but Jessie waved them in and shooed us away. "Get on out of here, you bad for business."

Back in the car I asked what kind of business Jessie was in.

"Numbers," Will said. "He runs it, I back it. I'm the bank."

"You don't look like a bank."

I'd heard the phrase "numbers racket" but hardly knew what it meant; I was only partly enlightened by the explanation Will delivered as we raced at terrifying speed through the back streets of South Memphis.

"Jessie was the groundskeeper on our place. He was the one who turned me on to the blues. All the time I was growing up he said he could get rich if only somebody'd back him in a numbers game. They all play the numbers—it's like, I don't know, a lottery. Pick three numbers and if they come up you win, a few hundred, a thousand, depending on the bet. Jessie just needed a bank. So I went to my uncle Jerome and asked to borrow ten grand and told him I'd pay him back in a month with interest. Well, old Uncle J., he gave me my first drink and my first cigarette and he was always crazy as a bedbug and hot on the idea of corrupting minors. So now Jessie and me got so much money we don't know where to hide it."

He threw the car into a hard left turn, which slammed me up against the door.

"Where do you get the number," I asked after I had regained my balance.

"The *Wall Street Journal*. Last digit of three Dow-Jones averages—industrials, utilities, transportation. Bets close at three p.m. Memphis time. An hour later when the exchange closes in New York you got the number."

This fact suggested an intriguing if tenuous linkage between the poor sporting blacks of Memphis and the financial barons of Wall Street, and explained Will's unlikely subscription to the *Journal*.

Will and I sat quietly through dinner that night—leftover turkey—while Cheryl smoldered innocently and Elbridge tried to explain to his father why he was taking a poetry class.

"Seems like a damn waste of time and money," Mr. Savage said.

"For a nineteenth-century southern gentleman," Elbridge claimed, "having a dozen or two poems committed to memory was as important as knowing how to shoot."

Mr. Savage turned to me. "Fine piece of wing shooting," he declared. "Now you're blooded." Tired as I was, I believe I blushed. As soon as we could, Will and I excused ourselves and crawled upstairs.

"I'm so goddamned tired," I declared, "if Cheryl Dobbs spread herself naked across my bed I'd tell her to go find her own place to sleep."

"I don't know that I'm quite that tired." Will opened a window and took a pack of cigarettes from a bureau drawer. I shook my head when he offered me one. I'd done enough smoking for one year.

"She's not so hot," he said suddenly.

"Not so hot? Are you crazy?"

"She's got no spirit, no soul," he said, blowing smoke out the window. "She's like a pinup."

"Exactly," I said. "That's what I mean."

"Two-dimensional."

"That girl's as three-D as they come," I insisted. "What do *you* like, that scrawny little colored girl?"

He narrowed his eyes and looked at me. "Maybe," he said. I couldn't tell if he was serious or just trying, as he often did, to get a rise out of me.

Suddenly the door burst open and Elbridge bounded in. "Hey, what you faggots up to? Shit, Will, you better put out that butt before I call your headmaster."

Elbridge plucked the butt from Will's fingers and took a drag. Beneath his other arm he cradled several books.

"If you didn't know better," Will said, "you'd think L.B. was a redneck."

"Don't go blowing my cover," Elbridge said. "Next you'll be telling people I know how to read and approve of desegregation."

"What have you got?" Will demanded, grabbing for the paperbacks under his brother's arm. After a brief struggle, Will claimed the books— Jean Genet's *Our Lady of the Flowers,* Henry Miller's *Tropic of Capricorn* and Richard Brautigan's *A Confederate General in Big Sur*—which were apparently intended for him all along.

"Don't go telling anyone where you got 'em, little bro."

Will admired the volumes with undisguised relish. "Thanks L.B."

"You boys up for a party in town," he asked. "See some of the quality? I don't want your friend to get the wrong impression of us, think we're all a bunch of Negro musicians and dope fiends." I was flattered that Will's older brother seemed to care about my opinion. Minutes later, as we roared out into the night, I sat quietly in the backseat of the Cadillac with Will, watching Cheryl's golden hair bouncing in front of me for miles like a prize that would always be just out of my reach. This reverie was broken when Elbridge pulled through a set of stone gates and drove up to a luminous white mansion floating on a wide dark lawn, its circular drive an enchanted ring of white Cadillacs, red Mustangs and a matched pair of British racing-green MGs. This looked remarkably like the world to which I wanted to belong.

Raucous knots of clean-cut revelers loitered in the two-story entry hall, which was dominated by a circular staircase. A boy in a crewcut waved from the stairs and called out to L.B., who bounded up to meet him. I felt I had walked into a movie set, but at least, in my chinos and button-down shirt, I looked like the other boys. My first impression of the girls was that they all came in pastel shades—turquoise, peach and pink. The boys were essentially unchanged from that breed William Tecumseh Sherman had identified a century before, in a letter to Lincoln, as the "young bloods of the South: sons of planters, lawyers about town, good billiard-players and sportsmen, men who never did work and never will."

One of them was introduced to me as Spook Lawson. "You still up at that Yankee homo ranch," he asked Will.

"Spook," Will said to me, "was, as you may have guessed, unable to gain entry to any of the nonmilitary schools up east."

Somehow Will disappeared and I found myself standing alone, acutely self-conscious, with Cheryl. I wanted to take the opportunity to impress myself upon her, to tell her who I was, to tell her *that* I was; she couldn't possibly imagine the sheer vivacity of my being, the poetry of my fierce yearnings and fears, or she wouldn't simply be standing, half ignoring me. If she were to register a fraction of my tortured essence surely she would throw her arms around me. But I was at a loss for conversation, and I found it difficult to look at her directly. Beauty often affects us like deformity; we are afraid to seem to notice.

"Nice house," I said, swiveling the beam of my gaze around the hall and beyond.

She nodded. She was probably even more daunted by the surroundings than I was, though at the time I was aware only of my own awkwardness.

"You want a beer or something," I asked.

"I don't drink alcohol," she said. "I'm a Christian."

A Yankee, I was both puzzled by this non sequitur and stymied in my fantasy quest for Cheryl's attention, for I couldn't even *imagine* a girl yielding to me, except under the influence. Never mind that she was dating my friend's older brother; I was able to conjure away such minor logistical problems. But sobriety seemed insurmountable; and I was running out of time.

"Hey, good-looking," said an older boy in a dark suit who seemed to stand several feet taller than me. "Where'd you come from?"

"Hopkinsville, Kentucky," she answered, taking him at his word.

I felt I should say something to assert my presence, to affirm my role of temporary chaperon, but suddenly another boy had approached, nudging me with his arm as he inserted himself into the company. "Don't mind my friend here. Prescott goes to Dartmouth and doesn't know how to behave around the fair sex. Pack of wild Indians, literally. Uncivilized brutes. Say the word, darlin', and I shall forcibly eject him from the premises."

Prescott grinned at this dangerous sketch of himself, while the newcomer bowed deeply to Cheryl: "Jim Cheatham at your service."

Cheryl was blushing, and in her nervous excitement, she nearly curtsied, clutching the sides of her dress. "Cheryl Dobbs," she said, looking at the floor.

"I'm Patrick Keane," I said, holding out my hand.

"Pat, why don't you get me a beer?" Cheatham turned away from me, deftly sliding toward Cheryl and cutting me out of the circle. At that moment I saw Elbridge approaching with several friends.

I turned and slipped away, chagrined at my dereliction of duty. Unable to find Will, I wandered through the house admiring the furniture and the art, studying the paintings—dour portraits, rural landscapes and hunting scenes—as intently as a visiting art historian. My tour led me into a parlor of sorts, occupied exclusively by couples, draped on the sofas and stuffed chairs, making out. Retreating, I found a refuge—a book-lined, masculine den which was miraculously empty. I scanned the titles: old leather-bound sets of Dickens, Fenimore Cooper, Washington Irving and something called *Tennessee Torts*.

"Careful," said a gravelly, female voice behind me. "No one's touched them in years. They might explode or something." A girl about my own age was standing in the doorway holding a glass full of ice in one hand, a pack of Winstons in the other. Having so far formed an impression of Southern Womanhood as fair-haired and brightly clad, this specimen seemed unusually dark and angular, her straight, shoulder-length hair as black as her turtleneck. She dropped into an armchair, spreading herself like butter over its leather surface, and lit a cigarette.

"So what are you?" she said, leaning her head back to exhale a cloud of smoke. "An intellectual?"

I haltingly introduced myself.

"I'm Lollie Baker," she said. "If you open that cabinet to your left, you'll find a glass and some whiskey."

I hesitated. "Are you sure it's okay?"

"Well, if you mean would Daddy mind, he might, if he knew, but that's what makes it fun." She studied her cigarette as if it were an exotic insect that had just flown into the room and landed unexpectedly in her hand. "It's like," she added, "who'd bother to start smoking if you didn't have to sneak them. That's my philosophy. Anything worth doing's usually prefaced with the words 'thou shalt not.' Except maybe reading." Delivered with a drawl, these sentiments seemed particularly radical. She paused to reconsider. "Hell, even reading's supposed to be done only in moderation in these parts. And of course, well-bred southern young ladies aren't supposed to tax their pretty little brains. Southern gentlemen don't like them too educated." She examined the perilously long ash on her cigarette, then tapped it into the narrow throat of a bronze urn on the table behind her. "How about you? I'll bet you just love these blonde belles with cotton between their ears?"

"I'm just . . . visiting," I responded to this accusation. "I'm a friend of Will Savage."

"Will's all right." Somewhat mollified, she said, "He just borrowed my car."

"What? Where'd he go?"

"Don't worry," she said. "He'll be back. He's probably gone over to the Bitter Lemon, to try to score some dope."

I handed her a bottle of bourbon from the liquor cabinet. "Get yourself a glass," she commanded, then shook several cubes into my tumbler and poured us both a drink. I took mine more in despair than with delight, upset with Will for abandoning me.

"I actually do like to read," I said, after I'd ventured a sip.

"Such as?" She was now studying her glass of whiskey.

I quickly edited a list of my favorites. Salinger seemed too predictable. "Dylan Thomas . . . ," I finally said.

She nodded. " 'The force that through the green fuse drives the flower / Drives my green age . . .'"

"Ayn Rand."

"That crazy old dyke," she barked, then noticed my shocked expression. "I don't know, you get the idea that the Empire State Building's her idea of an excellent dildo."

I've tried to read Ayn Rand several times since that night, but somehow the charge, however reckless, sent her plummeting down the face of a skyscraper into the gutter reserved for embarrassing former enthusiasms. Then, out of local consideration, and because we'd just read "A Rose for Emily" in English class, I proposed Faulkner.

Lollie rolled her eyes. "Yeah, right. Strangle me with kudzu. You should read Kierkegaard"—a new name to me—"and Baudelaire. And maybe some Hammett to toughen you up." She reeled off this eclectic list with the gruff confidence of a doctor prescribing a medication for a specific, if rather common, affliction.

"Are you a writer," I asked hopefully, for this was my secret vice at the time. I wrote poetry. Certainly I had the kind of "Negative Capability" commended by Keats, if not, perhaps, the imagination.

"You ever read Anne Sexton," Lollie asked. "I'm studying with her at Harvard this summer."

I had, in fact, and I was particularly impressed to learn that Lollie was in her junior year at Miss Porter's. "She's good," I allowed. "But I prefer Lowell."

"He's okay." She shrugged, and I saw, with some relief, that I'd discovered one of the boundaries of her reading, though I barely knew Lowell's work myself at the time.

Under the influence of the whiskey I eventually confessed to being something of a poet, and we ended up talking for more than an hour. Lollie discoursed about the dangers of regionalism—"I ain't gonna be no damn southern lady writer, that's for sure," she insisted, after we'd consumed half the bottle of bourbon. Her intention was to move as soon as possible to Greenwich Village, where she would write tough but lyrical, nonprovincial poetry. I became increasingly confident in my own aesthetic, showing off my reading as well as dropping the names of authors who were little more than names to me.

In my tipsy admiration I wanted to impress her, quote her some poetry from memory. But all that came to mind as I watched her light up another cigarette: *Winston tastes good like a cigarette should, no filter, no taste, just a forty-cent waste.* And that Ogden Nash chestnut: *Candy / Is dandy / But liquor / Is quicker.*

Eventually we were climbing the circular staircase under the guise of consulting some volume in her shelves and then we were groping athletically on her bed. My hand slipped beneath the waist of her corduroys and crept stealthily up the smooth skin of her belly until, after long minutes of kissing, she impatiently guided it to its object. I would have been happy enough to lie there kissing her till morning, my hand cupped on the astonishingly soft and amazing curve of her breast, even as I began to wonder if something more might be possible, or even expected of me.

"Don't go away," she whispered, climbing out of bed. "I'll be right back."

I had many restless New England nights, after lights-out, in which to imagine her return to my arms. But it was Will Savage who roused me some time later and dragged me down to the car, and since there was no sign of Lollie I didn't know whether she'd abandoned me before or after I passed out.

V

Back at school that December, Will seemed to draw away, as if compensating for the intimacy of my visit to his home. Or perhaps it was simply that I was playing soccer and studying for finals, while he, though barely passing his required courses, was increasingly involved with such arcana as Buddhism and Beat poetics. His mentor in these esoteric pursuits was his older brother, who seemed to be the leader of a cult of guerrilla intellectuals based in the hills of southeastern Tennessee. My own reading was taking a different turn, under the influence of Doug Matson, our housemaster and my English teacher, a recent Amherst graduate who'd spent a polishing year at Oxford, where he'd acquired, among other things, a new set of vowels. Prematurely curmudgeonly and stately at the age of twenty-three, Matson was as worldly a person as I could imagine, a sort of preppie dandy who wore a neat mustache and favored bow ties and Harris tweeds and, no matter what the forecast, carried an umbrella with which he, in the manner of a Venetian gondolier, propelled himself across the flagstone canals of the campus. In class he recited great swatches of Shakespeare, coughed up gouts of Pater and Ruskin from memory. He was said to have had a short story accepted by *The New Yorker,* although it hadn't actually been published and so far as I know never was, but over the years this rumor became part of the lore of the school, its eternal imminence more intriguing than the consummated fact could ever be.

Matson had studied with Richard Wilbur at Amherst. One day after class, when I confessed my interest in poetry, he directed me to Shakespeare's sonnets and then to Eliot, Berryman and Lowell—scholar poets bristling with canonical learning. The fact that I was as yet largely unfamiliar with the canon didn't discourage me in the least. I particularly liked Lowell, the renegade patrician, who conferred on the relatively familiar landscape of Boston an antique dignity. Like Matson, I preferred the clotted sonority of his earlier work to the more recent confessional free verse. When Lowell lowered the net on the prosodic tennis court, in *Life Studies* and *For the Union Dead,* Matson felt the betrayal as acutely as did folk fans when Bob Dylan went electric. Ginsberg and Ferlinghetti, Will's poets, were naturally anathema. I followed my mentor in such matters, though I secretly loved the unbound final lines of "For the Union Dead," with its indictment of the shabby present:

> Everywhere,
> giant finned cars nose forward like fish;
> a savage servility
> slides by on grease.

But this was recreational reading; when the first snow fell, I was desperately struggling with calculus, French and a paper on *Macbeth.* Will, sitting across the room at his own desk, was reading a subversive pamphlet called "The White Negro."

"Listen to this," he said. " 'The source of Hip is the Negro, for he has been living on the margin between totalitarianism and democracy for two centuries.' Is that great or what?"

"What course is it for," I asked.

"It's for the course called Life. You should take it sometime, Patrick."

"You're going to flunk out if you don't start your term papers."

Will fixed me with a wry smirk. "If you just said that in a phony English accent you'd sound exactly like Matson." Will and Matson could not abide each other. Matson was sarcastic about Will's musical and literary predilections, which he deemed crude and vernacular, and awarded him a stream of demerits for curfew and noise violations. Will found Matson pretentious and obtuse and refused to pretend otherwise.

"It's not an English accent."

"No? Where'd he learn to say *shedule*—at Amherst? 'I say, old man, we're bloody well running a bit behind *shedule*, what?' Did his parents teach him to talk like that? He picked up the fucking accent in the duty-free shop at Heathrow."

"He lived there, for Christ's sake." Even at the time, I knew this was lame.

"Bad enough he carries that fucking umbrella everywhere. What's really bogus is he calls it a *brolly*."

"Does not."

"There are certain words no American should be allowed to say under pain of death. Under pain of being beaten to death with their so-called brollies. Of having their so-called brollies shoved up their—"

"Look, I just don't want you to flunk out. Is that so uncool?"

"I'm not touching that question. But, hey, not to worry. I have a plan." He held up a bottle of green-and-white capsules. "Diet pills," he said, when I gazed at them blankly. "On the seventh day God rested and on the eighth day he opened the pharmacy." He laughed. "Enough to keep me up for finals week." Standing up, he pushed his hair out of his eyes, threw his shoulders back and smirked at me. "Excuse me sir," he said, "may I go to the loo?"

"Fuck off."

"Very good, sir." He marched toward the door, then paused. "Cheerio."

Will made good on his promise, staying up every night that week, camping out in the library till ten and then returning to the dorm, where I coached him through a half hour of calculus. After lights-out he would read all night in the wedge of light from his hooded desk lamp while I slept with a pillow over my head. His blue eyes rimmed with red, he would capsulize his reading for me the moment I woke up, declaiming that our American history texts were riddled with propaganda. "The whole shiteree started off with the thieving of the land from its rightful owners. And guys like my father have been perverting the democratic process for years," he said one morning as we crunched across the frozen snow to the cafeteria for breakfast, his voice hoarse with sleeplessness. "Checks and balances my ass. It's a cash and carry system."

"Maybe," I suggested, "where you come from it is."

"Don't be an idiot. It's just more open where I come from. Doesn't mean it's more prevalent. Like racism. Yankees are just more subtle about it. More hypocritical." This was the first time I'd heard Will defensive on the subject of the South.

When my mother arrived to pick me up for Christmas vacation, wearing her old mink stole and a nervous bright red smile, Will was in the library knocking out his last paper. From my second-story window I saw the car pull up, and watched her check herself up in the visor mirror. Anticipating the teary gleam in her eyes, I ran down the stairs and met her halfway up the walk. Surprised at how happy I was to see her, I felt my own eyes glisten as I submitted to her great bosomy embrace. I hadn't seen her in three months; although home was less than an hour away, I had not allowed myself a visit.

"Look at you." She held me at arm's length, as if to read some text on my forehead. "You look so handsome."

It was snowing lightly. I invited her in, anxious about the collision of the only two worlds I'd ever known, even though the house was almost deserted—except for Matson, who poled up the back hall to the living room with his famous umbrella. He bowed from the waist, then stepped forward to take my mother's hand. "Ah, Mrs. Keane, a very great pleasure indeed. Young Patrick is a gentleman and a scholar, and I can see where he comes by his pulchritude."

My mother blushed with confusion and pride. "Well, I'm awfully grateful to you for taking care of him," she said. "I hope he's a gentleman. We tried to drum some manners into him, but I don't honestly know where he gets his brains."

However we feel about our parents privately, when we are sixteen they are without doubt a public liability. But when my mother looked down at her shoes and apologized to Matson for tracking a little snow into the living room, my chilly teenaged heart thawed and I had to struggle to control my emotions.

"A lovely figure of a woman," Matson said when she went off to "powder her nose," and at that moment I experienced a flash of double vision: my mother *was*, in fact, an excellent woman and Matson was a pompous asshole because he was so insincere in saying so. I wish I could claim this was a lasting insight.

But I was also furious at Will, who'd promised he would be there to meet my mother and say goodbye. When he failed to show after half an hour I said we should leave. I was damned if I was going to chase him up in the library.

Once in the car with my mother, her cologne mingling with the familiar vinyl-and-cigarette-smoke smell of the Impala, I felt I was already back home.

"The strike was settled on Tuesday," she said, "but the men won't go back till after Christmas and it's already taken its toll on local business. Your father hasn't sold a thing in three weeks, so try to be considerate, Pat. Luckily I bought your presents before the strike." Though she'd mentioned the strike frequently, on the phone, I had barely registered it; my mind crowded with what I imagined to be higher concerns. Taunton was a company town, its health tied to the redbrick paper mills which every year employed a few less heads of household. Although no one in my family worked in the mills, this sense of creeping extinction lent a strange morbidity to my childhood and helped form my resolve to escape.

In the center of town, the brick and limestone Victorian storefronts with their lights and decorations had an air of gaudy desperation. The incandescent Santa atop Chilton's, the local department store, seemed to become more ghostly and insubstantial with each passing year as more and more of his bulbs burned out, never to be replaced; he finally died a few years later when the store filed for bankruptcy.

Hearing us in the hall, my father hoisted himself up from his recliner to greet me. He shook my hand, regarding me with what seemed to me an entirely appropriate air of suspicion, as if I had just returned from the camp of his enemies. "So," he said, "how's our preppie."

"I met the headmaster," my mother interjected. "He told me Pat's doing super."

"*Housemaster*," I corrected her. "Matson's just the housemaster."

"Well, anyway, he certainly spoke well of you."

At the time the distinction didn't seem to interest my father, any more than the football game he went back to watching interested me, but the term stuck with him; he would remind me several times over the next few days who was the housemaster in *this* house. Meanwhile my grandmother had emerged from her bedroom on her cane to welcome me home, kissing me dryly on both cheeks with her papery lips. "How are you, dear, you're getting so big. Did you run into any of the McCabes at your little school?"

I shook my head. Nana Keane had once dated a boy who went to Harvard, and she never quite got over it. She believed, not entirely incorrectly, that the network of New England prep schools and Ivy League colleges functioned as one big happy fraternity. Now that I'd been admitted, it seemed only a matter of time before I would bring back news of her long-lost beau.

"I believe Dave McCabe has three grandsons who would be just about your age. I'm sure they're all very good-looking. Dave was so handsome, and of course he was considered the most elegant dancer in all of Boston." She sighed. "Dave thought the world of me." All of her fond recollections ended with some variation of this concept: *He was so fond of me. . . . She thought the world of me.* If Dad was vaguely unhappy about my defection to prep school, Nana Keane felt that it was only my due as her grandson. After dancing with a Harvard boy, she had never quite reconciled herself to marrying a mailman. Nana Keane never tired of telling me that we came of noble Irish stock, that in Galway stood a castle where our ancestors had flourished before Cromwell's invading beastly horde had stolen it away. I sometimes consoled myself with this notion of our ancient nobility, but I was more interested in joining the winners than in wallowing with the losers.

After a single morning's regal sleep-in I took up my traditional holiday job. For the next four days I woke early to ride shotgun in a florist's
delivery van with one-eyed, foul-mouthed Al Wijtowski, in whom the
holiday spirit did not flourish. Al had been laid off at the paper plant
three years before and drove as if he were competing in a demolition
derby, cursing everyone and everything in his path. Between blasts of
his horn he preached an amalgam of anarcho-socialism and misogyny;
women and the rich were the enemy. "They got something you need
and they know it," he said as he pulled on a pint of Old Mr. Boston Pep-
permint Schnapps. "The rich got money, broads got pussy, and either
way they got you whipped." He urged me to profit from his wisdom.
And I didn't question it; it was just that I intended to be rich myself.

A minimum-wage Santa, I knocked on the doors of dilapidated row
houses and aluminum-jacketed ranch houses where suspicious house-
wives in curlers half opened the door on scenes of domestic chaos,
redolent of diaper pails and cooking grease, backlit by the blue light of
the television set. Some thawed at the sight of the little baskets of holly
and mums and glass balls, breaking into smiles and touching their hair,
suddenly self-conscious. Others, mired in domestic circumstance, were
immune to these festive tokens, stoically signing the receipt with one
hand, holding a hip-slung baby with the other. You sometimes sensed
the male animal in the background, torpid and menacing, like some
toxic, bottom-dwelling ocean creature who lies motionless in the sediment for hours only to explode and seize any smaller creature unlucky
enough to swim within reach. Infrequently the husband roused himself
to answer the door, beer in hand, unshaven and hostile—as if you yourself were responsible for the fact that he wasn't drawing a paycheck.

One day, out near the plant, the door of a double-wide trailer was
opened by Karen Santone, who had been my true love for six delirious
days before her Jehovah's Witness parents discovered I was Catholic and
banned our romance. Stunned, I stood there holding a basket of spruce
and holly. She wouldn't look at me, whether out of shame for her surroundings or of proud contempt for my Catholic soul. At that moment
I felt my heart go out to her all over again as I imagined her aging and
thickening before my eyes, Christmases winging past like the pages of

calendars in old movies while she remained framed in that doorway, going nowhere.

When Al dropped me off at six-thirty on Christmas Eve, I was greeted at the door by Mom's sister Colleen, who lived two hours away in Dorchester and who inevitably burst into tears whenever she saw me, as if years had passed and we had improbably survived wars and famines to attain this happy reunion. On this occasion she wept and crushed me to her bulging equator while her son, Jimmy, hovered just behind her like a dim moon. At the age of thirteen, he still wore short pants and an Eton jacket and seemed stunted by the attention his mother had lavished on him ever since his father disappeared, shortly and not coincidentally after his arrival on earth. Aunt Colleen spoke for him, adjusted his clothes and hair and generally treated him so much like a puppet that he seemed not to have developed any volition of his own. He shook my hand with a kind of fetal languor.

After our turkey dinner came the inevitable moment when Aunt Colleen seized a lull in the proceedings to ask, "What about some music?" And when no one could think of a polite way to disavow any such desire, she nudged Jimmy right out of his chair. "Go get your accordion, darling. You know how Aunt Jean and Uncle Mike love to hear you play."

And so I offered Nana Keane my arm and we adjourned slowly, slowly, to the living room, where once again I failed to scream in frustration that I did not belong in this upholstered oubliette where the Christmas tree blinked away and the beatified likenesses of John Kennedy and Pope John XXIII beamed down upon us from above the fireplace and little Jimmy Boyle unpacked his monstrous instrument of torture. We settled in for the long haul as Jimmy, suddenly animate, perched on the ottoman. Nearly obscured behind the dreadful device, he coaxed forth a series of preliminary sighs and moans. No matter how many times I was subjected to this instrument I could never quite get used to the sight of it—spawn of some violent coupling of reptile and pipe organ.

Glowing with proud anticipation, Jimmy's mother proposed "a nice polka."

"What about some Christmas music?" my mother suggested.

Aunt Colleen observed generously that there was plenty of time for both. My father and I, for once of one mind, exchanged sinking looks, and at that moment I felt almost achingly close to him, my own flesh, and all the more so for knowing that I could not express it. Awkward reticence was part of the nature he had bequeathed to me; neither of us was likely to announce: *No fucking polkas in our house, thanks, and get that nasty box out of here before we smash it to pieces.* For all my adolescent disgust I was as big a coward as he was, and so we sat and listened to "White Christmas," "Hark! The Herald Angels Sing," "The Beer Barrel Polka" and a half-dozen other selections whose names have blessedly faded with time. Colleen led the applause after each number and then called out the next tune. If Jimmy resented any of this, if he had any notion of how ridiculous he appeared to us, he didn't let on. He rocked back and forth on the ottoman, embracing his squeeze box, impassive. I squirmed on the sofa. Tiny as he was, my cousin seemed at times merely a passive appendage of the respirating instrument, a freakish child attached to a primitive life-support machine, trying to eke out another day on earth. Finally, Mom suggested we ought to be getting ready for Mass.

"Just one more," said Colleen brightly.

My father was caught standing. With a guilty look, he sank back in his recliner and listened stoically to the final, rousing polka while I blamed him for everything that was weak and yielding in my character.

Mass was another torture. Father Ryan preached at interminable length about the Holy Family while I daydreamed helplessly about sex. In recent years the sight of stained glass, the sound of the liturgy, aroused a perverse stream of carnal reflections. As if sensing my defection, my spiritual mentor Father Ryan had questioned me in the supposed anonymity of the confessional about impure thoughts and impure deeds, assuring me that these were mortal sins. Having no control over my thoughts, at least, I began to question the idea of involuntary sin and other aspects of supposed and actual church doctrine. I stopped going to confession, and would have stopped going to communion except I was afraid of what my parents would say, so that each

Sunday I approached the altar rail, a would-be apostate terrified of the sacrilege of taking communion unshriven. Now, on Christmas Eve, I was faced with a new dilemma; as the ushers moved backward down the aisle toward our pew, I found myself with a painful erection, which persisted as the rows immediately in front of us each emptied, until finally my mother and father and Aunt Colleen were rising and I was forced to a decision.

"Aren't you coming to communion," little Jimmy asked loudly, from the aisle.

The next morning, opening presents my parents could barely afford—including the London Fog raincoat I'd requested—I found myself weighed down with shame for all my betrayals and denials, from asking my mother to change her dress as we were about to drive to school that September, to passing my father off as a General Electric executive. And my ears still rang with what my father had said, driving back from church—"Preppies don't take communion?" I solemnly vowed to be a better son in the coming year.

I was under the influence of this resolution and still miffed at Will when he called to wish me a rockin' good Christmas and to invite me down to "the farm"—his homey euphemism for Bear Track, the Mississippi plantation where his father had been born. Though I badly wanted to go, I heard myself telling him, with a defiant pride in my station in life, that I was grateful for the kind invitation, but I didn't have the money for a plane ticket.

I knew my mother would be crushed to lose me again, so soon. Going away to school had been my own idea—and she was clearly delighted to have me in the house again.

Will solved the first problem immediately; he'd pay the fare out of his ill-gotten numbers gains. When I coldly informed him that I didn't want his money, he claimed he needed my help and explained that I could work off the debt. That, somehow, made all the difference. I didn't cloud the issue by asking him what it was he needed me to do.

The other obstacle was more difficult to surmount, but over the next couple of days I managed to imply to my folks that I knew they weren't the kind of parents who'd want to deny their son the broadening travel and social opportunities that his expensive prep school education had opened up for him—thanks to their generosity and sacrifice—which they themselves could not necessarily afford to provide. I was almost brought short by the look in my mother's eyes when she told me I could go, a look that indicated she knew she was losing me. My father, too, became misty-eyed as he drove me to the airport. In his relations with me he seemed to lurch between the poles of stern disciplinarian and moist sentimentalist, with no comfortable middle ground. It was all very Irish. I wanted to comfort him in some way, but we had no history of verbal intimacy, and my excitement at escaping the cramped sphere of his influence was only too palpable.

VI

We left Memphis behind us on the high ground and suddenly I was confronted by the vast bottomland of the Mississippi Delta. In its dusty brown winter cloak it seemed almost featureless, but under the irrigation of Will's rambling commentary fabulous growth sprang forth on the fruitless plain: a lost jungle of cypress, tupelo, sycamore and sweet gum flowered again out of a rich stew of flood-water, alluvial sediments and decomposing vegetation, stitched together by a chaos of vines and cane, trafficked by deer, bears, panthers, water moccasins, alligators and black clouds of disease-bearing mosquitoes. The Choctaw camped on the sedimented high ground near the banks of the river, but the fecund interior languished well into the last century until white men from Tennessee and the Carolinas arrived in flatboats from the river, having worn out the cotton lands to the north and the east, lured by the rumor of the richest soil on the planet. No yeoman farmers, these—the clearing and farming of this jungle required capital and slaves. "The Negroes die off every few years" noted one early visitor, whom I later quoted in my Yale senior thesis, "though it is said in time each hand makes enough to buy two more in his place."

All I could see now across the flat plain of the Delta was the long ridge of the levee, off to our right, like the edge of the world. The leading roadside industry seemed to involve the slaking of thirst and the recent advent of refrigeration, judging from the hand-painted signs advertising COLD BEER and COLD COKES. The bare cotton fields were studded with shotgun shacks, some swarming with black children, others abandoned and overgrown, tin roofs seemingly held up by bowers of kudzu vines. As we drove through a tiny settlement, Will pointed to the spot where a freedom rider had been gunned down the year before. "This is the south of the South," he warned, spraying potato chip debris on the dashboard. "Last unreconstructed spot in America."

Will had been almost two hours late picking me up at the airport. Cooling my heels outside the baggage claim in Memphis, I saw the Cadillac rocket up the arrival ramp and shoot past me before dodging a taxi and screeching to a halt several feet from the curb. When I ran up, the passenger window slid down. "I'm wasted," Will said. "You better drive." He briefly lifted his dark shades to reveal the pink filigree in his eyes.

I told him my learner's permit was only valid with an adult copilot.

"They don't care about that down here," he said. So I took the keys and followed his instructions, nosing the big, cushiony-riding Caddy down the ramp and out to Highway 51.

Will lit a cigarette and debriefed me as we drove south. "Got the house nearly to ourselves. Dad's in New Orleans and Elbridge has gone down to Destin with his buds. The beauteous Cheryl spent Christmas with us. At one point she tells us she forgot her baton. To which my old man says he's got a baton she can use, which sends Mom off to her room for two days. Then Dad gets in a swivet about L.B.'s draft status. He wants to use his connections to get Elbridge in the reserves so he can dodge Vietnam after he graduates, and Elbridge says that's cheating and Dad says that's just smart. Got pretty hot there at the old dinner table."

Once we were in the Delta, the highway was so flat that we seemed, curiously, to be driving uphill. The distance between objects—houses, cars, a stand of trees—seemed enormous, and I sensed a pervasive lassitude. In the harvested cotton fields ragged bits of white fluff clung to the cut stubble, like millions of tiny, tattered flags of surrender. The black man who filled our gas tank in Tunica seemed to make an epic meandering journey out of the simple trip from his seat inside the door to our car. The door itself was dangling on one hinge, rather like his overalls, which hung on a single raggedy strap from his shoulder, the other having frayed away. The RC Cola ice chest standing out front was full of trash, the lid long gone. Encrusted with vegetation, several automobiles were rapidly becoming part of the landscape.

Located some twenty miles north of Greenville, Bear Track had been in Will's family since the land was cleared in the 1850s—one of the first plantations in the region, three thousand acres of sandy loam planted in cotton. We drove through the naked fields up a long red drive. I was disappointed at first sight of the house itself, a yellow-brick ranch which, except for the surrounding pecan and magnolia trees, hardly answered my notions of an antebellum plantation.

"You were expecting columns and verandas?" Will said slyly as we parked out front. "The old house got torched by Yankees. Its replacement fell down after the flood of 1927, and that house burned to the ground after a drunken overseer fell asleep smoking in his bed. Which is actually pretty typical Delta history. You hear these fucking people round here carrying on about the glories of Dixie—shit, this was one big swamp. They weren't even fucking *here*. Forget that *Gone with the Wind* shit. Best thing ever happened to the South was getting beat so we could piss and moan for the next hundred years about our mythical lost glory."

We stopped in the kitchen to greet Eula and to steal two Schlitz out of the refrigerator.

"Breakfast of champions," said Will.

"You're gonna get me thrown out of the house," Eula complained. "Your mama, she think *we* be drinking all the beer."

"My mama hasn't set foot in the kitchen in twenty years."

"Maybe not, but your daddy, he measures the liquor every time he comes down here. I seen him do it. Turn the bottles upside down and make a mark with a pencil."

"When are you going to stop pandering to the oppressors," Will asked. "Don't you know the revolution is coming?"

It took me a moment to see he was teasing her. Eula had heard it before, and clearly didn't want to hear it again. Putting her hands to her ears, she said, "Onliest thing coming here is trouble if you don't leave me be."

If we had been a few years younger I suppose we would have rushed out to explore the land in the remaining daylight; instead we closed ourselves in Will's room listening to the Stones. Will showed me the collection of Indian artifacts—arrowheads and beads and shards of pottery—that he scavenged around Bear Track.

When his mother knocked on the door we scrambled to hide the beers before she came in. Dressed in a flowing kimono, she inquired minutely about the weather and apologized to me for the dearth of social activity.

"You boys should go riding," she said.

"We don't want to ride," Will said.

"Well, it seems like a terrible waste," she said, wandering around the room and frowning at the posters that adorned the walls. "All those perfectly wonderful horses out there. Somebody ought to ride them. You do ride, don't you, Patrick? Or don't they ride in your part of the country?"

"We just don't *feel* like it," Will said.

"Well, I think it's a shame," she said dreamily, pulling the door shut behind her.

"She wasn't always like this," Will said softly.

"Like what?"

"I don't know. Like a ghost. Cordell met her after his own father had pissed away most of the Savage loot and he was struggling to make it back. Mama was one of the richest and prettiest and funniest girls in Memphis, and the most generous by a long ways. She was twenty-one when she came into her first trust fund and she spent most of it on a Negro orphanage. Nobody'd ever done anything like that before. Everybody would've thought she was crazy, but because it was my mother they thought it was wonderfully eccentric and Christian of her."

Will reached in his bedside drawer, pulled out a pack of cigarettes and lit one.

"Dad went after her like I don't know what. Borrowed money to follow her to Europe—this place was mortgaged to the hilt—and sent her a poem every day for two years; finally she canceled her wedding to this guy from Chattanooga and eloped with my old man. He's been trying to drag her down ever since—like he had to spoil what he loved so he wouldn't need it so much. He started sleeping with her friends before long and made damn sure she stopped giving her money away. Just slowly wearing her down. And then, when A.J. died it was kind of the last straw."

This was the first time I'd heard Will speak of his mother. He was always dutiful, and later he would draw closer to her, almost by default, as he pulled farther away from his father; gradually I came to understand that he loved her for what she had once been even as he hated her for letting herself be defeated by Cordell, and for remaining in love with him to the end. But I remind myself, too, that this was *Will's* version of the marriage, and that it could hardly be unbiased.

"Let's drive," Will said, suddenly intent on some mission.

I waited for him in the driveway, and after a few minutes he jumped into the shotgun seat clutching two beers. I sailed out to the open road, the headlights conjuring up the faded white line out of the blackness.

"Faster," Will commanded. I glanced over to see him pull a revolver out of the waistband of his jeans. Surprised as I was, I thought it would be unmanly to inquire about our mission.

"The thing is," he said, "you've got to keep driving no matter what."

At that moment I slowed at the sight of a stop sign marking a crossroads. "Go through it," he said, leaning out the side of the car as I cautiously accelerated.

I braked at the sound of the report.

"Goddamnit, how do you expect me to hit the motherfucker with you driving like a box turtle? Back up and do it over."

I did as I was told, thankful there were no other cars in sight.

Finally, when we were fifty yards back from the intersection, he ordered me to charge the stop sign again. I floored it, and the sign was just a blur as we roared past and he fired again.

"Go back," Will said. "I think I got it." He reloaded as I reversed and stopped just behind the sign, which was unmarked.

"Fuck!" he shouted, enraged and wild-eyed. Climbing out of the car, he stalked up and fired all six rounds into the sign at point-blank range. Silhouetted against the vast night sky of the Delta, pistol in hand, he seemed to be enacting some outlaw ritual of vengeance.

Finally he lowered the gun and returned to the car. He seemed satisfied that he had won this particular skirmish in his ongoing war.

Will and I were alone at the dining room table on New Year's Eve. Cordell was still in New Orleans on business and Mrs. Savage had dinner sent up to her room. We sat at opposite ends of a table that could comfortably seat twenty, shouting to each other as we got drunk on champagne, toasting the ancestors whose likenesses hovered around us, all of them glowering as if they had anticipated this long flat afterlife of staring at the living.

Later we went out back and lay on the cold ground beside the gazebo, throwing pebbles up at the gourds which hung from a wire strung between the gazebo and a pecan tree. In the spring the gourds served as lodges for the mosquito-eating purple martins, door holes bored in the middle of the pendent fat ends. Soon tiring of this, we gazed up at a sky teeming with more stars than I had ever seen, bright gems overflowing the cloudy smear of the Milky Way.

"Intoxication eliminates the distance," Will said, "between us and the heavenly bodies."

"Like Cheryl Dobbs," I suggested. More than actually *feeling* this, I was performing for Will.

He seemed not to have heard me. "If you get high enough, you can touch them."

"God, I'd love to touch her heavenly orbs," I said, finding myself hilarious.

But Will was on his own planet. "You have to leave intellect behind," he said. "That's what soul's about—pure feeling. It's about freeing your slave."

"What the hell are you talking about?"

"About being drunk." Suddenly he stood up. "Look, I'll show you."

Pointing at a stand of trees behind the house, he announced that we would run through it as fast as we could. He let out a big, night-splitting rebel yell and I whooped back as we sprinted for the dark curtain of the trees. I had no doubt I could pass this test. With this warm spirit in my belly and the cool air on my face, there was nothing in the world I couldn't do. I ran as fast as I could through the wood, effortlessly dodging the massed dark trunks that hurtled harmlessly past, Will locked in step beside me, charmed against collision. I was invincible—until I cut left and Will veered right and together we tumbled to rest side by side in the damp leaves, gasping for breath.

"See?" Will said. "You have to trust your instincts."

I considered this, still exhilarated. Then suddenly Will said, "Would you let a guy suck your dick for a thousand dollars?"

"Hell no," I said.

"How about ten thousand?"

"No way."

"Would you let a girl?"

"Are you kidding?"

"But let's say if you closed your eyes. If it feels good when a girl does it, why wouldn't it when a guy does it?"

"Because." I wasn't comfortable with this line of speculation. "I don't know."

"But what if nobody would know?"

"I'd know. What are you—a homo?"

"I'm just saying—it's just this fucking . . . convention. We're all trapped in what we're supposed to think."

"Would you?"

"Maybe not. It's strange everybody thinks it's so terrible, is all."

"It just is," I said. "By definition."

Suddenly he stood up and brushed off the leaves. "More champagne for the Olympians."

After another bottle of Moët we each made a resolution to get laid in the New Year, and later I threw up in the wastebasket I'd been prescient enough to place beside my bed.

The next day we watched the Rose Bowl and manfully compared

notes on champagne hangovers, which we decided, in our extensive experience, were the worst except maybe for gin.

On Saturday evening we drove to Clarksdale to hear Lester Holmes. My heart sank when I saw the windowless shed hard up against the railroad tracks. A knot of black men slouched around the door like languid sentries, passing a joint among themselves.

"You white boys must be lost," one of them muttered as we approached.

"We're here for Lester," Will said confidently.

"That right?"

Reluctantly they shifted positions so we could enter. At first I could hardly see anything inside, though I was acutely aware of being seen. The voices fell below the music coming from the jukebox glowing at the far end. Dark faces took shape in the gloom. I nearly tripped over what appeared to be a V-8 engine sitting in the middle of the dirt floor. A single light shone on the stage, which was empty save for some amps and drums. We found Lester sitting in a corner with two female admirers.

"You following me," he asked, as Will pulled two folding chairs up to the wire-spool table.

"How else I'm gonna learn?" said Will, talking the talk.

"You got that right," Lester said. The women laughed appreciatively. "Ladies, this here's my protégé, White Boy Willie. He wants me to teach him all the shit that I know, but I tell him, some things, you either got it or you don't."

"You got that right, Lester," said one of the women.

"He sure do."

"I tell him—'Hey, some shit a white boy can't never get.'"

"That the truth."

"Wants to know my secrets with the ladies. But the thing is, I'm just a natural-born lover, is all."

The women greeted this announcement with derision.

"But I might could give him a few pointers."

"I'd be much obliged," Will said.

"The thing is, I gotta go play. You boys just watch and could be you learn a thing or two. Sometimes you want speed and sometimes you want to go *real* slow."

Will bought beers from the cooler that served as the bar, while I scrupulously studied a sign taped to the wall beside it: IF YOU WANT TO ACT LIKE A FOOL, DO LIKE YOU DID IN SCHOOL. SAY YOU GOT A STOMY ACK AND GET A EXCOUSE. THIS IS A FUN PLACE.

We sat with the women, who shouted at the stage. Suddenly I knew, viscerally, that what Will had told me once was true—the music *was* all about sex. Not necessarily the words, although that was sometimes true—but the rhythm and the feeling, the ebb and flow and destination. I was amazed. Now, I felt, I had the key. Will probably always had it. As the set progressed, he was leaning closer and closer to the girl beside him. When I glanced away from the stage a few minutes later, I found that the two of them were gone.

The other woman looked at me and smiled. "You wanna dance?"

"No thanks."

"Come on, honey," she said, standing up and tugging on my arm. Suddenly I realized that everyone in the room was watching, and it would have taken a substantial application of physical resistance to refuse the offer, dearly as I wished to. My apprehension only increased when the couples who'd been dancing seemed to disperse at a signal, as if they didn't want to be seen with us, or else wanted to watch from a safe distance. I was hoping for a slow song. We were alone out there when the band kicked into a fast, upbeat number.

Trying to mimic the gestures of my companion, I briefly felt I was doing all right. I recalled my dancing triumphs with Belinda a few weeks before, at Lester's house. For a moment I nearly lost myself in the rhythm. But as my partner's movements became increasingly complicated, my own tenuous confidence faltered, until finally I began to suspect she was deliberately making a spectacle of me. I persisted gamely, no longer following her lead, increasingly aware of the laughter from the tables around us. When at long last the song finally ended, my partner collapsed into the arms of a friend, incapacitated with mirth, while I was accosted with a chorus of hoots and jeers. As I slunk toward the table, my face burning, Lester announced over his mike, "Damn, that *hurt* to look at. I'm talking *ugly* here now."

In the car heading back to Bear Track, Will thrust his hand at me from the driver's seat. "Hey, man. Smell my finger."

"Watch where you're going," I said. When he continued to stab his finger at me I slapped his hand away, causing him to swerve off the road onto the shoulder before he regained control.

"What's your fucking problem?" he shouted.

"My problem? I don't have a fucking problem."

"You're just jealous."

"Yeah?" I yelled. "I wouldn't have touched that girl with a stick."

"That's cause you're a fag."

"Fuck you."

"Fuck *you*."

Ah, yes—those were the days when this seemed like a crushing and eloquent rejoinder.

We drove home in silence and went to bed without speaking. I was mad at Will for so many reasons I could hardly begin to sort them out, not least because I blamed him for my humiliation, but I wasn't about to tell him that, since I didn't want him to know about what had happened in his absence. When he had finally returned to the table I was sitting with two friendly young bloods who had hit me up for three beers apiece and a pint of gin.

My anger dissipated in the night; I awoke at dawn in a state of frantic anxiety, fearing that I had permanently damaged our friendship. When Will finally emerged from his room three hours later I apologized for my outburst.

"That's okay," he said, with a shrug. "We were drunk."

I'm not sure this explanation exactly covered the case, but I was happy enough to pretend that it did. In the middle of the night I had realized that Will had become my best, and practically my only, friend.

*   *   *

Will announced over breakfast that he was driving back toward Clarksdale to attend church. Was this a matter of penance for the previous night's activities? I'd been subject to compulsory Sunday Mass up until the moment I left home for prep school, where I shunned the stigma of the special van that took Catholics into town. I couldn't imagine voluntarily driving half an hour to sit inside a church, which, by Will's standards, could only be regarded as deeply uncool.

"There's this choir I want to check out," he said bashfully, or so it seemed to me. "You ever heard any gospel music?" Sensing my doubt, he said, "Man, you think rock and rollers have groupies—gospel singers get more pussy than anybody on the planet."

This was a side of the religious vocation I'd never considered. "You've got to be kidding."

"Kid you not," he said.

He told me I was welcome to stay at Bear Track, and I think he would have preferred me to, but I was eager to repair any damage that had been done to our friendship the night before, and I was curious to experience this cocktail of sacred and profane. In the car he expounded further. "What the musicians call soul, the colored ministers call the Holy Ghost. But it's basically the same thing."

A white box made out of aluminum siding, the church stood on cinder blocks in a field on the outskirts of the town. The hand-painted sign outside said ALL WELCOME; I was more surprised than I should have been, when we entered the service which was already in progress, to find that we were the only white people in attendance. There was a palpable tear in the fabric of the congregation as we tried to slip in quietly. The minister paused at his lectern as an usher rose and escorted us to the front pew, where we were seated as honored guests.

"I don't know about you but I been thinking," said the minister, a powerful balding patriarch with graying temples.

"*Tell it,*" called a voice from the back.

"I hear people complaining all up and down about the heaviness of they load."

"*That's right,*" shouted a fat woman in our pew.

"I'm thinking God's been too good to me for me to be complaining."

"Now you're talking."

"Go to somebody's house, they complaining 'bout this and that."

"Say it. That's right."

"Any old body can be religious in church. But it's what you do in your house. It's what the friends see and it's what the neighbors see. That's where your religion gonna show and tell. When you feeling things is bad, stop a minute. Don't let the situation dictate to you. Enlarge the place of your tent and your habitation brothers and sisters. You got to get to a place of not letting your barrenness dictate to you. Lengthen thy cords and enlarge thy habitation. You got to break forth. The more you break forth the more you get a crop that breaks forth. So when you want to break through what do you do?"

"*You break forth,*" a dozen voices responded. "*Praise the Lord.*"

The minister surveyed the congregation and nodded approvingly. "The more excited you get the more God gonna give you an excited crop. The more you act reserved is the more you gonna get a reserved crop. The more all fire excited you are the more it gonna break forth to the left and to the right. Where's it gonna break forth?"

"*To the left and the right.*"

"All around you brothers and sisters. Now the devil, he want us dignified. He don't want us excited. He don't want us filled with the Holy Ghost. If we complain in the house we gonna get a crop that's a complaint. As long as we just sit here and complain that's all we gonna get is a failure of crop. The more we praise God the more crop we gonna get in the house of God. It's gonna break forth in my church and it's gonna break forth in my home and when I go to my home I'm not gonna go complaining and when I go home it's gonna break forth in my home."

The woman beside me was crying beneath her white veil; looking around I could see tears on other cheeks. I'd never heard a sermon delivered with such conviction—except perhaps when Father Ryan was railing against sex—nor had I heard a congregation talk back like this one did. Beside me, Will was less animated than anyone in the church, and yet he seemed utterly rapt.

"The Lord know you too well. And the devil he know you gonna go home and turn on the radio and you got to tell him he don't know you.

I want you-all to keep praising God when you go home today and to-morrow and the next day and all the days of your life. Brothers and sisters, let me hear you say 'Amen.'"

The congregation crowned the sermon with a chorus of *amens*, and then the choir rose to sing, the voices washing over us like surf. Along with the others I started clapping. A sweet, powerful voice persistently soared above the rest, and eventually I recognized the tall, elegant girl it belonged to as Lester Holmes's niece. I nudged Will quizzically but he refused to look at me. The volume swelled as those around me joined the singing. Will stood stock-still as the congregation bobbed and swayed around him.

When we were driving home I asked him what was the point of attending that kind of church if you were just going to stand there like a pillar of salt. When he didn't answer I said, "Was this about the girl? Is that why we went?"

"I think she's got a future as a singer," Will finally said.

"Have you been talking to her?"

"Colored folks, when they say, 'You been talking to her?'—they mean, 'Have you been fucking her?' They say, 'I ain't been talking to her. No way.'"

I wasn't going to let him dodge my question with this nugget of anthropology, but then I saw his expression. I saw, to my amazement, that he was in love. Far from enraptured, though, he looked ill, like a man who has just been given the opportunity to confess to a terrible crime.

That afternoon and evening we drove up and down Route 1, along the river, "looking for music," as Will put it. Will would turn off the main road and cruise slowly down the side streets, stopping whenever he saw a cluster of lounging black men. Then, after chatting about the weather and the crops, he would ask whether they knew any musicians. Climbing back in the car, where I was happy to sit reading, he'd scribble in a spiral notebook. Finally at one little town we stopped in front of a boarded-up storefront from which we could hear the muffled wail of the blues. PLAYBOY LOUNGE was painted in crude letters over the door.

As we watched, a man staggered out of the place, blinking in the low sunlight, and fumbled with a pack of cigarettes.

"You coming," Will asked.

"Someone has to notify your next of kin." I'd had my fill of juke joints for the moment.

I locked the doors behind him and tried to concentrate on my French, but I kept wondering what I would do if Will didn't come out. Actually, at that time—'66—Will was fairly safe, beneficiary of a feudal system which was, despite recent challenges, still in place. After nearly an hour, he emerged in a state of high excitement, having learned that one of his blues heroes was living nearby. "He was recorded by Alan Lomax back in the forties," he explained. "Everybody just figured he was dead."

As the evening drew on we drove out into the middle of a cotton field, stopping in front of a tiny unpainted shack on cinder blocks. A wizened old black woman in a dirty pink dress answered the door. Between her accent and her thorough lack of teeth I couldn't make out a word she said, but I gathered from Will's responses that she didn't know where her husband was.

"Damn," he said. "Says he's on a drunk and she hasn't seen him in three days. I can't believe he's been living not ten miles from Bear Track all these years." Will's eyes glittered with a sense of quest, like a collector in pursuit of a rare piece of porcelain. He proposed that we conduct a town-to-town, juke-to-juke search for the missing singer, but I persuaded him to drop me off at Bear Track first. As the sun disappeared over the levee, Will dropped me at the house and set off into the cool Mississippi night.

VII

The firm is in a quiet uproar. This morning's tabloids are shrill with lurid details of Felson's murder. The motel where his body was found murdered was a notorious haunt of homosexual prostitutes, and Felson was apparently a regular patron. A variety of gay pornography and sexual paraphernalia had been discovered in the room, which explained several of the questions the detectives lobbed at me when they came to my office. A few hours after they left, I was brooding about the whole sorry business when I remembered something I could have told them. One morning—it must have been six or seven years ago—I rode up in the elevator with Felson and noticed that he had a black eye. And then, a few months ago, when he was working on a trust for one of my clients, he came in with a bruised and puffy face, which he explained as the result of a mugging outside his apartment building. I don't know, I suppose it doesn't matter now. But I wonder, Didn't his family notice anything? Didn't they wonder?

My wife, Stacey, is on the board of the Metropolitan, and opera has become a regular feature of our evenings. Last night was *Carmen*. Naturally, the plight of lust-addled Don José led me to thoughts of Felson. How did he manage? Where did he find the time? I hardly have the time for my weekly squash game, and I try to devote weekends to my girls.

My attention drifting momentarily back to the opera, I found myself entranced by a song in which Micaëla, Don José's childhood sweet-heart, prays to heaven for protection: *Je dis que rien ne m'épouvante* . . . and some quality in the voice and inflection of the soprano reminded me of Taleesha's gospel performance all those years ago in that Mississippi church. My God, could it really be almost thirty years ago now?

Returning to school after my interlude at Bear Track, I was astonished to learn Will got a grade of A on the previous term's American-history paper, although his other grades were unimpressive. For his part, Will would have been no less surprised had he known that I'd exchanged several letters with his father that spring, sending cheerful news of our academic idyll, mythologizing our prep school days in the Booth Tarkington manner and receiving in return wry and philosophical missives from Memphis.

One night Will slipped soundlessly into the room and caught me reading *Stover at Yale.* "Dink fucking Stover," he repeated again and again, after lights-out, emphasizing a different syllable each time and inventively giving each of these three words an ugly new inflection with each repetition. "Dink *Stover. Dink* Stover. *Man,* I am so disappointed in you."

Finally Matson opened the door and told us to be quiet.

"Tell *him,*" I said.

"Tell *him,*" Will mocked, as soon as the door closed. I stayed awake for what seemed like hours, furious with Will and with myself.

"*Dink* Stover and *Doug* Matson," Will whispered, long after I thought he was asleep. "Cute couple."

A few days later I came back from class to find Will smoking a joint. "Are you crazy," I hissed, grabbing the joint and throwing it out the window. Then I tried to fan the smoke from the room. "You want to get us kicked out of here?"

He looked slowly up at me with amused detachment. "Gosh, that would be terrible."

"What's the matter with you?"

"Obviously I'm crazy," he said.

"Well I'm not."

"Don't worry, Patrick," Will said. "Nobody's ever going to accuse you of that."

He was right; I couldn't afford to be crazy; that was a luxury my children might have.

And so we went our separate ways that summer, me to work at my uncle's Chevy dealership. By day I washed cars, changed oil and swept the service bay clean. Every night at six I scrubbed the grease from under my fingernails, then at six-thirty I ate dinner at the kitchen table with my parents and my grandmother, whose meat I would dutifully cut. Afterward I would retreat to my basement room.

"What the hell is it you do down there," my father demanded one night, his tone and my mother's sudden blush implying that it could only be solitary sexual vice that kept me so busy and sequestered. In fact I would have rather admitted to the masturbation which occupied a portion of every evening than to have been caught in the performance of my other chief activities, which were reading poetry and writing to Will.

Satirizing my life in Taunton seemed the best way to distance myself from it. I wrote grotesque descriptions of the troglodyte clientele of my uncle's car dealership, suggesting unctuously that when the revolution came it should ban madras shorts on fat people, although my best and fiercest letter was inspired by a visit from my cousin Jimmy and his accordion. I neglected to tell Will, however, that I spent weekends playing lacrosse with some kids from the local Jesuit school; I had learned the previous year that the lacrosse team was essentially a fraternity composed of exactly the kind of careless blue bloods I wanted to count among my friends.

Will reported that he was cruising around Memphis and the Delta, scouting for musical talent. Once liberated from school, he informed me, he intended to start a management company and maybe even his own record label. The next letter came from the family's camp in Ontario, a long tirade against his parents and their lakeside compound, which, to me, in my subterranean particle-board-paneled redoubt, sounded like paradise. He enclosed the lyrics to "All Along the Watch-tower,"—not yet released, and evidently obtained by some Woodstock samizdat—and underlined the phrase "Businessmen they drink my wine." This seemed to be an oblique reference to his father, whom Will described elsewhere in the letter as an "authoritarian reactionary pig. Speaking of pigs," he continued, "former creep veep Richard Nixon came for a few miserable days along with some other hideous Republican Nazi types. Nixon and my old man are undoubtedly planning a right wing coup." By Will's account the former vice president was a lousy fisherman with a great store of dirty jokes. He closed on a more inspiring note. "Cheryl 'baton' Dobbs arrives tomorrow for a week. Now, if I can just arrange to drown L.B."

In July the Savages returned briefly to Tennessee, then hied themselves to the mountains of North Carolina; our correspondence accelerated until we were writing every other day. And so, after a week of silence on Will's part, I wrote: "Fall down the stairs and break both wrists? Post office burn down? Hit by a car and suffering from amnesia? Well, just to refresh your memory, my name is Patrick Keane and I'm still waiting for a response to my last missive." Ten days later I was unable to disguise my sense of grievance: "If our correspondence has become wearisome you might at least have the decency to tell me so."

Finally, as I was packing to return to school I received a note from Cordell Savage.

Dear Patrick:

You will understand and forgive me for not writing earlier; Will was involved in an automobile accident and for more than a week we were not at all confident that he would survive. Happily he has regained consciousness and appears to be out of danger. He will certainly be late going up to school but I trust you will help him catch up upon his return. I know he would want me to send you his warmest regards, as do I.

I waited a week before calling Memphis. As from a vast distance, Will's mother told me he was doing well but was unable to come to the phone;

she wished me luck at school and would tell him I had called. Repentant about my earlier peevishness, I wrote lighthearted epistles intended to distract and divert the convalescent.

It was strange returning to school without Will. The bed on the other side of the room lay empty. In Will's absence I decided to take advantage of other social opportunities. For example, I made the lacrosse team. I spent most of the season on the bench, but after I proved that I was willing to put up with a certain amount of gratuitous physical abuse in practice and that I was willing to share my class notes, I was allowed to take meals with my teammates. I aped their shambling posture, cultivated the almost imperceptible sneer of the loutish patrician. When I set up James "Trey" Bowman III for the winning goal against Hotchkiss he actually congratulated me. Trey was team captain, and in this, his senior year, he was the king of the campus. His father, James II, managed the Wall Street empire founded by his grandfather, James I; James III had grown up in a huge apartment on Park Avenue and gone to Buckley before following his forebears to our school. That he was also tall and athletic hardly seemed fair, but most of us were willing to overlook these flaws in exchange for a smidgen of his attention and approval.

"Whatever happened to your friend Savage," he asked one evening in the dining hall. "Get his hair caught in somebody's zipper?" Everyone at the table laughed, myself included, although I didn't get the joke—to my deep shame—until later that night.

"We were beginning to wonder about you and Savage," Trey said. "The way you guys homoed around together."

"Don't worry," I assured him, "Will gets plenty of pussy."

"Right. In his dreams."

"Oh, man," moaned Collins, "I had a wet one the other night"—and the conversation propitiously drifted away to safer subjects.

In Will's absence I also spent time with Matson, who'd started a new club called the Auden Society to advance the appreciation of poetry on campus and to expose philistines everywhere. Through the club I met Isaac Mendel, who would eventually beat me out as valedictorian of our class. I had history and English wrapped up, but he was a math

and science whiz. There was something impressive about the way
Mendel didn't even try to conform to the sumptuary laws and Waspy
etiquette of the school. He was a Jew from Brooklyn, and he didn't care
who knew it. He seemed almost to pity the rest of us slow-witted con-
formists; I was amazed when he brushed off my initial overtures, imagining myself to be condescending from a more advantageous social
station. "Sure," he said, "you talk to me now when your jock friends
aren't around."

Fuck him, I thought. But a few weeks later when the lacrosse table
began to lob taunts at him, sitting alone at the next table, I surprised
myself by saying, "Hey, leave him alone, he's a friend of mine."

I held my breath; not quite believing I'd said it. But Bowman sized
me up, then said: "Okay, amnesty for Mendel."

Matson fell in beside me one afternoon as I was walking to the library.
Tapping the ground with the tip of his umbrella, he said, "I talked to
Dick last night. I told him about you, and he's looking forward to meet-
ing you."

After a puzzled moment, I realized he was referring to the poet
Richard Wilbur, whose reading the Auden Society was attending the
following night in Amherst. Only later did it occur to me to wonder
what he might possibly have "told" the poet about me—what was there
to tell, really?—but I was briefly flushed with a warm sense of self-
approbation, though if the majestically urbane Richard Wilbur had
ever heard about me he gave no particular indication when he shook
my tremulous hand after his reading. For my part I was struck dumb; it
seemed incredible that high scholarship and fastidious craftsmanship
could be combined with such grace and fluency and sheer charm.

"Look at this guy," groused Mendel, standing beside me. "It's like they
asked Cary Grant to play a poet." Wilbur embodied a sort of neoclassi-
cal idea of the poet which was then being called into question by the
new hairy romanticism. Standing in his lustrous presence, sipping from
a plastic glass of rosé and nibbling cheese which was neither presliced
nor orange like the cheese of my youth—cheese which might just pos-

sibly be foreign—it seemed hard to believe anyone would want to be authentic if they could be so *cultured*. In Matson you could see the aspiring version of this ideal. The poet was clearly acquainted with our leader, if not quite on such terms of intimacy as we'd been led to expect. As they conversed, I was astonished to see that, although Matson held his arms folded tightly across his chest, his hands were shaking.

Driving us back to school in his Volkswagen van, Matson regained his composure and regaled us with tales from the lives of the modern poets, emphasizing their minor eccentricities—Roethke's love of plants, Auden's shuffling up St. Mark's Place in bedroom slippers. No career seemed so worthy that night as the vocation of poetry. Halsted kept saying over and over again that he was damn well going to be a poet, that was the job for him all right. But Mendel, who hadn't had any of the wine, asked—If being a poet was so wonderful how come they all ended up drunk and crazy?

Muddy and bruised, I returned from lacrosse one day to find Will sitting on his bed looking as if he'd just materialized there briefly and might disappear at any moment, so pale and gaunt that he seemed like an apparition, although his eyes were if anything more startlingly blue than ever. A fresh pink scar zigzagged across his cheek. He smiled up at me serenely and all I could think of to say was "You're back."

"Either that or I'm astral projecting."

"You sound like yourself," I observed happily. "Who else would even know what that *means?*"

"What's with the webbed stick, white man?"

I felt the heat rise to my face. "I'm, uh, on the team."

"I *have* been gone a long time. What year is it?"

I changed the subject. "What the hell happened to you, anyway?"

"I don't remember. They say I hit a truck." He fixed his eyes on me and smiled puckishly. "Actually, it was a cement mixer."

"A cement mixer?"

He laughed, evidently delighted that his peculiar obsession had been somehow validated by the accident. All he knew for certain was that he'd been at a juke joint in Memphis and that he'd started back for his family's house in the early morning hours. When he regained consciousness a week later five of his ribs were crushed and one of his lungs was collapsed from the impact of the steering wheel.

"Jesus," I said. "You're lucky to be alive."

"Actually I was dead," Will said. "I came back." He seemed perfectly serious.

"You mean you were *almost* dead."

"No, I mean I *was* dead."

I decided not to pursue this. The look in his eyes scared me. Not that it was frightening per se; he looked like he did when he was stoned, somehow widely diffused and narrowly focused at the same time, like a cat in repose.

We resumed our routine. But Will seemed different—older and otherworldly, as if he'd actually begun to inhabit one of the regions of higher consciousness to which he was always alluding. I struggled to return our friendship to its familiar footing, and to this end, one night after lights-out I asked him if he'd gotten any nooky over the summer.

After a long pause, he whispered across the darkness, "I finally lost my cherry."

"Bull*shit* you did." I sat up eagerly in my bed. I was thinking—It's true then. It *does* change you. "With who?"

"You mean 'whom.'"

"Come on, Will. With whom?"

"Would you give your left nut to sleep with Cheryl Dobbs?"

"You didn't."

"No, actually it was Lollie Baker."

I was glad he couldn't see me. I could've killed him in his bed.

"Her family came up to Ontario," he whispered. "Everybody was out fishing and I stayed behind at the camp. I had some Panama Red I'd brought up from Memphis out to the woodshed. Lollie walked in on me, right after I lit up. So I offered her a hit . . ."

"What happened?" I said finally, trying to control my voice.

"Hey, I'm a gentleman."

If a moment ago I hated him for what he had revealed, I was now furious at his sudden reticence. "Tell me," I demanded.

"Hey, calm down. It was nice. It was great."

I couldn't believe this was all he had to say about the momentous event, but within minutes I could hear him breathing in sleep. It was not fair; for the first time I resented Will's good fortune in this as in everything. Lollie was mine. If Cheryl was the remote dream of carnality, Lollie was the practical embodiment of my nocturnal yearning. With Lollie I had a concrete foundation on which to construct my fantasies—the memory of her flesh and a sense of possibility—which Will had suddenly taken away from me.

Or so I told myself. In fact my jealousy was far knottier than I was willing to admit, even to myself, at the time. Lying awake, listening to the last sad crickets of the Indian summer, I was in no way prepared to entertain the possibility that it wasn't Will Savage I was jealous of, but Lollie Baker.

VIII

The leaves turned ruby and gold, then gathered themselves in fragrant heaps while I was filling out applications for college. Walking to the dining hall the morning of the first frost, with Will limping elegantly alongside me, I could see my breath and hear my steps on the crunchy turf. The chapel bells were ringing eight o'clock, the sound crisp and bright in the lucid air. I felt a flash of clairvoyant nostalgia, imagining my aging self hunched over a desk in some stuffy office.

"We'll be gone from here before you know it," I said to Will.

"Not soon enough," he answered.

Booking hard for grades that fall, the last semester that would count toward college, I felt myself drifting away from Will. I wasn't at all happy when our room became headquarters for a band of disciples who gathered to listen to Will's records and talk about black music and Indian religion and Beat literature. This was the first incarnation of the entourage which became a feature of Will's adult life. His very aloofness seemed to attract those who were less self-contained, and he did nothing to discourage these satellites. Incredibly, the chief disciple was Jack Stubblefield, who, under the influence of my roommate and the Zeitgeist, had quit football and grown out his hair.

"It's dangerous to introduce new ideas to a guy like Stubblefield," I complained one evening when we found ourselves, briefly, alone. "It's like sending a balloon up into space—it'll expand and explode in the void."

"Stubblefield's cool," Will said, staring out the window over the snowy lawns. "It's like starting with a blank slate." And indeed he did have a certain vacancy that made him the perfect athlete as well as an exemplary follower.

Shortly before Thanksgiving Will proposed to lead an expedition to hear Buddy Guy and Junior Wells play at a coffeehouse in Boston. To nearly everyone's surprise, permission was granted after Will secured Bubble Head Wilson, the music teacher, as chaperon. I was annoyed that I'd first heard about this adventure from Stubblefield, who asked me if I was going. And I was deep in the middle of two term papers. Toward the end of the week I had made enough progress on my papers to consider going. If Will had asked me to join him I might have, but when I mentioned I might not be able to go he said, "Whatever you feel like, man."

I didn't want our friendship to wither away. But neither did I want to become just another one of Will's hangers-on. Let Stubblefield kiss Will's ring and carry his water. And so I stayed.

Will and his disheveled band trooped into lunch on the Saturday after their concert, an air of jaded conspiracy emanating from their table. Back in our room, pride prevented me from asking any questions, but the campus was soon humming with wild rumors: Will had given everyone LSD. . . . Will had gone backstage after the show to smoke dope with the performers. . . . They'd all gone to the Combat Zone and gotten drunk. . . . He'd picked up a girl at the coffeehouse and taken her back to their hotel. . . . Will had incriminating photographs of Wilson in a strip joint that he threatened to release if the teacher didn't keep quiet. . . .

Wilson himself assured the headmaster that the outing was uneventful, but for weeks thereafter he seemed chagrined and dazed, and the trip became legend. Will's own renegade luster was further burnished, if not his standing with school authorities. His influence on campus was considered subversive. It was almost inevitable that the rumor of drug dealing would attach to him. Not long after the Boston outing Matson, in his role as housemaster, conducted a search of our room, and though, remarkably, no drugs were found, he did discover Will's large stash of small bills. We'd just returned from dinner when our triumphant housemaster confronted us in the entry hall.

"The headmaster would like to see you immediately, Mr. Savage." Will stared at Matson, unmoving, until the housemaster began to turn pink. "If you'd like I can summon security," he said.

Will turned to me with a comradely look and said, "Can you believe what a dickhead this guy is?"

"It was not without difficulty that I convinced the headmaster you had nothing to do with your roommate's activities," Matson said to me after Will had turned and marched out. "But if you know anything about this matter I'd advise you to cooperate."

"Will hasn't done anything wrong," I insisted, then turned and ran up the stairs. My own possessions were relatively unscathed, but Will's were strewn across the room. I began to put things away as I waited for him to return. Twenty minutes later he came in and sat on the bed. He seemed unnaturally calm.

"Did you tell him where the money came from?" I demanded.

"I told him I wasn't a drug dealer. That was all he needed to know."

"You've got to tell them something."

"I don't see why. It's my money."

"They'll kick you out for sure."

"Do you think numbers running would be viewed more favorably than drug dealing?"

"Maybe, if it's off campus."

"And if it doesn't involve any white people."

"That's not the point."

"It's almost always the point."

"Get real, Will."

I was furious at Matson, of course, but no less furious at Will for his refusal to defend himself. The discipline committee was scheduled to meet in two days. Will snored soundly that night, but I was unable to sleep. In the light of morning, only one plan of rescue seemed feasible. I skipped breakfast to call Will's father; if I got to him before the headmaster did I thought he might be able to devise an explanation for his son's cash. I didn't tell Will, since I was pretty certain he would be violently opposed to the plan.

"Well, where did he get the damn money," Cordell asked, after I assured him that Will was no drug dealer. "I know he's not the type to save up his allowance."

"I'd rather not say, sir."

"Patrick, if you want to save Will's ass you better tell me everything."

And so I explained the numbers operation, though I pretended not to know the identity of Will's partner. I was relieved that Cordell sounded more incredulous than angry—if anything he seemed proud of his son's enterprise. He made me promise not to tell Will, or anyone, that we had spoken.

Cordell flew up for the hearing that night. I was downstairs in the common room, pacing, when father and son walked in. Will was as sullen as his father was cheerful. "Well, Patrick," said Mr. Savage, "we seem to have convinced them to keep Will on until he decides to do something truly heinous. I thought you might like to join us for a little off-campus celebration at the Inn? They used to serve a nice prime rib in my time."

I studied Will to see if his father had betrayed me, but his air of smoldering resentment was not directed at me.

At the time the restaurant at the Inn represented, for me, the apex of public dining. The Inn was a vast, three-story, white clapboard affair with green shutters, a sort of hypertrophied New England whaling captain's home. The site of generations of family reunions and celebrations, it was a shrine to red meat and brown drinks. The dining rooms were Tudorish, with exposed round beams crisscrossing the white walls, and dim enough to seem candlelit. We sat in black Hitchcock captain's chairs. Tall as an open newspaper, the menu featured such wonders as filet mignon and veal cordon bleu. Over several Johnnie Walkers, Cordell explained how he had charmed the board out of expelling Will. "Told them I played the ponies from time to time and that in a fit of generosity I'd sent the young scholar my winnings from a trifecta. All small bills—straight from the betting window. And of course I didn't think it hurt to inquire about fund-raising and finances, given certain family bequests to the old school over the years."

"You didn't have to say anything," Will said. "Nobody asked you to lie on my behalf."

"And if I hadn't, you'd be out on your fanny."

"What if I *was* dealing drugs? Don't you even care if I'm guilty?"

"Would you tell me the truth?"

"Probably not."

"Well, then, I guess the wise man doesn't ask."

I tried to look like someone who had no particular stake in this conversation. I've never considered myself an especially skillful dissembler—though perhaps I am. Will apparently never suspected my involvement. Two weeks later I listened with sympathetic amazement when Will told me that Jessie Petit had been roughed up by the cops and jailed. He couldn't understand what had gone wrong, because the police were paid off regularly. Someone had targeted them; Will naturally blamed his father.

"He never liked Jessie; he came with my mother, part of her dowry." He slapped his hand into the pillow. "Shit, how'd that bastard find out?"

Lying in my bed across the room, I was grateful he couldn't see me in the darkness. "How can you be so sure it was your father?"

"I just know, that's all."

I rolled over and tried to fall asleep. And in the years since, whenever Will seemed to be exaggerating his father's malevolent influence, I recalled that on this occasion he was right.

I never did get around to telling Will that his father wrote me a letter of recommendation to Yale, his alma mater. Will himself seemed indifferent to higher education. Bad enough, in his view, that he came from a privileged background. Eventually, in order to get Sipwick the guidance counselor off his back, he applied to Reed and Bennington—the only progressive schools in the country, he boasted, but he had no intention of actually going. He still planned to manage the career of Lester Holmes, with whom he often consulted after supper on the dormitory phone.

Christmas was enlivened by the news from Bear Track that Elbridge had announced his engagement to Cheryl Dobbs. Returning from break, I settled into my last term, spending most of my time with the lacrosse boys or camped out in the library while Will and his entourage took over the room, discussing Zen Buddhism and the cultural significance of Lash LaRue, attuned to the high-pitched frequency of change and unrest coming from beyond the campus. I didn't even want to know what drugs they were doing.

I hardly felt the need to revise my dour opinion when Stubblefield solemnly informed me, the day after Otis Redding's plane crashed, that he was the greatest singer since Caruso. "And how do we know it was an accident?" he said. "Look at Sam Cooke, man. There's, like, a pattern there for anybody who wants to see it." A month before, he'd never heard of Otis Redding or Sam Cooke. Will's own judgments and pronouncements were rather more temperate by comparison. A great many of the figures he admired were to die abruptly over the next few years, and he always believed that he too would join the ranks of the talented young dead.

Will was allowed to use one of the music rooms for a kind of memorial service for Otis Redding. Some fifty of our classmates showed up to listen to Will play records and talk about rhythm and blues. I doubt more than half of them had ever heard of Otis, but Will had acquired a reputation as an oracle—or, at the very least, a spectacle. Even the jocks and the young Republicans among us were curious. But it's also true that Will was canny enough to let it be known that a truckload of ice cream and soft drinks was being delivered to the common room for the occasion. Modest as it was, I suppose this was Will's first gig as a producer.

As the ground thawed and the New England mud season approached, I was dismayed to realize that our lives seemed to be diverging irrevocably. One night, when I complained yet again about Stubblefield's constant presence, Will said, "At least he's not a fag."

"What's that supposed to mean?"

"I mean unlike certain housemasters."

"Matson's not . . . a fag," I said, stumbling over the word partly out of delicacy, partly out of a sudden uncertainty.

We hardly spoke to each other in the weeks leading up to the spring dance. Girls in white gloves from several nearby private schools were bused in for our wholesome, strictly chaperoned amusement. Will was disdainful of the entire concept.

I was beating him at squash one day when he said, "You don't really plan to attend this quaint ritual, do you?"

"Why not?" I tried to sound casual about it. Puffing from exertion, Will was still limping from his accident; a moment before, I'd felt bad about taking points from him in his convalescent state, but I suddenly wanted to thrash him.

"It just seems pitiful," he said.

"Lately, everything seems pitiful to you." I dealt up a violent overhead serve, which he bobbled. "Academics, sports, social events—it's all pathetic."

"I'm just asking you not to be a slave to convention, Patrick. If you weren't so damn smart I wouldn't care. But you're trying to buy a ticket on the fucking *Titanic*, man."

I didn't say anything; it was easy for him, from his privileged position, to devalue the whole social order. I served again; Will ducked just in time.

"You're a real quick study, Keane, that's for sure," Will said, giving me a look that would linger long after he opened the door and limped off the court.

The night of the mixer, Matson led a nondancing delegation into town for pizza and a movie. He, too, seemed disappointed that I was bent on attending. But I was eager to celebrate my acceptance to Yale, to claim as my prize the heart of a young princess. To that end, I joined the other young swains in the parking lot outside the auditorium, feeling especially dapper with my new Branford College tie, a gift from Cordell; it had been his college at Yale, and was soon to be mine. At length the buses arrived, two of them, and the girls filed off, holding up their skirts and scanning the mob while we murmured and whistled. Dickinson the math teacher tried to remind us that we were gentlemen.

"Look at the tits on that," Trey Bowman said, and suddenly I found myself staring at Lollie Baker, who stood in the door of the bus casting a skeptical eye over all of us, then spotted me and waved.

If I was ambivalent about our last encounter, torn between a sense of failure and one of pride at my only erotic adventure to date, I was wholly demoralized by Will's revelation that he'd slept with her.

Suddenly she was standing in front of me, smiling.

"Aren't you-all going to escort me in?" It took me a moment to realize the second-person pronoun wasn't plural. The increase in my standing among my peers was almost palpable as I offered Lollie my arm, my reservations swept away by a rush of gratitude and pleasure.

"Studly Keane," Bowman said, and an envious pall fell over the others as we strolled off to the auditorium.

Lollie looked much as I remembered her, if perhaps not quite so pretty in reality as in my fantasies. More rounded—Bowman hadn't been kidding about the tits—but still somehow masculine and angular, even in her pink dress. I had forgotten, or softened, the thin prominent nose which seemed, I now remembered, a projection of her aggressive manner.

Though I wanted to appear cold and aloof, in fact I was happy to see her and vastly relieved to find a friend amidst the pink and white ranks of the visiting team. When we started to dance I smelled liquor on her breath. Then, after an awkward fox-trot, silently counted out on my part, she said, "Let's get the hell out of this damn sock hop." Out in the parking lot the spring air was spiced with the scent of new growth, and darkness was falling. Thinking again of Will's conquest, I asked—with a marked formality, I thought—how she liked Miss Porter's.

"The pits," she sneered. "A deb factory. A mare farm for Locust Valley and Greenwich and Grosse Pointe. When I first got there my roommate asked me if we wore *shoes* in the South. I heard that question three times my first year. Louisa May Alcott's still big in the lit curriculum. The headmistress imagines herself to be the center of this reverential cult, we're all supposed to just worship her or something, the old prune. Give me a damn break. And a kitchen raid is everybody's idea of an outrageous good time. I just love the hell out of it," she concluded.

She also had a kind word for Yale, when I offhandedly mentioned that I'd been accepted. "The West Point of East Egg," she observed, although at the time the reference escaped me.

"What the hell's wrong with you," she asked, finally noticing my chilly manner.

"I thought you might rather be talking to Will than to me," I said stupidly.

I'm afraid I've never been very good at hiding my feelings; certainly Lollie didn't need any additional hints.

"Oh, sugar. . . ." She put her arms around me, drawing a finger-wagging rebuke from Colbert, the earth sciences teacher who was policing the lot.

"Hell, I grew up with Will," she said, after Colbert had receded.

"Oh, well that explains it," I said bitterly.

She put her arms around me and pressed her body against mine. "Will's . . . just a friend."

I snorted. "A friend. Right."

"Look, he's a sad and screwed-up boy," she said. "And maybe he's had a harder life than you know. And maybe I just . . . I don't know. I don't want to say I feel sorry for him, but I do care for him."

I was shocked at this view of Will, whom I considered the most self-assured person I'd ever met. But as soon as she said it I realized she was right, though I couldn't say exactly how or why.

"Hey," she whispered. "I got a flask of good whiskey in my purse. Let's go back to your room."

"The dorm's off-limits," I said.

Lollie rolled her eyes. "Gosh, *really?*"

She scanned the quadrangle. "What about the chapel? Maybe you and I could do some serious praying."

I had no idea if the chapel was locked or not, but I wasn't going to blow it this time. She told me to wait for her inside and she'd meet me there in ten minutes. As a boy, it didn't behoove me to be less daring than she was, and, as Will's rival, I was emboldened by a sense of competition. I watched her sneak back on the bus before I headed off on a roundabout route to the chapel. The door was open, but as soon as I looked inside I knew I could not go through with the plan. Whether it was the residual sanctity of the place or the simple fear of being caught or perhaps the fear that here, finally, I might be about to lose my own sanctity, I did not want to take Lollie in there. I went outside and waited, half hidden behind a yew.

Somehow she evaded the cordon of chaperons around the parking lot and ran up the walk, now dressed in a black turtleneck and black capri pants.

When I hissed her name, she dove on me and kissed me passionately, thrusting her tongue into my mouth. After perhaps a minute of this I told her that the chaplain was inside performing vespers.

"Shit," she said. We ducked farther behind the yew, which offered us moderate cover. She sat down in the mulch, her back against the foundation of the chapel, and handed me the flask.

"What's so screwed up about Will," I asked, having gulped as much whiskey as I could.

"One thing that's not screwed up about him." She took a long sip from the flask. "He knows when to talk and when to shut up."

At that I rolled on top of her and kissed her violently. For the season the night was chilly, but not excessively so, not for two young bodies stoked with hormones and alcohol. I've often wondered, since then, why we couldn't have stayed where we were, or found a dark patch of lawn or an empty building. But after ten minutes in the bushes my common sense was thoroughly obscured by lust. Going to the room was her idea, but I would have followed her anywhere, obsessed as I was with finishing what we'd started a year and a half before in Memphis.

We managed somehow to get to the room without being spotted. Matson and the nondancers were still at the movie. Upstairs, we finished the whiskey and were grappling on the bed when Will burst in. I was not entirely happy to see him—Lollie had just finished undoing my belt buckle. At the same time I was also relieved, if the truth be told, and I certainly didn't mind him finding me so successfully engaged.

"Jesus," he muttered.

"Hey, Will," Lollie said, as I struggled to extract my hand from the tight elastic of her bra.

"Matson's heard there's a girl in the house," Will said, "and he's checking rooms."

This news sobered me immediately. With less than three weeks to graduation I saw my academic career, my entire future, snatched away from me.

"Get in the closet," Will said. He pulled me off the bed and shoved me in among the clothes, then slid the door shut behind me.

I heard the knock on the outside door, then Matson's voice.

"Mr. Savage, I presume."

"Mr. Matson," Will said, in a courtly tone, "may I present Lollie Baker, of Memphis, Tennessee."

"Delighted," Lollie said.

I tried to convince myself that Will would talk his way out of it, that his superior rhetorical skills and charm would somehow save him. But even then I knew he was sacrificing himself, and that by remaining in the closet I was allowing him to do so. Though I suppose I might have had the excuse of drunkenness—of not really understanding the consequences when Will shoved me in the closet—in truth I felt acutely, painfully sober as I listened from my hiding place. I became more deeply ashamed of myself with each passing minute, but I stayed put until long after I'd heard Will and Lollie agree to follow Matson downstairs.

I was still in the closet ten minutes later when Will returned. Opening the door, he said, "All clear," and flopped on his bed with his hands behind his head.

"What happened," I asked idiotically. Having a girl in the room was automatic expulsion.

"Don't worry about it." Will smiled. "We both come out exactly where we want to be, and Lollie can take care of herself."

"What about the draft?" I said. It was the spring of 1967.

"There's plenty of ways to dodge the draft."

Stunned with self-loathing, I collapsed onto my bed, hugging my knees against my chest. I couldn't bear to look at him.

"Besides," he added coolly, "you're my best friend."

I probably would have lived through that miserable scene again to hear this admission.

Over the next two days I was tormented with the idea of turning myself in and, finally, with the realization that I would not do so. My life has been shaped by that decision and by Will's sacrifice, and though I'm fairly sure he never regretted it, I am still unable to think of that moment without shame. Several times in my career when I've been tempted to suppress evidence or lie for a client or otherwise take the expedient path I have turned back, haunted by the memory of that failure of honor. On the other hand, the lesson I learned was hardly a simple one because I would violate almost any of my principles, professional and otherwise, on behalf of Will Savage.

IX

Parents and siblings alike were baffled by the airborne FREE THE SLAVES banner, dragged by a small plane that buzzed back and forth over the fieldhouse lawn. But a cheer rose up from the rows of the begowned graduates, who understood that Will Savage had found his own way of making his presence felt at the commencement ceremony. I could see, from my seat in the third row, that this bit of theater had a mortifying effect on some of the faculty onstage.

Three weeks before, on the very day that Will had left campus for good, a collective derangement had spread through the professoriat. It was eventually determined that the brownies beside the coffee urn at the weekly faculty meeting did not originate in the dining hall. When Matson, who was notoriously fond of chocolate, failed to appear for lights-out that night we did not question our good fortune. Hall hockey, poker and general hilarity prevailed well into the night. Only the next morning, when several classes were canceled, did the rumors begin to circulate. Perhaps they were *only* rumors; there was no official confirmation or inquiry, and I had almost come to regard the story of the hashish brownies as one of those legends which spontaneously combust from time to time within enclosed communities. But Stubblefield was even more smug than usual the day afterward, and Will's profession of innocence over the phone a few days later was remarkably coy and unconvincing.

Airplane or no airplane, for my mother the commencement on the lawn was an unalloyed triumph. I had won the history and English prizes and graduated second in my class. Immediately after the ceremony she congratulated valedictorian Isaac Mendel and his parents, eager to show there were no hard feelings about his academic victory.

"I thought Senator Kennedy was wonderful," she said, after she'd shanghaied Trey Bowman's Chanel-suited mother into taking a picture of the three of us. "Just push the little button, it's all automatic. So intelligent and articulate. Wasn't he just wonderful? If anything I think he's handsomer than Jack and Bobby. I mean, than Jack used to be, of course."

This speech was ostensibly directed at her immediate family, though it was freely shared with Mrs. Bowman and all around us. Like a geyser, Mother projected herself into the spring morning in her pink-and-turquoise dress, fizzing between her skinny son and her shorter husband, her bosom threatening to burst with pride. Not only had her son graduated with honors from this Waspy redoubt, but Teddy Kennedy of the Boston Irish-Catholic Kennedys—one of our own, as yet unmarred by major scandal—was the commencement speaker.

"Just one more, come on boys, smile now," she urged us, as Mrs. Bowman readied the camera again. "This is a graduation, not a wake. Pat's poor father looks like he's thinking about how much the tuition costs at Yale," she confided to Mrs. Bowman, who was beginning to look dazed by all this Hibernian bonhomie. I was afraid Mom was also going to tell her that one of her distant cousins was married to one of the Kennedys' distant cousins, but she was saving this news for the senator himself, whom she managed to corner shortly before he escaped in his limousine. My father and I refused to accompany her on this mission—I experienced a rare flash of kinship and warmth for the old man when he rolled his eyes. "What do you think?" he said. "Teddy will probably want to invite us all down to Hyannisport once he hears how close we are." Mom got someone to take a picture of this meeting, and it's still framed on the mantel at home—a thin, boyish, slightly dazed-looking Ted Kennedy smiling crookedly at my mother's chest while she beams at the camera.

My graduate cynicism was a bit of a sham; I'd found myself misty-eyed at the end of the senator's speech, and while the immediate stimulus was the senator's oblique reference to his murdered brother, I was also mourning my departure. The melancholia was amplified by Will's absence, and by the fact that I was responsible for it.

That morning I had received a congratulatory telegram from Cordell Savage. If there was anything he could do for me at Yale, he wrote, I shouldn't hesitate to let him know.

My letter of apology to Lollie Baker caught up with her in Memphis, to which she had retreated—or, by her account, returned in triumph—after being thrown out of Miss Porter's.

Yeah, yeah, there was a show of perfunctory and strictly pro forma rending of garments and beating of breasts, but nobody's heart was really in it. Basically no big deal. It's a good old tradition in our good old family getting thrown out of good old schools, although largely, till now, a male tradition. And it's not like there's a big imperative vis-à-vis higher education for the womenfolk. So don't weep on my behalf, sugar. I'm actually relieved the decision about college has been made for me; staid Smith and wonky Wellesley, having been notified by prissy Miss Porter's of lascivious Lollie Baker's expulsion, are withdrawing their invitations to matriculate, but Bennington is notoriously more tolerant of human frailty. Which undoubtedly makes it the appropriate place for yours truly.

It was the postscript that intrigued me the most. "Do you know anything about this colored girl Will's gone crazy for? Lord, that boy surely knows how to stir things up." While I had my suspicions, I learned nothing definite for almost a year. Will had announced a grand pilgrimage through the Far East as his nongraduation present to himself, and by the time I heard from Lollie he was gone.

Throughout the summer and fall, news of Will's adventures dribbled in on postcards. The first came from Japan, where he was studying Zen at Daitoku-ji in Kyoto and cornering the market on used silk kimonos; apparently he could buy the latter dirt cheap at flea markets and sell them at a huge profit to a buyer in San Francisco. His next stop was Bali, where he spent a month sheltering in a hut on the beach and feeding on psychedelics. The last postcard was from Chiang Mai, in Thailand, and then—nothing for months.

In September I went off to Yale. Arriving at my assigned room on the Old Campus, I was less ashamed of my parents than I had been two years before, not because I'd become a better person but because I was determined to believe that I truly belonged at Yale. In any case, my parents were gone by the time my prospective roommates arrived. I was unpacking in one of the two single rooms when Aaron Greeley alighted in the doorway, unaccompanied, puffing from his trip up three flights with two suitcases. Within minutes I'd learned that he was from Evanston, Illinois, played lacrosse and wanted to major in English. Like me he was turned out in the uniform—Weejuns, chinos, button-down shirt—and among the possessions he had toted in his first trip up the stairs were a Jack Kramer tennis racket in its wooden press and a lacrosse stick. Statistically speaking, he was a very conventional Yale roommate, except that he was black, though he did not seem particularly aware of it himself. It took the advent of Dalton Percy and his father to remind him.

They appeared as Aaron and I were arranging the few pieces of basement-salvaged furniture I'd brought down in the station wagon and gaseously discussing the plays of Edward Albee. Dalton Percy was the very image of the roommate I had envisioned for myself: expensively dressed, haughty in bearing. His cruel, handsome face conveyed the impression of someone who engaged in duels over obscure breaches of honor. Although it was quite warm he wore a long topcoat of toasted-nut color and an old Yale scarf. His father was built along much the same lines, but fiercer: rather than a duelist he looked like someone who had people killed by his subordinates.

I had plenty of time to observe the Percys at rest; they seemed paralyzed after we introduced ourselves. They were cryptic and clipped when we offered Dalton his choice of rooms and invited them to share a bite with us downtown. Both men kept their coats on. Finally Percy Senior said, "If you'll excuse us, we have a previous engagement at Mory's." I was sorry to see them go. Though I liked Aaron, Dalton seemed the kind of boy who arrived already plugged into everything worth aspiring to socially, and I dimly suspected I was going to have to choose between them. Fortunately, perhaps, the choice was made for me.

Dalton never returned to our rooms. Exactly what channels were employed remained a mystery, but the younger Percy received a new room assignment the next day. Aaron and I knew how to interpret his defection, though we pretended to be happy about not having to share one of the bedrooms.

We were both eager to be remade in the image of Yale, though we were of scant help to each other in this regard, and ultimately Aaron became frustrated in the attempt. And yet, he started out so very close. He *looked* Yale. I don't mean that his features were Caucasian, but neither were they insistently Negroid, and to me he seemed indisputably princely. Although he'd attended a public high school in Evanston he seemed terribly preppie: he played lacrosse and spent summers on Martha's Vineyard, where he raced Flying Juniors. On land he retained a sort of nautical aspect. He wore dock shoes and often sported a blue blazer. He owned two dozen Brooks Brothers shirts—I was amazed to hear that Brooks had a branch in Chicago—a gray herringbone Harris tweed jacket and a gray flannel suit, with the appropriate accessories, all of which at any given moment were filed in closet and dresser according to an immutable code.

Among Aaron's vital possessions was a stereo, but he was not interested in the music that Will had taught me to like. Trying to casually establish my credentials as a soulful roommate, I spun my "James Brown, Live at the Apollo" as we unpacked the first day. Aaron closed the door to the suite and said, "You don't mind if I turn it down a little, do you?"

He fingered the volume knob with a fastidious gesture which suggested a desire to keep his distance from the noise. I wondered if James Brown was already passé with his own people. Eventually I understood that Aaron was embarrassed by my blues and soul records; he was afraid that our dormmates might associate him with the music. "I'm not a big fan of folk art," he announced one day after enduring a side of Sonny Boy Williamson. "All that raw, unmeditated emotion." His own record collection favored the Everly Brothers, Johnny Mathis, the Beatles, Simon and Garfunkel.

I invited him home with me for Thanksgiving, a gesture more complicated than even I was willing to admit at the time. I would have been ashamed to reveal my modest roots to Dalton Percy or any of his fair-haired ilk. Though I knew from his snapshots that Aaron's own home was more impressive than my own, he too was an outsider, and I trusted him not to betray me. Still, on the train I warned him not to expect much. "Sartre says hell is other people," I quoted, repeating something Matson used to say. "But I think it's a split-level on half an acre."

My parents in fact were more elegant in their hospitality than I was in describing them. My father was delighted to have someone in the house with whom to discuss the fine points of pro football, which interested me not in the least. My mother confided to me shortly after we arrived that she thought Aaron was extremely handsome, and she was hooked from the moment he held her chair for her at supper. Even Nana Keane was impressed, noting that he was "very polite and seems to be quite attentive to me." By the end of the weekend, it seemed clear that he was the son and grandson they deserved.

"Did you ever think a mistake had been made," he asked the second night. "A switch, a last-minute bungle—and you were dropped down the wrong chimney, into the wrong house, the wrong time, the wrong body, the wrong skin?"

"God, yes." I nodded madly, even as I supposed he was talking about a more acute sense of displacement than my own. We were parked above the reservoir in my dad's Chevy, bloated with Thanksgiving dinner, finishing a six-pack purchased from a package store renowned for its laxity about IDs.

"My father grew up on the South Side," he confided. "He was a good student, made it all the way to Howard University. Then his father died and he had to come home to support the family, six younger brothers and sisters. All he could find was janitorial work. Within three years he started an office-cleaning business and not long after I was born we moved to Evanston."

"Admirable," I mumbled.

"Yeah." With an exasperated sigh, he ripped the fliptop off a final beer and dropped the tab into the foaming slot. "He chose it because the school system was good. And he got Mama fixed after my sister was born—no way he was going to breed himself back into poverty. And I grew up playing tennis and taking piano lessons with white kids, so I could look down on my relatives on the South Side. And even look down on my old man because he can't play tennis or sail a boat." He took a long swig of beer. "And because he's a *Negro.*"

I didn't know how to respond to this last statement. I wasn't sure if he meant that his father was of the older generation that identified themselves with that old-fashioned appellation—*black* being the fashionable new term—or whether he meant, more spectacularly, that he somehow considered himself white. Afraid of asking, instead I confessed to similar feelings, acknowledging that my parents had nurtured a sensibility delicate enough to be embarrassed by them. But at least, I thought with sudden, unexpected gratitude, we were the same color.

Later, we used our high beams to harass the couples making it in their cars above the reservoir. "If we aren't getting any," Aaron declared, "then neither should these other bastards."

When Aaron talked about women, the referents were deities who transcended race. He carried a picture of his prom date, a pretty blonde he said was his girlfriend. Our junior year, women were finally admitted as fully vested, if not fully accepted, members of the college. Before that, sexual anthropology involved a field trip to Smith or Vassar. At my roommate's instigation, I assayed a couple of miserable road trips. We were late for our first mixer at Smith, having spent more than an hour by the side of the road changing the tire on the Dodge Dart we'd borrowed for the occasion. Making up for lost time, Aaron immediately approached the prettiest girl in the auditorium, a blonde whose hair turned up in a perfect flip, as did her nose and her breasts.

"What's shaking?" Aaron said, staring at the latter. She seemed amused. Introducing herself as Cameron DeVeere, she directed my attention to her friend—a plain-looking girl in a polka-dot dress. When Aaron and Cameron sauntered off without a backward glance, I asked the other one to dance. Far from deeming this an honor or a pleasure, she seemed merely resigned to her fate—and remained so indifferent and distracted that I persisted in dancing with her to prove that I was not merely settling. When I finally kissed her to the lugubrious chords of "Whiter Shade of Pale," she submitted to my tongue, her acrid breath unfriendly, her upper lip curiously abrasive, her lack of response irritating me to greater effort. And when that interminable song which inevitably signaled the end of all college mixers in those years was finally over, she curtsied stiffly, and said, "I better find Cameron."

But neither Cameron nor Aaron was to be found. I spent a sleepless night shivering in the backseat of the car. When Aaron finally appeared in the miserable gray dawn, chirpy and bright as the birds, I pointedly did not ask him about his night. He talked about everything *but* for the first half hour of the drive, until finally he couldn't contain himself. "I think I'm in love," he said, only partly in jest. They had spent most of the night in the yearbook office, to which Cameron had a key. He did not say whether he had actually screwed her, but he seemed far too animated to have gotten anything less than a hand job.

After that my weekends were spent alone in our suite or in the library, while Aaron was usually off with Cameron. And to this day I feel a tingle of melancholy panic when I hear the first organ chords of "Whiter Shade of Pale."

Will turned up in Memphis early in the New Year, delirious with hepatitis and the wisdom of the road. He wrote me a long letter which even at the time seemed less a letter to a friend than an attempt to mythologize his *Wanderjahre.* I saved it for a number of years, rereading it one maudlin, drunken evening in law school, though it has long since disappeared. The highlights, as I recall them now, sound like a kind of greatest-hits-of-the-hippie-trail, though at the time I'd hardly heard of most of the ports of call. As I recall, he reported he'd spent a month living in a tent with a band of Pathan tribesmen who ran guns and drugs through the Khyber Pass and were big fans of American rock and roll; after a hard day of smuggling and robbing they would listen to Chuck Berry and Elvis around the campfire. He'd then trekked the Himalayas to Ladakh, where he had meditated with Tibetan monks. Rolling overland by train and by thumb, he had lingered on a Greek island and in a squatters' commune in Amsterdam, whence he had taken a steamer to Rio. In a village in Ecuador, stoned out of his gourd on mushrooms, he was captured by a band of guerrillas, who took him to their mountain camp and interrogated him for three days as a suspected CIA agent. More than merely convincing the guerrilla leader of his innocence, Will had by his own account worked up for this charismatic warrior/scholar a New Left reading list which emphasized Marcuse and the rest of the Frankfurt school. And he had apparently promised financial and other support upon his return to the States, though, of course, he explained to me he was sure I would understand that he could not be specific about this.

My adventures at Yale were somewhat pale, by comparison, though at that moment the climate at Yale and elsewhere was just progressive enough that I suppose I did not feel penalized by those whose acceptance I craved for hanging out with my roommate. But Aaron was increasingly reminded of everything he wished to forget by the more militant black students, who wanted to claim him as their own.

One lunchtime our second semester, a tall angular young man from the Afro table muttered "Oreo" as he passed our group. The rest of us were indignant and would have leaped to Aaron's defense if any other issue had been involved—if he'd been called a fag, for instance. But our bookish little confederation was uncertain of the new etiquette, and, with the exception of Aaron, we were white as plucked poultry; half of us had never heard the word used in this context. Aaron himself pretended not to have heard. It seems odd to me now that Aaron and I never talked about any of this. But, then, young men seldom talk among themselves about the things that matter the most to them.

My attempt to accommodate divergent loyalties and ambitions was challenged that March by the arrival of an invitation to Dalton Percy's birthday party. Our near roommate had become the center of the Brahmin, rakehell set in our class, the boys whose ancestors were Old Blues and who themselves would soon fill the ranks of the secret societies. Dalton owned an old fire engine, and on Friday nights he and his friends would gather at some exclusive location to drink themselves into hilarity, after which they would climb aboard and race around the campus throwing water balloons at passersby. I'm sorry to report that this seemed to me the height of stylish fun at the time.

I'd never manned the fire engine, but Dalton had been in my history class in the first term, and I'd lent him my class notes on one occasion. Our initial encounter was never mentioned, and for some reason I had extended myself to be friendly, as if I were the one who had rejected him as a roommate. He in turn seemed eager to communicate, in his own careless way, that he had nothing against me, and always said hello. But I was still surprised to get the engraved invitation—black tie at Mory's, the venerable private club on York Street.

I didn't need to ask Aaron if he'd been invited. And in a momentary flash of lucidity, I wondered if that was *why* I had been invited, to sharpen the point of my roommate's exclusion. This anxious thought was immediately suppressed, as anticipation about the party swirled across the Old Campus. Participants were to be picked up in front of their dorms by the fire engine; prostitutes and strippers were forecast.

"Ask Patrick," Peter Barnholtz said to our table, one day at lunch. "He's going."

"I'm not going," I said, glancing at Aaron's face and just as quickly turning away, already angry that I'd been made to blurt out a denial when in fact I was still trying to work out a Missouri compromise with my conscience.

"I mean, I was invited," I added. "Don't ask me why. I hardly even know the guy."

"Don't stay away on my account," Aaron said coldly, as we got up to walk to class.

"I wouldn't think of going," I lied. The salient point, I suppose, was that I hadn't mentioned the invitation before, hadn't held it up and laughed in derision when I had opened it a few days before with Aaron standing right beside me at the mailboxes, tearing the wrapper from his latest issue of the fucking *Boating News*. Obviously, I was considering my response, and by the time Aaron heard that, from Peter, it was already too late.

In fact, I was not among the celebrants. Seldom has an intended good deed, modest though it was, been performed with such tortured reluctance. Then again, the older I get the more I suspect that many genuine heroes have sulked onto the field of glory, that famous stands of principle have often been hunched over with doubt. I wanted to go, was dying to go. But I couldn't find a place to hide my scruples. Finally, the night before the party, I called Dalton with an elaborate story of a dying grandfather—the classic failure-to-produce-homework story, which sounded no less hackneyed in this case.

"Too bad," Dalton said. "You're missing a bash."

"If it were *anything* else . . . ," I croaked.

"Yeah, well, catch you later, guy."

I returned to our rooms and paced, waiting for Aaron to come back so I could tell him what I had done and thereby alleviate in some small measure the sickening feeling of loss in my chest. I waited until midnight, unable to concentrate on *Beowulf* or Aristotle or the Dred Scott decision. I went to the library to look for him, then rushed home to silent, empty rooms. I hardly slept that night, imagining all the splendor and *bon* vivacity I would be deprived of in twenty-four hours.

In the morning, Aaron's bed had clearly not been slept in, and he was not at lunch. No one knew where he was. Indignant at his disappearance, I began to reconsider. The afternoon was ruined by indecision and the certain knowledge that I would regret either choice. At four I called the formal shop, expecting, and half hoping, to be told that all plausible sizes and types were unavailable due to a major undergraduate party. But in fact they had my very size, available in both shawl and notched lapel; I should have known that most of Dalton's friends would own tuxedos. At six-thirty I went to dinner, but I was unable to eat or to listen to anything said at table. When I raced back to my room there was still no sign of Aaron.

Finally, the fire engine, preceded by its siren, pulled up on High Street. I watched from our window as the boys in their evening wear climbed onto the side of the truck, holding the rails with one hand and clinking their beer and champagne bottles together as the flashing red lights disappeared into the festive night.

Aaron sauntered in an hour later to change his clothes.

"Where have you been?" I practically shouted.

He stopped and turned in the door frame. "I was with Cameron," he said. "What's the big deal?"

"I didn't go to the party." I didn't know what else to say. Angry as I was at him, the ostensible cause and beneficiary of my decision, I wanted him to make me feel better about it.

"What party," he asked.

"Dalton Percy's birthday," I said incredulously.

After a moment he nodded slowly, as if on reflection he dimly recalled hearing something about the event. "Bully for you," he said jauntily, and disappeared into his room.

X

"You know anything about this nigger girl?"

When Cordell Savage called with the offer of dinner in New Haven, I was flattered that he'd make the detour from New York. It wasn't until we were tucking into our steaks at Mory's that he revealed what was clearly the true purpose of his visit.

"I have no idea what you're talking about," I said, hoping the flush I felt rising in my cheeks wouldn't betray me.

"Hasn't he talked to you about her?" He paused as if to try to sniff my sincerity. I developed a sudden interest in my plate. "Well, he will sooner or later. And when he does I want you to remember what I'm about to tell you." He waited until I looked up expectantly. "We've heard tell Will's infatuated with this . . . girl. I don't exactly know your sympathies, whether you cotton to all this civil rights business. I don't expect you share my convictions. But most of our people do. They don't believe that God intended the races should mix—I'm talking coloreds as well as whites."

When he took a breather to fill our wineglasses, I conducted a quick reconnaissance of the immediate tables; no one appeared to be listening, but I still felt awkward hearing these sentiments expressed in this privileged outpost of the great institution of liberal education from which Cordell himself had graduated. *Lux et Veritas,* that was our motto. And yet Cordell was a charismatic man. He sounded reasonable. It was difficult for me to discount his opinions, particularly within the force field of his presence. Those of us with democratic temperaments are handicapped in the face of the autocratic personality.

"It may be up here you think there's nothing wrong with it," he continued. "But I'm telling you that down south this is a very grave matter. We have a heritage. We live in the world that was given to us. Even if I wanted to give my blessings, the fact is Will would have to contend with the judgment of an entire society. In fact I cannot give my blessings, and if Will continues on this course he's going to find himself cut off from his family and his people and his patrimony. And I don't think I have to tell you, Patrick, it would kill his poor mother."

"Don't you think all this is a little premature?" I said. "We don't even know if he's dating this girl, let alone—"

"We know he's seeing her," Cordell interrupted. "Memphis is a small town and Will is, need I mention, a conspicuous figure. Driving around town in a goddamned cement truck wearing some British officer's uniform—you think people don't notice that, don't tell us what he's up to? What worries me—we both know that Will is given to bold dramatic gestures."

I winced at the thought that this might be an allusion to Will's sacrificial expulsion, though on reflection, I doubted he had ever heard the real story.

"If he is serious about this girl," I said, "I doubt my opinion is going to make any difference."

"Of course it would. You're his best damn friend. And you're an outsider. Right now he's not listening to his own people."

"Will doesn't listen to anybody."

"He'll trust you to be objective." Having said this, Cordell tried to compromise my alleged neutrality. "Patrick, you've broken bread and hunted with us. I think you understand us, and I know you'll do right by Will."

This shameless appeal to my vanity did not entirely miss its mark. As we finished the excellent wine, I promised to find out what I could, though it seemed ridiculous, since Will was living in Memphis, right under Cordell's patrician nose.

Once his hepatitis cleared up, Will established a talent management and production company, Cement Mixer Music, and started cruising the back roads of the Deep South in a two-tone, cream-and-beige '55 Packard, scouring the dives for talent. In February, he had called me to report, with uncharacteristic pride and exhilaration in his voice, that Lester Holmes had a single on the R-and-B charts.

After Cordell's visit, I dutifully dialed the number of Will's office and left a message with someone who sounded too stoned to remember it. I had no home number for Will, and I wasn't sure where he was living. Shortly after Christmas break I received a package from Memphis. Inside was a record, a 45. The photograph on the sleeve looked familiar, but it was not until I saw the name—Taleesha Johnson—that I realized the singer was the shy, beautiful girl who'd once slapped Will's face. Examining the label, I found that Will had both production and cowriting credits.

Home for a long weekend, I was sitting at the dinner table with my mother and father, Nana Keane, my aunt Colleen and her son, Jimmy. Aunt Colleen had just said, "How about a little music?" when the phone rang, alleviating the dreadful silence around the table.

"I'll get it," I said, jumping up.

"What'd you think of the record," Will asked, without preamble, once I picked up.

"Hey, it's great," I lied, having been far too busy to even think about listening to it. "Of course, you know me," I hedged, "I'm no expert or anything."

"It's not meant for experts, Patrick. It's for everybody—even you buttoned-down guys. She's crossed over to the pop charts, and we're following up with another single next month."

All he wanted to talk about was Taleesha and her career, and I began to think his father's suspicions were well founded. He asked me if I could meet them in New York in three days; Taleesha was doing a gig at the Apollo. When I told him I'd try, classes would've started up again by then, he said:

"I need you to be there, Patrick."

On a Wednesday afternoon, I met Will under the clock at the Biltmore. My idea: I liked to picture myself as the kind of guy who hopped on the train from New Haven after classes and casually met his friends under the famous clock, like a character in an O'Hara story. My train was late and Will was waiting when I arrived—the only time he's ever waited on me. Normally he was at least half an hour late for any rendezvous, and often never turned up at his appointed destination. Days or weeks might go by before he called again. Drugs had something to do with this, but the condition was chronic—an unconscious function, I think, of the inherited sense of entitlement. Moreover, he was utterly convinced of the importance of his mission, of the work he needed to perform in the world, and immune to the fear of inconveniencing his fellow creatures, that nervous lower-middle-class anxiety which plagued me as I pushed through the throng of Grand Central beneath the dirty blue zodiacal dome on my way to meet him.

"I feel like a fucking cliché," he complained when I ran up, breathless, "waiting under the damn clock at the Biltmore. It doesn't get any more Dink Stover than this."

"Well, you look like a freak." He was gaunt, almost spectral. His hair was longer, draped thickly around his shoulders, and he was further shrouded in a long black cape over a lush paisley shirt.

"That's what I've been telling him," said the young black woman who rose from an armchair, bathed in the spotlight of Will's rapturous gaze.

"Taleesha Johnson, may I present Patrick Keane."

She took my hand. "So you're my big rival."

More than faintly pleased to hear this, I smiled. "And you're the owner of that amazing voice. I'll never forget the first time I heard you sing in that little church in the Delta."

"Wait till you hear the shit we just recorded," said Will, squeezing her to his chest. "She's even hotter singing the devil's music."

"Will, you know I don't like when you say that," she said, pushing away from him.

"She's a believer," Will said fondly. "Lord knows what she's doing with this heathen."

"You know I'm only interested in your money," she said. "Anyhow, you're no heathen."

She was right. Will was actually the most religious person I knew, though his belief in a submerged and spiritual order in the universe was neither readily apparent nor easily comprehended.

Cordell was also right. Things were pretty far advanced between them. And I could feel the logic of it. They made a potent couple. An inch or two taller than me, Taleesha seemed even taller, the verticality of her long limbs and regal carriage crowned with a sharp chin and a rich swell of lips and flared nostrils beneath the horizontal slash of her cheekbones. You simply had to look at her.

We took a cab to the Village and walked around, past Sheridan Square. "A barbaric Yankee general," Will said, pointing at the statue at one end of the park. "And in this corner—my people." He gestured toward the longhairs and the low-lifes congregated around the benches.

He was exuberant. The furtive mournfulness he carried like a hump on his back seemed to have lifted away. He was in love and the scent of marijuana was in the air. The slaves were growing their hair out and marching on Washington. The Pentagon would shortly be levitated. Robert Kennedy and Martin Luther King, Jr., and Jimi Hendrix were still among us.

We wandered the downtown streets for hours, pausing in front of various nightclubs which Will considered hallowed, until he finally suggested an early dinner at the Cedar Tavern, which he commended as the watering hole of artists and hipsters.

"They look pretty down and out to me," Taleesha said, observing the clientele. Over the course of the afternoon I'd been impressed with the way Taleesha managed Will and teased him, cheerfully squelching his wilder fantasies without mocking his hopes. She'd been considerate enough to annotate the music-biz talk for my benefit. Even by my conventional standards she was accomplished. At one point, when Taleesha ducked into a store on Bleecker to look at shoes, Will informed me that she'd been a National Merit scholar at Booker T. Washington High and that she'd received scholarship offers from all over the country. Except when she giggled at Will, a high, birdlike sound, it was hard to believe she was our age, so canny and self-assured was she. Her voice was rich and authoritative. At times her grammar was almost stiltedly correct, her diction chiseled. And then suddenly she would sound both south-ern and black—the slang, the melting elision of consonants and the lazy vowels. She tended toward the latter when deflating Will's pretensions.

A look passed between them and she excused herself from the table. Whatever was coming I saw they'd agreed that this was the moment for it to start.

"What do you think," he asked foolishly—not a question a man can ever answer honestly, when his best friend asks it about the woman he loves.

"What can I say? She's beautiful." This was one of the rare moments since I'd known Will that the balance of power had shifted to the point that he needed my approval; love had made him vulnerable.

He leaned forward, fixing me with those unnaturally blue eyes. "We're making it official."

I can't say I was entirely unprepared, but I was still surprised to hear him say it. And I suppose I felt a twinge of loss, a jealous fear that I was losing him.

"We're going to city hall tomorrow and I'd like you to be my best man."

"Honored," I said, once I'd regained some portion of my composure. "But what?"

"No buts . . ."

"Come on, goddamnit!"

Whether out of pique or good sense, I felt irresistibly compelled to play superego, or at least to test his resolve. I had, after all, accepted his father's commission. And so I reminded Will that he was only nineteen, that they'd known each other just a few months, that on many occa-sions he'd proclaimed marriage an outmoded bourgeois convention.

"And of course," he sneered, "there's the racial question."

"That's the least of it," I lied. A counterattack suggested itself. "Is that why you're marrying her? Because she's black?"

"Fuck you, Patrick."

"It *is* a great way to say 'Fuck you' to everybody, isn't it? A great big statement—"

"If you don't want to be my witness—"

"I'll be your witness," I shouted. "I'll follow you off a cliff if you want me to."

I paused, wary of Will's rage; it was always near the surface, and another sharp cut would have unleashed it. Softly, I said, "Just tell me what I'm witnessing."

He settled back into his chair, swallowed half a mug of ale. "Look," he said, "I just know this is right. Okay? I feel it all the way down. You know I operate on instinct. Taleesha's what I want in my life and marrying her's the right thing. Her old man's very religious, and she has pretty strong spiritual convictions herself. It's gonna be hard enough living together. But being married will make it easier."

"What about *your* family?"

"They'll learn to live with it," he said. "Or they won't."

Taleesha returned cautiously to the table. "I stayed in there about as long as I could," she said.

I rose from my seat. "Congratulations."

She took my hands and I leaned forward, and upward, to kiss her cheek.

Will reminded me that one does not congratulate the bride, that the groom is presumed to be the lucky one, citing polite convention even as he prepared to fly in the face of all of his breeding and upbringing.

"I told the boy—'You're crazy,'" Taleesha said apologetically. "I tried to talk him out of it. Tried and tried."

Will nodded happily. "She did."

"But he *loves* trouble."

"Just paying my dues."

I had never seem him giddy before. It was, on him, a bizarre mood to behold.

"I still think we should keep it a secret," Taleesha said, "least for a while."

"Why the fuck should we," Will declared. "I'm not ashamed."

"No, of course not," she said, puckering her lips at him. "But has it ever occurred to you I might be? What do you suppose my friends are gonna say? 'Shit girl, you gonna marry a *white* man?'"

Her humor and her prudence would serve them well, I thought. Will had little of either. I ordered a bottle of champagne, something I'd never done before. When Will went to the men's room I asked Taleesha how her family was likely to react.

"Well, my mama isn't likely to know. And Daddy don't approve of anything, he's real old-fashioned. Momma used to sing the blues, but he made her give it up when they got married. She tried, I guess, but when I was seven she up and ran off—just disappeared."

As if to make light of this fact, she suddenly adopted a breezier tone.

"Daddy's always been kind of high hat, anyway. A pillar of the black community, and all that, very—I don't know—*white* in his behavior, and even though he'd never admit it he's secretly proud as hell of his light skin, he's about three shades lighter than me. His great-granddaddy was probably some white planter in Greenwood, Mississippi. But that doesn't mean he believes the races should mix any more than Will's father does. In his own way he's as conservative as an old peckerwood."

Will returned, seeming a little stoned, a little broader of smile. After the champagne arrived I toasted their future—imagining their love as a noble cause, a force for healing the jagged rift across the face of our land.

What can I say—we were all very young at the time.

They dropped me off at the Yale Club, and I watched the cab pull away, feeling the bittersweet loneliness of the city as the champagne faded from the sooty canyon of Vanderbilt Avenue. In the bar upstairs I might find company, but I chose to indulge my solitude and wander uptown. At that time, before catalytic converters, the New York air was an even thicker medium than it is today, granular and purple with petrochemical by-products and particulates. You could practically taste it. Underdressed for the evening chill in my tweed jacket, I saw myself, not unhappily, as a poignant figure, a mendicant wandering the cosmopolitan streets where no one knew me, no one waited for me.

The city was an ontological challenge, defying you to prove that you existed.

Someday these would be my streets. Meanwhile, I found myself on Fifth Avenue, moving with a crowd admiring the lavish windows of Saks. And suddenly I was in front of St. Patrick's Cathedral. The city of my aspirations was a godless metropolis composed largely of Protestant landmarks—the University Club, the Stock Exchange, the Plaza Hotel—and encountering this monument to my native faith was something like spotting one's parents in the midst of an orgy.

I climbed the steps and joined the few souls within, dipping my hands in the holy water and blessing myself, genuflecting in the aisle and kneeling with my head in my hands, listening to the rustling echo of whispering voices. Raised a strict Catholic, I no longer had quite enough faith to pray for myself, but I said a prayer for Will and his fiancée and lit a candle for them on the way out.

The next morning—an overcast day threatening rain. I shivered nervously outside the club, surveying the grimy west flank of Grand Central. They arrived twenty minutes late in a chauffeured Rolls. Even as Will handed me a glass of champagne I couldn't shake the thought that someone was going to try to stop us. Taleesha seemed as nervous as me, all scrunched up inside her lanky self, wearing a smart, proper white suit with a hat and veil. But Will was as flamboyant as the brightly striped gambler's vest he wore beneath an ancient morning suit complete with silk top hat.

We climbed out of the limousine in front of a dour, block-long office building which hardly answered my Jeffersonian notion of city hall. Inside, we followed the ruffled shirts and the white dresses to the appropriate office. Seeing the lines in front of the registration windows, Will seemed to experience a moment of doubt about the demotic venue. I paced back and forth, unconsciously guarding the door and admiring in this drab and soulless setting the physical and sartorial variety of the matrimonial candidates: an Indian woman in a chartreuse sari and her bridegroom in white; a black man in a pink tuxedo that matched his bride's dress; a pale, trembling Slavic bride in a beaded floor-length gown with tight braids and flowers coiled atop her head.

When we finally entered the so-called chapel a hush fell over the half-dozen wedding parties, followed by furtive glances and whispered comments. I wanted to tell them to mind their own goddamned business, but I realized this was only the preview. Will and Taleesha were about to embark on a lifetime of being noticed. Will had long since gone silent and drawn into himself, a dangerous sign. Taleesha looked miserable.

Finally their names were called. As we rose and stood up before the judge, the voices subsided once again. Will looked back and scanned the faces in the room, as if to demand in advance whether anyone knew any reason why he and his bride should not be united in matrimony. Taleesha's hands, clutching a bouquet to her chest, were trembling. Will leaned over and kissed Taleesha's neck, then nodded defiantly to the judge.

The service itself took only a couple of minutes. When the judge said, "I now pronounce you man and wife," everyone in the room seemed paralyzed, including the newlyweds. Neither of them moved until a voice called out, "Right on," breaking the silence and sparking a volley of applause that continued as the bride and groom—as if awakened from a spell—finally turned toward each other and kissed.

We walked out between the rows of folding chairs. It was a fairly extraordinary eruption—perhaps a dozen couples and their witnesses clapping and cheering, the black man in the pink tuxedo shaking Will's hand and slapping Taleesha on the back, escorting them to the door with a bright proprietary air, a benevolent stranger launching them into their hazardous new life.

"Peace, brother and sister."

"Be cool," Will said.

"We did it," Will said uncertainly, as the driver closed the door behind us. He opened another bottle of champagne and poured each of us a glass.

"Oh, shit, Will," Taleesha said, "are you *sure?*" She was dazed, not certain whether she should allow herself to be happy.

He said, "Sure as I've ever been in my life."

"Well," she said, "we all better fasten our seat belts and hold on is all I can say."

Will leaned over and kissed her again, licking the champagne from her lips. "Let us not forget our best man," he said. Taleesha removed from her purse a tissue-wrapped package, which proved to consist of two leather-bound volumes. The first was the 1909 Doves Press edition of Shakespeare's sonnets, in full vellum with gilt title. "I'm afraid the actual first edition proved a little beyond my means," Will said. "Just promise me you won't show it to Matson."

The second volume was a notebook of some sort. Opening it up, I read, on the brittle title page, handwritten in sepia ink: BINNIE PILCHER SAVAGE, HER PRIVATE DIARY, 15 FEB 1861 A.D.—

"You told me you were thinking of majoring in history. Well, there's a little piece of history you might find of some interest."

Despite my protests that it belonged to his family, he insisted I keep it.

"It's better off with you," he said, with a cryptic smile.

They dropped me at the club; I had a paper to finish so I would never know how sweet Taleesha sounded at the Apollo on her wedding night. The next day they were on their way to Paris for their honeymoon. It seemed there should be something more than this dangling curbside parting to publicly mark the beginning of their wedded life; I suddenly understood the purpose of the big wedding with its sense of communal witness and closure.

As the limousine pulled away they were snuggled—or was it *huddled?*—together in the backseat, but as I rattled toward New Haven in the cigarette-stinking train, I couldn't shake a plummeting feeling of anxiety for their future.

XI

The Saturday after the two detectives interviewed me about Felson, a young man came calling on my daughter for her first date. My wife, Stacey, was picking up our youngest from her playdate. I was already in a morbid frame of mind; Felson's funeral was scheduled for the following Monday. At that moment in particular you'd think I would have been reassured by the sight of the handsome boy who arrived at our door in his blue blazer and chinos. Except for the annoying backward baseball cap, he was the very image of the boy I'd always wanted to be; and the cap was itself testament to his insouciance, his easy certainty of his place in the world, which allowed him to affect the generational flourish. I'd already heard his vitae, and the surname announced by our doorman was one that would have been familiar to Edith Wharton. His father had a seat on the exchange, his mother served on several boards with Stacey, and the young master himself attended Buckley. Of course I disliked him immediately.

True, my whole life had been directed toward acquiring just this sort of escort for my daughter, but suddenly that seemed like a sad, even shameful, realization.

He looked me in the eye, shook my hand firmly and removed the stupid cap at the threshold. "Very nice to meet you, Mr. Keane."

We sat in the library and talked about the prep schools he was applying to, while Caroline strategically postponed her entrance. She finally appeared in the doorway wearing jeans and a faded denim shirt over what appeared to be a tie-dyed T-shirt, her wrists adorned with colorful string bracelets she'd woven at camp last summer. It's been several years now since I had any input in the matter of her wardrobe and I have learned not to try. But what really got to me somehow was the beaded choker she wore around her neck, from which dangled a bronze peace sign. She looked like one of the groupies that used to attach themselves to Will. Like them, the stoned chicks I met backstage with Will, Caroline was a vegetarian prone to lecture me about health and ecology.

Trying to be a semi-cool dad, I squelched the reflex to inquire into their plans. But if my restraint was noted, I was not rewarded with the customary kiss on the cheek.

Although I almost never take a drink before six, I mixed myself a scotch and soda after Caroline and her date hurriedly departed. It would be at least an hour before Stacey came home. Not that talking to my wife would help. Suddenly I thought of calling Lollie Baker, whom I hadn't spoken to in more than a year. I dialed information in Los Angeles and then called the Chateau Marmont, the return address of her last Christmas card. Lollie had been living in Los Angeles for more than three years—doctoring scripts for obscene wages, procrastinating the commencement of her fourth play—but she continued to live in a hotel, as if to proclaim her transient status.

"'ello, Chateau." The voice, which I recognized from my last call, suggested a curious amalgam of doped languor and haughtiness. When I asked for Lollie and was told that she was not on the premises, the tone of the response seemed to hint that even if she were, it is unlikely that she would wish to receive my call.

Then I called Will in Malibu. I didn't want to talk about anything special, certainly not about the sources of my dark mood. Small talk was what I needed, pleasant and aimless distraction. Will's line was answered by a surly character, one of his functionaries, who said Will was out of town and asked, when I tried to find out where, what my call was in reference to.

"It's in reference to my life, smart-ass," I said, and slammed down the receiver.

For almost thirty years, through all the erratic twists and turns of his curious journey, I've always sensed that Will was out there somewhere, and that I would hear from him in due course, but just at that moment I would have liked to verify it.

After the wedding, Will had checked in from the Crillon in Paris. "Fat, happy and disinherited," he pronounced himself. The night before, he said, they'd hooked up with two of the Rolling Stones, one of whom was smitten with Taleesha. Before that they'd been in Morocco, where Will had recorded some of the native music and smoked an immense quantity of hashish.

Cordell was drinking scotch, I would guess, when he called a month later to inform me "just for the record" that Will had disgraced the family and was henceforth no son of his. He did not refer to my part in this *travesty,* or ask about my knowledge, and I certainly didn't volunteer any information. But as I listened I couldn't help feeling chastised. "His mother is absolutely devastated," he said; apparently, if I could take his word on the subject of his wife's feelings, horror over Will's marriage apparently was one of the few things they'd been able to agree upon in years. "Bad enough Elbridge getting kicked out of Sewanee for damn marijuana and liable to get drafted any minute. Get himself killed in Viet-fuckingnam unless I can pull strings to keep him stateside. Then . . . *this.* And Will actually has the balls to stay on in Memphis. He's bought a big piece of land in Germantown, not ten miles from where I sit— planning on building some goddamn eyesore is what I hear."

He paused to take a drink. "Tell me this, Patrick. Would you say he did this thing specifically to mortify his mother and father. Was that the primary motive here?"

Not the primary motive perhaps, though surely not irrelevant. "I think . . . I think he's in love." I knew this would not be a popular answer.

"Don't give me that shit, Patrick. You're pissing me off now. Would that be your intention, here?"

I couldn't imagine anyone but Will who would go out of his way to piss Cordell Savage off.

"Does he think the two of them can just walk around the streets holding hands? That the decent people he was raised among are going to stand for this?"

"I really don't know, sir."

"Because they're not."

I didn't ask what, precisely, the decent people of Memphis were going to do. I listened patiently, and conceded that it was a difficult and even a foolish course that Will had chosen, and then I resumed my safe and cloistered pursuit of Light and Truth.

BINNIE PILCHER SAVAGE, HER DIARY

Bear Track March 11th 1861

Just returned from a splendid frolic at the Harkness place in Washington County. Accompanied by twelve fiddlers danced till the daylight with Tom Cook, Griffin Trenholm, James Harkness favoring the latter, and a half a dozen other young gentlemen. My sister Juliana of course was there with her new husband and I flatter myself that she was a little jealous of the attention I received; the role wife sits somewhat uncomfortably on one who so brilliantly played the coquette, which part now falls to me. A midnight feast of roast beef, bear, venison, oysters, chicken salad, jelly, charlotte, pound cakes, sponge cake, figs, dates, oranges and nuts. There were gallons of eggnog and champagne and many of the young men had brought their own whiskey with the result that several of them were hardly fit for dancing or conversation. The house, newly finished, is alleged to have cost more than fifty thousand with furnishings, quite the melange of architectural styles, betraying elements Florentine, Greek, French and what I can only describe as hill country rustic. The furnishings, though, all from France and Italy, were worthy of one of the great houses of Charleston. We are gradually civilizing this wilderness.

The young Harkness boy lured me out to the garden near dawn and then seemed not to know how to press his advantage until I finally pretended to stumble on the path and topple directly into his arms. This after young Trenholm lost consciousness on the veranda. I like a gentleman as well as the next girl, but I think our local swains carry their diffidence too far. Juliana discovered me in the garden being kissed, but I have no doubt her look of disapproval reflected more jealousy than censure. In any event, I am safe on that flank, ever since I found her with Mulligan the overseer.

Matson came to New Haven to visit that spring. Bearing a bottle of single-malt scotch, he arrived on a Friday night shortly after Aaron had decamped for Smith. After a white-clam pizza downtown, we sat in the living room which Aaron and I had turned into a gallery of posters and lithographs: Picasso, Giacometti, Braque, Buffet, Huey Newton on his rattan chair throne and Raquel Welch in a revealing bearskin wrap from the movie *One Million Years B.C.*

In his three-piece tweed suit Matson looked smaller and more artificial than I remembered, and I had forgotten the way he wet his lips with his tongue between sentences, a tic that seemed to have become more pronounced in the year since I'd seen him. Though flattered by his visit and eager to show him the campus, I also felt a new sense of equality. We stayed up half the night drinking the single malt and discussing poetry, gradually increasing the volume of the *Brandenburg Concertos* and the "Moonlight Sonata" as I became increasingly brilliant and vocal, grateful for the opportunity to show myself off. Here was someone who could appreciate my learning and discrimination.

"I see your taste in music has improved since you've been away from Will Savage." Matson relit his pipe. "His embrace of popular culture and black music was obviously some kind of Oedipal reflex—a blatant attempt to thumb his nose at his family background."

"That doesn't mean it isn't genuinely felt," I said, the whiskey making me feisty.

"Oh, I don't necessarily deny it's genuinely felt—the great problem with pop culture is that it's *only* about *feelings*. Civilization is constructed on the premise of subjugating the emotions, is it not?"

"I guess Will would say we've become too civilized."

Matson laughed. "You can't be *too* civilized. Which is not to say I'm in favor of repression. There's a public, civil self and then there is the private realm, and the twain need never meet. That's where Will and his fellow primitivists go so wrong, trying to collapse the distinction. Here, for instance, in this room, we happily occupy the private sphere." And with that he poured us another drink.

Aaron spent most of his free time with Cameron, the blonde princess of Smith College, until she broke up with him just before midterms. Having felt left behind, I experienced a brief surreptitious thrill when he told me she had refused to come down from her room that Friday when he arrived at her dorm at Smith. When he finally reached her on the phone, she said, without explanation or apology, that she didn't want to see him anymore.

We went out and had a good drunk, and all at once our friendship seemed renewed, but for the first time since I'd known him, Aaron began to assert his racial identity. "It's like, she wants to flirt with the taboo," he said, "have a taste of the dark meat, but when it's getting down to summer vacation and Mummy and Daddy and Bar Harbor—hey, we can't be having no Negro hanging round the yacht club."

A few nights later Will called the dorm just as I returned from the library. Martin Luther King, Jr., had been shot dead at a motel in Memphis. My first thought, after the initial shock, was to wonder how this would affect my friendship with Aaron.

But Will's worries were far more apocalyptic. "I know what this is about. My old man and his cronies are behind this." He claimed that Cordell was involved in a secret, ultra-conservative, white-supremacist network whose tentacles reached from the Tennessee State House to the CIA and the FBI. He raved on for twenty minutes about high-level conspiracies. I didn't say anything, not wanting to exacerbate this nuttiness.

When Aaron appeared, shortly after I hung up, it was difficult to know what to say. He threw his books down on the battered trunk that served as our coffee table and fell backward on the couch. I couldn't read his mood at all.

"Did you hear," I asked.

"Hear what?" he snapped.

"About Dr. King."

"Yeah, I heard." More than anything he seemed irritated.

"I'm sorry," I said.

"Why?" he said. "Did you shoot him?" Suddenly he stood up. "I'm beat," he said, retreating to the bedroom.

Aaron and I would room together the following year in a suite we shared with two public-school boys, but we were never again as close as we had been that first year. Late that spring he became involved with the Black Alliance and began spending most of his free time with its members. I always wondered if it would have happened anyway, if his sudden discovery of his own people had only to do with having his heart broken by a beautiful blonde, or if it was inevitable, a sign of the times. Sharing quarters in the gorgeously faux-Gothic Branford College, we went out of our way to accommodate each other, like an old married couple honoring a truce in an undeclared war. As room selection approached the following spring, he announced that—no offense, it had been great—but he was rooming with two of the brothers.

The night after King's murder Will called back and said without preamble, "There are tanks on the street, man. Fucking tanks. This is it, Patrick, the shit coming down. . . ." He sounded seriously fucked up, high on something. A long silence on his end was underlined by the sound of a vast bellowslike inhalation.

"You there, Will?"

"The cities are burning," he said in a deep, smoked voice. "And all these fucking white people can say is, 'It's a shame it had to happen in Memphis, ruin our fair name.'"

"How's Taleesha bearing up," I asked, hoping to change the subject.

"*Fair name. What fair name?*" There was another hiatus. And then, "She's good, she's wonderful. She's a much better person than I am. She's convinced me not to go out and start shooting white people."

"I think she's right on this one, Will."

March 20th 1861 Warmer today. A foretaste of dreadful summer. Mother in bed with her drops. My brother John morose and broody past bearing. After years of roaming woods and field with Clarence, the slave charged with hunting and fishing for our table, he has been told that he must pursue his sport on his own. Clarence has been John's constant companion for years to a degree that all of us had begun to question; it is one thing for a boy, but John is nearly fifteen and it is time as father says to put away childish things and cultivate the society of his own people. As for the exact circumstances of the estrangement, I have been piecing this together from the reports of the house servants. It seems that Father took the unusual step of selling the woman that Clarence calls his "wife." Since then the big negro has been exceedingly morose and perhaps as a consequence has withdrawn from all around him but most particularly from John, finally taking the unusual step of requesting that he be allowed to hunt alone, which request seems to have suited Father's purposes.

April 13th So we have fired on Fort Sumter and war would appear unavoidable. Father says no good can come of this and thinks the interests of the Delta are best served within the Union.

I next saw Will and Taleesha in New York; she was performing at Max's Kansas City, but they were staying uptown, in style, at the St. Regis. Both seemed to have grown into their marital state; she was more confident, at least in that setting, and he was obviously proud of her. She was, I gathered, on her way to becoming a star, and she told me rather breathlessly that two college boys had recognized her on the plane. Even if you didn't recognize her, she and Will were an extraordinary sight, walking arm in arm up Fifth Avenue: she colossally long-legged in a white minidress, he with his dark hair overflowing the shoulders of a Sergeant Pepperish bright red British army officer's coat. They seemed to accept the attention they received as tribute. Both would have been conspicuous no matter how they dressed or comported themselves, and so they decided to push it to the limit. It was partly the times, I suppose, and partly Will. He would have hated not to be noticed, and Taleesha, after all, was a performer. And in New York they could flaunt themselves relatively safely, which was not advisable in Memphis.

New York is a challenge for the exhibitionist: it's easier to make a U-turn on 42nd Street than it is to turn heads there. And Will and Taleesha turned heads. Alongside a review of Taleesha's performance, the *Village Voice* was to run a picture of the two of them: *LONG DISTANCE INFORMATION: Soul Diva Taleesha and Music Mogul Will Savage, of Memphis.* This was probably the first time Will was referred to as a mogul, and the first evidence I had that the world might take him at his own—and my—valuation.

I met them in the King Cole bar at the St. Regis; brilliant as tropical birds amidst the gray-suited businessmen, they looked as if they might have just stepped out of the Maxfield Parrish mural on the wall behind the bar.

Will rose to greet me, enfolding me in a bearish embrace. "Hey, if isn't old Dink Stover from Yale. What's the word, Dink? How does your ivy grow? You get that record I sent you?"

Of course I hadn't. Will was a fount of good intentions, but his attention was easily distracted and he didn't yet have the staff to implement his whims before he forgot them. He was stoned on something, the brilliant focus of his gaze slightly diffused, talking animatedly about a singer he'd just discovered, running down a disc jockey who'd failed to give Taleesha enough play even after Will had plied him with a gold Rolex President. "I bought a damn gross of the fuckers in the last year," he complained. "All these hip DJs gotta have their big old tacky Presidents."

Taleesha listened to her husband with an air of amused pride, occasionally spraying down the flames of Will's hyperbole. Everyone in the room seemed to be watching his performance, certain only that a rare beast was among them.

Downstairs in the men's room, a man asked me if I was sitting with one of the Beatles.

I had meant to ask Will if he had ever read the diary of Binnie Pilcher Savage; having read it carefully, I was curious about his motives in giving it to me. But before I'd gotten around to it I made the mistake of asking if he'd had any contact with his parents.

"I haven't had the pleasure of direct communication," he said, smiling expansively. "But I wouldn't be surprised if I hear from my old man soon. I've written a letter to the U.S. attorney general's office proposing him as a prime suspect in the King assassination."

Taleesha rolled her eyes for my benefit and stroked Will's arm soothingly.

"Jesus, Will," I said. "Maybe you should stop projecting your problems with your dad onto the global scene."

"Maybe you should just suck my dick, Patrick."

Taleesha said, "Don't talk like that to your best friend."

"Who said he's my best friend?"

"*You* did. Lots of times."

"I must have been stoned."

"*No*," said Taleesha. "You? Stoned? I can't imagine."

She was bantering Will out of his mood, but I felt as if I'd been slapped. Pushing my drink away, I stood up and stalked off in a huff.

Taleesha caught up with me in the lobby and clutched my arm. "Patrick, you can't go. He'll be miserable, and then I'll be miserable. If nothing else, please stay for me. You know how he is."

I *did* know how he was. And of course I stayed—to listen to Will explain the conspiracies, the hidden springs and trapdoors of the body politic . . . stayed to hear Taleesha sing that night to an enthusiastic crowd of shaggy cognoscenti—because at that moment in the lobby of the St. Regis I couldn't help being a little bit in love with her, if only because she was my best friend's wife, imagining in that first moment of real intimacy how I would comfort her at Will's funeral and take care of her, until, drawn to me initially by our mutual love of Will Savage, deceased, she would eventually realize that she loved me, possibly more, even, than she'd loved Will, though we would both always respect the memory of her love for Will.

With such ludicrous, morbid fantasies did I fool myself, and while away the long mud season of my unwanted chastity.

XII

"*H*ey, boy," drawls the unfamiliar, disembodied voice. "You know what we do to nigger-loving, longhair scum?"

Unconsciously, I have answered the ringing phone. I stare into the dark, while the voice, dry and spiked as a thistle, goes on to describe a crude, if specific, surgical procedure. ". . . Tell you what, your brother weren't no accident. You best watch your ass or we 'gone burn it up." At this point I hang up the phone and grope for the bedside light.

Five in the morning. I'm nauseous, in part from the motion of the water bed rolling and sloshing beneath me. I am, I discern, in Will's house in Memphis. The call was intended for my host, who at the moment is at large.

By the spring of my sophomore year Will and I had fallen into a routine in which I'd write regularly and he'd call whenever the inspiration seized him. One afternoon in May I'd just returned from the stacks in Sterling when I was summoned to the phone. Taleesha had never called before, and I soon wished she didn't have occasion to, now. Distraught, she informed me Elbridge had died behind the wheel of Will's car. She hadn't seen or heard from Will in the two days since he'd learned about the accident. "I thought maybe he would have called you," she said hopefully.

I then spent a sleepless night attempting to study for my philosophy exam the next morning and to convince myself I couldn't possibly go to Memphis. As usual I didn't have the airfare; what I did have, in addition to the test, was a term paper in English.

First thing the next morning, I found Professor Egan, my English professor, in his office. He caressed the edition of the bard's sonnets I handed him as if it were a living thing—the same appreciative touch with which he stroked his own beard in class. Finally, delicately, he coaxed it open and turned to the title page, which he rubbed between his fingers. He granted me an extension on my final paper. I staggered off to take my exam, an exercise in automatic writing, and afterward met Egan at his bank, where he gave me two hundred dollars in cash.

Though this was the year of hijackings, I made Memphis without incident. At the airport, Taleesha was waiting for me at the gate. She looked older, as though she had suddenly become a woman with adult anxieties and responsibilities in the year since I had last seen her. We embraced awkwardly—somewhere between a hug and a handshake, and I wondered what local protocol governed how a black girl and a white boy should walk to the car.

Outside the air-conditioned terminal, it was warm and muggy as only Memphis can be. Once we were sealed in the car—a green Dodge Charger I'd never seen before—I finally asked what had happened.

"I guess you heard," she began, "about Elbridge getting kicked out of Sewanee for smoking pot. He was getting pretty far out there, hanging out with the Bitter Lemon crowd, doing acid. When L.B. got his induction notice Will started begging him to go to Canada. Night before he's supposed to report for his physical he comes to Will and asks to borrow Will's car—he wrapped his little sports car around a tree the week before. And now he's high as a kite. Will asks if he's going to Canada and L.B. says he's going to fly away. Those were his words, Will said. *Fly away.* He'd gotten weird, lately. So Will gives him the keys to his Packard, asks him if he needs money, wishes him Godspeed. This is maybe midnight. Next we hear—it seems about three a.m. he's trying to outrun a police car and he hit a tree doing over ninety miles an hour."

An unidentified witness had been quoted in the paper that morning claiming the crash had been preceded by an exchange of gunfire. Even before he heard the details, Will was convinced that the police had been after him, in his well-known vehicle. He blamed himself for what had happened.

"After he heard, he threw a chair through the back window of the house," Taleesha said. "Then he punched the wall so hard he broke his hand. And after he'd hurt himself enough to stand it, then he called up his daddy. And not his daddy nor his mama would come to the phone. I guess they blame Will too. Who can know, a family like that? Half hour later he took off without a word and I haven't seen him since."

Taleesha slapped the steering wheel in frustration. "It would be hard enough if Will was an easy person to live with," Taleesha complained, nearly rear-ending the car in front of us, lurching into the passing lane at the last minute as I jammed my feet into the floor in front of me. "I'm trying to convince him to move to Chicago or New York."

"What does he say?"

"Will says the music is here. He says Memphis has the groove. I don't know. It's an excuse. It's bullshit. I think he likes the conflict. He needs to have the enemy around him, within range. Including his crazy family. Especially his crazy family. And here we are in lovely Germantown."

We were driving through rolling countryside now, just off the interstate, past horse farms and broad rolling pastures which sprouted the occasional big, showy house of recent construction, which, for all its stridency and even ugliness, mimicked the antebellum plantation house and reflected the essentially conservative aspirations of new money.

Will's new house, visible from a great distance across a hay field, was so incongruous it might have dropped out of the sky. It was a fantastic sight, the roofline turreted and crenellated and arched against the horizon, seeming to combine Moorish, Tuscan and Bavarian motifs, like something designed by Antoni Gaudí on assignment for Walt Disney.

"You believe this shit?" said Taleesha, with an air of one long suffering, as we approached the gate and turned into the long drive. They'd been living in a small farmhouse on the property during the construction of this implausible residence, which after a year was nearly complete. Two workmen were perched on scaffolding, finishing off a section of mosaic which constituted part of the variegated skin of the edifice.

Parked near the house was a cement mixer, which at first glance seemed part of the construction site. But it was painted black, and a second look showed Plexiglas windows set in the sides of the drum. Seeing the target of my gaze, Taleesha walked me over to the machine.

"He has himself driven around town in the thing," she said, gesturing toward the ladder. I climbed up and opened a hatch in the back to discover a chamber with two couches, carpeted with kilims, hung with dark paisley fabric.

The house was no less bizarre. She took me on the grand tour, a bemused chatelaine attempting to do justice to her husband's stupendous folly. I recognized Will in every room, or rather, I began to see the elements of what would become his imperial style: a kind of haute-hippie, opium-den look in which Indian, Ottoman, William Morris Arts and Crafts and medieval decor all seemed congruous, held together if nothing else by the sheer force of Will's enthusiasm. It was a nighttime aesthetic, all heavy velvet drapes, intricate burgundy carpets and dark carved wood, painted mandalas and carved heraldic shields. The sun was not meant to penetrate far into these rooms, not even the huge common rooms—the oval ballroom with its Baccarat chandelier, the dining room with its massive ebony table, and especially not the play room, also known as the drug room, with a Berber nomad's tent standing in the middle, tent spikes nailed into the wooden floor.

Out in back, beyond the terrace and the black swimming pool, like a rebuke to the whole gigantic enterprise, stood a small, unpainted hut—an exact replica, Taleesha explained, of a teahouse on the grounds of a Zen monastery in Kyoto where Will had once stayed.

"I think I like this little house the best," she said. The bright, spare interior was indeed a relief after the baroque excesses of the main house: mud-colored stucco walls, crisp yellow tatami mats with black borders, a small copper-lined pit for a fire, an alcove displaying a pen-and-ink landscape scroll. Taleesha knelt down and ran her finger across the textured surface of the tatami. "I like that there's this part of him, even if I don't understand it yet."

* * *

Searching for Will that night we went to the Bitter Lemon, a tiny coffee-house full of hippies where the ancient bluesman Furry Lewis was playing. Will had been there the night before and had made a strong impression.

"He was cooking," said the doorman.

"Even for Will," someone chimed in. No one knew where he was now.

As Taleesha's escort, I oscillated between anxiety and a strange vicarious pride. She was a celebrity in this world.

In the steamy red-carpeted murk of another club, I was accosted by a raging drunk. While Taleesha signed an autograph, a frosty-haired black man rose from his stool like a rocket, lifting off slow, in stages, and stuck his face in mine. "What you think—you special? You better than me?"

"It's turned ugly these last few months," Taleesha said, after she'd rescued me.

Returning finally to the two-bedroom farmhouse beside Will's castle in progress, we found it uninhabited.

That night I was awakened by the threatening phone call intended for Will. Unable to sleep with that parched voice in my ears, I lay in bed and watched the sun come up over the roof of Will's new palace.

"We get a lot of those calls," Taleesha said, over breakfast. "Some folks get the welcome wagon, we get the Shelby County chapter of the Ku Klux Klan."

"Do you think they had anything to do with Elbridge's death?"

She paused, her coffee cup halfway to her lips. "No, I don't think so." She took a sip from her cup and put it down on the table. "But I don't think Will is crazy, either. I know—sometimes he seems paranoid to you."

I was willing to accept this characterization of my views.

"But if you were me . . ." She paused. "White people been telling us for years there ain't no fire where there's smoke, even when we're burning. If you were black, his theories might not seem quite so crazy. You know what I'm saying?"

Actually, despite my essentially empirical cast of mind, I could never dismiss any of Will's ideas completely. Certainly, it was more interesting to imagine the Mafia in bed with the CIA than it was to accept the findings of the Warren Commission. I envied him the power of his convictions—the conspiracy theories as well as his messianic belief in music—even if I couldn't quite suspend my own disbelief.

Taleesha had to stop by her father's house and asked me if I wanted to come along.

"Dad's real CME," she said as we drove into town. Seeing my bewilderment, she discoursed on the Colored Methodist Episcopal Church. The ministers tended to be light skinned, she said, and the parishioners formed the heart of the black middle class, the merchants and business leaders whose churchly comportment was self-consciously more dignified than the highly emotional revival-meeting behavior of the African Methodist Episcopalians. It was at one of the latter churches that I'd heard her sing. Her father, when he found out about it, was furious at her for attending the African service, and especially for singing—behaving, as he put it, like "some crazy field nigger."

Taleesha's family lived on Southern Parkway, a broad boulevard lined with substantial, middle-aged, self-important houses in diverse states of repair. "Used to be a white street," she noted, as we turned into the driveway of an immaculate Tudor.

We entered through the garage, emerging into the kitchen. Taleesha's sister, Daisy—an older, thicker version of herself—was flattening dough on the counter. After dusting the flour from her hands, she embraced Taleesha. "Fixing chess pie," she said. "I know you'll want to stay for a piece." To me she said, "Hah! She don't hardly eat enough to keep a hummin'bird alive."

Taleesha introduced me as Will's best friend and explained that she had to drop me off at the funeral.

Mr. Johnson marched in, stopping short when he saw his youngest daughter. A tall, stately, light-skinned man with a severe expression and military posture, he was wearing some kind of uniform—a ceremonial outfit with gold buttons and braid, insignia and epaulets. What appeared to be a tricornered hat was pinned under his arm.

"I wasn't aware that we were expecting company," he said to Daisy.

"I just came by to corrupt my siblings," Taleesha said. "This is my friend Patrick Keane."

"How do you do, sir," I said. "I'm a friend of Will Savage." I extended my hand and held it in midair.

"Music business?" he inquired coldly.

"We went to school together."

"Patrick goes to Yale," Taleesha noted. Indeed I looked the part in my rep tie, blue blazer and gray flannels.

He finally took my hand, engulfing it in his own large palm.

"I knew Yale would do the trick," Taleesha said blandly.

"You'll excuse me, Mr. Keane. I'm on my way to a meeting. A benevolent society which I have been associated with for some years." He turned and left.

"You two are like to break my heart yet," Daisy said. "I wish you'd *try* to get along."

"I wish *he* would," Taleesha said. "He looks at me and thinks I'm Mama."

"Hush, now."

A lanky young man sauntered into the kitchen, as if he had been waiting for the cue of his father's departure, and opened the refrigerator.

"Ain't you got nothing for me?" Taleesha said.

He shambled across the floor into her embrace, then stared at the linoleum as he shook my hand.

"Bud's shy," Taleesha said.

"Am not," he said, looking up defiantly.

"I been his mama over ten years now," she explained in the car. "He's the only one who comes to visit Will and me. My father—we haven't gotten along since I was thirteen."

We crossed Beale Street where a crane assaulted a brick storefront with a wrecking ball—in pursuit of what was then called urban renewal. "*A benevolent society which I have been associated with for some years,*" she mimicked. "That's how he actually talks. And how about that outfit? Spiffy!"

"Looks like something Will would wear." We were both briefly diverted by this notion.

She dropped me at the church, making me promise to call immediately if Will showed up. And, in fact, all through the service I expected him to crash through the door at any moment and commandeer the organ that groaned and shrieked above us. Sweating liberally in my blazer and flannels, I kept glancing over my shoulder as the minister and the high school football coach eulogized Elbridge as a team player, a natural leader, a true Christian, a son of the South. The reader of subversive literature and psychic explorer, beloved of his younger brother, was never mentioned.

The service at an end, Cordell Savage nodded at me as he led his wife, hunched and rigid, out of the church. I was riveted by the sight of Cheryl Dobbs in a black dress, struggling down the aisle on the arm of one of the ushers. Grief had only refined her appearance, and I couldn't help but be dazzled by the thought that she was no longer spoken for. Dizzy and torpid from the humidity, I was looking across the street at a civic building of some sort, its Doric entrance flanked by alabaster figures—fluid feminine LIBERTY on the one side and stern patriarchal JUSTICE on the other (well, *which* is it going to be?), like the household deities of Savage *fils* and *père* respectively. Was it possible, after all, to have one nation with liberty *and* justice, conflicting ideals that they were? I was pondering this when Joseph, the Savages' houseman, tapped my shoulder and said Mr. Cordell would be much obliged if I would come on to the cemetery and then along to the house where a few friends were gathering.

By the time we reached the Savage residence it was evening and slightly cooler. I'd driven back from the cemetery with Lollie Baker, who'd come down from Bennington. She'd gained weight—if not quite the proverbial freshman fifteen—and her hair was shorter, à la Twiggy. If anything, her self-possession was greater than ever. "Don't worry, Will's always disappearing," she assured me. "It's one of his defining characteristics. You go to a party and somebody says, 'Where's Will?' 'Well, hell, he was here just a minute ago.'"

"The mortality rate for Savage sons is running kind of high," I said.

"He'll turn up."

I asked her about Bennington.

"It's not bad," she said. "Everything's elective, except the lesbianism requirement. I could do without that shit. How's Yale? White bucks and blue balls? I suppose you go to mixers and all that?"

"If I ever hear 'Whiter Shade of Pale' again I will be forced to kill myself."

"I want to hear *all* about it," she said, in that wonderful tone unique to southern women, attentive and dreamily dismissive at the same time, as we pulled into the driveway. "I might could do about ten minutes here, tops."

We joined the subdued gathering inside. Nearly concealed behind a thick mask of bright makeup, Mrs. Savage nodded stiffly at my mumbled expression of sympathy. Cordell took my hand in both of his own. He looked haggard, but there was a hard, undefeated resolution in his bearing and expression. "Thank you for coming, Patrick. It means a great deal to us to have you here. Are you staying for any length of time? Of course you're welcome to lodge with us."

Without going into my lodging status, I explained that I had to hurry back for exams. A young soldier in uniform came over to express his sympathy, one of several; their shaved heads and Deep South accents made me nervous. And I didn't like this talk about the enemy, suddenly conscious that my hair was longer than any man's in the room. Seeing Cheryl Dobbs languishing on a sofa, leaning back on her chignon, I sidled over to express my sympathy.

"I remember you," she said thickly. "You were the boy who passed out at that party." She seemed similarly inclined at the moment. "You were really sweet."

"Thank you," I said, the heat rising in my cheeks.

"No, I mean it," she insisted, touching a finger to her lower lip. "You were just so, I don't know . . . *sweet.* You know? Some people just aren't very nice. You get a bad feeling from them. But you . . . you're . . . *sweet.*"

"That's really . . . *kind* of you to say that," I said, ringing a slight variation on the adjective.

At that moment Lollie tugged on my sleeve. "Hey, sweetface. You ready to blow?"

"I think maybe I should stick around awhile," I said.

"What are you, a necrophiliac? These people are stiffer than El-bridge."

I put a censorious finger to my lips. "I really think I ought to stay."

"Suit yourself, Aeneas. I'm heading for the surface." I watched her leave with the sinking feeling that I was making a mistake. Anything might happen if I joined her now. I might even lose my virginity. At the very least I'd have a ride and a familiar companion. I was throwing this away, for what? I told myself I'd come all this way for Elbridge's funeral and it behooved me to spend time here, with his family, though in fact I found myself riveted by the presence of Cheryl and entertaining a ridiculous notion of impressing myself upon her. Just then she was speaking to an elderly couple. They all seemed to be crying.

I went to the bar and got a bourbon from Joseph. Cordell introduced me to the relatives, boycotting Will's name—I was "a friend of the family."

By the time I escaped an uncle with an obsessive interest in garden-ing, I couldn't see Cheryl anywhere. After getting another drink, I found myself holding a defensive position against the fireplace, pinned down by heavy artillery: a pimpled soldier was discoursing on the Southern Military Tradition. Stonewall Jackson holding the line at Manassas. . . . Jeb Stuart riding again, dashing across the Chickahominy on his roan mare in plumed hat and silk cape, mocking the ponderous Yankee be-hind his own lines. . . . A wounded Bedford Forrest at Shiloh, musket ball lodged against his spine, scooping up a hostage under his arm as he gallops off to fight another day. . . . All the *beaux sabreurs* of the South.

"It's in the blood," he insisted. "From that day to this—the military man is respected and honored in Dixie. I'll tell you what—we don't have no damn peaceniks down here dishonoring the flag and burning their damn brassieres." Though his arm was draped fraternally around my shoulder, his tone was becoming increasingly strident, his face dan-gerously red, the slits of his eyes narrower. Afraid I might at any mo-ment be accused of brassiere burning or worse, I claimed to need the bathroom and retreated to the back of the house.

Hearing a feminine sob from one of the guest rooms, I nudged the door, which was slightly ajar, and found Cheryl lying on her back on the bed, feet on the floor. Mascara had run down her cheek, and her hair was in disarray, but she was no less beautiful for that. She lifted her head and smiled wanly. "It's you."

I walked over and stood beside her. "Will you hold me," she asked. "I want you to hold me." Unable to believe my ears, I sat down gingerly on the bed beside her. She opened her arms. Slowly, incredulously, I lowered myself slowly into her embrace. All at once she was kissing me wildly, probing my mouth with a furious tongue. I knew she was drunk, and I knew that this had everything to do with a boy lying in a coffin a few miles away and nothing to do with me, but I didn't pause to worry about that. Suddenly she took my hand and thrust it into her blouse, under her bra and into possession of the miraculous swelling of her breast. Even as I tried to abandon myself to the moment I felt almost frightened by her morbid intensity. I have never been kissed, before or since, with such swallowing greed. It was as if she were trying to perform resuscitation, bring me, or someone else, back from the dead. I rolled on my side to help her rip the clinging blouse away from her flesh.

Something caught my eye: Mrs. Savage was standing in the doorway. I froze as Cheryl continued to struggle with her shirt. If I've ever been more mortified I can't remember. "I think that's quite enough," Mrs. Savage commanded.

Cheryl turned slowly, mechanically, toward her ex-mother-in-law-to-be. I sat up on the bed.

"I believe it's time for you to be leaving, Patrick," Elbridge's mother said, her face an impassive mask.

Cheryl appeared to be in a daze, slack-mouthed and glassy-eyed, Sleeping Beauty arising from her coma. I took her hand. "Will you be okay," I asked.

"That's none of your concern," said the mask.

I staggered down the hallway and let myself out the sliding door in back, emerging into a dark garden spangled with fireflies. The setters in their kennels began to bark, scenting my fugitive anxiety. Out on the road I tried to hitch a ride. Sometime after midnight a guy in a pickup truck brought me to a gas station where I called a cab.

"What the *heck?*" exclaimed the cabbie, as we rattled through the fields past the invisible horses: although it was only a little past midnight, dawn appeared to be glowing over the ridge to the east. A few minutes later we saw the flames, stark and beautiful against the blackness of the surrounding countryside. Will's castle was burning, throwing flames a hundred feet into the sky. The cab pulled to a stop beside Taleesha, who was standing in the driveway a hundred yards from the conflagration. The cabbie and I stood beside her and stared at the flames. Finally she said, "They waited until we were just about finished."

"What happened," I asked.

"What do *you* think?" she said impatiently. "Loose wire, maybe? Is that a *plausible* explanation?"

The fire engines arrived a few minutes later, almost an hour after Taleesha had called. No one was surprised when the police investigators concluded that arson was involved, nor was anyone particularly amazed that no suspects were ever apprehended.

XIII

The summer that men walked on the moon, Edward Kennedy drove his car off a bridge and I drudged for my father in his store, selling washers and dryers, yearning to be a young oligarch—a loafered lizard sunning on a rock in Bar Harbor . . . guzzling southsiders in Southampton.

Taleesha sent a postcard from India. "Hot, dusty and dirty—just like home. Will is collecting weird antiques and auditioning holy men. He says to tell you don't be fooled—the moon landing was staged in a TV studio in the Nevada desert to distract people from the real problems. Jes' thought you'd like to know." She concluded by inviting me to meet them in August for a big music festival in upstate New York, but for reasons I can't remember now I didn't attend what was later regarded as the seminal event of my generation.

To alleviate my boredom that summer, I interviewed Nana Keane, who told me among other facts that two of my immigrant forebears, newly escaped from the famine, arrived here just in time to help fight the Civil War. Her grandfather, my great-great-grandfather, was wounded at Gettysburg. A blacksmith, he had lived with a gangrenous leg wound which his wife washed and dressed every day for twenty-six years. His brother had died somewhat more rapidly from a bayonet wound suffered in the battle of Franklin, Tennessee.

Back at school again, I hunkered down in the stacks, shuttling up and down High Street between Branford College and Sterling Library, the carillons of Harkness Tower providing the only music in my life. For economy's sake, I had decided shortly before entering to complete Yale in three years, which required an academic load of six courses each semester. All of Yale's secret societies somehow failed to tap me for membership, and in response I threw myself into academic life with a vengeance. For a variety of reasons, I declared history my major. My excursions into the South had reawakened a childhood interest in the Civil War. Then, too, I felt I'd been born too late, imagining myself not as a serf, but as a kind of Jeffersonian gentleman with a book in one hand and a riding crop in the other. But even *I* was beginning to suspect that the old order to which I wanted to pledge allegiance was crumbling. When I spoke to Will I advocated my choice of majors in contemporary terms: the study of the past, I told him, would illuminate the present struggle. And not least, I hoped it would help me get into Harvard Law.

I didn't see Will for six months after his house burned to the ground. Ravaged and reticent, he'd come back to the ashes after a fierce, week-long bender in the Delta, crawling the juke joints. He would call me often enough that fall—seldom before midnight—that I think of him as nearly present that year, living in the hall phone booth with its locker-room/ashtray smell, its carved initials and graffiti: WHEN BETTER WOMEN ARE MADE YALE MEN WILL MAKE THEM, and late in the following year—WHEN BETTER MEN ARE MADE, YALE WOMEN WILL HAVE EQUALS. After the fire, he and Taleesha had moved into a suite at the Peabody Hotel. I wrote him letters, carbons of which I haphazardly saved along with English and history papers, like this representatively embarrassing note:

Dear Will:

It's the tail end of one of those Sunday afternoons which was supposed to have hosted all kinds of achievements—paper writing, letter writing, extracurricular reading, room cleaning and general lubrication of the wheels and cogs of day-to-day life. But I went to a fairly boring party and got blasted last night so the mind somewhat fuddled, the synapses encrusted with carbon.

Speaking of extracurricular reading, I just finished a book you would thoroughly approve of, if indeed you have not given up on the written word, though this is the very book about your brave new world—Norman O. Brown's *Life Against Death.* A remarkable book, ideas-wise and aesthetically. Argues for a new non-hierarchical society and "polymorphous perversity" that will free us from the so called reality principle. Right up your (back) alley.

Loved that line from Furry Lewis. Got to use it in a paper. Great to hear the biz is going so well—I keep hearing T's latest on the radio and I don't even listen to the radio. Your brand of R and B is more popular here in Ivy land than yours truly would have imagined. You and James Brown and Norman O. Brown are avatars of the same *Weltanschauung* and you seem to be slipping it over on the rest of us. Hark, I hear the Philistines knocking at the gate. But meantime, the reality principle still obtains and I've got to go grind. After I sing a few bars of the Whiffenpoof song, of course. Love to your better three quarters, meaning Taleesha.

What seems interesting to me about this now is the way I was straining to find the bridge between Will's world and my own. Or perhaps I was cooler than I remember; I haven't thought of Norman O. Brown in years, but the fact that I read him then would seem to indicate that I was less of a nerd than I remember. In retrospect, maybe I've made the oppositions more stark, given where we both ended up. Besides this I notice the uneasy tension between self-mockery and showing off; clearly I was very pleased to deploy the word *Weltanschauung,* with its Panzer division of vowels—in fact the whole sentence seems to exist for the purpose of using it.

Will was present also that year in the form of his great-great-grandfather John Savage, who as a boy featured prominently in the diaries of Binnie Pilcher Savage and whom I could only envision in Will's precise image. The diaries rambled innocuously enough except for their news of the distant war, until this entry from the spring of 1861:

April 27th Great excitement here. Father has convened the gentlemen hereabouts for a Home Company to investigate the planned insurrection of the negroes. So far it is only the testimony of young John which points to such a conspiracy, but in the present wartime atmosphere suspicion reigns and his report is taken most seriously. At table last evening Father chastised him for his sullenness and table manners John then burst forth declaring he would be glad when the negroes rose up and killed him, that is Father, with an axe as they were planning to do. When questioned by Father about this extraordinary prediction he claimed to have heard Clarence and another negro from the Yancy place hatching that very scheme not three days before.

Within weeks of this event, according to the diaries, Clarence and seven other slaves at Bear Track and two adjoining plantations were hanged. The subject of slave rebellions was an increasingly fashionable one toward the end of the sixties, and it occurred to me that this remarkable slice of history which had fallen into my hands would make a fine subject for a thesis. I began to spend most of my time in the stacks, poring through slave narratives and old WPA interviews with former slaves. Will promised he would try to find more material, though the Savage archives, I suspected, were closed to him for the indefinite future.

Shortly before Thanksgiving, almost two months into my search, I found what I was looking for on a Library of Congress microfilm—a short interview with a slave named Prince Johnson who had grown up at Bear Track plantation, the first independent confirmation of Binnie Savage's story of the alleged slave insurrection:

113—Autobiography of an Exslave
Prince Johnson—Isaqueena County 1937

Ma'am, I's named Prince Johnson on account of I was named after Prince Albert, [sic] *the famous royalty. They say I was born in*

Charleston and moved to Bear Track when I was a bitty thing. Closes' I can figgers I's nearly one hundred year old. I b'longed to Marse Elihu Savage, he was de riches' and highes' quality gent'man in de county. He had de blues' eyes you ever seed. Same as young Marse John. Ever'body knowed him all round the country and nobody wanted to cross him. He had some kind of temper, Marse did. But mostly he was good to us. We ate good grub and the slave quarters was tolerable snug.

Marse he married Miss Julia who was a Trenholm. She lose one baby girl. De two young ladies was de prettiest young ladies in dem parts, wid big brown eyes and black hair. Den came young Marse John. He was de secon' boy, de firs' he up and die from de fever. And same wid de firs' born girl. Most all of us niggers and white folks back den, we got de fever ever' spring.

Miss Eliza was a wild one. She married young Mr. Alcorn over to Coahoma County. But she was a han'ful, no mistake. Dey all was. Dem Savages, dey was quality, but dey was de wildes', cussinges', fightenes', hardes' drinkin', fastes'-ridin', outspendinest folks you ever seed.

They was nearly two hundred head ob folk living in de slave quarters. Us heard about ol' Hones' Abe de rail splitter but we didn't pay much mind, 'cept some ob de younger boys dey get to talkin' 'bout 'mancipation when dere weren't no white folk aroun'. I never hear bout no rebellion, but dere was a boy named Clarence, big fella used to do de' huntin and fishin'. He use to take young John out to de woods like he was his own son and den one day dey question us all and dey say Clarence he plottin' a rebellion to kill de Marse and rabish de white womens. Well, I ain't heard no such talk but Clarence he was mighty het up when they done sold his woman off to a place down Vicksburg way. And dat weren't like Marse Savage to do a t'ing like dat at all. No sah. A young nigger name of Abraham testify against him but he was a worthless no count nigger and wouldn't no black peoples b'lieve a word he say. Dey say hit went hard for Clarence when dey found two guns and a hatchet 'neath his cabin, but I says, hit were his job, huntin' for game for de table. But I don't say hit to anyone but keep my own counsel, like always. And d'at's why I's here today. Not like some of dem young bucks, like Clarence. Dey hung him and seben, eight others.

After de 'mancipation most of de niggers dey run off but me I stayed on. Hit were my home.

One snowy night shortly before Christmas break I returned to my room to find Will waiting with pinwheel eyes and a black velvet cape, sitting in a lotus position on my bed, the stereo blasting some funky new record of his. Unfolding his legs and rising slowly from the bed, he clapped his hands on my shoulders and attempted to look into my eyes, his actual focal point somewhere outside the walls behind me.

"Looking very Yale," he said.

"You look . . . medieval," I said.

He seemed to like this idea. Any sane person would have felt absurd floating across the Yale campus dressed as Will was, but you could sense immediately that he didn't. And in his company you became a little self-conscious about your own appearance, your conformity, even on this, your own turf. I would have blamed this on my own insecurity, but Aaron, whom we ran into in the Branford courtyard, commented on it the next day after Will was gone. "Guy's from another planet," Aaron remarked, "but he makes you feel like he's the one that belongs."

Of course, to Will the campus must have seemed half real at most, the right-angled brick melting softly, the gray stone dressed up in brilliant chemical hues—his mind being literally elsewhere. Or so I imagined. I didn't know what he was on. He was whacked out and yet he was coherent and self-contained.

I wanted to show him Yale or, rather, show him *me* at Yale. But he'd already seen it once with his father, well before Will had chosen a very different brand of higher education, and he was invariably condescending about the whole thing. "Kind of a big museum to Apollonian culture," he said. "Sarcophagus of the status quo."

I, for one, was hoping this relic would last long enough to award me a diploma. Twenty-five years later, I'm still not sure which of us picked the winning side. At the time, Will definitely had the edge. Yale is still

Yale, but I suspect that the world my daughters are inheriting has been shaped more by Will's followers than by Old Blues like his father. Or me. After his visit I sent Will a letter quoting a tract that I suggested could serve as a fine description of the Age of Aquarius, declaimed at a convention of southern states by one Leonidas Spratt of South Carolina in 1860:

> I have perfect confidence that . . . when the peerage of England shall have yielded to the masses—when democracy at the North shall hold its carnival . . . when women shall have taken the places and habiliments of men, and men shall have taken the places and habiliments of women—when Free Love unions . . . shall pervade the land—when the sexes shall consort without the constraints of marriage, and when youths and maidens, drunk at noonday, and half naked, shall reel about the marketplaces—the South will stand, secure and erect as she stands now.

At Rudy's, an off-campus dive, Will kept leaning farther and farther forward across the table until his chin was almost in my beer, the scar beneath his left eye seeming to pulse under my nose. He assured me a revolution was at hand and worried that I might end up on the wrong side.

"I'll just tell them I know you."

"Better not," he said. "People around me have a tendency to get hurt."

"Look, I'm sorry about Elbridge," I said. "But you know it wasn't your fault."

Will reared back in his chair as if I'd slapped him. He swallowed half a mug of beer and shook his head.

"Thank you for that absolution, Father Keane. But his blood is still on my hands."

"He could have borrowed anybody's car," I pointed out.

"But he borrowed mine," Will said. "And I let him." He leaned even farther forward and hissed, "And they were after *me*."

"Who was after you?"

"L.B. was in my car. Everybody knew that car. They were tailing him." He paused one of his long pauses, staring off into the ether. "Out there

on the highway they thought they could take me down and say whatever they wanted later."

"Will, he was high," I said. "He was speeding and the cops gave chase."

"Were you there?" Will demanded.

"Were you?"

"You've got to free your senses from the official version of events," he
said. "Sacco and Vanzetti, Sam Cooke, Medgar Evars, John and Bobby
Kennedy, Martin Luther King—there's always a cover story. Resisting
arrest . . . lone gunman . . . drugs." He looked around, reconnoitering,
and whispered, "They always try to make it look unconnected."

"Was there an autopsy or a coroner's report?"

"Haven't you been listening?" Will rolled his eyes. "Quis custodiet
ipsos custodes?" he quoted, retrieving a chestnut from senior-year Latin
class. "It's the motherfucking foxes guarding the henhouse. Hell, L.B.
was the guy who first clued me in. He lent me the books, showed me
how to look behind the veil." He fell silent, and for a moment I was
afraid he might cry.

"Maybe you should move out of Memphis."

Will sighed and settled back in his chair. "Maybe so." Will's lips disappeared as he sucked them inward. "L.B. was always telling me to get
out of town. I don't know why he couldn't take his own advice." After a
long pause, he said. "It's in the blood. You can't run from a curse."

This emboldened me to ask, "Did you ever read that diary you
gave me?"

"I might have looked at it." He smiled cryptically, then reached down
into his shirt and extracted a hoary, carved stone which hung from a
thong around his neck. "Remember this? The uzat, mystical eye."

I nodded, having seen it in his father's collection on my first visit to
Memphis.

"Protects against ghosts, snakebites and envious words."

"You ought to give one to Taleesha," I said. "She's the one who needs
protection."

He smiled as if at a dim child. "You see her as the noble victim," he
said. "But, let me tell you—she's way better than that. She could eat you
for breakfast. Hell, she could eat me for breakfast. Fact, she nearly did."

He suddenly pulled off his jacket and rolled up the sleeve of his vivid shirt; on the inside of his bicep was an ugly bruise that looked exactly like the imprint of a set of teeth.

He grinned as if he were immensely proud of this trophy.

"Taleesha did that," I asked.

"Don't worry about Tally. She's gonna be fine."

He was right: Will himself was the one to worry about. When he still had a brother he was free to be the errant son. Now that he was the last of the Savages, he had to struggle even harder against his heredity, and I could see that it was wearing on him.

"Who are these people?" he demanded, looking around us. To my horror he suddenly stood up on his chair and shouted, "Hey, Yalies, you think you're so fucking smart—who here knows where the Southern crosses the Yellow Dog?"

I thought for sure we were in for a fight, but the comparative hush which this exclamation evoked was suddenly broken by a rebel yell. A big jock at a nearby table stood up on his own chair. "Moorhead," he shouted. "Any good ole boy knows the Southern crosses the Yellow Dog at Moorhead, Mississippi."

The Mississippian lumbered over to our table with his pitcher and soon we found ourselves carousing with several members of the football team. Incredibly, Will seemed delighted with this company and they with him. I was amazed not only that Will got along with these guys better than I could, but also that he knew how to talk about football, while our new friends proved to be extremely well versed in soul and blues. They were, in fact, big fans of Lester Holmes. After an eternity of bonding, I tried to extract Will; I had classes in the morning.

He said he'd be back in my room within the hour. I did not see him again for several weeks, although the football player from Mississippi always had a hearty greeting for me after that whenever I saw him on campus.

XIV

For Christmas that year my parents gave me a '63 Corvair that my uncle had taken in trade on his lot. In this Ralph Nader—condemned chariot—bidding farewell to my folks, little Jimmy, Aunt Colleen and Nana Keane—I set out a few days later for Jackson, Mississippi. My plan was to visit Will in Memphis and then follow the river south through the Delta to Jackson, there to scour the Mississippi Department of Archives and History for further clues about the alleged slave uprising at Bear Track.

Three hours short of Memphis I pulled off the interstate and made my way to Franklin, Tennessee, site of one of the bloodiest battles of what was still known in these parts as "the war." The man who would have been my great-great uncle died there. In the years since, the postcard-perfect Victorian town had spread over much of the battlefield, and I stopped at a gas station to ask directions. The attendant asked, "You one of them reenactors?"

"Beg your pardon?"

"Reenactors. Those folks dress up in uniforms, do the battle. There was a big one here a few years back—must have been five thousand of 'em, blue and gray, camped out in the field there, drinking and carrying on. Next day they acted out the battle, realistic as hell, carrying the colors, marching up against each other firing their muskets, falling over like fainting goats. It was a hell of a thing to see."

After I disclaimed any such affiliation, he directed me to Carnton, an antebellum mansion where four Confederate generals had been laid out on the porch, and where thousands of lesser rank lay buried. As we do in such places, I tried to conjure up from the serene landscape some mystical sense of connection to the hallowed bloody past, but I couldn't feel anything except a vague reverence until, on my way out of town, I encountered a young soldier in the olive-drab uniform of the U.S. Army standing beside his car at the pump next to mine. Inside the Pontiac a fat girl in a white dress was dabbing her eyes with a dirty handkerchief. He was about my age, nineteen or twenty, crewcut and skinny, with a thin face that seemed to be all pimples and bones. Young as he was, his face had a wizened quality; it was easy to imagine him in a daguerreotype, leaning on his musket, a member of the doomed Army of Tennessee.

He suddenly looked up at me, nodded and said, "How you doing?"

All I could manage was to blush and mutter some pleasantry—suddenly ashamed of the educational deferment which would keep me out of Vietnam while boys like him went in my place. According to Nana Keane, a Boston banker had bought an exemption from service in 1861 and sent my great-great uncle as a substitute to be killed here in Franklin. For all I knew the descendants of that banker were known to me from school. And I couldn't help wondering if this boy would be so friendly if he knew he was my substitute.

If this were another kind of story, the protagonist's life would be forever changed by this political epiphany—Saint Paul dashed from his horse. But for most of us these moments of clarity fade as quickly as the flash of a camera, recollected, if at all, as a faded picture in the album of memory. The young soldier dutifully paid the attendant and drove away to his fate as I proceeded toward mine.

Dusk was falling on New Year's Eve as I arrived in Memphis. I succeeded without much difficulty in finding the Peabody Hotel, one of the more prominent features of the Memphis skyline, but there was no answer to my calls in the Savage suite.

I think it was Faulkner—usually a safe bet in these matters—who said the Mississippi Delta originated in the lobby of the Peabody. Certainly no one would have mistaken this for the Boston Ritz-Carlton, or for the Plaza in New York. That curious and beguiling southern blend of ease and formality were in the air—that rhythm oscillating between languor and hysteria. The lobby was thronged with revelers in evening dress. Sitting in a leather chair, I watched an elderly couple step from the elevator. In a tuxedo which looked as if it had been handed down through half-a-dozen generations and might dissolve into dust at any moment, the man bowed gallantly from the waist to a pair of women getting into the elevator. When the women had passed, his silver-haired spouse assisted him in regaining his upright posture. Young women in ball gowns wafted about the two-story lobby, while their male counterparts lurked in corners, conspiring and breaking out into sudden fits of suppressed hilarity. These young swains applauded as a tiny man in livery marched the ducks from the fountain in the center of the lobby across the floor and into the elevator en route to a pen on the hotel roof. The ducks were the descendants of a batch of live decoys—or so Cordell Savage once told me—which had been dumped into the fountain one afternoon by a band of liquored-up hunters fresh from the duck blind who wanted to continue drinking at the hotel bar.

After I grew tired of sitting, I orbited the lobby, looking in the shop windows and seeing only myself in the glass, a ridiculous figure pretending to be occupied while the festive couples swirled past, too busy to notice. Finally I took to the streets, which seemed desolate. Beale Street, the scene of Will's initiation into the blues, was being sanitized and demolished. Only after lingering over a dinner of ribs in a tacky restaurant catering to tourists did I return to my vigil at the Peabody.

I tried the house phone every fifteen minutes, and finally claimed a stool in the bar, sorely tempted to press on with my trip and say to hell with Will. I was tired of living on Will Savage time, being always the one left waiting and wondering whether he would show. And I was tired of being alone again on New Year's Eve, that most melancholy of holidays. I had a terrible premonition of a solitary life, of dinners on TV trays and odd-smelling, transient rooms. Something was wrong with me; I was afflicted with a terrible self-consciousness which seemed to set me apart, doomed forever to be a spectator at the ball, watching the dancers from the sidelines. I tried not to inquire too closely into the sources of my alienation, but sometimes, as on this particular evening, it was impossible to resist the pressure of self-knowledge. I tried to divert myself rereading Binnie Pilcher's diary:

May 10 Outside my window the scraping sound of the hands hoeing. Already the mosquitoes are a plague. Human beings were not meant to live here. Law, take me back to Charleston! Whatever the issue of the current strife, this country will always be ruled by insects. And I shall die a maiden. And Mama shall become invisible under the influence of her drops. Clarence was hanged to day also Abraham, and two other of our field hands, plus the Yancys' Thomas, who ran away last year and was recaptured. Plus two of the Johnsons' slaves and the Platts' carriage man. And old Red who died of heart attack under examination makes nine. The other negroes, our own and the Yancys', reprieved. The size and scope of the conspiracy still in doubt, but after a week of hearings the desire to preserve property i.e. able-bodied male negroes has somewhat overtaken the zeal for lurid revelation and retribution.

Father refused to let the committee depose John, saying he was too young, and in the end it all came down to Ben the Yancys' driver who said he heard Thomas say that the federals are coming and the negroes should kill Mr. Yancy and ravage Mrs. Yancy and the girls. I wonder if I was to be ravaged or rather ravished as I think is the proper expression? To the end, Clarence refused to testify, even under the lash. The gentlemen of the committee urged him to acknowledge and meet his Maker with unburdened heart to no avail. Sissy the kitchen maid says that his heart was turned to stone when Father sold off his woman and that he didn't care what happened after that. This morning John tried to lock himself in his room but Father forced him to go to the courthouse to witness the hanging, he said John had started this and that he must see the consequences through to conclusion. We ladies staying home sewing haversacks. John returned at midday ashen and silent, blazing eyes banked low for once and dim. Took to his room. I could almost feel sorry for him then. Clarence was once his constant companion, taught him to ride and fish and conjure while Father was off in Memphis or Vicksburg or New Orleans. John spent so much time in the slave quarters and so often cited the authority of his friend Clarence that Mother and Father began to fear for his morals though for a negro he possessed a high degree of intelligence and dignity.

Looking up from my drink, I found myself being studied by a woman with a shock of vivid red hair two stools away.

"Whatsa matter, honey? All alone on New Year's Eve?" Her drawl was pronounced, her eyes animated with a quick and predatory curiosity that seemed at odds with the torpid voice. I was not good at judging the age of women older than myself, but I guessed her to be about thirty. Her skin was fair and freckled, and her eyes had tiny sun wrinkles; she seemed far too pretty to be talking to me, except that this was the South, whose natives were known to talk to strangers for no particular reason.

"Actually, I'm waiting for someone," I explained, as she slid across to the stool beside me.

"Aren't we all, honey? Aren't we all?" Her name was Janie Thompson, and she was from a town called Indianola in the Delta. "I come up here with a friend for a little New Year's festivity but he got a little too festive right off the bat, and here I am—all dressed up an' no place to glow." She shrugged her shoulder and grinned at me impishly. "So allow me to buy you a drink." Waving to the bartender, she pointed at our glasses.

When she leaned forward to squeeze my hand I was treated to a glimpse of the freckled valley of her cleavage and the lacy scalloped edge of her brassiere. "Did you see that sign out in the lobby—now appearing in the something or other room, Lash LaRue?" she said. "I couldn't hardly believe my eyes—Lash LaRue, that old lariat thrower. I used to watch him on the TV when I was about this tall." She lowered her hand to the vicinity of my knee. "I always had a little crush on ole Lash. Well, I'm on my way to the bar but then I see this sign and so off I go to see the great man. And there he was signing autographs, in the flesh, more or less, looking like they pickled him and put him up. So when it's my turn I say, 'How's it going Lash, what you been up to?' And he says—get this—he says, 'Well, ever since they shot President Kennedy I been spending a lot of time on Mars. The streets are cleaner up there.' At first I think he's pulling my leg but then I look in his eyes and see he's serious. Crazy as a betsy bug. Lash LaRue." With that she drained half the drink the bartender set before her. "Where you-all from," she asked.

"I go to school in New Haven," I said.

"I like college boys," she said. As a Yale man I found her enthusiasm for male academia rather too broad based, but so pronounced was Janie Thompson's affability that I suspected she was also in favor of many other categories of male. "I guess your little friend isn't going to show, is she?"

"It's not a she," I said.

"Oh. Well, different strokes for different buckaroos."

"No, it's not. . . . That's not it," I stammered. "I'm waiting for an old friend from prep school."

"Well, hell," she said, "what's this old buddy of yours called. We all know everybody down here."

"Will Savage," I said, supposing that he and Janie traveled in very different circles.

"Will?" she exclaimed. "He's practically a legend in these parts. My daddy used to raise hell with his daddy. They used to fly their little planes up and down the Delta and over to Nashville, just going to parties. They were *wild*." She pronounced the adjective with an emphasis that suggested she was something of an authority on rash behavior. "You've heard the story about how he shot his own daddy."

Stunned, I shook my head. "You mean Cordell?"

"Well, they ruled it accidental, but Cordell's daddy was a mean drunk, and some say he took a hand to Cordell's mama one too many times."

I questioned her further about this alleged patricide, but she'd told what she knew and seemed to feel that it was an old story, and not particularly an unusual one in her experience.

"So how is old Will? I haven't seen him in aeons. He sure did cause a hell of a fuss marrying that colored girl. What's she like, anyway? Is he really in love with her?"

We drank and talked about Will, four scotch-and-waters' worth. Finally the bartender turned up the volume on the television set as Guy Lombardo counted down the minutes to the not-a-moment-too-soon New Year of 1970, and not long after the stroke of twelve my companion was kissing me, probing remote crannies of my mouth with her tongue.

Only moments later, it seemed, we were kissing in the elevator on the way up to her room. She held her finger to her lips as she turned the key in the door, then dragged me over to the bed.

With a drunken fluency and much help from my new friend, I squirmed out of my clothes and assisted her out of hers while managing to keep my tongue in her mouth—as if I believed that the whole process would surely grind to a halt the moment contact was broken. I couldn't believe it was finally happening, though my excitement was adulterated by a nagging fear about my performance. When she broke free of our lip lock and kissed her way down my chest and belly, I lay back, rigid with astonishment and anxiety. In a sense, it was, indeed, too good to be true. It's hard to say who was more surprised when I came a moment later.

"Hey," she said, raising her head from between my legs. "That was supposed to be the warm-up, not the main event."

I mumbled some kind of apology.

"You wouldn't by any chance be a virgin, would you?" she said brightly, sliding up to face me, a new and—to me—embarrassing tang on her breath.

"Sort of," I said.

She laughed. "Seems like either you are or you aren't. That's okay. I don't mind. We can try again."

Like a schoolboy, I asked if I could go to the bathroom, desperate for a moment alone to compose myself.

"Sure," she said. "If you gotta go you gotta go."

I was just inside the door when I heard her whisper something cautionary, though I couldn't make out the words.

The bathroom light revealed a young man in a tuxedo sprawled in the bathtub. Pausing just long enough to verify this seeming hallucina-

tion, and recover the use of my limbs, I turned off the light and retreated.

"Don't go, that's just Lance," Janie said, as I searched in the dark for
my clothes. Frankly, I couldn't see how these two clauses fit in the same
sentence.

"I've got to meet Will," I said.

She tugged at my arm in the dark. "You still owe me one," she said.

"Sorry," I said. At that moment, I felt that my sexual career had ended
about the same time it had begun.

Remembering my manners, I thanked her as I was leaving.

Out in the lobby I dialed Will's suite again, and then, as a last-ditch
measure, his office. Just as I was about to hang up someone answered. I
asked for Will, but the din on the other end was so great that I doubt he
heard me. I listened to the music and the competing voices of a party
for some minutes before giving up. Replacing the receiver, I felt stunningly sober.

Will's office and studio was a short walk from the hotel, in a derelict
part of town, an old limestone hulk just off the river. Gargoyles grinned
down from the portico and from the elaborately incised rooftop cor-
nice. The mullioned windows were pulsing with music from within.
Two white men of menacing demeanor stood on the sidewalk, passing
a joint. "I'm looking for Will," I explained. Nobody said anything, but
there was just enough room to slide through the door without violating
anyone's space. Downstairs, a logo stenciled on the glass identified the
offices of Savage Management & Cement Mixer Music.

Behind the first door I opened I surprised a couple making love on a
desk, or rather they surprised me; the woman turned and grinned at me
through the cascading ropy strands of her partner's greasy hair while he
went on about his business. It seemed a night designed to put me off sex
forever.

A door opened behind me, unleashing a blast of sound. Stubblefield
stuck his head into the lobby, reconnoitering. "Keane," he said, as if he
had seen me the day before. Even as a hippie he looked preppie; his utterly limp, straw-colored hair was reminiscent of much-washed chinos,

and his self-contained, slightly smug expression suggested that any-thing that you might think of doing had already been achieved by his ancestors. I followed him down a hallway into an open studio, where five or six musicians were jamming and dozens of bodies churned in a choppy sea of strobed light.

Finding nothing to moor myself to, I was grateful when a skinny white girl with a blond Afro suddenly held out a joint. I took a quick hit and attached myself gratefully to her group.

"When my pop died Will said I'd see him on the other side," the girl said. "He's so spiritual. It's incredible. He died himself on the operating table that time after he got stabbed—you know that scar on his face, from when what's his name, the blues guy, cut him?"

She looked vaguely around the room as if the alleged perpetrator might still be among us, knife dripping. "What was I saying? Oh, right, Will said he was lifted up out of his body and looked down on the earth and saw that it was just, like, a phase, you know, our physical exis-tence on this planet." She sucked in on the joint which I had returned to her.

"That's cool," said a fat guy with a long matted beard. "He was telling me this story about the Monterey Pop Festival in '67," he said, taking the roach from the girl.

"Who was?"

"Who was what?"

"Telling you what you just said about Monterey."

"It was Will, like I said. It's like, Hendrix got in from playing with King Curtis at four in the morning and he walked into his bedroom, and he saw this cat in bed with his old lady. He went and got his pistol, stood over the bed, cocked it and turned on the light. He's just about to shoot but then he says to himself, 'Damn, that's Otis. Shit, I can't kill Otis, man.'"

"That is so outrageous. Was Will there?"

"I don't know, man. Maybe."

"But what does that have to do with reincarnation?"

"I don't know. I thought we were talking about Will."

"Where is Will," I asked.

No one seemed to know, though they assured me he was around. I left this group to free-associate amongst themselves and strolled around, trying to assume a casual, funky gait, feeling conspicuous in my crewneck sweater as a topless woman with small, asymmetrical breasts danced past me.

Spotting Lester Holmes conferring with two white girls, I sidled over and reminded him that we'd met. He regarded me for a moment with mild irritation, then sloped off without saying a word.

"Will says Lester could be the biggest thing since Ray Charles," said one of the girls, to no one in particular, "except he's lazy and won't travel more than a few hours from Memphis."

People kept saying that Elvis was going to come by; if he did, I missed him. But in fact I was surrounded by people who were much cooler than Elvis, though few of their names were familiar to me at the time. Some years later in New York, when we were both sitting up late over a bottle of cognac, I asked Taleesha to run down the guest list that night.

Among those she recalled being present were Duck Dunn and Don Nix, along with another founding member of the Mar-Keys, Steve Cropper, who became famous as a producer and studio guitar wizard for Otis Redding and others at Stax. Also Jim Dickinson and Jimmy Crosthswait. Alex Chilton, who at the age of sixteen was the lead singer of the Box Tops and later played with Big Star and Panther Burns. Bowlegs Miller. And Bukka White—who supposedly stabbed Will— whose 1940 Vocalion sessions helped define the Delta blues. The great Sleepy John Estes even brought his guitar; Will paid for his funeral when he died in poverty some years later. Hound Dog Taylor, from Chicago. Chips Moman, the producer and songwriter, and fellow Alabaman Dan Penn, with whom he wrote "Do Right Woman." Issac Hayes, of imminent "Shaft" fame. The guitarist John Fahey, who found Skip James, long presumed dead, on a plantation in the midsixties. Jerry Phillips, son of Sam, of Sun Studios.

Fresh from his appearance at the Peabody, Lash LaRue made a big splash with the Memphis hipsters—the cowboy from outer space. William Eggleston, the photographer, arrived in a hearse equipped with an oxygen tank, accompanied by the writer Stanley Booth. I remember seeing Eggleston, an anomalous, razor-thin figure in an elegant black suit, dripping anomie and looking askance at the hippies.

Wading blindly through these legends-in-the-making, I spotted Stubblefield leaning against a wall watching the proceedings with stoned intensity.

"Will around," I asked.

"Somewhere. How's Yale," he asked, drawing forth a long earnest answer from me before I realized that he couldn't care less, that he was stoned out of his mind. "My old man went there and so did his old man," he said, as if to drive home the point that I needn't have bothered to yammer away about it.

"So what do you do for Will," I asked, with what I hoped was a discernible measure of contempt for all mere functionaries, subordinates and flunkies.

I thought he hadn't heard me, but finally he turned to me and said, "I ball all the chicks is what I do."

Finding no niche for myself in this bacchanal, I explored the edges until I found Taleesha in an office, curled up in a beanbag chair, improbably reading Samuelson's *Economics*.

"Hey, Patrick," she said, looking up and grinning, scrambling to free herself from the grip of the chair. "Oh, shit! We were supposed to meet you, weren't we? God, I'm sorry. Living with Will I start to get on his schedule, which is no schedule at all. Anyway, it's good to see you"—she shook her head—"in this zoo."

I hadn't seen her since the fire, and I was happy to discover that my residual guilt—about not having been there to prevent it—seemed to dissolve in her presence. I gave her a hug. "Happy New Year."

"Have you seen Will yet," she asked.

"I haven't been so blessed."

"He's doing his Buddhist Rasputin thing tonight. Come on, let's find him."

We took the stairs to the basement, where a red sign glowed above a door: RECORDING! DO NOT ENTER WHEN LIGHT IS ON. Taleesha pushed on through. Dressed entirely in black, Will was sitting astride a stool in front of the console of a mixing board, one hand on the board, a huge joint in the other. Jessie Petit sat in the corner reading a newspaper.

"Play that last track again," Will said to the middle-aged man sitting beside him.

"Will, it's Patrick," Taleesha announced.

Turning slowly, Will registered me with a complacent look. Making a minute adjustment on the board, he stood up and held his arms open. I walked awkwardly into his fleshy embrace.

"Dink Stover, I presume."

"I went to the hotel," I said, trying unsuccessfully to keep the frustration out of my voice.

Will nodded, as if misdirection were all part of a larger plan. "It's good to see you, Patrick," he said. He offered me the roach, which I accepted. "You gotta hear this," he said. "This is cooking."

Later, after listening over and over to various takes of the latest song Will was producing, we were in the car and Will was driving very fast the wrong way down a one-way street. Taleesha was trying to convince Will that this was a bad idea, particularly since his license had been suspended recently for similar behavior. Besides, she said, Jessie was supposed to be Will's driver. But if Will heard her, he gave no indication.

Dozing intermittently in the backseat, I awoke when the car stopped, blue light flashing in the rear window.

"Everybody be cool," Will said, stepping out of the car. I waited with Taleesha and Jessie, none of us daring to speak. I had more than enough time to wonder what kind of controlled substances might be in the car with us, to consider the charged racial climate of the South, to contemplate how a felony conviction would look on my law school applications.

Finally Will returned, slipped into the driver's seat and eased the car into gear.

"What'd you say," I asked as we pulled away.

"We talked some politics," he said. "Each contest calls forth its own tactics. You follow your *chi*. Sometimes you thrust, sometimes you yield."

"Sometimes," Taleesha said, "you just confuse the living shit out of everybody."

"And mostly, you just pay the motherfuckers off," said Jessie.

Back at Will's hotel suite, shortly after dawn, I seem to remember Taleesha screaming at Will and slapping him, but I may have been dreaming.

Waking up in the Savage suite, a sprawling set of grand, tatty rooms atop the Peabody, I stepped over several bodies in the living room. Crippled with hangover, I went back to sleep for several hours. When I woke next, it was to the sound of Taleesha's voice.

"Get the fuck out of here, everybody," she screamed. "I mean it, get out!" When I finally emerged from my chamber, Taleesha was alone, sipping coffee in a kimono.

"I can't even remember the last time Will and I were alone," she said.

"I can leave," I said, "if this isn't a good time."

"Not you, Patrick." She sighed. "Hey, what do you want? I'll call down for room service."

That afternoon I watched football while Taleesha mastered economics. She explained she'd started taking classes that fall at Memphis State. Although the big windows looked out over the city to the east and the Mississippi and Arkansas to the west, the rooms had been customized and day-proofed to Will's womblike specifications so that it was perpetually twilight within. The dark Persian carpets and the upholstery were speckled with burns. I sprawled on a fusty-smelling couch with a vicious headache, sucking down Cokes and tomato juice.

Will appeared about four, wafting into the room in a dark blue kimono. "Happy new decade, my friends. Any signs of the dawning of the new era?"

"There was a big old bodhisattva here looking for you earlier," Taleesha remarked, "but he got tired of waiting."

When I saw the red welt on Will's face I remembered the argument I'd heard in my early morning stupor.

"Are we doing something today," Taleesha asked. "I mean what's left of today? If any damn thing's dawning out there we'd never know it in here. We're just like fucking movie stars," she remarked to me. "We can't go out in public. And even if we could, Will's too busy playing tycoon."

As if to illustrate the point, Jessie Petit came and spent a half hour closeted with Will, who then talked for an hour on the phone, tending to his growing empire while we two students studied. Finally Taleesha, beckoning me to come along, walked into the parlor where Will was conducting his business and ripped the phone cord out of the wall.

"Goddamnit, Taleesha." He threw the useless receiver on the table.

She looked over her shoulder at him with defiant, haughty mien as she disappeared down the hall and, after a moment, he followed. Back in the living room, I closed my book and stared at a football game in which I had absolutely no interest. At halftime, I went to my bedroom, ostensibly to get a book—or so I made a point of telling myself. It now seems comical that I would fabricate an excuse solely for my own benefit, even as I crept along the carpeted hallway in stocking feet toward their door, stopping just outside to listen to their syncopated grunting. Leaning close to the crack I had a narrow, vertical but no less startling view of brown and white flesh intertwined, rising and falling on the crimson spread.

I determined that she was on top, her breasts hanging pendulously above his hair-stippled white chest. This seemed a fabulous inversion to me, as marvelously perverse as the juxtaposition of skin colors. Even more fantastic—Will's arms were stretched back behind him—his wrists bound and fastened to something just out of the picture. To this day I don't quite know how to interpret this partial composition, or whether to trust my memory, but I now understand all too well that you can never predict the geometry of appetite, or know for certain what secret passions may roil within the breast of even your best friend. Certainly the wife of my murdered colleague Felson must be pondering such matters at this very moment. . . . Felson in his ill-fitting suits and his devotion to the driest regions of the Law. . . .

That evening Will went to the studio for a few hours. At eleven Taleesha and I were sitting on the floor of the living room picking at a room-service dinner.

"So, what's happening with your singing career," I asked Taleesha, whose mood had brightened considerably once she reappeared from the bedroom.

She laughed. "My singing career's mainly a fantasy of Will's—kind of a Josephine Baker/Ronnie Spector deal. I just got tired of it. Singing and dancing used to be the only way up, the only door open. I want to get my B.A. Then I'd like to do something . . . original. Something a black girl isn't *supposed* to do."

"You already did that," Will said, standing in the doorway, "when you married me."

"And look what a good idea *that* turned out to be."

Will bowed theatrically.

"Irony isn't Will's strong suit—is it honey?"

The tension between them had disappeared, and they suddenly seemed as carefree as they had been that first day in New York. While he was still in a good mood I told Will that I was planning to stop at Bear Track the next day to pay my respects to his parents. "You don't need my permission, man." He smiled. "My sympathy, maybe."

"Plus a heavy-duty suit of armor," Taleesha said.

"A garlic necklace," Will suggested, grinning at his wife.

"And a sharp wooden stake," she added, walking over and kissing him, a kiss which was to continue on and off for the better part of the next hour, until I finally took the hint and retreated to my solitary bed.

XV

When I arrived at Bear Track early in the afternoon, Joseph directed me out back to the stables, where Cordell was conferring with a groom. A plump, jowly pink man sat astride his horse.

"You're just in time," Cordell said, thumping me on the back, "to join us on a little afternoon shoot. Have you eaten? I can have some sandwiches packed for us. Cobb, this is my young friend Patrick Keane. Patrick, Cobb Hilton. Cobb owns the next piece over. His great-granddaddy carpetbagged down from Ohio or some damn place after the war and picked it up for ten cents on the dollar. Now he's got more prime land under cultivation than anybody in the whole damn Delta."

In response the man grunted and spit, his eyes buried deep in the pink recesses of his cheeks. I would have found him more plausible as a foreman or the proprietor of the feed store than as a planter.

I was relieved to hear that the sport of the day was shooting rather than riding. But when Cordell said, "You take the roan gelding," I realized I was not to be spared. I should probably have confessed that I'd never ridden anything except a pony at a petting zoo, but I think I wanted to present myself as the kind of guy who could jump right on a horse and take charge. As a direct result of my experience that day, my older daughter now takes riding lessons in Central Park.

The groom helped me up into my saddle and adjusted the stirrups, asking me if they felt right. I managed well enough as we trotted over to a little cabin, where two pointers hurled themselves against the chain-link fence of their kennel, causing my horse to start turning in nervous circles. Cordell had dismounted to talk to a wizened old man with a disintegrating straw hat and gray-black skin. I'm not sure what provoked my horse to take off suddenly at a gallop. I tried to stay upright as I pulled back on the reins, but it didn't seem to slow the horse, who I later learned had a "hard" mouth and was responding to the pressure of my knees clutching his flanks, which acted as an accelerator. I was maintaining an increasingly precarious balance; the ground was a blur, loud and hard and distant beneath his pounding hooves. Finally a drainage ditch accomplished what I could not, bringing my horse up short and throwing me down against his neck.

When Cordell caught up, I had nearly recovered my composure.

"Wait up for us older folks," he said. "It's five months yet to the Kentucky Derby." Cobb Hilton bounced up like Jell-O on a stick. Noses to the earth, the two dogs traced manic figures in front of us. Cordell introduced me to Solomon, the straw-hatted dog handler, who rode over and slipped a double-barreled shotgun into the scabbard on my saddle.

As we trotted out over the cut winter fields, my fear and unease started to slip away; my horse settled down and I began to feel competent—after all, at least I had managed to stay on the beast—and to see myself as a romantic figure, astride a fine-looking animal with a gun at my side, Nimrod on his steed. The furrowed fields were punctuated by stands of trees, hedgerows and giant rolling sprinkler rigs that looked to me like the vertebrae of some prehistoric creature. The vast Delta landscape with its huge cerulean dome seemed a canvas for heroic horseback deeds.

"This is the richest soil on the planet," Cordell announced. "Yank on your left rein, Pat, don't let him walk you sideways like that. Give him a good pull—don't be shy. He's got a hard mouth."

I did as instructed.

"Topsoil's forty foot deep hereabouts," he said. "Ever since the last ice age, the big river's been collecting sediment from a watershed covering some part of thirty-seven states, then flooding its banks with blessed regularity and precipitating the very best soil right about here. Considering all we lost, I think it's only right and meet that we've spirited away millions of tons of Yankee topsoil over the millennia."

Solomon chuckled, amused by this trope.

"Only thing good ever come down from up north," drawled Cobb, who seemed to have forgotten his own provenance.

The two pointers appeared to be plowing a patch of tall grass with their noses.

We were riding through a cornfield which had been left standing, the dry husks hissing against the flanks of the horses, when Solomon said, "Point," in a quiet, urgent tone. One dog was locked in a rigid, quivering pose in front of a patch of scrubby cover; the other stood motionless behind him. We rode up to within some twenty feet, or, rather, most of us stopped at that distance; my horse kept on going, as I nervously squeezed on his belly with my legs, trotting inexorably to where the lead dog crouched.

"What in hell's he doing?" Cobb hissed behind me. I yanked back hard on the reins just as the covey broke—an eruption of wings, a dozen mad drumrolls launching as many blurred brown projectiles over the field. Although I knew the birds were there I was so startled by the rise that I nearly fell off the gelding. Watching them disappear, I wanted to follow them, to ride off and hide in the high grass and the cotton stalks and the lespedeza, eating bugs and seeds. I sat there staring out into the empty sky, then yanked on the reins again, gratuitously, almost viciously, in an attempt to share the blame.

"Actually, Patrick," Cordell said as he rode up, "that's not quite how we do it down here."

At dinner that evening, I had many reasons to be inconspicuous. I was still stinging from the afternoon's humiliation in the field, and the conversation was hardly calculated to put me at ease. Cobb Hilton had stayed on, and we were joined by two gentlemen from Arkansas. I gathered that a business deal might be pending. They were a good deal younger than their host, in their early thirties, young men who seemed impatient to rush all things, including their own middle age, even if the rest of the country was joining a cult of youth; proud of their new paunches and the boozy accretion of flesh around their faces, they were relentlessly loud, confident and eager to impress Cordell Savage, vying with each other to damn Washington, Wall Street and, for all I know, the Enlightenment. Cordell remained aloof, though I don't think either Arkansan realized it.

"What do you think of the wine, Patrick?" he said abruptly. "Mouton Rothschild 1928."

"Damn good" and "Excellent" opined the Arkansans. Cobb had refused the claret, insisting that bourbon and branch was good enough for him.

"I don't know much about wines," I said, looking back into Cordell's cruel eyes. This was a quiz and it definitely counted toward the final grade.

"I didn't ask how much you knew about wines, did I? I asked what you *think*. I don't know much about wines either, boy, but I know what I like."

We call this leading the witness. I had my clue. "It tastes a little sour to me, sir."

"Me too. It's turned. Joseph, take this shit away and bring me that other I brought up."

The wine probably *was* off, though I suspect he would have sent it away even if it wasn't. This was Cordell's way of giving me a chance to redeem myself after the hunting debacle.

"Beautiful silver," said one of the boys from across the river. "I got a venison dish at home that's the spitting image. Fellow in Savannah told me it used to belong to the Queen Mother of England."

Cordell directed a skeptical look at his guest in which anyone else would have read chastisement; you only had to look at him to realize that it was terribly *common*, as his wife might say, to compliment your host's home furnishings.

But the man from Arkansas was undaunted. "Where'd you pick it up?"

"Well, I *picked it up,* as you put it, at the home of a friend from Yale. It had been in his family since the end of the war and before that it had been in my family. It's an interesting story, actually. When I accepted the invitation to my classmate's home in Boston, Massachusetts"—this last word pronounced, as it so often is in the South, with an overenunciated sarcasm—"I had no idea that on his mother's side he was a Butler."

Cobb Hilton broke his corpulent silence with a grunt of distaste.

"You may recall from your history, Patrick, that General Butler occupied New Orleans, among other distinctions. I can't recall his Christian name just now, but down here we normally call him Beast Butler for reasons we needn't go into at the table, or sometimes Spoons Butler on account of his tendency to confiscate the silverware and other valuables of prominent Confederate families in the course of duty."

He paused to examine the wine that Joseph had just poured for him, nodding toward my own glass. Joseph poured some for me, which I tasted and, with some trepidation, pronounced suitable. Cordell smiled and nodded his approval.

"Now, my great-great-uncle was in New Orleans during the war, and eighty-odd years later, when I went home with Toby Farwell for Thanksgiving, I was rather surprised to find myself eating from Savage-family silver. They hadn't even bothered to remove the family crest. I didn't say anything then but on the evening we were to return to school I requested an audience with Toby's father and offered to buy everything back from him. He was quite indignant and sent me on my way. Well, a few years later Mr. Farwell Senior suffered some terrible reversals in business. I was of course deeply saddened to hear of this misfortune, but my distress did not prevent me from picking up the family silver at auction in New York."

The next morning, over breakfast, Cordell filled me in on the later stages of the evening; I had gone upstairs to read when the poker started. "I apologize for the company," he said, languidly buttering a piece of cornbread. "Not very stimulating. Those boys hoped to engage me in a business proposition. They were eager to demonstrate they were men of substance and daring, and I was more than happy to take their money at the poker table. Then Tupper, the short one, wanted to cut cards for a hundred dollars. You know, pick a card, high card wins. An idiot's pastime—if ever there was one. Then he wanted to cut for a thousand. Finally, just to get rid of him I said, 'Tupper, how much exactly are you worth?' Well he puffed himself up and started figuring his assets, I was half expecting him to start counting on his fingers any minute, and finally he says to me, with all false modesty, he says, 'Well, all told about two million, I reckon.' And I said, 'Tell you what, I'll cut you for it.' Well, that got him out of the damn house, finally." He inserted a slice of bacon into his mouth and chewed with evident satisfaction. Then, looking away, he said, "How's Will?"

I offered the usual response, that he was thriving and happy.

"Will? *Happy?* Now I *know* you're bullshitting me, son."

"Relatively speaking. Happy for Will."

"I would appreciate it if you don't tell him I asked."

I nodded.

"You know he's writing letters to the attorney general blaming me for everything from the Kennedy assassination to the Chicago Fire."

"He does tend to take historical events personally," I said.

"Thinks I'm the damn Antichrist."

Seeing him across the table looking at me with Will's eyes, I suddenly arrived at my thesis. Intuitively, I felt I knew what had happened at Bear Track a hundred years before.

XVI

C ordell Savage's disappearance a few weeks later was the talk of Memphis and the Delta. He'd driven off to the Rotary luncheon one day and hadn't been heard from since. Will phoned from his mother's house, which was itself indicative of the gravity of the situation.

"Maybe he's just off on a binge," I said. "Surely *you* could relate to that."

"Not the old man's style."

"Foul play?" I suggested, lawyerly.

"Smells rank, on somebody's part."

The missing person, I gathered, was himself one of the prime suspects in the matter of his own disappearance. Will said he'd let me know of any developments, and I asked if there was anything I could do.

"Keep in touch with Taleesha," he said. "She likes you."

I suppose he knew this would please me. After all, even fans need acknowledgment sometimes—an autographed picture, a kiss blown carelessly from the bright center stage.

The Savage clan was much on my mind that semester as I worked feverishly on my thesis. Cordell's vanishing act emboldened me as a historical analyst; I didn't think he would approve of my project, and this prospect made me nervous. Will claimed that his father was a Bones man, and I was enough in awe of this fact to imagine his reach extending to the campus; I could imagine him looking over my shoulder as I wrote, barking his disapproval. All I had told him, as I departed Bear Track for Jackson, was that I had developed a keen interest in southern history.

I had been none too comfortable pursuing my research at the Mississippi Archives, though no one seemed particularly hostile. A middle-aged librarian named Lizzie Tyre ostensibly assisted me, glaring at the card catalog through her pointy Cadillac-fin glasses, making me wait for documents while she talked with friends and relatives on the phone. I started by asking for letters and diaries of planters, which were well cataloged and preserved. To locate the interviews with ex-slaves conducted by the Works Progress Administration took much longer. When eventually some of this material surfaced, it came in the form of faded and crumbling carbons on yellow paper fastened together with rusting staples and paper clips. Amazingly, most of these had never been forwarded to the Library of Congress in Washington, and thus were not part of the collection I had seen on microfilm in New Haven. This was particularly the case with those interviews that cast plantation life in a harsh light. This evidence of censorship at the state level was itself an interesting discovery, one which was noted later by George Rawick in his classic *American Slave*.

I took time out from my thesis only to apply to law school and to campaign for the newly formed school senate. Not being a candidate for any of the secret societies, I'd run for election in an attempt to expand my orbit on campus and to bolster my undergraduate resume for my law school applications. Shortly after I was elected by classmates who did not necessarily covet the honor, various members of the Black Panther Party were charged with conspiracy in the murder of New Haven party member Alex Rackley the previous year. Initially, like most students, I didn't assume that the trial concerned me in any manner. Yale was Yale, aloof from merely local events.

The first scheduled meeting of the senate was canceled for lack of a quorum, and for some reason the second was canceled as well. In the meantime I received acceptances from Virginia and Michigan Law Schools—but no word from Harvard. When we finally convened in April, more than a hundred spectators—half of them black—awaited us in the lecture hall. The agenda for the meeting included a number of resolutions formulating Yale's response to the Panther trial, but the chairman of the steering committee, intimidated perhaps by the clamor from the back of the room, announced that he would entertain motions from the floor. This immediately proved to be a mistake. A shaven-headed black man demanded we vote for a university-wide strike in support of the Panthers.

"We don't recognize your authority," shouted a white man on the other side of the room who was draped in a red hammer-and-sickle flag. It was hard to believe he was a student—certainly I'd never seen him before.

"This body is irrelevant," he proclaimed, "an artifact of the corrupt, discredited power structure. It should be disbanded immediately. Power to the people!"

At this point the floor exploded with shouts and jeers. Our chairman pounded his gavel and pronounced the mob out of order. But it was a little late for that. Everyone was shouting. Looking down from the raised platform, I saw a black woman in the second row looking directly back at me, screaming "Fuck you fuck you fuck you. . . ." I was startled by the hatred in her face. So far I hadn't even said anything. And the senate hadn't opposed the strike; we hadn't yet had the opportunity to consider it. Who were these people, I remember wondering. Had they been at Yale with me all this time?

Prevailing over the mayhem, a black man with an Afro every bit as impressive as his dashiki addressed his remarks to the podium. "You pathetic lackeys—go home to your white corporate masters. Go lick the boots of the masters of the military-industrial complex." He held the commandeered microphone in one hand and thrashed the air with the other. Standing beside him I suddenly noticed Aaron Greeley.

Without thinking, I waved to my former roommate—and then instantly dropped my hand, realizing how inappropriate this gesture was under the circumstances. However, it apparently confused the speaker and created a strange hiatus in the proceedings. For just a moment, the noise subsided, no one knowing quite what to make of my inexplicable semaphore. Aaron stood there rigid beside the orator as if immobility would disguise him.

Looking directly at me, the man in the dashiki regained his composure: "You make me sick. All you privileged fucking honkies with your pathetic parliamentary bullshit. You wanna debate rules of order while the pigs are breaking their clubs on our heads. We're done with bullshit. You got that? In the name of the people I hereby declare this meeting adjourned. The black student union will hold a press conference at ten tomorrow morning and introduce a little reality into this fucking university."

He jumped down from the podium and walked out, trailing dozens of the spectators, including Aaron, in his wake. But the lecture hall still seemed on the verge of a riot. Somehow the chairman was able to shout out a proposal endorsing a strike, which most of us timidly voted for, if anyone cared. And then we ran for cover.

Shaken as I was after my close encounter with the revolution, I had naturally called Will. Taleesha answered at the Peabody and told me with no discernible goodwill that he was at his mother's house. Cordell Savage had surfaced in London with Cheryl Dobbs, his dead son's recent fiancée.

"Some Memphis people saw them at the American ambassador's in London," she said, "and the old bastard's lawyer has contacted Mrs. Savage to ask for a divorce."

This incredible news served to promote the tenuous reconciliation between Will and his mother; at the cost of a difficult and unloving husband, Mrs. Savage seemed to be regaining a son. This amnesty did not extend to her daughter-in-law, who had yet to meet Mrs. Savage or set foot in her house. "I understand," Taleesha claimed, unconvincingly. "He's all she has left."

She'd spent Easter with her own family while Will stayed by his mother's side. The good news was that he'd finagled a special compassionate exemption from military service on the grounds of his mother's recent loss of Elbridge and fragile health—an exceptional dodge which probably, ironically, had much to do with Cordell's residual political clout.

"So you got the Panthers on trial up there in New Haven," she noted.

"I didn't put anybody on trial. As far as *I'm* concerned they can all go free tonight."

"Sorry. I was just making an observation is all."

When I told her about the disrupted senate meeting, she sighed audibly. "There was actually a moment, right before I married Will, when I thought everything was getting better."

I thought I knew what she meant. "Then King was shot."

"Yeah, that and a lot of other stuff."

I called Memphis several times over the next week, but Will was never at home and I didn't want to call his mother's house for fear she might answer. He finally called me to hear firsthand about events in New Haven, so intrigued by the prospect of anarchy and revolution, by the putative alliance of ruling-class students and black revolutionaries, that he was planning to fly up to add his body to the fray. "Didn't I tell you the old ivy walls would come tumbling down?"

"And what are you going to put in their place," I asked, "communal farms?"

"Poppy fields," he proposed.

"Get real, Will."

"You're just afraid you might not get your precious Yale diploma."

He was half right. The events of the week were leading me to believe Will's interpretation of the momentum of recent history; the times were beginning to seem apocalyptic. The strike—supported by much of the faculty—was in effect, and that morning only three other students turned up for Professor Morgan's class on the American Revolution. Since I'd mostly been hiding out in the stacks, my front-line information was scant, but I dutifully repeated all the rumors I'd heard at meals: that the Hell's Angels were roaring into town en masse for May Day, that the three Weathermen who'd fled the exploding townhouse in

Greenwich Village were already here; that gelignite had been stolen from the chem lab, although no one stopped to ask what gelignite was doing there in the first place.

"What news on your father," I asked, thinking that if I ignored it, the revolution would go away.

"There's nothing to say about my father. I don't have a father anymore."

"That's exactly what he said about you two years ago."

"You're going to have to unlearn this habit of quoting deceased authority figures."

"Is he *definitely* in London with Cheryl?" I was riveted by the magnitude of the scandal; despite my feelings for some of the principals in this drama, it was a delicious spectacle.

"He's declared his intention to be married by the archbishop of Canterbury once the divorce goes through," Will said, temporarily raising him from the dead.

"Maybe he loves her," I said—the same observation I'd made to Cordell about Will's marriage.

"And maybe Nixon is really a compassionate and caring human being."

The following day I received a letter from the Harvard Law School. Hyperventilating all the way up the stairs, I carried it to my room and set it down on the desk, while I myself sat on the bed, looking across the room at the envelope which seemed all too light and insubstantial to bear the life-transforming news I so fervently hoped for. Finally I carried the letter into the bathroom; standing in front of the sink, I ripped open the envelope and learned that I'd been accepted.

Will never made it up for the May Day protest, but thousands of others did. The bombings in Cambodia and the subsequent killing of four students at Kent State threw high-test gasoline on the fire of the rebellion. What pissed me off, personally, was the announcement of grading modifications; because of the disruptions and the strike, undergraduates were to be given the option for each course of dropping, completing over the summer or taking a grade of "satisfactory" or "unsatisfactory" for work done so far. Even though I was en route to Harvard Law, I'd been busting ass all semester, and this seemed to cheapen my achievement.

That Saturday night I was walking back from Sterling, exultant at having at last finished a draft of my thesis. The clear spring night was fragrant with the smell of the freshly mowed grass. Strolling up High Street, I was overtaken by a dozen students running past me, shouting as they ran and scattered throughout the Old Campus. Hearing a thud on the lawn beside Saybrook, I saw the teargas canister just as the first fumes reached my nostrils. Half blinded, nose and mouth burning, I stumbled away from the expanding cloud of gas, clutching my briefcase to my chest. Someone took my arm and dragged me into Durfee, dumping me in a bathroom where I coughed and vomited in the shower, cursing the revolution, the counterrevolution and all the combatants.

My thesis makes for somewhat specialized reading, particularly the first twenty-two thousand words, in which I examine and eventually discount the idea of an organized slave conspiracy at Bear Track. In the penultimate section I advance a psychological solution for the historical problem. I see now that I projected Will and his father onto the figures of their ancestors, though I'm not sure that this bias necessarily invalidates the thesis.

His nearest white playmates being miles away, I wrote, John Savage passed much of his childhood with the black people of the plantation. John and the slave Clarence spent their days in the fields and on the rivers—I compared them to Huck Finn and the slave Jim—away from the social strictures of the big house to the point that Clarence became a kind of surrogate father for John. Even a man as thoroughly imbued with the idea of the inferiority of the Negro race as Elihu Savage must have felt jealous of the relationship between Clarence and John.

Shortly before the outbreak of the War between the States, when John Savage was going on fifteen years old, Elihu Savage sold Clarence's wife off to another plantation, a fairly drastic action even for the time and place. This event would surely have traumatized Clarence; he could not have been kindly disposed toward John's family, or to white people in general, and John could not have failed to notice this chill, which he would have blamed on his father. At about the same time Elihu tells him, to quote Binnie's diary, "it is time . . . to put away childish things and cultivate the society of his own people."

Within days or at most weeks of this break, war was declared, making Elihu Savage and other Delta planters, who were outnumbered nearly ten to one by their slaves, more nervous than ever for their safety vis-à-vis the newly restless Negro population. When John Savage blurted out word of a slave conspiracy, Elihu and his white neighbors must have been all too ready to believe, particularly since the alleged ringleader was a man with fresh cause to hate.

"Is it shameful of me to mistrust my brother's motives," asks Binnie Pilcher Savage in her diary. It's unfortunate that she was the only one, so far as we know, to raise this question; John Savage is an adolescent who is angry at both his real father and his surrogate father. Both have let him down, though he knows that the blame ultimately rests with the former. When his father criticizes his table manners his accumulated resentment and anger find expression—I proposed—in an Oedipal thought, instantly repressed and transformed. At that moment he wishes his father dead, and he attributes the wish to Clarence, who has reason to hate his father. Perhaps he is at that moment also angry enough at Clarence to place him in jeopardy, or perhaps he does not consider the implications of his statement for Clarence. Perhaps he once heard Clarence mutter some dark imprecation or overheard Clarence discussing the war and the prospect of emancipation. But when he is questioned about this wild accusation it seems likely that he panics and begins to embroider his lie in self-defense, to tell a story which answers the great archetypal narrative of southern life: "The slaves are going to rise up and murder us in our beds."

All the repressed and inchoate guilt of an unjust society found outlet in this single fear—they will do to us as we have done to them. Elihu Savage and his neighbors have been waiting all their lives for this mo-

ment, dreaming about it, like a tribe that lives in the shadow of a smoking volcano. Elihu was a small child living in South Carolina when Nat
Turner and his followers hacked up white women and children with
axes and bayonets. And thereafter he never slept as deep and righteous
a sleep as the man who is not surrounded in the dark by two hundred
souls in bondage.

Once John Savage had transmogrified his Oedipal struggle into the
collective myth of his people, events moved rapidly. We can only imagine his surprise at how thoroughly he was believed, his torment at the
inexorable chain of consequences—the long dark nights of the rest of
his days stalked by the ghosts of nine innocent black men. . . .

I went on at numbing length, but that is the gist of my thesis, which
was very well received by Professor Kaufman, my thesis adviser, who
was impressed enough to submit it to the *Yale Review*. And that's where
the trouble began. On the editorial board of the *Review* was a history
professor, whom I will call Jenkins. One of the more radical members of
the faculty, Jenkins had played an inflammatory role in the Panther proceedings, and he now turned his flamethrower on me.

Professor Kaufman called me into his office a few weeks before graduation to inform me that not only would the *Review* not be publishing
my thesis but also that his recommendation that I graduate with honors in history had been challenged. Jenkins had written a letter to the
chairman of the department in which he attacked me for marginalizing
the role of the slaves. A bearded gentleman of the Samuel Eliot Morison
school, Kaufman was deeply embarrassed as he fussed behind the paper
towers on his desk.

"Let me just say, Patrick, I am surprised and appalled by this unfortunate development, and I of course intend to defend you and your
scholarship all the way to Brewster's office." He took out his handkerchief and blew his nose, then opened the folded linen as if to read the
contents. "But I'm afraid that for the moment the question of your
graduating with honors is being put before the next full meeting of the
department."

Jenkins's central complaint, as contained in the letter Kaufman read
to me, was this: *Once again, a white scholar has placed white men at the*

center of the narrative. (I should mention in passing that Jenkins was no less white than myself.) An actual conspiracy involving Clarence and his fellows, Jenkins argued, was a far more plausible—and, of course, heroic—conclusion, based on the evidence.

Kaufman cleared his throat. "I am concerned that at the very least, the matter won't be resolved in time for graduation."

And he was right. I graduated summa cum laude, and I still have my Phi Beta Kappa key in my cuff link box, but the controversy over my thesis dragged on well into my first year at Harvard, when I finally received an apologetic letter from Kaufman. As a budding lawyer I thought about pressing my case. But illegal immigrants tend not to resort to courts of law to redress their grievances, and I still felt like an alien in the world I wished to occupy.

Like his polar opposite Cordell Savage, Jenkins was a man of righteous conviction, but I am a man of the middle, which is why I suppose I failed to follow up on this. While I am proud of my alma mater, my own small rebellion dating from that time consists of dropping each annual fund-raising solicitation into the wastebasket, a practice I have followed to this day. Maybe it was an early grounding in the concept of original sin which makes me susceptible to doubt as to my own convictions. Or maybe it is a sense of my own fraudulence that prevents me from asserting myself even when I believe I may be right. In fact, I had interpreted the evidence of the diaries according to my extratextual knowledge of Will's family, just as surely as Jenkins had decoded the same data on the basis of his political convictions. I take comfort in the belief that, in the end, history may be better served by those of us who are able to see through our own convictions than by the passionate believers.

Somehow the whole incident filled me with shame. What I'd expected to be the jewel in my undergraduate crown had, in effect, served only to tarnish it. On the other hand, I had done in three years in New Haven what usually required four; I had, along with my Yale diploma, acquired a first-class ticket to the world I so fervently desired. And I had, or so I imagined, polished the veneer which concealed from that world the base materials of my nature, and the darkest enigma of my being.

XVII

Amidst the bleached tribe at the Harvard Club with their larval winter faces, Taleesha cut a striking figure as she strode in to meet me, her height exaggerated by a dark halo of hair and tight pink hip huggers that flared out to meet a pair of red platform shoes. A few months short of receiving my degree, I was in New York interviewing with law firms. She was assistant to a vice president at one of the big record companies. Still a recent immigrant to the North, Taleesha found it amusing—or perhaps she defensively pretended to be amused—to integrate such a WASPs' nest. I hadn't seen her in three years.

"The job's great," she said, after we'd observed the pleasantries and ordered iced tea from a uniformed black waiter. He and Taleesha exchanged a fleeting look that seemed to me like a secret signal, and then suddenly she was back with me. "I've had a promotion and two raises in less than a year and I'm learning the business. Everybody at the company's fascinated that I quit singing. But I never really had that hunger. I'd rather be backstage, thanks."

"Like Will," I said, experimentally, dropping the taboo name. Though they were living apart—Will was still in Memphis—the terms of their separation were still not clear to me, and Will had been characteristically obscure on this subject.

She laughed mirthlessly. "No, not like Will. I don't need to pull every-body's strings. Will wants to set the world free, but strictly on his own terms. He can't make up his mind whether he wants to be a preacher or a politician or a rock star." Eyes bright with vexation, she seemed on the verge of an angry outburst. I watched as she paused to let the emotion subside. "Anyway, nobody's like Will," she said, in a subdued tone. "Even here I can't . . ." She let me complete the thought. "Everybody at my company worships him, thinks he's some kind of outlaw genius."

I waited, glancing up at the stuffed head of a wildebeest.

She sucked in a deep breath, preparing for a sprint. "It just got to be too much. All of it—Will's family, my family, the entourage, the South. His father leaving—that was the beginning of the end. Will started spending all his time trying to take care of his mother, but maybe that's my fault. I don't have much of a pattern for being a good wife. Then my brother getting killed in Vietnam. At first they told us he was missing and finally they sent him home in a box." Her face grew taut. "The god-damned box was stinking by the time it got to us. There we were crying and sweating in the church on an August day and trying to hold our breath with my brother stinking in his coffin."

She paused and smiled at the busboy as he filled our water glasses. "I don't know," she said once he'd gone. "Maybe we're still stuck some-where back there in history, somewhere between here and the Emanci-pation Proclamation."

"I thought Will lived in the moment," I said, playing dumb.

"He tries. That boy sure *does* wear it out. God, it was exhausting. Wake up in the afternoon and step over the bodies. Specially after we bought that old house outside town—it was like a transient hotel for musicians and dope fiends. I mean I could almost handle the drugs and the crazi-ness, the groupies and the hangers-on, even the disappearances. But honey, Memphis was wearing us down. You don't even know. Down there, white folks are still pissed off about sharing their precious lunch counters, let alone their blue-eyed sons. There'd be these remarks, you know, just loud enough so you could hear them, people spitting on the ground. Will would get in fights, if somebody says something he'll be right in their face, but it just plain wore me out." She glanced around the room. "Not that it's a fucking bed of roses up here in Yankeeland."

Indeed, it was difficult to make a case for great racial tolerance in the North; my Irish-Catholic brethren in South Boston would soon be setting fire to school buses and beating up Negroes with an ardor that would surely thrill and inspire the rednecks of Mississippi.

"So," she said impatiently, "have you seen the great man?"

"The mighty mogul?"

"Big guy, about like this." She held out her hands to indicate a paunch. "Smokes a big fat spliff. Best friend of Mick and B.B. and Elvis."

"You mean the guy who invented rock and roll?"

"With a little help from his friends."

"But not much."

"No. Mainly him."

Our sudden laughter dispelled the tension; both Taleesha and I realized, I think, that we were and likely always would be caught up in his powerful gravitational field.

When I was in law school, he always invited me to the shows when he came through Boston with Sam and Dave or Bobby Blue Bland. Once he took me backstage when the Rolling Stones came to Boston. I tried not to let myself mind the fact that he was sometimes barely there with me, his mind already racing ahead to the next concert, the next act he would sign, the record he was about to produce.

I think he appreciated me as a foil; he tried to shock me once by saying that Lester Holmes had shot someone in New Orleans and that he paid off Jim Garrison, the notorious district attorney, to quash the indictment. Relating this, he grinned across the table of a club in Cambridge, eager for my reaction. Whether it was true or not, he wanted to challenge my Ivy League law student worldview. He told me about having bags of cash delivered to disc jockeys, record company executives and indie promoters. "But hell," he said, "I come by it honestly. One of my earliest memories is being in the car with Cordell when he drove to an abandoned construction site with a suitcase stuffed with small bills."

Invariably there was a girl, some pale, longhaired waif or more often an African queen, whose name he could scarcely remember. He was constantly gobbling handfuls of pills—"feeding the beast," he called it.

One night he arrived at my apartment with a musician named Stevie Ray Vaughn and another guy, who pointed a pistol at me and then threatened to jump out the window. On another occasion I bailed him out of jail after he had punched a security guard and busted up assorted furniture at the Ritz-Carlton; he'd been asked to leave because of his flamboyant disregard of their dress code, and as I drove him back to my place he raved on about the great unfinished, unwashed revolution, about buying the damned hotel and showing the bastards. A few months before my lunch with Taleesha he was back at the Ritz-Carlton, his previous visit apparently forgiven.

I arrived that night to find a party in progress, a half-dozen figures lurking within the smoky gloom. Will was on the phone in the living room, a stunningly pale and lanky blonde creature draped on his shoulder. How he could hear anything above the music I can't imagine. The power source of the gathering was a pile of white powder on the glass coffee table; one by one the revelers knelt down at this altar and partook, as Stubblefield obligingly held their long locks back behind their heads. Will finally lifted himself from the couch and, still attached to the girl, lumbered over to embrace me. Though he was clearly pleased to see me, I also sensed that, given his state of mind, we might as well have been in two different cities. Not bothering to introduce his companion, he offered me a hit on his joint and then pointed out several of the males in the room, members of a then-popular band. I took the joint, but declined the offer to kneel down at the table.

He frowned. "Are you judging me?"

"I'm not judging you."

"Here I invite you to my party and you won't accept my hospitality."

"I'd just rather not," I said. "That's all."

The benevolent glaze in his eyes had suddenly given way to a menacing intensity.

"You've got to learn to trust me," he said ominously. "You think I'm the devil, trying to tempt you in the desert, or something?"

One of the guys in the band came over and held out a rolled hundred-dollar bill, tinged with blood, which he had just extracted from his nostril.

"Patrick doesn't do drugs," Will said, by way of introduction. Rubbing his nose and sniffling ostentatiously, his guest regarded me with amazement, as though Will had just identified me as a hermaphrodite.

Fortunately, at that moment Stubblefield called Will to the phone.

Compensating for my squeamishness about the cocaine, I smoked the rest of Will's joint while Annalina, his companion, quizzed me about our friendship.

The bass player, hearing that I was a law student, came over to ask my advice about certain fine points of legal practice. "Let's say you throw something out of your car window," he proposed. "I mean, how can they say whether it's yours or not?"

Soon I was engaged in a monologue touching on search and seizure and probable cause. This musician, I decided, was actually an excellent fellow. Will reappeared at intervals. I waved from the couch, eager to show him what a grand time I was having.

Later I found myself standing in front of a bathroom mirror, staring at my own face, which seemed unfamiliar, trying to reclaim it. Stumbling out, I took a wrong turn and ended up in a bedroom. I thought it would behoove me to rest for a few minutes to regain my edge. I don't know how long I'd been lying there when I suddenly realized Annalina was sitting on the bed beside me, stroking my forehead.

"That better," she asked. Standing up, she stepped out of her jeans and shucked her T-shirt.

"Wait a minute," I said, as she straddled me and began to unzip my jeans. "Aren't you Will's girlfriend?"

She shrugged. "He told me to take care of you."

"Are you sure?" I said, reaching down to stop her hands. "I mean, are you sure this is what he meant?"

"He said I should ball you," she replied matter-of-factly. "He said you needed it."

I pondered this as she unpeeled my jeans. "Do you *ball* Will?"

"When he's in the mood," she said, lying down beside me. "Actually I've only known him since Thursday."

At the start, I was too amazed to assist or resist. But I was removed enough from my own body to simply observe as it seemed to respond

THE LAST OF THE SAVAGES

and, then, to perform with a will of its own. Under the mounting influence of undeniable physical pleasure I lost my self-consciousness and
rejoined my body as it merged with Annalina's, surrendering to the moment and then actively participating until I dimly heard her say, "Whoa,
Mr. Stallion," even as she bucked harder beneath me.

Afterward, she retrieved a joint from her jeans and rejoined me on
the bed. "Will said you were probably a virgin. But, hey, I never would've
guessed it."

"Jesus," I said. "What else did he say?"

She shrugged. "What's with you guys anyway?"

"What do you mean," I asked, after taking a hit off the joint.

"I don't know. It just seems a little weird. I mean, maybe you guys
should sit down and talk."

A glazed look of recognition crossed Will's face as I rejoined the party
with an air of cocky modesty, but I left soon afterward to try to salvage
some portion of the coming academic day, and we never did talk about
Annalina, or that night.

Will was off in Memphis, or Muscle Shoals or Managua, when I attended our fifth reunion, though of course technically he was not a
member of the class. Matson was still teaching English, still a housemaster, a less romantic figure than I remembered—slightly ludicrous
now in the same bow ties and English country tweeds that had once
seemed so sportif, speaking in the same convoluted locutions that had
once been so charming. I was nervous about seeing him—our last
meeting had not been a thoroughly happy encounter, but to my surprise he was effusive in his greetings. "We expect you to be nothing less
than the next Oliver Wendell Holmes," he declaimed. "Still finding time
for your poetry, I hope."

I mumbled something about keeping my hand in. As I had drifted
away from Yale's English department to history I stopped sending him
poems and essays, partly because of the strangeness of his visit to New
Haven, and partly because I felt I was betraying youthful ideals of which
he was the executor. I felt that embarrassment still, simultaneous with a

feeling of condescension. Having finished my second year at Harvard Law, I imagined myself to be part of the wider world from which Matson had sought shelter. I was more than a little smug.

Had I attended my twenty-fifth reunion a few years ago, I might have looked at myself from the perspective of youth and found I was not quite the giant I might have hoped to become, back when everything seemed possible. But as a scholarship boy five years out of prep school I was by no means displeased with myself, which was one reason I had gone to the reunion in the first place—to demonstrate that I was making good on my promise.

At the cocktail reception, I felt obliged to come clean with Matson about the incident with Lollie Baker. "I was in the closet that night when you came in," I confessed. "The girl, the, uh, young lady was with me, not Will."

I wanted to shock him. I wanted him to know that I wasn't the person he took me to be.

He touched his glass to mine and winked. "I know," he said, his pink face beaming. "I knew it then, my boy."

If I'd been a man at that moment, instead of a lawyer manqué, I would have decked him.

Will grew larger in every sense—fatter, richer, more successful. He founded his own label, and eventually branched out to the white artists who were influenced by his black artists—this despite his oft-quoted remark that white boys just couldn't sing the blues. He bought his first private jet, helped bankroll and organize the abortive presidential campaign of George McGovern and later threw benefit concerts for Jimmy Carter. And, to the despair of his accountant, he became a devotee of the Dalai Lama, whom he followed around the globe. In Will's mind this was all part of the same plan.

His fame was not broad, and he took pains to stay out of the spotlight, but those who were truly famous often prided themselves on their acquaintance with Will Savage and spoke knowingly of his fortune, his excesses, his influence and his genius. Once he took me to a party given by an English lord in a townhouse on the Upper West Side. Everyone wanted to meet the rock stars; all the rock stars wanted to meet Will. While supplicants and well-wishers surged in and out, Will sat in the lotus position in the middle of the Persian carpet in an unfurnished parlor. Finally Mick Jagger arrived, slouching in a corner and pouting through that mouth which looked like a reptile sewed on his face, lethally bored until someone told him Will was in the next room.

While many of the new heroes of show business and rock and roll had utter faith in the efficacy of Will's benediction, old-style tycoons and entrepreneurs were also grudgingly respectful of what they took to be Will's canny discovery of a new vein of wealth. *Fortune* devoted two pages to his empire. He remained more interesting than anyone I'd ever met, and he was still two steps ahead of his demons in the midseventies—no small feat in itself.

Will and I never discussed his father. I didn't tell him, for instance, that Cordell had sent me an alligator wallet from Asprey's when I graduated from Yale. By all reports he had prospered in his new home. Having left all of his fortune but for a hundred-thousand-dollar grubstake to his ex-wife, he had proceeded to accumulate another by somehow managing to make himself the synapse between large bodies of international capital and commerce. Will, who still refused to see or speak to his father, insisted that arms dealing was at the center of his activities and sometimes attributed his success to the Bohemian Grove Club, a semi-secret society of movers and shakers who periodically met at their retreat north of San Francisco to dance naked and perform pagan rites amidst the redwoods. Certainly Will had his sources. Cordell's name came up in connection with a case I handled involving the transfer of funds to overthrow Allende in Chile; later, I would hear him linked with the Rothschilds and Niarchos in perfectly legitimate capacities. Throughout these years we exchanged Christmas cards, and once, while taking a break from Torts or Contracts in the law library, I came across a picture in *Town and Country* of a beaming Cordell and an anxious Cheryl with Prince Philip at Ascot.

*   *   *

The summer of my graduation from law school I took my first trip to Europe, previous breaks having been devoted to earning my tuition. I was almost relieved when I failed to land one of the prestigious but poorly paid federal clerkships. I was tired of eating TV dinners in a tiny cell without TV. All along, the law for me had been a kind of airship—a shiny vehicle of upward social mobility. In August I would begin working for a white-shoe firm in downtown New York. In the meantime, I finally assayed the pilgrimage to the Old World that most of my peers had been making for years.

Though I stayed in a damp, fusty-smelling hotel staffed by furtive subcontinentals, though the city that summer was plagued with brown-outs and intermittent phone service, I felt at home in London. I bought a stout umbrella and sauntered Matson-like through the Georgian streets of Mayfair. In my tweed driving cap I walked the gaudy length of the King's Road, half expecting to see Will among those I thought of as his tribesmen, and trudged dutifully through the British Museum. The day before I was to leave for Paris, I called Cordell Savage, having thought about it all week.

It took more than an hour to get a connection; after being disconnected once and auditioned by three successive secretaries, I was about to hang up when a piercing squawk came over the wire. It wasn't until I heard Cordell's voice that I recognized the duck call. "Is this Patrick Keane, Bachelor of Arts, Member of the Bar, late of New Haven and Cambridge?"

I told him I hadn't actually passed the bar yet. When he heard I was leaving London the next day he chastised me for not calling earlier and insisted I come for dinner that night.

Arriving in Eaton Square promptly at seven-thirty, I was greeted by a butler who led me to a room which exactly answered my notion of a grand London townhouse library, except for the tattered Confederate flag over the mantel where one would have expected the Gainsborough portrait. Cordell appeared as I was examining the volumes in the shelves. Still daunting, he hadn't aged since that Thanksgiving almost eight years before. I had almost forgotten how aggressive his casual scrutiny seemed, though he shook my hand warmly.

"I read your thesis," he said, after the butler had brought us our drinks and I had capsulized my own recent history.

I was shocked. I certainly hadn't sent him a copy. "What did you think?" I managed to mutter, running my fingers nervously over the etched ridges of the crystal tumbler.

"Crock of shit," he said cheerfully. "I think maybe you should have been a novelist instead of a lawyer. Basing everything on the scribblings of old Binnie Pilcher and Dr. Freud. I knew Binnie. She was crackers, completely out of her tree. One story crazier than the next."

"She would've been ancient by then."

"Older than the flood." Then, after we had complained about English food, and the weather: "Have you seen Will?"

"I see him from time to time."

"And?"

"He's doing well," I ventured. "He's got a new distribution deal for his record—"

"I know all about his career," he snapped. "I'm not without my sources, and any idiot can hire a clipping service. I'm asking you about his soul."

This was not a word you expected to hear on Cordell Savage's lips, and I almost said so. I was inclined to the belief that he'd relinquished his claim to this kind of intimacy when he left Memphis with his eldest son's fiancée. But I'd made my pact with Cordell many years before.

"His vices and virtues are almost indistinguishable," I offered. "The qualities that have made him so successful will probably kill him." I was deliberately striving for effect. "He's driven in every sense of the word."

"And you blame me," he said without inflection.

I shrugged and took a sip of my scotch. I didn't particularly like scotch, which was one of the reasons I drank it—this practice keeping me temperate. "You have more in common than he'd care to admit."

"Let me tell you something. My eldest, whom you met—I guess I favored him. I don't say I was right. But there you have it. He was everybody's golden boy. I'm afraid I placed too many of my hopes on his shoulders. I expected him to carry on the family. You never expect you'll have to bury your own children. I hope you'll never know that pain, Patrick." He took a deep breath.

"The youngest—well, I was all wrapped up in business when A.J. came along, and his mother raised and spoiled him and turned him away from me. I don't know that the genes were at their strongest proof in his case. But Will . . ." He paused and sipped his drink. "I knew Will was bright. Real bright. And he had that orneriness you often see in second sons, the irritation at finding that someone else had come down the road before him, having to compete for the love of parents that a first child takes for granted."

He emptied his drink and pulled on a cord which summoned the butler. Once the servant had replenished his glass and left us alone, he resumed. "I wanted him to be his own man. And to do that he had to overthrow me. That's the way it's always been with fathers and sons, even before all this youth revolution stuff, before we'd ever heard of a generation gap. Isn't that right? Can you tell me honestly that that's not part of your story—of who you are now? Didn't you sit down one day when you were a boy and disown your father in your heart?"

I drained my own drink to cover the rising blush.

"But you didn't have to pull very hard against your old man," he continued. "You're not really angry with him anymore. He's not as big a tyrant as me and that will limit how hard you push yourself and how far you go. I made it easy for Will by making it hard on him. Made it easy for him to hate me. Will's a champion, a producer. It's the same as with bird dogs. You got your spaniels, your setters and your pointers. Your spaniel works close, you keep him within ten, twenty yards. He's a good, hardworking dog. He'll find anything in that range and point it or flush it, depending on how he's trained. A spaniel will make a pet, you can let him indoors, let the women and children fuss over him and not ruin him for birds necessarily. He wants to please you; he finds the birds for you. Then you've got your setter, who likes to work farther out, range around the countryside a little, cover some ground. Some people keep setters in the house, some kennel 'em."

The butler returned with fresh drinks, spiriting our old glasses away on his silver tray.

"Then you got your pointer. You don't want to coddle him and he doesn't want to be coddled. You don't bring him in the house. He's a working dog. He lives to hunt. You need a horse to keep up with a pointer. Your pointer's a wide ranger, works way out there, sometimes that dog is working half an hour's ride ahead of you. But he finds twice the birds the other dogs will, and he'll hold a point all day if he has to. But, make no mistake, he's doing it for himself. He doesn't give a shit what you want. He's working, buddy. And Will's like that. A.J, I knew he'd stay close to home. And Elbridge could do it all, he was an all-purpose champion. Or at least we thought he was. But Will's got that restless drive. Will, you wouldn't want him sleeping in the bed with you. I was tough as hell on the little bastard and it worked. I gave him that drive."

I looked up at him, amazed at this rationalization.

"You think I'm bullshitting you?"

"You wouldn't ask if you didn't have some doubts yourself," I finally answered.

"You'll make a fine fucking little lawyer," he said, smiling.

It was too easy, his little retrospective, and I was not about to absolve him on Will's behalf. "I don't think you need to explain yourself to me."

"What about his love life," Cordell asked. "I suppose he's just fucking like a tomcat, now that he's free of that . . ." In deference to my sensibilities, I think, he left the sentence dangling. "Free love and all that? Or will he settle down someday?"

"I doubt his views on marriage are very favorable." I hadn't exactly intended to sass him—as Cordell might have put it—but we both realized this was exactly what I'd done.

"I'm afraid his mother and I were ill suited from the start," he said. "Could be I cared too much about her family—what she represented to me was somehow more real than she was. When we finally got to know each other . . ." He paused and looked into his ice cubes. "But if Will were to ask me now I'd tell him that marital bliss is an attainable state."

It occurred to me that in his present bliss Cordell might be indebted to Will and his kind for unlocking the shackles of social convention; that he was, in a way, the surreptitious beneficiary of a revolt which he stridently opposed. But before I could pose the question he said, "Well,

I don't suppose you have to be married these days to have children." So, he was thinking dynastically. Breach or no breach, he wanted to continue his line, and Will was his only chance. He was afraid that Will would be the last of the Savages. I wondered if Will might deliberately hold the bloodline hostage so long as his father was alive.

I was not courageous enough to tell Cordell that I thought Will was still in love with Taleesha, that he would always be in love with Taleesha, and at that moment, fortunately, the first of the guests was announced. We went out to greet them. As I was introduced to the marquis and his wife, Cheryl appeared at the top of the curving staircase, arresting the conversation.

"Hello, darling," Cordell called. She started down the stairs, watching the hem of her long dress and stepping tentatively from one high platform heel to the next, like a country girl not quite used to shoes. If she intended a glamorous Hollywood entrance, she didn't pull it off—but she was more beautiful than ever. She greeted me shyly and looked down at the carpet when Cordell reminded her that we had met. I wondered if she remembered our morbid little grope in Memphis. In addition to my chagrin, I was prepared to feel disdain, but instead I felt sorry for her. She did not belong there, in that mansion or on that continent, and she seemed to know it even if her husband did not.

At dinner Cheryl was cautious and polite. As if nervous of making some faux pas, she spoke little, mainly answering queries lobbed her way by her husband. "I was just telling Bartholomew how much you love to ride. Isn't that right, honey?"

Certainly the company was daunting to me, as it must have been to her—an expatriate American merchant banker, a Conservative MP, a playwright, their bejeweled and entitled wives. A pretty, irreverent blonde from Tennessee studying at the London School of Economics was provided as my dinner partner, and in attending to her I nearly forgot about my hostess until dessert, when Cordell tapped a glass with his fork and announced that his wife would perform for the company.

"No way," I murmured.

"Oh, yes," said my amused companion. "It's a regular little feature of dining chez Savage."

Cheryl withdrew, emerging several minutes later from behind a gold-leaf screen in what looked like the same outfit I'd seen in Memphis, twirling a baton which was on fire, flaming at either end. Cordell's recorded voice boomed forth over hidden speakers: "Ladies and gentlemen, Cheryl Savage, former runner-up Miss Kentucky, performs with the fire baton."

A burst of music followed, a familiar patriotic march—Sousa, perhaps—which only increased my sudden discomfort at being an American. Cheryl's diffidence and nervousness were gone. She circled the table, high stepping in her spangled boots and twirling the baton with supreme confidence, occasionally flinging it to within inches of the frescoed ceiling and then gracefully snatching it out of midair. Cordell nodded along to the thumping beat, smiling slyly. It was impossible for me to tell whether he was truly proud of her or whether he was having a laugh at her expense and ours. The other guests watched with frightened, rigid smiles.

When the performance was finally over, a faint sprinkle of applause soon gave way to an awful silence. "That was just wonderful, darling," said Cordell, raising a glass of champagne to his child bride. Suddenly self-conscious again, she curtsied and disappeared behind the screen.

"Well," said the marchioness to my left, who could think of nothing more to add.

"Indeed," said the MP. "Quite remarkable."

I took my dinner companion back to her flat in Kensington, and to my astonishment she invited me to stay. Perhaps I shouldn't have been surprised, it was the seventies after all, and love was still rumored to be free. Or so I'd heard. For me the carnal arena was anything but carefree.

She didn't give up easily, but like her forebears she was gracious in defeat. Such was her southern grace she nearly had me convinced that failure was the norm rather than the exception, that in fact it was pretty unusual, practically unheard of, for a man to achieve and sustain an erection which culminated in an ejaculation inside an actual living woman.

Lying in bed beside me as the rain fell in the garden behind her flat, she steered conversation to our real point of contact, asking me about Will. She'd known the family all her life, and when she arrived in London Cordell had taken her under his wing, inviting her to dinners and the theater. When I asked if his attentions were entirely innocent, she laughed.

"No, it's nothing like that. It's a southern thing. He's just taking care of me. Besides, he's madly in love with Cheryl."

The exhibition I had seen again tonight, she claimed, was also uncalculated. He was actually inordinately proud of her baton-twirling abilities. His friends and business associates indulged it as one of his milder eccentricities; still, I was inclined to the theory that he staged Cheryl's performances as an elaborate way of pulling their legs, as a way of asserting control by throwing everyone off balance. As for Cheryl, I was told, she tried hard to fit in but was happiest in the company of her hairdresser, who traveled everywhere with her.

"He's not a bad man," my companion said. "Look at what he had to live down." When I asked what that might be, she picked up the story that I'd first heard in the lobby of the Peabody one New Year's Eve.

When Cordell was twelve, his mother had been charged with killing her husband, Will's grandfather, who was found dead in his bedroom with a chest full of birdshot. According to this version she was acquitted on grounds of self-defense, her husband being a notorious alcoholic and bully. In Memphis and up and down the Delta, however, it was whispered that the son, rather than the mother, had pulled the trigger. She said, as if in partial explanation, "Delta people are kind of . . . extreme."

Lying awake beside her that night, worried about making my flight the next day, I kept thinking about that long-ago morning in the duck blind, Will Savage silhouetted against a dawning pink sky, holding a shotgun aimed at his father's head. And that is the image that sprung to mind when the police arrived at my office to question me about Felson. I was afraid that Will had finally pulled the trigger.

XVIII

The shabby glamour of New York seemed all the more poignant to me as the city shambled toward bankruptcy. Having at last arrived in the capital of fresh starts, I worried that I might be too late. And yet I was reassured whenever I walked into the marble lobby of my downtown office, when I looked out from the thirty-second floor at the massed Constructivist mountains of the cityscape. On those rare weekends when I was not in the office, while others were strolling in Central Park, I walked up the limestone canyon of Park Avenue, peering into the emerald-canopied portals of metropolitan wealth, imagining my future. It was comforting to think that the city, like the edifice of the law, would survive me and all of its puny tenants. Perhaps this is why Will never liked New York—because he couldn't dominate it. In any event I was only fitfully aware of my surroundings, regularly billing fourteen and sixteen hours a day. I gained a certain renown in the downtown legal community for once billing twenty-five hours in a single day: I had woken up in New York and flown to California, thereby adding three hours to the working day. Almost by accident, I found myself on the way to being a corporate lawyer. And while it had always been a lucrative field—more akin to investment banking than to the drama of litigation—it became absurdly rewarding in the eighties, the wave of mergers and acquisitions showering us with fees and, eventually, with percentages of billion-dollar deals. But that was later.

If the city itself seemed luminous at times, my own life was as drab as my standard gray suit. Opera once a month and the museums furnished me with all the beauty I allowed myself. Except for the occasional drink at the Yale or Harvard Club, mine was the New York of solitary coffee-shop meals and Laundromats and subway commutes. While waiting for my Yorkville lease to begin I took a dingy room in the Van Cortlandt Hotel on Broadway, one of the dozens of flyblown weekly rate hostels that used to be such a prominent feature of Manhattan, populated by those either at the beginning of their adventures in the great metropolis or near the ragged end. I shared the bathroom down the hall with a small-time pot dealer who introduced himself as an anarchist; a male dancer; and an alcoholic silent-film screen star who shambled up and down the hall in floppy slippers and a terry bathrobe cursing us all for befouling the WC. Once a month she painted and combed herself into a brittle semblance of her lost beauty and posed in the lobby to wait for the limo sent by a former producer who was either kind enough or sentimental enough to dine with her.

The Van Cortlandt was about as close as I got to bohemia. I soon moved to a one-bedroom walk-up in the far-east Eighties, several critical blocks removed from the Côtes d'Or of my aspiration between Fifth and Park. I continued to go home for holidays, but it was more than a year before I felt established enough to invite my mother down for a visit. She insisted on taking the bus; it was the easiest and the cheapest, she said. So I met her at the Port Authority—not exactly the gateway to the great city that one wished for one's mother. The homeless and hopeless—then called bums—had not yet become general throughout the city, and the bus terminal was one of their traditional sanctuaries. Panhandlers were epidemic, the narrow end of a wedge of coercive enterprise in that sinister place. After a year, I had developed the gruff defensive street manner of a New Yorker. I would sometimes give out spare change on the subway, but now, in the Port Authority, it seemed smartest not to look at anyone, or acknowledge any request. So I refused to turn when a small, bundled figure edged into my peripheral vision and said, "Can you spare some change? I'm hungry." The voice sounded pathetic, but I had already made up my mind. He continued to hover beside me long after I had shaken my head.

Finally the bus arrived; my mother waved from the window. Clearly she had befriended the bus driver, with whom she exchanged a farewell, holding up the other passengers before climbing down to enfold me in her large embrace and claim her suitcase. "Look at you," she said. I expected her to say how big I'd grown, and I think she was on the verge of it when she caught herself.

At that moment the little man drifted up again. "I'm hungry. Could you—"

"No, we couldn't," I said, in a tone that surprised even me. I'd like to think my protective instincts were overengaged on behalf of my mother. She looked at the man and then back at me, stunned at my vehemence. I glanced over at the mendicant with a scowl I hoped would seal my refusal and saw him through my mother's eyes: a wizened little man with the face of a bewildered child, clearly retarded and now scared, clutching to his chest a shopping bag overflowing with rags and scraps of paper. When I turned back to my mother her expression wrenched my heart. I saw that she was ashamed of me. She was wondering how she could have raised a son who could respond so heartlessly and brutally to one of God's needy creatures. I think she was too surprised to reach into her own purse, and I was too mortified to repair the damage by giving the poor bastard some money. I took her by the arm and led her away. "A lot of these guys are just con artists," I said. "You've got to be careful."

My mother never mentioned the incident, but it shadowed her visit to the city. My worldliness was abruptly discredited. The slightly imperious manner I had been cultivating now seemed merely rude. My budding command over waitresses and cabdrivers was gone, though until that moment in the bus terminal I was hardly aware of having become so thoroughly condescending.

She stayed in my bedroom while I slept on the couch, and her company made me realize not only how lonely I had been but also how she must have felt after I had gone away. I'd felt homesick before, when I first went to school, but never quite so acutely as I did that night in my New York apartment with my mother sleeping in the next room. Eager to show her I was a better man than I had seemed, I tried hard to make her trip a success. For once I was not too sophisticated for a trip to the Statue of Liberty or a meal at Lüchows. And I would like to believe I shed a layer of callowness back then, sloughed it off like a snakeskin. Back at the Port Authority two days later, sending her off, I blushed when she said, "I'm proud of you."

And now I remember a curious fact—that Felson was drudging in the office on the Saturday I took my mother for a tour, and though I barely knew him she would often ask after him when I called home. "And how's that nice Jewish man in your office?" And she would always quiz me about Will, though she had yet to meet him.

Busy as I was, I did my best to keep in touch. Will usually called when he was in town—with the Dalai Lama, with Eric Clapton. Though he had a team of lawyers in Memphis, he often consulted me on questions of finance. In '79, when he needed capital to expand, I arranged a private placement, and much later, when he was spinning into bankruptcy, I arranged the sale of his catalog to one of the major labels.

Unofficially, I kept up through Taleesha, with whom I dined once or twice a month. I felt a sense of custodial responsibility—as if I were keeping her safe for Will—as well as a kind of vicarious thrill of possession: I enjoyed the veiled glances on the street, the secret stares and whispered conversations in restaurants. She took me to the Cellar and Mikels, the West Side hangouts of the black middle class in those years. Flirting with the taboo of miscegenation, I imagined myself in touch with the whole terrible history of race, until Taleesha herself disabused me of my illusion. "You have no idea what you're talking about," she would say, when I blithely ventured too far across an indiscernible border. She did not suffer wise men gladly.

When I think of Taleesha in those days I see her looking out past my shoulder. She always seemed to be scanning the room; the sound of the front door in a restaurant or a bar never failed to draw her attention. She had several good reasons to be in New York, but one of them was her mother, whose last postcard had come from the city many years before. On the street, she was always searching the faces of the onrushing crowd, although I don't think she was aware of it.

Taleesha and Will talked almost every day; theirs was a curiously intimate and fond separation. They replayed their failures in exquisite detail, Will blaming himself, Taleesha insisting it was really her fault, though I actually think they were able to stay in love partly because they considered their marriage a casualty of larger forces. The world they lived in was not good enough for their love. And so they mourned their separation, and yet at a distance of a thousand miles they attained a new and previously unimaginable intimacy, comforting each other over their mutual loss by insisting that they still had each other. Free from the erosion of daily life, they were free to paint each other as romantic figures in a great love story. As if in anticipation of that unspecified day when they would be gloriously reunited Will kept her apprised of the most minute details of his business life, and was at any given moment aware of her location in the city. I discovered this one night when he called her at the restaurant where we were having dinner. I thought it must be an emergency, but he just wanted to chat with us, serially, while we leaned our elbows on the reservations book and the captain glared at us through fastidious wire rims.

"He likes to know where I am," she explained when we were back at the table.

"Don't you find that a little inhibiting," I asked.

"But I also find it sweet. If I ever decide to disappear, don't worry, I know how. It's a little gift that runs in the family. Maternal side."

To lighten the mood, or so I thought, I reminded her of the first time we met, or rather the first night I saw her, leaning motionless against the wall at Lester's house amidst the dervishes. "Will went over and asked you to dance, and you slapped him. I've always wondered—what did he say?"

At first she looked blank. I thought she had forgotten until her eyes suddenly brimmed with tears. I handed her my handkerchief. "Goddamnit," she murmured, then regained her composure. "He told me . . . his name was Will Savage and he said he was going to marry me someday."

"Why don't you just get back together," I suggested. "Save on long distance."

She dabbed at her eyes with her napkin. "He's a big asshole is why, which you should know as well as I do. And he's impossible to live with," she said. "I don't know who could put up with it."

"Well, then, maybe you should just divorce him and get on with your life."

"On the other hand," she said, "after you've lived with Will, everyone else seems kind of . . ." She shrugged, leaving me to supply the diminutives.

"Oh, thanks," I complained. "As your date—"

"Oh, come on, Patrick. We're both here because we love that big bastard. Don't start acting gallant on me because neither one of us believes it."

Several years after my visit to London the big bastard came through New York. Through my firm he engaged my services for the afternoon for what was billed as a meeting with his record company. Shortly after lunch he picked me up in a chauffeured Rolls. Only in girth did he resemble a tycoon. The gaunt beauty of his youth had dissipated. His face was puffy, his eyes like twin patches of troubled sky glimpsed through a wild thicket of beard and hair.

"Happy as I am to see you," I said, "you must be aware that I don't know anything about the record business."

"All you need to know is that it's about as venal and corrupt as Louisiana politics. And bear in mind that attorney-client privilege will absolve you of having to testify about anything you might see or hear today."

"You're not planning on killing anyone, are you?"

"If I told you that," he said, "wouldn't it make you an accessory before the fact?"

The office suite which was our destination belonged, according to the plaque on the door, to the executive vice president of the label. The secretary was clearly daunted as she announced Will's arrival. A moment later her boss came bounding out of an inner office—an eager, fuzzy man in a leisure suit. At least I think that's what it was—a beige two-piece garment of dubious cut over a white silk shirt open to the sternum. He moved as if to hug Will, then seemed to realize that this was not a good idea. Will was forbidding at the best of times, but he seemed particularly austere at this moment.

Stepping back as if to get a better look at the legend, the executive held open his arms in an expansive welcome: "Will, Will, Will," he said. "What are you, visiting from Nashville? Memphis, I mean. It's Memphis, right? Great to see you. Been a long time, man. Too long. You should have called."

"Tony, Patrick Keane, my attorney."

Tony didn't appear to notice that he had not been accorded the courtesy of a surname. In fact he seemed like one of those men—I associated them with the entertainment industry—who didn't have a surname and considered the whole notion of family names hopelessly Old World and formal. I held out my hand, and this, too, apparently struck him as a quaint custom.

"You want a drink, a joint, a snort," Tony asked, once we'd settled into his shiny, bland office, decorated primarily with gold records and framed photographs of smiling Tony with his arm around sneering or dazed-looking rock musicians. "Anything you want just name it."

Will had not taken a seat; now he walked over behind Tony's desk and grabbed hold of his fuzzy muttonchop sideburn, yanking him rudely to his feet. "What I want, *Tony,* is to throw you out this fucking window."

"Will, hey, buddy, what's with the negative vibes?"

"*Vibes?*"

"This bad energy, man."

"Well, let's think about this, *Tony.*"

I was nervous, though I must say I admired the way Will had of turning his antagonist's name into an obscenity.

"You've been hitting on my wife is what, making life miserable for her around here. My *wife,* you understand? You've been telling her if she doesn't fuck you her career is dead. You should think twice about using that word *dead,* Tony. It gives crazy motherfuckers like me ideas. Do you know what we do where I come from to guys who fuck with our wives?"

"Will, what'd I do? Hey, a little kidding around, maybe. A little inno-cent flirting." Being held at an odd angle by his sideburn didn't make it easy for Tony to sound casual. "That's all it was, I swear. What can I say—she's a good-looking woman. Just a little fun was all. A little kid-ding around."

"Are you saying my wife is a liar? I hope that's not what you're telling me, Tony."

Will gave the sideburn another yank.

"Will, I swear to God."

"You better swear to me, Tony. You better swear to me that from now on you treat my wife with the utmost respect."

"Absolutely."

"Because here's your choice," Will said, finally releasing him. "You hit on her one more time or make her unhappy in any way you'll wish I'd thrown you out this window. I'll follow you to the ends of the fucking earth. And if she even *suspects* we've had this conversation I'll make the renewal of my deal at this company contingent on your ass getting fired. So if you want to stay alive *and* employed I suggest you promote Talee-sha right on out of here."

As awkward as it was to witness this scene, I found myself unprofes-sionally entering into the spirit of things. Smiling blandly, I shook hands with the vice president as we were leaving. "Tony, a pleasure doing business." And in what I thought was a very stylish coda, I handed him my card. Accustomed to polite mediation between warring fac-tions, I was exhilarated to observe this raw conflict.

In the car, Will lit a joint the size of an Esplendido. "Was I was too subtle, counselor?"

Taking a hit on the joint, I said, "I don't think you can be too subtle with a guy like Tony."

"You're probably right."

Because it had been so long since I'd seen Will, I booked out for what was left of the afternoon, and we toured the bars in the Village, where Will seemed to be known. Taleesha was out of town, which fact had dic-tated the timing of Will's appointment with Tony. I wasn't sure what he'd done was wise, and it certainly wasn't diplomatic, but I was proud of him and after I'd had a little too much to drink I told him so. And when I was fairly certain that Will was drunk I described my visit to London. He asked few questions, though I sensed that he was eager for information. He was greatly diverted by the baton-twirling story.

"Is Cheryl still the creamiest piece of cheese from the state of Kentucky," he asked. "Or was she one of those early bloomers?"

"Pretty as ever," I said.

"Shit," he said. "I've been looking forward to the day my old man wakes up in Belgravia and looks across the Porthault pillowcases to discover that his cheerleader's done frumped up on him."

Much later, when we were both very drunk indeed, he rose up suddenly from the bottom of some deep well of reverie. "Have you ever heard the expression, Patrick—'Revenge is a dish best served cold'? Let's drink to that one." And I raised my glass, imagining that he was referring to the loathsome Tony.

Will proposed another toast. "Jessie Petit always says 'What goes over the devil's backbone is boun' to pass under his stomach.'"

Cryptic as this was, it didn't occur to me until years later that he was thinking of his father.

Then we were in his limousine on our way to the Upper East Side. He wanted to show me a townhouse that had been owned by his mother's father. "He had a private railroad car he took all over the country . . . railroad track built underground . . . private spur that went right into his own basement. The old coot would roll right into his own house in his very own railroad car and scoop up a bottle from the wine cellar on his way upstairs." This seemed preposterously elegant, and I was all for seeing the house. Will had the limo driver prowl along 72nd Street and then 73rd, looking for the house. Finally he thought he recognized a limestone facade between Fifth and Park. Jumping out of the car, he ran up the steps and rang the doorbell.

"Will, it's two in the morning."

"Come on," he shouted from the steps. "We gotta see this."

The third-floor windows suddenly went bright. Drunk, I sprawled slackly in the limousine. "Let's go, Will. They're asleep. Will?"

But he wasn't about to abandon his quest. The police arrived, it seemed, within moments.

"Break down the door, officers," Will commanded.

"Had a few drinks, have we?"

Will explained to them about the railroad track. "It's still under there, it's gotta be. Wouldn't you like to see a fucking thing like that?" Standing on the doorstep waving his arms, he looked like one of those wild-eyed prophets such as you see in Washington Park.

"Pipe down, you fucking freak," said the smaller policeman.

"Pipe down yourself, fucking pig."

From my vantage in the car I couldn't follow the exact sequence of events, but it looked as if the smaller man shoved Will against the door and Will shoved back, sending him tumbling backward down the steps. The tall officer dropped Will with his billy club, at which point the fallen officer came back to kick him in the ribs. I leaped out of the car and started up the stairs, stopping on the first.

"You want some of this," asked the little guy, pausing in midkick to glance back at me.

"You want a five-million-dollar civil suit?" I said. "I'm his attorney."

A braver man might have thrown himself into the fray, but my remark had the intended effect. The big officer pulled Will to his feet and read him his rights while the little one handcuffed him and glared at me in my lawyerly pinstripes.

I was unable to make bail till the next morning. In addition to resisting arrest Will was charged with possession of marijuana, an ounce or so having been found in his pocket. He was subdued until we got in the car, at which point he began punching the seat in front of him, vowing to wreak havoc on the ruling order.

I was irritable with hangover. "You can't call a police officer a pig and expect to get a medal."

"No? You ever hear of the First Amendment?"

"Not my specialty."

"I can see that."

"We're not in Memphis anymore," I said, a little smugly—the adoptive New Yorker.

Not being a criminal attorney, I referred Will to a Yale classmate who'd studied at Fordham and served in the D.A.'s office. After his arraignment Will was allowed to return to Memphis; his lawyer informed me he hoped to plead down to misdemeanor possession, drawing a fine and six months' probation. But prison remained a possibility. He postponed the trial twice. And eventually, quite by accident, I found a way to make Will's legal problems disappear.

XIX

I t was one of those tropical, malodorous August evenings in the city
when I ran into Aaron Greeley for the first time in ten years. I was
sitting at the bar of the Yale Club waiting for a client when a hand
pressed my cooling, sweat-soaked shirt to my back. He looked much as
I remembered him from freshman year—a preppie prince who just
happened to be darker complected than most Yalies. He greeted me
warmly, and I was happy to pretend that we had parted on the best of
terms.

Aaron was now an assistant district attorney; after Yale he spent a
year working with Alabama sharecroppers before going to Columbia
Law. I wondered what happened to the rage and dogma of '70, when he
and his compatriots had busted up our senate meeting. But then, the
same might be asked about the country at large. It all seemed as far
away as Gettysburg and Shiloh. Will was the only person I knew who
hadn't changed—still charging the hill, waving the colors.

"What's happened with your poetry," Aaron asked.

"Now I write briefs." I paused. "And you were quoting Huey the last I
remember."

"Yeah, well . . ." He shrugged. "Working within the system these days.
Can I buy a fellow sellout a drink?"

We were still checking each other out, reading the signs. My suit was standard issue J. Press. But Aaron's double-breasted blue-suit-and-spread-collar-shirt combo seemed very racy to me at the time—too European to pass muster in my office—but he looked better in it than anybody I'd ever seen outside the pages of a magazine. This difference in style might have been imperceptible to most observers, but I wondered if after his walk on the wild side he had become comfortable enough to modify the hard won uniform of the preppie. Or maybe he suspected that within a few years, the tribal dress by which members of the eastern ruling class had recognized its members for decades would be mass marketed to the rest of America, would become just another style to pick off the rack.

"Married," Aaron asked.

"Not yet. You?"

"Having *way* too much fun, man."

Aaron said he was late for an appointment uptown, but insisted I come to a dinner party at his apartment the following week. "Just a few friends for spaghetti, no big deal." This must have been just before spaghetti became pasta. "Bring a date."

As it happened, both Aaron and Taleesha lived in the same thicket of postwar apartment towers around Lincoln Center.

Twenty minutes early as I staggered up out of the purgatorial subway tunnel at Columbus Circle, I dawdled up Broadway. Waiting at the light two blocks north, I noticed a kid I'd seen on the subway. Actually he might have been my age, but he wore tight jeans and cowboy boots, a T-shirt with a pack of Marlboros rolled up in the sleeve. He was regarding me with what seemed to be hostile intent, and my first thought, the instinct of a New Yorker, was to reach down to feel my wallet.

Then he smiled and held up a cigarette. "Got a light?"

I shook my head. He was a curious combination of thuggish and fastidious; his white shirt was immaculate, and his short hair looked like it had just been cut.

"How about a drink?"

I patted my pockets reflexively, not quite sure what I was doing, as if I might indeed have a drink stashed away on my person. Then I realized this was an invitation. "No thanks," I said, blushing. "I've got a date."

"Lucky guy," he said.

Stepping out into the street, I was nearly hit by a cab speeding up to make the light. The cabbie slammed on his brakes and hammered his horn. "You stupid shit," he screamed. I shrugged and jogged to the far corner, feeling incredibly foolish—like a tourist. When I looked back, the T-shirt waved. Suddenly I was struck by the ambiguity of the phrase "lucky guy." Indignant and shaken, I hurried up Broadway to Taleesha's building.

"He's really smart," I told Taleesha as we descended in the elevator from her apartment. "I think you'll really—"

"Is he by any chance *black*," she said. "Is that what you're *really* telling me, Patrick?" She took my chin in her fingers. "What kind of number are you running here?"

"No number," I said sheepishly. "I needed a date for dinner with my old roommate. I called you when Lollie Baker said she was busy."

Taleesha was on to me, but she laughed and agreed to go along for the ride. As an escort, she was eminently suitable, though I had to stand rigidly erect in order to be almost as tall as she was in her heels. A black man sauntering down Broadway turned as we passed and called: "Hey, baby, looking fine." And indeed she was—regal and unperturbed in a cream linen sundress, despite the wilting heat.

The dinner party consisted of five couples, several jugs of wine, disco music and spaghetti *bolognese*. At one point I saw Taleesha register a Marvin Gaye tune I happened to know Will had produced. "I love this song," said one of the women at the table, and I wondered if Taleesha would announce her marital connection. When she did not, I became suddenly proprietary.

"A friend of mine produced—"

But Taleesha cut me off. "You really shouldn't be serving this Gallo wine," she said to Aaron. "Haven't you ever heard of the United Farm Workers?" She seemed to have taken an immediate dislike to him.

"You're absolutely right." He stared at her with a barely perceptible smile. "However, it was brought by one of my guests, and I thought it would be rude to pour it down the sink."

"I'm sorry." Stacey Colchester, a pretty young intern from Aaron's office, hadn't said a word until that moment, and now she looked as if she were ready to cry. "I just completely forgot about the boycott."

"I always forget that stuff," I volunteered. "What I'm supposed to buy and not buy."

Taleesha looked at me and rolled her eyes; she might as well have said, *You're a wimp, Patrick.* But I couldn't help feeling solicitous of Stacey Colchester, the youngest and most demure member of the party, and wondering if she was Aaron's date, or just a friend. When she started to clear the dishes after dinner, I jumped up to help her. She was shy, but under cross-examination she revealed that she was from Marblehead, Massachusetts, that she had just graduated from Holyoke, that her father was indeed Judge Colchester of the Circuit Appeals Court, a jurist I had admired since law school. She didn't know Aaron very well but thought he was "like, a terrific guy."

"Like one, or is one?" This seemed clever until I said it, when it sounded merely mean-spirited.

"Oh, God, I sound like an idiot. It's just that I feel so much younger than everyone else and Aaron's my boss. Are you two good friends?"

"We met in New Haven," I said, employing the falsely modest euphemism for Yale. "He was my roommate."

"Doesn't he just think he's God's gift," said Taleesha later, when I was walking her back to her apartment. "Thinks he could walk from here to New Jersey without using the bridge."

First thing Monday morning Aaron called me at my office. "Listen," he said, "Taleesha isn't—I mean, you two aren't going out, are you? I mean, you're just friends, right?"

I laughed. "I didn't think you two exactly hit it off."

"She's definitely feisty," he said. "I don't normally go for black chicks."

"What about Stacey," I asked.

"Man, she's just an intern here. My date fell through, so I invited her at the last minute. Stacey's a good kid, but she's straight as a fucking arrow."

"Actually Taleesha's married to my friend Will Savage." I could hear resounding silence on the other end. After a sadistic pause, I added, "They're separated," then said I had to run to a meeting. I was uncomfortable with the whole situation, but I told him I would call Taleesha and feel her out.

She wasn't nearly as dismissive as I expected, when I reached her later. "Hell, give him my number if he really wants it."

"You sure?"

"I'm a big girl, Patrick."

Feeling belatedly guilty and protective of Will, I decided I would not call Aaron, but he called me again within the week. "So how does it look?" he said.

After I had given him the number he asked me about Will, and I found myself explaining Will's pending case—resisting arrest, possession. Although I had not intended to ask his advice, and certainly wished to avoid the appearance of a quid pro quo, I suddenly realized that Aaron might be able to help. "Do you think you could look into this for me, see what you can find out?" I had never really stepped into the back alleys behind the paneled chambers of the legal system before. But I was willing to risk offending Aaron if there was the slightest chance of keeping Will out of jail.

"I'll check around," he said tentatively.

Three weeks later Will's lawyer informed me the charges had been dropped. He vaguely attributed this victory to his own connections. But I heard the bravado of doubt in his voice. After hanging up I thought about calling Aaron, but I was uncertain whether it was appropriate to thank him or not. Over the next several days I found myself experiencing an overpowering sense of unreality as I sat through meetings, the world I inhabited suddenly seeming less solid and lawful than I had previously imagined. I would feel the same way years later when I heard about Felson's murder.

When I finally called Aaron it was ostensibly to ask for his intern's phone number. I didn't mention the other matter.

"Stacey? Sure. Hey, if that's your thing, be my guest."

Actually, I thought it might be my thing. Having learned from Aaron that she liked the opera, I called and invited her to *Il Trovatore* at the New York City Opera. By happy coincidence, it turned out to be one of her favorites.

"My father took us to see it when I was six," she said with sudden animation. "I loved the 'anvil' chorus. And I was so terrified about the gypsy witch who gets burned—I grew up a few miles from Salem, so witch burning was kind of a recurring theme in my childhood."

"So you'll join me?"

"That would be nice," she said, almost inaudibly.

Not counting Taleesha and Lollie Baker, this was to be my first real date in more than three years.

Lollie was in the city in those years—one of those florid southerners who seem to transplant so well to the pavement of the Upper East Side. She'd left Bennington in her junior year, and by the time I arrived she appeared to know everyone in Manhattan. She wrote famously scathing book and movie reviews and had spent years working on her first play. We would meet once a month or so. She took me to Gino's and Elaine's and El Morocco and half-a-dozen places I would never have seen the inside of otherwise. Occasionally I had to carry her back to her apartment—two soaring, frescoed rooms in a converted mansion between Madison and Fifth. I slept on her couch more than once. On those occasions when she served as my escort for business-related social functions—fund-raisers or dinner at a partner's apartment—she conscientiously restrained her exuberance. Until I met Stacey, I didn't seem to have time for romance, and for some reason Lollie remained fond of me. Perhaps it was nothing more than the fact that people like Lollie need an audience, a role to which I seem all too perfectly suited.

One Saturday night I was settling into bed with a novel when she called from Elaine's, which was in my neighborhood. Though it was past midnight she insisted that I come meet her immediately. I demurred, or rather, I tried to demur; but Lollie was a world-class bully and she was also drunk. "I'm with a bunch of dead people. I mean, honey, we're talking literally. Corpses. They're starting to stink and rot.

I absolutely insist that you come down here and rescue me." And with that she hung up.

When I arrived, she was sitting at the bar clutching a snifter of brandy. She insisted that I accompany her to a sex club downtown, a place so notorious that even *I* had heard of it.

"Why would you want to go there?" It wasn't that I was devoid of curiosity; quite the opposite. My carnal desires were as vivid as anyone's— I daresay more vivid—but I was unwilling to pay the price of their fulfillment. Better to suffer one's fantasies than to risk their grotesque translation into reality.

Lollie squinted as if to get a clearer view of the moron she had mistakenly called for assistance. "*Why* would I want to go? Because it's *there*. Because it should be amusing. Because life is fucking short, sugar, and I want to see as much of it as possible."

"Isn't it a gay place," I asked.

"That's why I need you," she said.

"No way," I said. "That's not in my job description."

"Come on, Patrick. It'll be a hoot."

"For you, maybe."

"I was thinking *you* might like it."

I felt as if I'd been slapped, but I maintained my composure. "What would possibly lead you to that conclusion?"

"Well, I don't see any of us girls catching your eye. It's like you and Will—"

"What about me and Will?" Now I was furious.

"He can't get it up for white girls and you can't get it up for *any* girls."

When she was drinking Lollie sometimes turned nasty, but this was more than I could tolerate. I stood up. "I'll see you later," I said, trying to sound less upset than I felt. I was hardly aware of leaving the restaurant. Before I knew it, I was striding down Second Avenue, a fine snow falling around me. Within moments, I heard Lollie running after me.

"Patrick, wait."

I kept walking, propelled by my anger.

When Lollie finally caught up, she took me by the arm and turned my face toward hers. "Patrick, I'm sorry." I could see she was near tears. "I didn't mean it."

"What part didn't you mean?"

"I'm just so damn drunk and lonely is all."

I was still angry—as only the guilty can be angry—but I wasn't about to leave her there on the street. I flagged down a cab and gave the driver her address after we got in. Lollie was still clinging to my arm, sniffling, but neither of us said anything as we rode crosstown to Fifth. I stared out the window at the snow falling like mist on Central Park.

At her building, I declined her invitation to come up for a drink, waiting until she was inside before I paid the cab and sent it off. Walking east, I watched the snowflakes fall in the lighted canyons between the dark apartment buildings, disappearing on the pavement at my feet. Passing cabs slowed down and then accelerated away from me, tires hissing on the wet street. In the uncharacteristic silence I was deeply conscious of the lives suspended in slumber behind the brick and brownstone, thousands of my fellow creatures stacked in rows like books on a shelf. Or rather—because I imagined them all in pairs—like matched objects: creamer and sugar bowl, salt and pepper shakers, all locked away snug and safe for the night in their conjugal cabinets, together. And I was filled with self-pity because I could only imagine myself alone, an unmatched cup in a discontinued pattern.

Chilled with loneliness, I turned and walked back to Lollie's place.

"It's me," I said into the intercom.

She greeted me at the door in a wildly festive kimono. I was grateful that she didn't question my reappearance, but merely held out her arms and enfolded me in her cushiony embrace.

"Sometimes," I said, "I can't stand myself."

"Well, I love you, if it helps."

"Do you think I could stay tonight?"

"Sure," she said. She gestured toward the bedroom.

I shed down to my boxers and crawled beneath the quilt on Lollie's bed. Suddenly I was exhausted. Lollie dropped her kimono and crawled in beside me. She stroked my head, and I pulled her closer. When she kissed me, I realized that I loved her too, though I did not desire her, much as I might have liked to pretend that I did. My most fervid cravings pointed in another direction. And yet, admitting that I didn't desire her and knowing that she accepted me as I was freed me of the fear of her carnality, and her judgment. And oddly, that freedom allowed me to want her. I found myself kissing her back and finally, with no discernible transition, making love to her.

It's a familiar trope that you can't sleep with a friend without ruining the friendship, but we disproved it that night and on several other occasions. Some nights I needed her, and on others she likewise turned to me for comfort. If sometimes we stopped short or faltered in the middle, it didn't matter. With Lollie I was somehow able to disregard the terrible awkwardness of physical contact between foreign bodies. And I was able to advise her without extreme prejudice about the other men who jumped in and out of her bed. Our own soothing interludes aside, she told me she liked it rough. And that Will, at least in her sole encounter with him, was surprisingly passive. And gradually I told her my own closely guarded secrets, which, lurid as they might be, were largely speculative. To my relief, Lollie was less shocked at my depravity than I was myself.

Every few weeks Lollie would declare that the theater was dead and threaten to move to Los Angeles to write for the movies. And I, sprawled on her bed, would patiently talk her out of it—the corporate lawyer making a passionate case for artistic integrity. I read the drafts of her first play and later forgave her when I recognized myself in her second, which ran for seven months at the Lortel down in the Village. We rented a house together in Bridgehampton that summer, and Lollie organized a small clambake one night for Jack Dupree and his wife, who had a huge spread on Dunemere Lane in East Hampton. Jack was the head of the executive committee at my firm, and a very important ass for me to kiss. He drank most of a bottle of Dewars and howled at Lollie's jokes; after they had left, she told me how he'd cornered her in the kitchen. "Copped a feel," she said, "then tried to perform a mouth to mouth tonsillectomy." It was part of her indisputable charm that she was more amused than amazed.

That fall I took her out to dinner at '21' to celebrate the acceptance of her first play at Playwrights Horizon. Suitably seated in the front room of the saloon after Lollie had refused an inferior table in the middle room, I confided in her my anxiety about making partner. I was in my seventh year. The coming year's review would determine whether I made the cut. Those associates who were not invited to join the firm began to take on the aspect of eunuchs. Everyone knew the story about the lawyer at Cravath Swain and Moore who had to be dragged from his office in a straitjacket after learning that he'd been passed over. My record, thus far, was excellent; I was billing almost three thousand hours a year and had sat on any number of stupid committees, entertained Jack Dupree and served as summer associate liaison; my annual reports had been good—the last two years I had scored eight out of eight points. But I was not particularly adept at office politics, and even a single dissenting vote at the annual partners' meeting was fatal. Somehow I didn't think I'd sucked up enough. And the phrase "partner material" implied a narrow range of social and behavioral variables. Partners were old boys. They played golf. They drank scotch. And they tended to be married.

"Better order another damn Dewars," Lollie advised.

"Maybe I better start thinking about another career."

"Hell, I'll marry you," Lollie said exuberantly enough to attract the attention of several adjoining tables. Even when she wasn't excited Lollie's voice tended to rattle the glassware.

Putting a finger to my lips, I whispered back that I might take her up on her offer if I didn't pass the next review.

"You don't think I'm serious. I *mean* it. We'd probably do better than most married couples. We could keep our own apartments and have dinner every Thursday night. That's pretty much my dream marriage anyway, if you really want to know. All I'd ask is enough notice to find another date if you couldn't make it for Thursday."

She persisted in describing the advantages of the arrangement, and then a bottle of champagne arrived, compliments of a couple across the room who believed they'd witnessed a betrothal. A well-tailored Park Avenue pair in their fifties, they waved to us as the waiter opened the bubbly.

I raised my glass to them, and then to Lollie. "To us."

"To fucking us."

Our benefactors stopped to congratulate us as they were leaving. Before I could stop her, Lollie had convinced them to sit down for a glass of champagne.

"Well, just for a minute," the Chanel-suited wife said. "It's our anniversary, actually."

"Twenty-two years," her husband added. Although probably a year or two younger, his wife looked somewhat older than her husband against the backdrop of prosperous businessmen dining with their second wives and younger dates. But in their patrician serenity they seemed precisely matched, as if over the years their marriage had transmuted into a blood relation. It did not take long to discover that she had been to Miss Porter's some years before Lollie and he had preceded me at Yale. My initial unease was replaced by a feeling of security; I felt myself slipping easily into the fiction of our engagement. Half persuaded that we could pull it off, I savored the irony of proving my establishment bona fides by entering into an unconventional marriage.

"I want a big tacky wedding," Lollie said when I dropped her at her door. "Twelve bridesmaids in pink taffeta and a dress with a train stretching the whole length of the church. And of course I will insist that you drink champagne out of my slipper and unhitch my garter with your teeth."

The next morning, waking up with a hangover and a somewhat refreshed sense of reality, I dismissed our little fantasy. But Lollie called me at the office to say her offer was still good.

A few weeks later I met Stacey, and Lollie embarked on a liaison with a married *New Yorker* editor. Three months after I started dating her, I proposed to Stacey at a bistro in the Village. Short courtship, long engagement; what with one thing and another, we set a date fourteen months in the future. Meanwhile Stacey accompanied me to firm picnics and happily served as hostess when I dutifully entertained the partners and their wives. Three weeks before my wedding, after a tense afternoon in my office while the partners met upstairs, I received a phone call from Jack Dupree informing me that I was now a partner myself.

XX

Saul Felson's funeral was held at Temple Emmanuel on Fifth Avenue. I don't know how we all got through it. A reporter for one of the local tabloids lobbed desultory queries at the mourners as they entered, chiefly pertaining to Mr. Felson's proclivities. When he spotted Davidson, our most prominent partner, he scuttled across the sidewalk and asked if the firm had a policy regarding the sexual preference of partners. Trudging up the steps, Davidson refused to lower his snowy head to acknowledge the man's presence.

Felson's wife and his two teenaged boys sat grave and immobile as statuary in the front row. The partners took up the first three rows on the opposite side from the family, showing the colors—a somber phalanx of expensive blue and gray suits. The rabbi dutifully praised the deceased's devotion to his family and his myriad contributions to the community, yet all I could think of—all anyone could think of, surely— was what Felson had been doing in that grubby hotel room. But we're all deeply schooled in suppressing our emotions—the Jews and the Irish Catholics as well as the genuine WASPs in our white-shoe firm. We drink scotch; we play golf; we are married. The law is the exoskeleton which contains the squishy offal of our animal nature and viscid passions. Control and conformity are our mantras, and they had served us well up to this point. Felson, however, had stepped outside the boundaries.

I wanted to say something to Mrs. Felson, but couldn't find a suitable opportunity. Under the circumstances, the family had decided not to compound the awkwardness with any further gathering of the bereaved.

My wife attended the service, though I told her it wasn't necessary. Stacey is a conscientious person, strict in her observance of the decencies, whether a thank-you note or a visit to the hospital. Some years ago, she left her job at Chase Manhattan to devote herself to the kids and to a literacy program in Harlem; if this seems old-fashioned I can only say that her selflessness is genuine; her charities are chosen not for their social cachet, but from the heart.

"Of course I'm going," she said, the night before, as we sat at the kitchen table. "He was your colleague." And suddenly, unexpectedly, my eyes blurred with tears.

"Are you all right," she asked, her forehead suddenly creasing with concern. She reached across the table and put her hand over mine.

In fact, I felt as though I were drowning in a flood of sadness, though I hardly knew for whom—Felson, his wife and kids, Stacey or myself. My lawyerly distance from my own life seemed, if only for a moment, to have deserted me.

"What is it, Patrick?"

When I could finally speak, I said, "You've been a great wife, Stacey."

The day after my engagement to Stacey had been announced in the Sunday *Times,* my secretary buzzed me during a closed-door conference. "I'm sorry, Mr. Keane. It's a Mrs. Cordell Savage. She insisted it was urgent." Indeed, it was hard to imagine a casual call from Will's brittle mother. Calling to congratulate me on my marriage might not be out of character for her, but it would hardly qualify as urgent. With no small sense of dread, I picked up the line.

She wasted no time on the pleasantries.

"Patrick, it's about Will. You must come down here immediately."

"Is he all right," I asked.

"Of course he's not all right. Why do you suppose I'm calling? I can't even get him on the telephone, all those crazy people around him, and I'm not well enough to go down there myself. I just hope he'll listen to you." Even now, as she was calling on my aid, she was clearly exasperated that such a blunt instrument as myself might actually be efficacious in such a delicate family matter.

I immediately rescheduled the week's appointments and booked myself on the afternoon flight to Memphis. I considered calling Taleesha but ruled it out until I could deliver a firsthand report. It had been months since I'd spoken to Will, which was in itself a bad sign; I'd heard he was having business troubles. Lester Holmes had been killed recently in a shoot-out; the *Times* had actually run a small obit. According to Mrs. Savage, Will had barricaded himself in his office, surrounded by armed minions, and refused to come out or to let anyone else into the building. Things had gotten so bad that old Jessie Petit had walked away, telling Will he wouldn't stand by and watch him kill himself. It was Jessie who'd gone to Mrs. Savage.

Memphis was hellishly steamy. After checking into the Peabody I changed into jeans and knocked back a drink at the bar. Seeing the ducks in the fountain reminded me of how many years had passed since I first came south with Will. I wondered if any of them had survived from my last visit, years before. How long does a duck live, if it doesn't get shot? How long, for that matter, would we keep on splashing in our respective ponds before they took us up the elevator to the roof once and for all?

At the pharmacy I bought half-a-dozen packages of Contac cold capsules and a small box of baking soda. My clothes were drenched with sweat as I approached the Gothic facade of Will's building with its lurid gargoyles. Two black men in army fatigues and wraparound shades lounged inside the door, both wearing shoulder holsters with automatic pistols.

"Delivery for Will Savage," I said.

"Leave it," hissed one of the men.

"This isn't the kind of delivery I can leave."

"Orders is nobody goes up."

I held up two plastic bags, one full of capsules and the other white powder.

"You ain't the reg'lar."

"He called me and said bring it up personally."

"Got enough shit up there to kill a elephant already."

The two sentries looked at each other, and through some telepathy which passed the impenetrable lenses of their glasses decided to let me up. The speaker jerked his head to indicate the door behind him. I hiked up a long wooden stairway. Opening the door on the first landing, I glanced into a large studio, empty except for a microphone stand and the shattered remains of a grand piano, which seemed to have been attacked with a sledgehammer; sprung strings swarmed out of the black wreckage in exclamatory coils. Assaying the next flight, I climbed toward the insistent bass notes that reverberated through the stairwell.

When I opened the door on the third-floor landing I was stunned by the tsunami of music—one of those lugubrious late-seventies synthesizer bands that new wave and punk was supposed to have already killed off: King Crimson, maybe, or Yes. Jack Stubblefield was standing in the middle of the rough-planked floor, his head rolled back, eyes closed, whipping the air with his limp tresses. At first I thought the noise was somehow emanating from his electric guitar; then I realized that it was a shotgun he was strumming. A football game was playing on a big TV set across the room. As the song climbed toward a garish crescendo, Stubblefield windmilled his right arm furiously across the stock of the gun. When the final chords had died away, several phones were ringing; Stubblefield shook himself off like a wet dog, lifted the gun to his shoulder and pointed it at an overhead light. Then he saw me.

"Goat boy," he said.

"It's Patrick."

"I know who you are." He walked over and turned up the volume on the television. "You're not a football fan, are you?"

"Not really," I said.

He snickered. "No, I guess you wouldn't be. You're never going to understand the South if you don't understand football." His jaw was moving quite independently of the demands of speech and his eyes were starting to look dangerous. "Are you a Capricorn," he asked.

"Where's Will," I asked in as delicate a tone as I could manage. I jumped when another phone started to ring.

He raised the gun suddenly and pointed it at me. "Ever heard about the goat and the stallion?"

I shook my head slowly, carefully.

"Say you got a really high-strung stallion, you know, one of those wild boys wants to kick the stall apart—well, you put a goat in the stall and he'll calm right down. Old Jessie told me that." He paused. "And guess what?"

I shrugged cautiously.

"I thought of you," he said. Lowering the gun, he planted the barrel on his own toe. "You know what I'm saying?"

"Where's Will?"

"He's achieving Rainbow Body."

"Is he in the building?"

"You're not fucking listening to me, man. I hate it when people don't listen."

"I'm listening."

"See, the being who is going to attain Dzogchen Rainbow Body, you got to be left alone in a cave for seven days. Nothing left but the nails and hair by the eighth day. I reckon Will's been up there about a week now."

Stubblefield abruptly raised the gun and walked toward me until the barrel was inches from my chest, his eyes vitreous as marbles, face glistening with a sheen of sweat.

"What you got there?" He was looking, insofar as he was looking anywhere, at the bag full of baking soda.

Cautiously, I extended my hand.

Laying the gun down on the floor, he crouched down to examine the contents.

I ducked back into the stairwell and took the stairs three at a time, then thrust my shoulder against the door at the top of the landing. The first thing I picked out of the cavernous darkness was Will, in three-quarter profile, sitting at a desk, a bottle of cognac on one side and a mirror piled with white powder on the other. The desk was a dark, elaborately carved library table replete with griffins and unicorns and mythological beasts. From beyond the grave big Bukka White was singing "Fixin to Die." I did not take this as an auspicious sign.

If Will was aware of my entrance, he gave no indication. I approached as you would a wounded buffalo.

"Who died," he asked without looking up.

"No one yet," I answered. "At least not that I know."

"Presumably that includes me."

"Looks like you're working on it, though."

Finally looking up at me, he took a swig from the bottle. "Lester's dead and my brothers are dead, so why not me?"

"It isn't for lack of trying."

"That what you think I'm doing?" he said after a long interlude. "I've just been living faster than you. Besides, this is just one plane. I'm not afraid to move on to the next."

"What happened to Lester," I asked, easing myself into an armchair across from him. It seemed like a good idea to keep him talking; and for me, hearing Will's familiar voice, edgy and hoarse as it was, somewhat alleviated the weirdness of the situation.

"What happened to Sam Cooke?" Will said. "What happened to the Scottsboro Boys? He got shot." He dipped the long curved nail of his little finger, grown out, I supposed, for this purpose, into the pile of powder, raised it to his nose and inhaled. "I hadn't seen old Lester in more than a year. He turned on me. Claimed I was ripping him off. Called me a white devil. Shit, I carried his lazy ass the last five years. Got him off with probation after he shot some pimp." He nodded toward the mirror. "He had a little problem with the powder. Maybe he owed the wrong folks money. Or maybe . . ."

He left the thought hanging. Looking around, I could begin to make out the features of the room. Will was sitting directly beneath the apex of a pyramid-shaped skylight made of tinted glass and steel which extended perhaps another story above the roof of the building. Daylight was otherwise pretty effectively banished by the blackout shades which covered the tall windows. On the wall behind the desk was an intricate diagram. At one edge of the posterboard was the name JAMES EARL RAY, from which locus dozens of lines branched out to other names. On the other edge of the diagram, connected via several routes through four or five names, was CORDELL SAVAGE.

On the floor nearby were several jars full of liquid. A Tiffany lamp burned dimly on a table at the far end of the room, just barely illuminating the front end of what appeared to be an automobile.

"Is that a car," I asked.

"Cadillac. Former property of the King himself. Colonel Parker gave it to me. Sixty-five Coupe de Ville. Had a bitch of a time getting it up here. That's another one, Elvis. He's dead. Course he died back in '58 or so. The pod people got him. So, you want a drink?"

"Not right now."

"A line? No, of course not."

I'd never seen him so strung out before, and it was beginning to scare me. "Talk to me, Will."

"You want me to pour my heart out while you sit there all sober and straight, judging me."

"I'm not here to judge you."

"Fucking Dink Stover, the All-American Boy."

"All right, Slim, fuck it," I said. "You want me to do a line, I'll do a line. Okay?"

Back then, in '81, people with regular jobs weren't au courant with coke etiquette. Will showed me how to stick the rolled-up fifty-dollar bill in one nostril and block off the other. It scared the hell out of me, seeing my face suddenly loom up from the mirror. I braced myself for a violent alteration of consciousness, but I didn't notice much at first except for the tickling and burning in my nostrils.

Will separated out another sinuous trail with his knife and snorted it himself. "I hear you've got a chick."

"Just got engaged," I said. "Stacey's a great girl. You'll have to meet her."

He stared at me balefully. "Taleesha wants a divorce."

I knew this and had been feeling bad about it for weeks. "You've been separated almost eight years," I pointed out.

"Is that supposed to make me feel better about it?"

"She needs to get on with her life, Will."

"Always the pragmatist." He held the knife up to his nose and sniffed at it. "Don't you ever get just a little bit tired of being practical all the time?" He laughed dryly, then frowned again. "Why does Taleesha want a divorce now? Who's the dude?"

Taleesha had been seeing Aaron for several months, and I suppose it was my fault. I didn't know how much Will knew, but this seemed like the time to come clean. "This guy she likes—he was my roommate at Yale."

"That's touching, Patrick. I'm really fucking glad you told me that."

"He was the one who got those charges dropped in New York."

"Who fucking asked him? I'll face the motherfucking charges. Give me back my wife."

"You know she's been seeing other people. You both have. God, you and your little groupies. Come on, Will. You don't expect her to wait forever, do you?"

"We talk almost every day."

"What do you want from her?"

"I want everything." He jammed the tip of the knife down into the surface of the desk.

"You can't have everything," I said reasonably. My teeth were starting to feel funny.

"Why the fuck not?"

"I refuse to be the parent here," I said. Under the influence of the drug, wanting everything didn't necessarily seem quite so crazy as it might have a few minutes before.

"What does she want from me?" He sounded bewildered, as if he could not begin to imagine why they weren't together still.

"What if she wanted you to be normal," I asked. "Could you manage that for her?"

"You think I *chose* who to be, like you choosing Yale?" He stood up and began to pace the room. "Maybe you're right. Maybe I could settle down and become an accountant."

I had to laugh.

Still pacing, he lit up a joint. "What I'm afraid is I'll ruin her life if I step back into it. What if she can't save me and I only drag her down with me?" Taking a long pull of cognac, he said, "Remember that asshole I threatened to throw out the window that was hitting on Taleesha?"

"Yeah, the leisure suit."

"Became president of the company last month and shit-canned my contract immediately. Had to put a fucking mortgage on Bear Track. Even before my deal was canceled that bastard had been making sure my records, my acts, didn't get any airplay. My people. And when they started to leave, what could I say? I couldn't even take care of my people. For the first time I couldn't take care of them. All I ever wanted was to be a conduit. . . ." He paused in his pacing as if to focus all his energy on what he was trying to say. "I always believed in what I was doing. . . ."

He sucked on the joint and held his breath. "But maybe it's all just commerce," he said, through the smoke. "Maybe I was wrong. Maybe I'm just another huckster. Another big massa."

"You're not that," I said. "I'll stake my life on it. You're the only person I know who really believes in something."

"But what the fuck is it? I can't remember." Will handed me the bottle.

"I believe in you," I said. "Even though I don't always know what you're doing."

But his mind had skipped to another track. "It's all fucked up. I can't make her happy when I'm with her, but I can't make myself happy without her."

"You've never been happy," I said, surprising myself.

Seeming to masticate this idea, he worked his jaw like a gum chewer. "I've had my moments," he finally said. "The day we got married—hey, that was one. The day Taleesha's first single hit the charts." He took a few steps and stooped for one of the jars standing on the floor. He turned away from me, his bizarre modesty still intact in this near delirium, unscrewed the top and unzipped his fly. Finally he screwed the top back on and placed the jar on the floor beside the others.

"You don't have a john up here?"

"It's somewhere over there," he said, pointing, "if you want it."

Actually I did, suddenly, but I wanted no part of this pissing in jars. Standing up, I felt it had been a long time since I'd been vertical. Briefly, I wondered what Stacey would think if she could see me now. I couldn't quite believe I was here myself. On my way I hoisted one of the window shades. In the deep twilight, the lights below me outlined the Chickasaw Bluffs. Scattered lights in the distance marked Arkansas, beyond the wide black plain that was the Mississippi. Off to the right, upstream, a suspension bridge spanned the void. My senses seemed incredibly crisp and quick, processing everything more efficiently than usual. My bladder, however, wasn't working properly. I felt like I had to go, but then I couldn't.

Coming out of the bathroom I saw Stubblefield waving his shotgun from the top of the stairs.

"Just let me shoot him," he said to Will.

"Give me the gun," Will said.

"We could have barbecue *cabrito*." He spotted me then, and leveled the gun at me. "There you are, you little prick."

Will advanced on him slowly, his arm outstretched for the gun.

I was too curious to be afraid. Was he really serious, I wondered. Had they gotten that far out there?

"Give it to me," Will said, stopping a few feet away.

"Please," whined Stubblefield, like a child pleading for a toy.

"Now," said Will softly.

He lowered the gun, and handed it butt first to Will.

"Go get some rest," he said.

"You don't need me?"

"Go on home, Jack."

Will waited until he was gone, then leaned the gun against the door-jamb.

"Haven't you ever wondered about your compulsive need for disciples? Look what happened to Jesus, Will." I *must* be high, I thought. This didn't sound like me.

Will was staring at the shotgun. "I'd trade them all in to get A.J. back," he said. "And I'd gladly give my own sorry hide for Elbridge. He was the man. Smartest motherfucker I ever knew. He could do anything. And I killed him."

"You didn't kill him."

"I might as well have. I killed them both."

"Come on, Will. Give it a rest." I was definitely emboldened by the drug; certainly I'd never spoken so bluntly to Will, or taken his sorrows at any but his own valuation. "How long are you going to wallow in that? I know you loved him. But it's history."

"That's exactly what it is," he said. "Your major, wasn't it? Well, here's what you should have learned: it's always with us. Right alongside us, like a ghost train. It's all still happening—everything that's ever happened." He had his nose in the mirror.

"Maybe I'll try another one," I said.

The night slipped away incredibly quickly. I couldn't believe it when I saw the daylight leaking around the edges of the shades. We were sitting in the front seat of Elvis's Cadillac. Throughout much of the night, Will had been clutching the steering wheel as though he were, at the expense of great effort, keeping us from spinning out of control and crashing. Periodically he called pit stops; he would go off, modestly turning away, to fill another jar. I explained at great length my interpretation of the so-called slave rebellion at Bear Track, which seemed to validate Will's long-cherished notion of the family curse.

"It's not just us," Will said. "It's the whole goddamned Republic. The curse came over to the New World with the first black slave and it's been here ever since."

"My ancestors were starving in Ireland," I pointed out.

"And when they got here they were thrilled to have somebody to look down on and shine their boots."

When I tried to tell him about historical indeterminacy, he informed me I was talking to somebody who dropped a thousand tabs of acid and that he'd forgotten more about indeterminacy than I ever knew.

Later we talked about love and about the difficulty of understanding women—how much simpler the love between men, like ourselves. "The only problem," Will said, "is I don't want to sleep with men."

* * *

Toward midday Will's mood turned dangerous. He jumped out of the car and began pacing back and forth demanding Aaron's phone number. "He's a friend of yours, you bastard!" He heaved a stereo speaker into the windshield, then took the shotgun by the barrel and swung the butt like a club at every standing object in the room, starting with lamps and finishing with the jars of urine.

After he dropped the gun I tackled him, pinning him to the floor. Because he was uncharacteristically thin, or because he'd expended most of his rage, I was able to hold him down as he thrashed and tried to throw me off, until gradually he yielded and began to sob.

Finally, I persuaded him to sleep. We took some kind of pills and climbed into the sleeping loft over the bathroom. As I drifted off I half dreamed that Will and I were floating down the river on a mattress, drifting past the high bluffs and the broad levees, two boys without past or future, leaving behind the lights of the river town where the families and fathers and fair young ladies were still sleeping.

XXI

I had forgotten that it was Halloween. On my way to meet Stacey at the very bistro where I had proposed, I decided to get out and walk, after stagnating in a cab near Washington Square for ten minutes. More than a little out of place in my lawyer's mufti, I struggled through the boisterous throng of the annual Village parade. It was difficult to determine the border between spectators and participants. Outnumbering the wolfmen, vampires, ghosts and witches were dozens of Ronald Reagan masks, the president reigning supreme in the local demonology. One man—at least I supposed it was a man—walked around inside a papier-mâché toilet. The females tended toward short hair, drab olive and denim clothes; a distinct minority among the men were brilliantly tricked out as women. Despite the chill there were a great many shirtless, muscle-bound torsos. At one point I was thrust up against a young man with the rear end cut out of his jeans; another, much appreciated by the crowd, wore nothing but a codpiece; yet another was in diapers.

After ten minutes I found myself trapped behind the blue police barricades along the main parade route on Sixth Avenue. A fleet of leather-jacketed women pedaled uptown under the banner DYKES ON BYKES, followed by THE HOUSE OF SCARLET—a troupe of black men in hoop-skirted gowns and brandishing parasols. I was just about to bolt through the lines of these mock southern belles when, to my horror, a man wearing feathered mask and a toga pointed and waved at me. He was holding a sign that said PEDAGOGICAL PEDERASTS.

"Patrick, my boy. Come aboard." The accent was unmistakable—it was Doug Matson, my old housemaster. Before I could react he'd taken my hand and pulled me through the opening between two barricades. "One of my protégés," he announced to his fellow Greeks.

"Let go," I shouted, and when he failed to, I pushed him, inadvertently knocking him over so that he in turn bowled over one of his fellow pedagogues. I ducked under the barricade and bored frantically through the wall of onlookers on the other side of the street, drawing scattered boos and jeers.

Matson was the last person in the world I wanted to see at this moment—as I was anticipating my wedding. I did not wish to be reminded of the night he had come to visit me at Yale, when, after many hours of talk, I found I was so drunk that I had trouble navigating to my bed. Matson, supposedly quartered in Aaron's empty room, had suddenly slipped into mine, sitting on the corner of my bed as I watched the room spin around me.

"What are you doing?" I said.

"Please, Patrick." He began to stroke my leg. I asked him to stop and he said he didn't believe I wanted him to stop. I remember debating him. I tried to convince him that I wasn't that way. He told me that I was hiding from my true self. At first I think I was vehement in denying this claim, but in my ductile state, I allowed myself to be swayed, or rather, I allowed myself to attribute to drunkenness my eventual acquiescence. Finally exploring that side of my nature which I had tried so desperately to deny, I found it was easier to pretend that I was not fully conscious, that I had not so much acted as yielded. And Matson made it easy. "You don't have to do anything," he repeated. "Just lie there." And he was as good as his word. Which is not to say that I did not recoil from the sight of him the next morning, full of remorse and self-loathing.

*   *   *

When I finally arrived at the restaurant disheveled and wild-eyed, Stacey regarded me with dismay. "I nearly got trampled in the parade," I explained.

"These people are out of control," she said, straightening my tie. "I mean, *really*."

With Stacey brushing my hair back into place I began to feel better almost immediately. It was an extraordinary gift, having a woman who cared for and took care of me. And for her part, traditional girl that she was, she'd been delighted to find someone so respectful not only of her, but also of her parents.

Nine years younger than me, Stacey seemed to hail from an era before mine; she had missed the great wars and bacchanals which had shaped my generation—the revolt of youth against age, of Dionysus against Apollo, *Lux et Veritas* versus rock and roll. With Stacey and her friends it was as if those years had been erased, as if the Beatles had never landed on these shores, as if the birth-control pill had never been invented, as if Vietnam were nothing more than an answer in a geography quiz. Insofar as they existed, Stacey's political convictions were more or less aligned with her father's. She worshiped her parents, and now I would inherit a portion of this fealty and devotion.

After guzzling a gin and tonic I felt better. Yes, this was what it was like to be engaged, this happy concourse. It was reassuring to hear Stacey discuss the wedding plans: invitations, flowers, music, catering, guest list, gift registry. I envisioned the stately spectacle of our wedding under a green-and-white tent stretched tight between the Colchesters' big white house and the ocean. It was reassuring to catalog Stacey's august clan, to hear that the governor of Massachusetts and several congressmen would almost certainly be in attendance. Sitting there, I knew that if I just concentrated on the nuptial details I could block out the image of Matson sprawled on Sixth Avenue and erase the memory of the weekend at Yale. It was certainly not the kind of thing I wanted to discuss over cigars and brandy with my future father-in-law.

As a judge, Carson Colchester had a reputation for toughness, a patrician manner and a scathing wit. I dreaded the moment when he would interrogate me about my motives in marrying his daughter— not that I necessarily believed they were dishonorable. Father of six, he was a handsome, weathered man who relished the role of patriarch, who expected obedience and respect, whose claim on authority was only emphasized by the fact that at fifty-seven he remained taller than his grown sons, as if by design. In conversation he tended to assume an impatient, knowing smile that stopped just short of a sneer, as if he had heard it all before and could, in any case, look right into your soul—but if you kept it short and lively he might hear you out. It was as if I'd found a more liberal, Yankee version of Cordell Savage for a father-in-law. Stacey was his youngest child, and if he largely spared me his withering skepticism, it might well have been because he didn't perceive me as a threat or because Stacey did not merit as much of his attention as her older siblings.

I had waited until we were engaged to take Stacey home to my parents, somehow fearing they might blow the deal, though in fact my father's fortunes had taken a dramatic upturn. He had opened three new appliance stores and was just then beginning to sell computers. My parents had moved to a large new house on a lake outside of Taunton. My grandmother Keane had passed away, rejoining all those souls who had been so very fond of her, who had thought the world of her before they left it. Her place had been taken by Aunt Colleen, whose son, Jimmy, had died of a heroin overdose, his body discovered in Tompkins Square Park, a victim either of maternal repression or of rock and roll, depending on your vantage point. Colleen lived in the so-called mother-in-law suite over the garage of the new lakefront split-level. My father was fiendishly proud of his pool, the game room in the basement and the golf cart in which he cruised down to the lake and back, and if anyone had told him that there was anything to aspire to beyond his present state he would have been politely and understandably skeptical. The first night home with my fiancée, I stayed up with him after the women had gone to bed. A sense of father-son business was hovering in the air.

"She's a great girl," he said, lighting a fresh cigarette. And then, "You know, I've always been faithful to your mother." I took this to be a piece of fatherly advice. "I'm not saying we haven't had our problems. With work and money worries, I haven't always come through for her when she needed me. But we've always loved each other. And we both love you." He paused. "Luckily she stood by me. If she hadn't, all this"—he waved his smoking hand to encompass the house and the lake—"it wouldn't be worth a damn. If the money was all gone again tomorrow, we'd still have each other."

"I love Stacey," I said, answering what I understood to be the question—was it a reproach?—embedded in his speech. And I almost believed it. I had convinced myself that the tender regard I had for Stacey was far more enduring than the usual hormonal fever, and indeed my affection for her has acquired depth and patina over the years. I was about to say she's my best friend—at any rate she's my second-best friend. That she is not the object of my desire incarnate does not invalidate our partnership. Most of the parents we see at our daughters' school are divorced. Sometimes I think the Japanese have it right, arranging their marriages like corporate mergers, without reference to the poets or the moon.

Looking at my father that night in the smoky den, I realized with a shock that after my long flight and all my fantasies of nobler parentage I still wanted him to be proud of me. Some part of me felt fraudulent, and yet for the first time in many years I felt almost comfortable in my parents' home.

I wondered if anyone was ever at ease with Stacey's father. After dinner one evening, on a long weekend at the family home on Nantucket, he invited me out to the porch for a brandy. The dreaded moment of inquisition was suddenly upon me. We sat down in rocking chairs on the big porch, the brightly lit windows of the gray shingled house glowing behind us, the ocean audible but invisible out beyond the white beach.

When he finally spoke he said, "This has been Stacey's summer home since she was born."

"It's a beautiful place, sir," I said.

"Stacey tells me you're planning to ask your friend William Savage to be best man."

237

"Yes, sir, I am."

"I know his father. Very shrewd businessman, and I gather young William has done well in his way."

I nodded.

"Quite the unconventional character, I'm told." He took a long sip of brandy. "That in itself doesn't concern me. However, I've learned that he has a drug conviction in California."

His intelligence was correct. Two years after his arrest in New York Will was stopped and searched by the state police in Sausalito. "It was a misdemeanor," I noted.

"Be that as it may, I sit on the bench of the second-highest court in the land. How do you think it would look if my son-in-law's best man had been convicted on narcotics charges?"

"He's my best friend," I said firmly.

"I'm not asking you to bar him from the wedding. But I don't think it would be appropriate for him to assume an official role. I know Stacey's brother Charlie would be happy to do the honors. In that way you might avoid offending your friend. If you wish you can always lay it at my doorstep. I'd like you to think hard about this, Patrick."

If there was another option, I didn't hear it in his tone. But I could hardly sleep that night or the next, wondering how to accommodate my divergent loyalties. Though the idea of defying the judge was daunting, Will *was* my best friend. And I had just resolved to tell Carson Colchester, respectfully, to fuck himself when a letter arrived from Will—a rare, almost unheard-of event—rendered in a nearly indecipherable scrawl:

Patrick:

You know how I hate committing thoughts to paper—from sheer laziness plus I find the written word slow and crusty. But it's not every day you tell me you're getting hitched. I spose congratulations are in order. No one will be happier than me yada yada yada if you're happy. But are you sure you're doing this for the right reasons? I mean, not to sound too boring, are you in love? You know, like in the songs? Ain't no mountain high enough . . . Layla, you got me on my knees, etc. Do you love Stacey or what she represents? Don't mean to rain on your parade but neither do I want to piss on your leg and tell you it's raining. This all may be heroic and stoic and very Dink Stover, but is it *you*, Patrick, my man? And what about Stacey? Forgive me if I'm full of shit on this, but just think about it, will you?

However much it angered me, the letter provided the solution to my dilemma. Feeling as he did, Will could hardly expect to be my best man. As for his concerns and reservations, I knew perfectly well what I wanted, thank you very much.

But I had already caught a glimpse of the demands that would be placed on me as a son-in-law. And in a rebellious frame of mind that Will might have approved I impulsively asked Aaron to serve as my best man. I was so pleased with this gambit that I forgot, until after I had asked him, that my best man was dating Will's wife.

In an unofficial capacity, Will did attend my wedding and even came to the rehearsal dinner at the Colchester house in Marblehead. Standing on the front steps with Stacey's father, I watched Will roll up the gravel driveway in a vintage maroon-and-cream Rolls. Having fortified the judge with tales of Will's business prowess and wealth in hopes of ameliorating his actual presence, I still hoped Will would seduce the company, charm them all into dancing to his own beat.

My father-in-law, however, was amused by neither the music that blared from Will's chauffeured car nor the purple smoking jacket and jeans he'd selected for the occasion.

"I know your father," the judge said, after I had performed the introduction.

Will shook his hand. "I won't hold it against you."

"That's quite an outfit you've got on."

"Tell me, Judge," Will countered. "What constituency do you dress for?"

"I beg your pardon?" A dark cloud passed over Judge Colchester's craggy features.

"You probably dress for your peers," Will explained. "I don't imagine you're wearing that penguin suit sheerly out of considerations of comfort. It's kind of a father-of-the-bride uniform in your circles. And I expect you wear black robes in court. Very appropriate for your role—dignity of the bench and so forth. We all have our roles, don't we?"

"And how exactly would you define *yours?*"

"I have many roles," Will said, but the arrival of several Colchester cousins thankfully abbreviated this discussion.

When I caught up with him a few minutes later he was in the library pretending to examine the books. I wanted to warn him that Taleesha was here with Aaron, but I was distracted by the sight of the white powder in his black mustache.

"Jesus, Will. Are you *trying* to ruin my wedding?" After our long, dark night in Memphis, I had found buyers for several pieces of Will's empire, and now I suspected that he was going to make me pay for helping him out when he was down.

"I'm here to celebrate your nuptials," he said, hoisting his glass.

"For God's sake," I said, reaching up to brush away the coke, or whatever. "The governor's here, and the attorney general."

"You must be very proud, Dink."

"That's not the point," I said. "The state police come with them, goddamnit. I told you on the phone—no drugs. Stacey's dad's a judge—"

"You still hear from that old bastard over in London," he asked abruptly. "That lecherous piece of right-wing shit? You tell him his happy days are numbered 'cause I'm coming to get him. I got a plan's gonna put him flat out of bidness."

Beyond the door I saw my own parents hovering, clutching their drinks with the fervor of those who wouldn't otherwise know what to do with their hands. I waved for them to join us, then turned back to Will. "Try to do a little better with my parents than you did with the judge."

Suddenly it seemed amazing to me that they'd never met. At some other point in the history of our friendship, I might have been more nervous about Will's impression of my parents; now I could only wonder what they would make of him—a wild-eyed, badly dressed hippie. But Will was on his best behavior, immediately shedding his anger and arrogance.

My father clapped both hands over Will's, one successful business-man to another. "Will, a real pleasure," he said.

"Likewise, Mr. Keane." Will bowed deeply. "And Mrs. Keane—an honor and a pleasure. Patrick's told me so much about you." He kissed her hand, then hugged her. In his bearish embrace, my mother giggled with delight.

"I see you both have a cocktail," he said after releasing her. "And I can't help noticing that I've finished mine. Perhaps you'd be so good as to accompany me while I freshen it." When I left them at the bar, Will and my father were discussing Caribbean real estate.

I tended to the new arrivals, most notably Lollie Baker, now a cele-brated playwright. I was touched that she'd come. I hadn't seen her in more than a year, and I was afraid that her new celebrity would keep her away.

"I take it as a flagrant insult, Patrick, that you'd think for a minute I might miss this. Do they by any chance have a bar around here? No, wait." She slapped a hand on my arm. "Can we take a little walk or something?"

We slipped around the back of the house and walked down the lawn to the seawall. The water was a steely gray, and Lollie held her hand over her short coif to keep it from rising in the salty wind. She put her other arm around me and we both looked out over the waves, hypnotized by the vanishing point of the horizon.

"I was so goddamn happy to get your invitation. I was afraid you hadn't forgiven me for the play."

"Is that your idea of an apology?"

I had my season of disapproval after seeing Lollie's second play, which involves a love triangle: a salty actress from New Orleans, a bril-liant Jim Morrison–like rock star and a repressed Irish-Catholic banker. Lollie had managed to absent herself from the matinee performance I attended; and on a hunch, I hadn't asked Stacey along. When the lights came up I cowered in my seat, certain that I would be pointed out and jeered. But in the end it seemed there were only three people in the world who recognized me as the model for Ian Rourke, the sexually confused banker who hangs himself at the end of the play.

"Just say you forgive me."

"No one would have ever guessed you were a fan of Tennessee Williams," I said, looking out over the water.

Lollie leaned into me, thrusting her breasts authoritatively into my ribs. "I just want you to know," she said, "my offer still stands. No, wait, hear me out. If you're ever going to have second thoughts they'll come in the next twenty hours or so. And I'm ready to stand in." From her capacious and cluttered purse she removed two airline tickets. "Round-trip to Paris, first-class, in the name of Mr. and Mrs. Patrick Keane. Say the word and we're out of here."

"It's tempting," I said. "A lifetime of watching my weaknesses revealed onstage."

"Don't be ridiculous, Patrick. Marriages don't last a lifetime anymore."

"Mine will."

"You don't have to tell me now. Offer good right up to the altar. My friend Sissie told me that's when you know, when you're walking down the aisle. That's when you suddenly realize you're making a hideous mistake. She should know, she's on her fourth husband."

I hugged her. Amazed at her offer, I could think of no way to adequately express my gratitude. "Am I doing a terrible thing," I asked, whispering into her hair.

She shrugged. "That's what I'm asking you to consider. Try to be honest with yourself, even if you can't be a hundred percent honest with her." Freeing herself, she handed me the tickets. "Your wedding present, if you go through with it. And don't forget, I was almost your first. Now, where can I get a damn drink?"

After showing Lollie to the bar, I saw Will through the bay window. Out on the lawn, Taleesha was restraining him as he lunged toward Aaron, who was holding a hand to his cheek. Having brooded about this possibility for weeks, I started toward the door, but I was intercepted by Stacey, whose obvious distress turned out to be related to a last-minute seating crisis.

"Don't worry," I said, steering her away from the larger disaster outside. "We'll figure it out."

Will's obstreperous behavior carried over into the rehearsal dinner. If the Colchesters had been as stuffy as I sometimes suspected, they would have called off the wedding that night. I'd seated Will at the second table facing away from Aaron and Taleesha, but this precaution proved inadequate. Halfway through the roast beef Aaron tapped his glass and made an amusing speech about what a geek I was at Yale. Then Charlie Colchester, the failed candidate for best man, described in clever detail the weaknesses of my tennis game. As the dinner plates were being cleared—just when it seemed I might be spared the ordeal—Will rose up like Banquo's ghost. I'd wanted to slide gracefully into my new life, and I was still secretly afraid that my qualifications for marrying Stacey Colchester would be called into question at the last minute. Standing up uncertainly, Will banged with a spoon on the bottle of Russian vodka which he was holding by the neck. "My name is Will Savage," he began, "of Memphis, Tennessee, and it is my distinct honor to be present at these . . . *nuptials.*" He paused, looking puzzled, as if he'd forgotten the rest. "And I would just like to say . . ." Again he paused, his features blurry, though he now seemed to be gathering his wits. And I was alarmed by the expression that settled on him then. I had seen it before, that look of diabolical resolution. "I'd just like to say that Patrick is a good man, damn good man. Lucky to get him, even if he doesn't know it."

For a blessed moment I thought this might be the end of his speech; he bent from the waist toward his seat—but only to put down his bottle. Righting himself, he scanned the dozen or so tables, and resumed. "Patrick is of Irish descent, as you may know. Not so very long ago, his people were spat on when they arrived in this city. Spat on, I might add, by the very kind of Anglo-Saxon bastards that drove them out of Ireland in the goddamn first place."

He retrieved his vodka and took a long swallow, then examined his audience. "Greeted by signs that said NO IRISH NEED APPLY and such. Treated much the same as the supposedly free slaves in the land of my own birth after the War between the, uh, States. We said they were too passionate, and unruly, too childlike in their emotions, too fond of music and drink and revelry. Ah, yes, sounds familiar. And yet, here we are today. Here *you* are."

Paralyzed by his performance, I sat there dying a slow death like the ice sculpture at the buffet table.

"Patrick Keane marrying Stacey Colchester with the blessing of the . . . *plutocracy.*" He winked, as if to congratulate himself on his vocabulary. "Almost makes you proud to be an American," he said, sounding anything but proud. "It makes me proud of Patrick. Smart as hell, old Pat. Worked hard. Studied hard. Doesn't smoke or drink or dance the hoochie-coo. Well, not hardly. Not for an Irishman. Brushed his teeth after meals, between meals. Whatever. And he stands here on the threshold of his own American dream. I wouldn't touch it with a fucking barge pole my own self. But Patrick, he's my man . . ."

Again he seemed lost, staring out into the crowd. Then he turned to me and smiled. "And I want him to be happy. Clutch him to your stony bosoms. Like I said, you're lucky to have him. Stacey, be good to him. He has a sweet disposition and a heart that's large and stretchy. Big enough for all of y'all . . . and even, I hope—for me."

Will sat down with the slow ceremony of the corpulent drunk, beaming at me as if the stunned silence were a tribute to his oratory. Stacey kicked me under the table, and when I finally dared to look at her I saw in her face the steely determination of her father. In this, our first crisis, I realized she was not quite the pliable helpmeet I had imagined her to be.

If Will was right that my affections were plastic enough to accommodate widely divergent objects, they had seldom felt so thinly stretched as at that moment when I was furious both with Will and with these unimaginative citizens who would judge him, who'd never seen him at his mesmerizing best. In fact I wondered if I had not reached a point in my life when I would have to choose between the twain. After my wedding it was a long time before I cared to see Will again.

Following Will's performance, Lollie Baker cantered to the rescue with a speech casting herself as the groom's first flame and ardent pursuer, the groom as a paragon of virtue. "We southern women," she concluded, after entertaining the company with bowdlerized versions of our adventures, "pride ourselves on our wiles and our charms and even our guerrilla tactics. But like Robert E. Lee before me, I have to admit defeat. Congratulations, Stacey. Now that you've retired from the field, I hope you'll give me a few tips on strategy." It seemed to me that Lollie was salvaging not only my honor but that of her homeland; her little speech nearly cleared the air of the lingering stench of Will's. And given her recent success, the very fact that I knew Lollie was seen as a credit to me.

After we rose from the table, Taleesha immediately pulled me aside. I was more than happy to avoid, if only for a few minutes, the impending private conference with my betrothed. In fact I gladly would have postponed speaking to anyone on the bride's side for several years.

Taleesha looked as distraught as I felt. "I'm sorry, Patrick."

I assured her it was not her fault. Will had been my friend before he was her husband. I asked about the fight on the lawn.

"Will took a swing at Aaron, luckily he didn't really connect."

"He was just saving his *big* punch for me."

"Patrick, I don't know what to do," she confided.

"What are your choices," I asked, avoiding Stacey's impatient wave.

"He needs me," she said.

Aaron joined us then, and our private parley ended. I was left to face my fiancée and her family.

Brides and grooms imagine that the dull ceremony which codifies their cooling romance is the main event, when, in fact, off in the coat closets and the bathrooms and out behind the elm trees the real drama takes place. My aunt Colleen, who had recently lost her own son, sobbed so loudly during the wedding ceremony that my father had to escort her outside. Stacey's thirteen-year-old nephew Brent was discovered in the boat house engaged in an imminent act of incest with his cousin Leanne. Returning from Bermuda, I learned that Will and Taleesha had slipped away from the wedding together and flown off to Mustique.

XXII

I didn't see Will again until he came to New York nearly two years later. By then, he and Taleesha were living in Santa Monica and Stacey was pregnant. I chose to attribute her bad mood to that fact; she was appalled that I was going out to dinner with Will. "After that awful speech he made at our wedding." I finally had to explain that it was business, which was only partly true.

Will had agreed to meet me at the Quilted Giraffe at nine-thirty. By the time he showed up at ten-forty I was nursing my third scotch. Draped in black, gargantuan in girth, he walked unsteadily toward the table, escorted by a nervous maître d'.

"Good thing for you I'm not billing these hours," I said.

I don't think he heard me. He hugged me, his face slick with sweat, then lit a cigarette and ordered a double vodka. When the drink arrived he used it to wash down a fistful of pills.

"Don't worry, Pat. Just vitamins." He winked.

When I inquired, he told me that business was terrific, and for the first time I didn't believe him. He protested too much. And I detected a lesion of his old self-assurance. Ordering a second vodka, he informed the waiter that he was a vegetarian, but it hardly mattered since he ignored the food when it arrived, and I could only wonder how he had managed to get so big.

When I asked about Taleesha, he fell silent and puffed away at his cigarette. "We lost one," he said.

"Lost what?"

"She had a miscarriage."

"God, Will. I don't know what to say."

"Just as well," he said gruffly. "I'm not sure I particularly want to continue the bloodline."

By now he'd had several drinks. "Can you imagine how fucked up my kid would be," he asked, loudly enough to draw the attention of nearby diners. When he lit up a joint, the waiter very politely asked us to leave, but Will ignored him. The manager was somewhat less polite.

"Come hear some music," he said, when we were out on the sidewalk, his hand seizing my biceps like a bear trap. "Iggy's playing downtown." His driver came around and opened the door of the Rolls.

"Will, I can't afford to get busted, and Stacey's home vomiting," I snapped, regretting it immediately. Feeling guilty about our reproductive success, I added, "Okay, let's go. Just for an hour."

By the time the car pulled to a stop in front of a club downtown, my mood had shifted from guilt to anxiety about the time and about Stacey's condition. Out on the sidewalk, at least a hundred scruffy kids were clustered on the otherwise deserted streets in postures of jaded yearning. On the steps above them, a white man in a black leather jacket and beret played the role of Saint Peter, standing guard in front of the steel door. The crowd, registering the arrival of Will's limo, parted grudgingly as he lurched forward into its midst—recognizing the air of entitlement, if not the face—closing in again before I had a chance to follow.

"Will Savage," he called to the doorman.

"Will *what?*"

"I'm Will Savage," he repeated, as a young woman with a clipboard appeared in the doorway

"You on the list," she asked.

"Fuck the list."

"Sorry," the woman said. "I don't see your name here."

"He knows the owner," I called out, hoping to spare him further erosion of his pride.

"Who doesn't?" said the doorman. Skepticism seemed to consolidate the individuals on the sidewalk, a chorus of sardonic laughter rising from the pack.

"Just let me in," Will bellowed, lurching toward the door. When the guy in the beret clutched Will from behind, three kids in front of the line bolted through the door. Locked in struggle, Will and the doorman tumbled down the steps, cursing each other. When the doorman started punching Will I shoved my way through the crowd and grabbed his arm.

Then an authoritative voice cut through the bedlam.

"Hey, enough already." This man clearly ran the club; he ran down the steps and pried the doorman away from Will, who slumped down on the sidewalk furious and spent, like a baited bear.

"Will, Jesus," he said, "what the fuck's going on? Look, I'm sorry, but you gotta understand. . . ." An emaciated Englishman with cockney vowels, he did not elaborate, nor did he seem entirely happy to see his old friend Will Savage.

Will rose unsteadily, righting himself with effort. "Duncan," he said. But the simple act of recognition exhausted him, so I went over and took his arm, guiding him to the car. He didn't seem to know where he was. For my part, I did not want to witness any of this.

Duncan followed us to the car. "You want to come in, I can give you some drink tickets."

Waving him away, I pulled the door closed behind us. I didn't think the evening could get any worse, but Will seemed determined to destroy everything in his path.

"Kind of ironic," he said, "*you* having a kid. Back at school, I didn't know just how incredibly fucking appropriate that was—you hiding in the closet."

The night was already so disastrous that I could hardly summon any further embarrassment. All I wanted was to be home.

I left Will at his hotel after arranging with the concierge to have a

THE LAST OF THE SAVAGES

doctor sent to check on him. I felt like one of Noah's children watching the patriarch lurch drunk and naked around his tent. It was as if, on the brink of fatherhood, I had felt the chill breath of doom.

Three months later I sent out announcements of our daughter Caroline's birth. I hesitated before addressing one to Will and Taleesha. I received a hearty note of congratulations from Cordell Savage, along with a Georgian baby spoon and dealer's certificate vouching that it was made by Hester Bateman. And in due course there was a monogrammed cashmere blanket and a note—"With love from the two of us"—from Taleesha.

For the first time since I had known him, I imagined myself to be looking down on Will from the high plateau of fortune. I can't say I relished this unaccustomed perspective, though I couldn't help positing a kind of moral balance sheet in which Will was finally being called to account. And I couldn't shake the peculiar notion that somehow our fortunes were inversely related, that the tortoise was finally claiming the prize. Stacey and I had bought a nine-room apartment on Park Avenue after having survived the intense scrutiny of one of the city's more formidable co-op boards, and within a year we would buy a weekend place in Connecticut; I was a new father, making more money than anyone had ever heard of before the eighties—though not half as much as Will pissed away in the seventies.

Checking with a Harvard classmate who was now an entertainment lawyer, I learned that Will was struggling to regain his relevance, that he was considered something of a relic at best, a wreck at worst. "Don't sugarcoat it for me, Tom," I said, irritated by his exuberant Schadenfreude. It was one thing for me to condescend—I was Will's best friend.

"Hey, man," he asked. "Is it true that he's the father of Aretha's kids?"

"Tom," I said. "I heard he's the father of your kids."

I kept meaning to call, but with each passing month it became harder, particularly after I heard, through Lollie, that Taleesha had suffered a second miscarriage. I imagined Will hiding out, licking his wounds. Sometimes I would think of him as a bearded guerrilla chieftain—resting in the hills between battles, planning his next campaign. When, a year after Taleesha's note, I finally dialed, a functionary said that Will was in London on business and that Taleesha was away on holiday. I had my secretary make a note on the calendar to phone three weeks later, when they were scheduled to return, but I was called out of town the day before.

The days disappear like newspapers, seasons like the leaves and snow. I was working harder than ever, devoting what was left of my time and concern to my new family. In the middle years, time can seem to stand still even as it relentlessly carries us away. And then one day the secret clock of our life tolls, and time starts up again.

Early one morning Savage *père* called me at my office. "How's the great white hunter," he asked, with what sounded like forced jauntiness. "I don't guess I'll ever forget the surprise on your face when your first duck fell out of the sky."

"I was even more surprised than he was," I said. "How's Cheryl," I asked, inadvertently touching his sore spot.

"Well, it's funny you should ask, Patrick." There was a long, transatlantic pause. "Is there any chance this line is secure?" he whispered. Once I would have considered this an absurd question, but since our firm had begun to get involved in mergers and acquisitions, some of them hostile, we had our lines swept regularly for bugs. "Can you be on the Concord this morning," he asked. "Of course I'll pay your retainer and expenses."

It was out of the question; I had meetings and clients . . . but six hours later I was sitting in the library of the house in Eaton Square. Looking at Cordell, I calculated the time that had passed since I had seen him, so much had he seemed to age. His temples had gone gray and his neck was shrunken and wattled. I'd never thought of him as having a particular age, but I realized then that he was well over sixty.

The butler brought me tea. Cordell was drinking scotch, and looked as if he'd been at it for days. "Please close the doors on your way out," he ordered. After the butler had sealed us in, he sighed and leaned back in his chair. "All my life I've tried to control my environment and the people around me. I don't believe that we were put on this earth to emulate the anarchy of nature, but to tame it. Will and his friends were always talking about liberation. But you and I—we know that control is what matters."

This wild conjunction of the personal and the metaphysical reminded me of no one so much as Will. Rather than point this out, however, I waited for Cordell to cut to the chase.

"A week ago," he began, "I sent Cheryl off to Saint-Tropez in the company of her hairdresser, who's her best friend and more or less a paid companion. Paid by me," he added. "In fact, I paid her to keep an eye on Cheryl, if you know what I mean. Cheryl wasn't very good at making friends here. You know the English, not exactly the warmest race on the planet. And Cheryl, with her background, was always self-conscious. If there has been a blot on our happiness . . . well, anyway, I hired a friend for her." He seemed to be pleading for a generous interpretation of this domestic espionage. "When I saw that she responded to Dora, the hairdresser, I put her on the payroll. To keep Cheryl company, and to keep me abreast. You're shocked, I can see—"

I shook my head in defense of my own worldliness, and my broad allowances for Savage behavior.

"An older man married to a younger woman, his own eyes aren't what they used to be—so he pays someone else to watch. And you trust her to protect your interests, goddamnit. Foolish of me. It's the inherent dilemma of espionage—the suspicious mind needs to trust its spies. I suppose Will told you I was OSS during the war? No? At any rate, someone turned my agent, my Cockney hairdresser. Obviously someone else was paying her more than I was. Not knowing this, I sent them off to Saint-Tropez together. I was planning to join them once I'd attended to some business here in London."

Usually, he told me, one or the other phoned in every day from the hotel. Cordell wasn't alarmed when a day went by, but after two days without word he called and discovered they'd checked out. The next day he received an anonymous call and then, twenty-four hours later, a package of photographs and an audiocassette graphically documenting Cheryl's dalliance with a sailing instructor.

"Whatever you may think of my May–December marriage," he said, once he'd collected himself, "I love my wife and I am deeply wounded by this. I know Will and his mother have demonized me. They think I ran away with Cheryl out of some monstrous perversity, as if I'd always dreamed of stealing off with my dead son's girlfriend. But I fell in love with Cheryl in spite of that fact, not because of it." He looked stricken, as if he had suddenly allowed himself to imagine that this wasn't true, that in fact there might have been some monstrous and perverse aspect to his attraction. "God forgive me if that's not the truth."

He drained his scotch in a single gulp. I could see his inward gaze swivel outward, as if he had turned away from whatever black truth he may have seen in his soul and was searching for others to blame for his present unhappiness. "If they imagine it was easy or pleasant to give up everything of value in my life and begin again, well, they are gravely mistaken. I wasn't happy about ripping apart what was left of my family. But I'd lost . . . I lost two sons. I suffered, too."

"I'm sure you did," I said, more out of polite reflex than conviction. Though there was a chance he was completely sincere, I couldn't help wondering if he'd noticed his suffering before Cheryl bailed out.

He saw this in my face and it seemed to steel him. "Leaving my feelings aside, there is the question of what has to be done. That's why you're here," he said, in a tone that reasserted command and reminded me that I was, after all, an employee. "I don't know how familiar you are with Fleet Street tabloids, Patrick, but they're shameless sons of bitches. And these blackmailing scum have threatened to distribute the pictures to the press. Along with some speculation about my business dealings—which is their real interest. I don't flatter myself that my private affairs are of burning interest to the public, but in conjunction with the names of some of my associates I'm afraid it would be a great three-day sensation and it would ruin me and many others. The repercussions would be . . . let's just say, *extensive.*"

"Who are they," I asked, "these blackmailers?" I was trying not to sound skeptical. "What is it they want?"

"*Who* is the sixty-thousand-dollar question. What they want is for me to refrain from a certain transaction. They're also demanding hush money of a million cash. But the deal is worth much more than that and it's part of a very complicated web of transactions. Not to be too cryptic about it, I'm supplying merchandise to one party in a dispute. The other party doesn't want me to." He paused. "Do you know how to reach Will?"

"What does Will have to do with this," I asked nervously.

"I have reason to believe that Will's in touch with the other side, the other party as it were. Or if he isn't, he could be. I need to know if the blackmail's coming from his friends. If it is, I'll have to do what they want, or possibly he can help me negotiate. If it's not coming from that quarter, then I'll know who else has a stake in this and I'll know what to do about it."

All this international intrigue, these sinister forces, sounded ludicrous to me. What seemed more likely was that Will might actually be behind this whole scheme—the opportunity to thwart one of his father's arms deals, if that's what we were talking about, being a perceived bonus on top of the destruction of his marriage. Certainly Will was resourceful enough to pull it off, and he'd threatened something like this many times over the years.

"I'd have to know more about what I would be getting involved in, Cordell." This was probably the first time I'd addressed him by that name. "Surely you understand that."

He considered this. "Right now all I'm asking for is that you help me find Will."

"As a friend of the family—that I could do."

"Thank you, Patrick." He stood up and grasped my hand. Then he lifted a book out of the shelf; a panel of the library wall opened out to reveal a hidden staircase that led down to an elaborately equipped basement office. Within an hour I had tracked Will to a recording studio in Miami. I had to insist that it was a family emergency.

"Who's dead?" Will said, when he finally came to the phone.

He listened while I brush-stroked the story, which sounded even more implausible in my telling. "Does this make any sense to you," I asked.

"Let's say I'm familiar with the terrain."

"Can you do anything to help?"

"Tell him to call me," he said. "I want to hear it from His Royal Selfness."

I delivered this message, lightly edited, to Cordell, who was waiting upstairs in the library.

Ten minutes later he returned, handing me an envelope. "I'm deeply grateful to you, Patrick," he said, his demeanor that of a man who had received the last rites of his church and was ready to accept his fate.

"You talked to him?"

He nodded. "He's coming in tomorrow morning."

He walked me to the hallway. I felt for some reason that I might never see him again, and the thought emboldened me even as it made me sad. "May I ask you a question?"

He shrugged. "I'm in your debt."

"I heard a rumor—" I began.

"That I killed my father."

"Well, yes," I said.

"And you want me to tell you whether it's true? Well, I'll tell you if you want. But why should you believe me?"

"At this moment, I think I would."

"My father lost his money and his self-esteem with it, and he turned into a drunk. He used to beat my mother, and one day he came after me. And that was the day she picked up the shotgun. She didn't mean to kill him, I don't think. I think she was as surprised as he was when it went off. But I'll tell you what . . ."

He put his hand on my shoulder and looked me straight in the eye. "If she hadn't, I would have. Does that answer your question?"

I held his gaze. "I don't know."

"Ah, you see?" He smiled, evidently delighted with my inability to fully trust him—as if it confirmed his view of human nature. Or perhaps he was merely pleased to preserve the mystery.

We shook hands and said goodbye. His chauffeur took me to Claridge's and I left early the next morning. The envelope contained a signed blank check.

* * *

I had several years to wonder about the outcome of this father-and-son reunion. In the meantime, when I spoke to Will, it was all business. Just when I thought he was down for the count, his business manager approached me about selling his second label, which turned out to be far more valuable than we imagined. Eventually it fetched over forty million, almost half of which Will immediately poured into a free clinic and hospital in the Mississippi Delta. Millions more went to the Dalai Lama and Tibetan refugees as well as less worthy causes—friends and hangers-on. He seemed to be trying to get rid of the money as fast as possible, and his accountant asked me to impress on him the wisdom of preserving his capital. But when I reached him at his office in Los Angeles, Will said of the money—"It's not mine, Patrick."

"Of course it's yours."

"I'm just a temporary custodian. My job is to distribute it. Don't worry—it all comes back to you in the end. Bread upon the waters, Patrick."

"I can't believe you're giving me this hippie shit after I busted my capitalist ass to make you rich again."

The conversation deteriorated from there. Somehow, after all these years of cherishing our differences, we seemed at that point in time to have hardened against each other. What, after all, did we have in common anymore, if ever?

My other life resumed, and another year went by. Until one day in August, when my family was in Nantucket, Taleesha called to say she was in town. I canceled a meeting so we could have lunch. It was an eerie day in the city: a hurricane was coming up the coast; the streets were unusually clear and windows all around town were crisscrossed with masking tape, in anticipation of flying glass. She took me to the Russian Tea Room, where she was greeted as a favorite. Other diners glanced up, trying to place her; this towering black woman so regal and elegant that she *had* to be a star of some kind.

When we'd settled in our booth, she admitted that she had come to town on and off, but that after the events of my wedding, she was reluctant to call. "I just thought—we thought—maybe you needed to get on with your new life."

"Maybe you were right. I haven't been very good about keeping up either."

She shook her head, absolving me. "Will called a few months ago and got your wife. She didn't sound too happy." Taleesha saw that this was news to me. "Oh, shit, I'm sorry."

I was surprised, and then again I was not. "No, *I'm* sorry."

"God," she said, "listen to how polite we've gotten." She laughed and I suddenly recognized the teenager I'd met under the Biltmore clock. Is it still there, I wondered. Had they taken it away?

She talked about L.A., where they'd been living for years now—they'd just bought a place on the ocean in Malibu—and I showed her pictures of my daughters, Caroline and Amanda. As happy as I was to see her, I needed time to feel the old intimacy; and Taleesha was, if anything, more reserved than me. I managed to wait until the borscht arrived before I asked the inevitable question.

She sighed and put down her glass. "He's in Kyoto, at that monastery of his. The free clinic was a wonderful idea, but if he doesn't stop giving away money . . . I think that's what he wants, you know, to give it all away, to wash his hands."

I hesitated. "Look, if he needs a loan, I could do it through you. He wouldn't have to know. Don't be so quick," I said as she raised her hand to brush this offer away. "I make a ridiculous amount of money."

"You have a family." She took a sip of her iced tea. "That's the problem, actually. Family. The family he *has* and the family that he *doesn't.* I've had three miscarriages, Patrick. Will blames himself. He's sure it's all the drugs and booze and what all that's fucked up his chromosomes. Basically he thinks it's karma. I think he's so conflicted that his sperm are paralyzed with fear. He's not sure he wants to turn any more Savages loose on the world and anyway he sure doesn't want to give his old man the satisfaction." She took another sip. "Or maybe it's me that's paralyzed, afraid I'll turn out like my mother. Not to mention the whole race thing. I mean, I can handle it if we never have any kids, but now that we've failed Will won't let go of it. When we're trying to conceive he lays off the drugs for months. And then after we fail, he goes on a binge to burn off the guilt."

She laughed ruefully. "I was about three minutes away from marrying Aaron," she said. "And then you had to invite me to your wedding."

After lunch we walked along Fifty-seventh Street, Taleesha towering over me in her heels. The sky was a dark green canopy above us, swollen with the impending storm. I put her in a cab at Sixth, and we claimed we would see each other soon, though at that moment I doubt that either of us thought it was likely.

XXIII

One autumn, shortly before Thanksgiving, the phone rang at three o'clock in the morning. The words were slurred, but I recognized the voice immediately.

"Do you have any idea," he said, "what it feels like to fuck your father's wife?"

"No, I can't say that I do." When there was no response, I whispered, "How does it feel?"

"Who is it?" said Stacey, rolling out of bed to check on the girls.

Will mumbled something I couldn't make out. "What?"

"Feels crowded."

I waited, listening to the static of a bad cellular connection.

"Feels like shooting a cat," he said. "Ever shot a cat? Even if it was a bad cat, doesn't feel like you thought it would."

The line went dead. Having no idea where he was I couldn't call him back.

"Who was it," Stacey asked again, returning from maternal reconnaissance.

"Wrong number," I lied, having discovered in my wife a recalcitrant core of willfulness that sometimes surprises me still. A child of privilege, she could be imperious on certain points, such as the care of children; when the girls were younger we went through nannies about as fast as they went through diapers. Will was another subject about which Stacey had strong feelings.

That phone call marked the midpoint of Will's final binge. A few weeks afterward Taleesha sent a Christmas card with the news that Will was in India with the Dalai Lama. Another year slipped away.

Then, at a word from my secretary, the seamless flow of the days stopped . . . blinked and started up again—though with none of the earthquake signs that announced the day the Mississippi River flowed backward. Will was on the line, calling from the Carlyle, just a few blocks from our apartment on Park; he sounded more embarrassed than proud as he explained he was about to be inducted into the Rock and Roll Hall of Fame over a big dinner at the Waldorf.

"Shit, Dink, I don't belong in this club. Can you imagine Charlie Patton and Robert Johnson sitting up there on some thundercloud, sharing a reefer, saying—'Savage, that ofay motherfucker?' I think when the decision was made the committee was under the impression that the honor was posthumous. 'Savage? Yeah, sumbitch died with a needle in his arm, didn't he?' Now they're hoping I'll make a big donation for the fucking museum in Cleveland."

Hearing his voice after so long, it was easy to imagine that he'd just gotten back to school from a family holiday in Memphis, that we were still dewy and ductile, waiting for our lives to begin. He preferred to meet me at home, saying that in his new sobriety he was avoiding restaurants and public places. Not at all sorry that Stacey was in Marblehead with our daughters, visiting her parents, I told him to come on over.

Though still stately and plump, Will had lost perhaps fifty pounds, and his eyes seemed to me to have regained the old clarity and focus. And yet I almost missed that fanatic blaze in his pupils, a certain manic rhythm of the limbs. But he refused the offer of a seat, preferring to stand and pace. "I've heard it said everybody in this life gets a bathtub full of coke and a swimming pool full of gin. I was starting in on my third tub and my fourth pool, not to mention a lot of acid and quaaludes and smack. Taleesha finally pulled me out of the deep end. Almost drove her away but not quite."

In my mind they had never really split. Their epochal separation seemed more fond and intimate than most marriages.

"It's funny," he said, "to look back now and realize I never really believed I'd see forty." We had both passed that melancholy milestone recently. "I think that's one of the reasons I nearly let Taleesha slip away when I did. I didn't want her to find me wrapped around a tree, or cold and blue one morning on the kitchen floor."

He continued to pace the room, stopping now and again to examine a picture or an object. Looking at my home through his eyes I saw a nest of haute bourgeois strivers, crowded with eighteenth-century English furniture, hunt prints and Audubon plates. It's fortunate that only rarely are we given the opportunity to see ourselves as types.

Examining the physical evidence of my life I couldn't help but feel a dichotomous sense of confusion and contentment. When the doorman smiles and says, "Good evening, Mr. Keane"; when, on those occasions that I am home early enough, I open the door to the squeals of my younger daughter; when, at night, I steal into the rooms of my children and watch them sleep—I sometimes feel as if this were someone else's good fortune, someone else's life. A cigar after dinner, the tongue-and-groove fit of precedent and new case, the easily stanched tears of Amanda, the melancholy soughing of the Atlantic from the porch of my father-in-law's house on Nantucket, the crisp, leafy air of Manhattan in October—these are the things that make me feel lucky. The fecund and portentous air of spring, on the other hand, makes me restless and sad, germinating a sensation of regret, stirring an awareness of all the roads not taken and all the desires stifled as if under perpetual winter woolens. It is in the spring that I cannot shake the sense of what I have surrendered. And if on an April day I am filled with desperate longing at the sight of a young man in a white cotton sweater strolling like a god across the Hellespont of Fifty-seventh Street, hailing a cab with his tennis racket, does that mean my life is a lie? If the love I feel for my wife is almost fraternal, if she often seems only half real to me. If I have been more or less in love with my best friend for thirty years? Studying the living room that night, I suddenly realized how feminine it was, all chintz and pillows, with its pale garden of floral Benison and Brunschweig fabrics.

"Let's sit in the library," I said. There, at least, we were surrounded by my books, by old leather and dark cherry paneling. It was also a cliché, but at least it was *my* cliché.

Looking through the framed photographs on the library table, Will spotted one of the two of us, taken that first year at prep school just before we went off to Memphis for Thanksgiving. He picked it up. And I was proud that it was there, signifying a small gesture of domestic assertion on my part. This and my refusal to accompany Stacey and the girls to church were among my few declarations of independence.

Gingerly replacing the photo, he laughed and shook himself like a wet dog. "Well, now that I'm saved, what are we going to do with the rest of our lives?" He rapped his knuckles on the table. "I tell you what, though, I feel like a whole different person than I was two years ago."

Slightly skeptical of this new-man notion, I said, "You still have the same father, yes?"

"Talked to him recently, matter of fact. Taleesha and I are planning a visit this fall."

After all these years, this simple declaration was quite astonishing, the banality of the phrase "planning a visit" quite inadequate to the occasion. I asked what had happened during his last visit, the one I had brokered.

"I never told you?"

I shook my head. "Sit down, will you, for God's sake."

Will lowered himself into a beat-up leather club chair which I'd had for years and fished his ivory cigarette holder out of his pocket, along with a pack of Camels and a Dunhill lighter. "How much do you know?"

"Just enough to be incredulous. Even after my long association with your family. As I recall, your father was being blackmailed." I paused, looked over at him enthroned in my chair, like a king returned from exile. "I always kind of suspected it was you."

"Good guess." He rubbed his hands together as if he planned to use them to tell the story and settled back in the chair.

* * *

After Cordell called and asked for his help, Will explained, he'd checked with his own mysterious sources and come up with nothing—the blackmailers were not "his people"—and evidently that cleared the way for his father to come down very hard on some of his own associates. In the end, Cordell was able to squelch the publicity for considerably less than the original asking price. Cheryl eventually turned up in Geneva, asking for a divorce.

"Didn't ask for a penny," Will said, "and married her sailing instructor the day the papers cleared. Funny thing is, she totally loved this guy, who didn't have anything to do with the scam. They're living in Maine or someplace, just had a kid. But these *people,* they'd been waiting for months to get something on the old man. They had the hairdresser on the payroll and when she saw romance developing between Cheryl and the sailing guy they wired both hotel rooms in Saint-Tropez and sat back to wait. The old man was fucking crushed, but then he got busy on some of his partners." He laughed. "More than this, my friend, you don't want to know."

Suspicious of all this intrigue and skulduggery, I said, "What are you telling me—people were *killed?*"

"You've never wanted to believe the worst about my father, Patrick, never wanted to look too deep under the surface of things. Don't start now."

I resented this. "I'm not inclined to invent conspiracies when there's a simple logical explanation—if that's what you mean."

"Lone gunman. Isolated occurrence."

"Sometimes, yes. In this case the least convoluted explanation was that *you* were the blackmailer."

He leaned back in his chair and laughed at the ceiling. "See," he said. "The obvious answer, in this case, is dead wrong."

"You didn't do it?"

"No, but I *am* the logical suspect. And hell, I almost pulled it off myself." At this he smiled cryptically.

"You don't happen to recall," I asked, "a certain late-night phone call to that effect?"

"Hey, you could fill a fucking library with what I don't recall. Volumes one through seventeen—*Late-Night Phone Calls.*"

"This was something about sleeping with one's father's wife," I said. "Sounded more than hypothetical." I took a Cohiba Esplendido from the humidor I kept on my desk, cut and lit it.

Will blushed, something I'd never seen him do, lowered his head and wiped his face with a hand. He sighed. "God, did I get into that—my brilliant campaign? I was almost beginning to think I dreamed it."

He watched the smoke from my cigar for some minutes. I'd long ago learned to wait.

"I schemed for years," he began. "Had private detectives map out the old man's schedule. Arranged to run into her on my trips to London. Just happened to be strolling down the street outside her beauty parlor. 'Wow, what a coincidence. How are you? No, we can't tell Dad. But great to see you. How about a drink?' I worked on her practically a year, flew to England three or four times. 'Hey, it must get lonely over here. Stranger in a strange land.' And she *was* lonely, totally out of place, the hairdresser the only person she could talk to. And even *she* turns out to be spying on Cheryl for the old man. Well, I suspected as much, I know my old man, so I paid her off, too." He laughed, fit another cigarette into his holder. "That bitch made out like a bandit, didn't she? Anyway, I told her my father wouldn't understand my innocent desire to see my step-mother, so why worry him about it? And Cheryl really *was* happy to see me. Always wanted to know all about everything back home. Did the dogwoods and the redbuds still bloom in March? Pining for the taste of collard greens. She was *ripe*. So finally I get her to my suite at the Dorchester. A couple drinks. Few lines, a lude. I've got three hidden video cameras covering the bed. Took twelve hours and three former British spooks just to set up the equipment. I wanted to make sure my old man got a clear picture."

"You were going to send him the videotapes?"

"That was the point." He shook his head ruefully. "But I couldn't go through with it. I mean, I did . . ." Will's peculiar modesty reasserted it-self at this point, so that *I* never got a clear picture. "Something weird happened to me in the middle. All of a sudden I was absolutely terrified. It was . . . I don't know how to describe it." As he stared into the middle distance, I noticed for the first time the gray in his sideburns.

It was as if, he said finally, he had discovered the ecstatic moment of union with the cosmos he'd been searching for all those years, through the mediation of all those chemicals and narcotics. But his epiphany was not euphoric or even benign. He was looking into the abyss at his own death, suspended by the finest of threads over a whirlpool of pain and despair and damnation. It was not his Buddhist Nirvana but the Christian perdition of his ancestors. Afraid that he would die in that bed, his flesh inside the flesh of his father's wife, he suffered a kind of seizure. He lay there for hours, paralyzed, drenched in sweat, trembling, his teeth chattering while Cheryl asked him what was wrong and tried to spoon him tea. But he was unable to speak, to describe to her his awful visions.

"It was like the worst motherfucking acid trip I'd ever experienced, only ten times darker." He lit another Camel, this time eschewing the holder. "When I finally regained control of my senses"—he exhaled a great cloud of smoke—"I destroyed the videotapes. I was blown apart from the inside. I'd lost it. Somehow I managed to get out of there, get myself on a plane. But it was a long time before I could pull myself out of that pit."

We sat in silence, me smoking.

"And then," he said, "a year later, two years, you call me from London, and then Cordell's on the line, my father—asking for *my* help. And even more incredible—somebody else had done essentially what I'd planned to do. What I did. And he sounded broken. The invincible, omnipotent bastard was wounded and bleeding. It was the moment I'd been waiting for. But I got no satisfaction when it arrived. The thing I thought I'd wanted for so long didn't fill the old hole."

He paused, examined the tip of his cigarette. "After you called I flew to London. Did what needed doing. And I never told him about me and Cheryl. And now I don't guess I ever will."

We filled the library with smoke. We talked business. Will was up to something utopian and profitable which I couldn't really understand—giving computers to kids from L.A. street gangs, teaching them to program and make music. Sony was throwing money at him, he said, and he'd convinced them to kick in another million to help keep his free clinic in Mississippi up and running.

For the first time in years I heard the old enthusiasm in his voice as he described how computers were going to free us all from the web of corporate power and democratize our atrophied political structures. This was essentially the same vision he'd been espousing since prep school—only the weapons were new. Kids already live in this wired world, he said. Then he asked me what it was like, having kids.

"It's great," I said, trying not to sound too enthusiastic. "Also a huge pain in the ass."

"I guess you know we can't," he said.

"There are always options," I said.

He fell into one of his reveries. "Do you think it's genetic," he asked suddenly.

"What's genetic?"

"What you're . . . well, *whom* you're attracted to?"

"You're asking if my daughters are likely to be dykes?"

"No, of course not. I just wondered if there was anything—"

"That made me"— I hesitated to admit what I had only to Lollie— "attracted to men?"

After his revelations, and after a moment of reflexive panic, I realized that if I was in fact Will's best friend I couldn't hold back on him now. Or maybe I'd finally come to terms with my own nature. I told him that there was no single event, no aspect of my relationship with my father and mother, that nicely explained this part of my emotional composition, only a gradual realization. Perhaps I felt to an unusual degree the anxiety that accompanies sexual awakening, the foreignness of women. Matson didn't really influence me, though he must have recognized what I was reluctant to admit to myself. I certainly didn't choose this preference and in fact I have been fighting it most of my days. But I could honestly tell Will that my life is not a total sham, that I have felt desire for men *and* women and that, in my own way, I am happy with Stacey, if not sated.

Will listened attentively, without judgment, and I found myself almost giddy with relief to finally unburden myself to my closest friend.

Later, conducting a tour of my apartment, I pointed out the Matisse, his wedding present, over the mantel. It was an odalisque, from his Moroccan period, hardly more than a foot square, in a massive gilded bib of a frame.

Will examined it with interest. "It's good to know where some of the money went," he said. Our most valuable possession, it had been dumped with all the other presents on the Colchesters' dining room table. He didn't remember it.

"So here you are on Park Avenue, Patrick. Is it what you hoped it would be?" There was something ominous in his scrutiny, that relentless, unblinking stare, those charged *longueurs*. "I guess I want to know—does it make you happy?"

I shrugged. "When you say 'happy,'" I said experimentally, "you mean ecstatic." This sounded true and even significant as soon as I said it. "You mean something bigger than I think we're capable of sustaining."

"Hell, maybe repression and conformity've made you happier than me." He smiled ironically. "Maybe I was wrong all along. I mean, look at me."

"You've already left behind a bigger footprint than I ever will."

"Will Savage, Bigfoot. Large, hairy and elusive, possibly mythical."

"And this is Caroline's room," I said, switching on a light to illuminate a divided realm of stuffed animals and pictures of handsome young thugs. Though I poked my head in here almost every day, I looked at the room with sudden amazement, unable to believe that it really belonged to my daughter. Will, too, seemed slightly awed. He examined the posters for Green Day and Boyz II Men and rubbed his hand along the nubbly pink bedspread.

"Do you know who her favorite band is," I asked.

"Pearl Jam?"

I shook my head. "The Doors."

"No shit." Will seemed pleased. He studied the room carefully, as if it were the lair of an alien creature that he might presently encounter.

"I have something I want to talk to you about," he said, picking up a stuffed elephant in overalls. "A favor to ask."

"Whatever it is, you got it."

"You haven't heard it yet," he said, squeezing the elephant.

XXIV

The equilibrium I have achieved is the antithesis of everything Will has believed in, a refutation of the liberation theology embedded in all those popular songs. And now the feel-good dogma of carpe diem is beamed into our homes by the corporate purveyors of goods and services, who bought the rights to his message, slimmed it down and mass-produced it. But are we any better off for it?

Inevitably, by virtue of not immolating himself in his own flame, Will has drifted slightly closer to my point of view. Does this mean that in the end I have won? If so, it is a melancholy victory that might to some eyes too closely resemble defeat. I think of my ancestor Donnell Ballagh O'Keane, who fought with Tyrone in the war against the English but who later changed his allegiance so far as to be knighted by James I. And yet, for all his adaptability, he spent the final years of his life a prisoner in the Tower of London.

Our desires are infinite and insatiable; it is only by mastering them that we stand a chance at happiness. Or if not happiness, then peace, for the pursuit of happiness seems to me a cruel and frustrating creed in the end, a terrible scam perpetrated on our callow polity. With few exceptions—Matson at Yale, a brief vertical encounter in the back room of an adult bookstore and another at a rest stop on the Merritt Parkway—my outlaw inclinations have been suppressed.

I, too, want to hear the gypsies play and the mermaids sing; I want to drink the magic tea and walk barefoot on the beach in Bali, watch the bronzed dancers dance for me. But I am not strong enough to invent a role for myself outside of convention, and I have watched others who have tried come to grief—Felson in his bad suits and his holy day yarmulkes. Even Will, as robust as he is. What many would call cowardice I style wisdom. If Don José had left Carmen's hands tied and turned her over to the dragoons, married little Micaëla . . .

That night several years ago, Will was back in his hotel before eleven. I realized later that this might be the last intimate conversation I would have with my best friend. Now we live for our families. He and Taleesha have a son—eked out with the help of the highest reproductive technology. We talk about the kids, about estate planning. *When* we talk, which is less frequently than we might like. The signal, shaping events of our lives are probably behind us. Speaking for myself, I have outgrown the turbulent emotions. Or at least I hope, I *pray* that I have.

I've started going to church again—part of a middle-aged quest for significance, I suppose, and a strategy for curbing the dangerous urgings of the flesh. One afternoon not so long ago, I had a strange epiphany in a doctor's office. Lying back on a vinyl recliner with my chinos around my knees, I experienced a powerful intimation of immortality, as if my soul for an instant vibrated to the music of its source. Not that I can say with certainty what I believe—only that I *want* to believe. I think of something the astronomer Martin Rees once said: "Absence of evidence is not evidence of absence." Still, I'd be grateful for a sign. As I wait patiently for grace, I pray for my best friend as well as for myself, even though his faith, if unorthodox, has always been deep.

Two years ago this spring, on one of the happiest days in my all-too-sober life, I stood godfather to Will's child in a church in Santa Monica. A shaven-headed Buddhist roshi stood beside me in an unofficial capacity while the Episcopal minister presided. Taleesha's father stood at the altar with us, along with old Jessie Petit, who by then was using a walker. Stacey stayed home with the girls. We have reached a tacit agreement on the subject of Will, as on so many other issues. Unless Stacey should suddenly surprise me—and I would be the first to admit it's possible—I think our marriage will endure. However, I decided not to tell her, at least not yet, that I am the biological father of Robert Johnson Savage.

I admit I was stunned and gratified that night at my apartment when Will asked me. I tried dutifully to summarize the hazards of the plan, even as I treasured the honor of his request. A few months later, during a business trip to Los Angeles, I consummated our long, strange friendship—and caught that fleeting glimpse of the cosmos—alone in the darkened office of a fertility clinic in Westwood.

After the christening ceremony, there was lunch on the beach at Will's and Taleesha's new home in Malibu. The old cement mixer was parked out front, a permanent installation which the neighbors were suing him to remove. Half the surviving rock stars of the past three decades were parading across the lawn, clutching children and soft drinks, tamed or perhaps just tired. Somehow the young women, the nannies and personal assistants and girlfriends, looked almost exactly like the girls of my youth—rail thin, with long straight hair and tie-dyed shirts. I don't know, I don't have much of an eye for fashion, but it was eerie, as if in some way nothing had really changed—as if the world hadn't aged, only we had.

At the center of the gathering was Will, running to fat again, sweating in a black braided military jacket and black collarless shirt, puffing like FDR on his long cigarette holder, making concessions neither to the climate nor the march of fashion, defiantly upholding the traditions of an era that didn't believe in tradition. His hair is still long, though it has started to march up his forehead, and he dyes it now, a surprising piece of vanity, along with his beard. That day he put me in mind of some great Georgian rakehell who discovers to his surprise that he has survived into the Victorian era. After lunch, I saw him sneaking a joint in the driveway with one of the nannies.

I sat on the porch with Taleesha, admiring the expensive Pacific while she nursed their handsome beige baby. Will's other idea for a name, she informed me, was Muddy Waters Savage.

I laughed. "Very catchy. I'm glad wiser counsel prevailed."

"I told him the kid would have enough to contend with as it is. And of course he pretended not to know what I was talking about."

"If it makes you feel any better," I said, "I'll take the blame for every rotten thing the little monster does."

"I'm not worried," she said, lifting the baby away from her breast to burp it. "Will won't ever tell you," she added, "but you know how grateful he is."

I'm sure Will's thankful to be absolved of the curse of his own lineage, just as I'm delighted to find myself a retroactive member of an old southern family and the natural father of my best friend's son. Is it possible we all get what we wished for? None of us have yet figured out how to comprehend this mutation of the traditional family which we've concocted. Then again, it probably can't work any worse than the original model. I do sometimes worry that Will might come to resent me. Certainly Cordell Savage has not yet come to terms with the fact that his only grandson is half black: and to this day he doesn't know that the child is not, precisely, his grandson. And who knows if young Robert will hate us all, when he is finally told how he came into this world. Will he combine our strengths, this mulatto boy, or be divided against himself? Looking hopefully that day into his light blue eyes for some trace of my blood, I wondered whether a child of two races might redeem the original sin of our heritage. Or whether, at least, he might be happier with who he is than we were.

After the last guests had gone I took a long walk down the beach with Will, who smoked a joint and held forth on the digitalized, postcorporate future when each of us would take control of our destiny—or, rather, when our children would. On the sunny edge of the continent, laved by the saline breeze off the Pacific, two thousand miles from the Civil War killing grounds of Tennessee and six thousand miles from the Yorkshire estate where Cordell Savage lives with his third wife, it seemed possible that afternoon to start fresh, to take twelve steps into a brave new life. If we log on to the Internet, eat the right foods and exercise religiously, surely we will forget our differences and begin to love one another. But then the riots break out again in the City of Angels, just a few miles south of this paradise, and sons stand trial for shotgunning their parents.

I think of Will pointing a shotgun at his father. And I ponder those weird hobbyists who dress up in the gray and the blue and shoulder muskets and regimental colors to reenact the battles of Gettysburg and Manassas. Our ghosts walk among us—soldiers and hippies, slaves and tyrants, moaning their griefs and rattling their sins like chains. Robert Johnson Savage will have no choice but to grapple with them. I can only pray that he fires no weapons in that contest.

After flailing so awkwardly against my own modest heritage, I know that my only contribution to the great tides of destiny will be to relay the message of my genes. There be giants . . . and there be the rest of us, drifting in schools with the dark currents beneath the waves. Passing the midpoint of a lifetime of small triumphs and failures, of pursuing false idols and common virtues, I see that cleaving to Will was the single daring and unpredictable choice I allowed myself along the way. If this has been the story of Will's life, more than my own, that is because he has lived.

Will wanted to liberate us all; no doubt he'd inherited a taste for lost causes. Yet there have been times—swaying at his side backstage in Boston; racing the wrong way down a predawn street in Memphis; cruising with the top down across the hot skillet of the Mississippi Delta in search of the blues—when I knew, at least for a little while, what it was like to feel free.

A NOTE ON THE TYPE

This book was set in Minion, a typeface produced by the Adobe Corporation specifically for the Macintosh personal computer, and released in 1990. Designed by Roger Slimbach, Minion combines the classic characteristics of old-style faces with the full complement of weights required for modern typesetting

Composed by N. K. Graphics, Keene, New Hampshire
Printed and bound by R. R. Donnelley & Sons,
Harrisonburg, Virginia
Designed by Peter A. Andersen